Praise for
West Newport Blues

"P.S. Foley has written a terrific novel here. Filled with engaging characters and cool prose, this is more than a coming of age story. It's a fascinating portrait of family and friendship on the level of the great Pat Conroy."

David McKenna, screenwriter of *American History X* and *Blow*

"*West Newport Blues* reads as easy as my own high school summer memories flow. The narrative may center around a beach town in Southern California but even a middle-aged beach bum from Tel Aviv can relate to the characters in this book. There is something unique that binds surfers around the globe into a tribe; this story is a glimpse into that something."

Oded Shakked, Surfer, Writer and Wine Maker Extraordinaire

"*West Newport Blues* is impossible to read without the reader becoming emotionally involved in the story, turning every page to find out what he or she can learn about the meaning of a remarkable friendship, which is the heart of the novel. And the good news is that Newport Beach hasn't changed much since the days of this story and magic of the beach town and the illusion of living in a world of endless summers can still be sustained there. Its children are still growing up and dealing with the same issues as did Scotty and Bobby, It is a tale of reminiscence but it is a tale that is just as relevant today as it was forty years ago."

Casey Dornan – Author and Editor of *The Lost Coast Review*

West Newport Blues

West Newport Blues

A Novel

P.S. Foley

WHISPERING
OAKS

Whispering Oaks Press, LLC
Whisperingoakspress@gmail.com
708 Gravenstein Hwy. N #242
Sebastopol, CA 95472

WHISPERING
OAKS

Individual Sales. This book is available through most bookstores or can be ordered directly from Whispering Oaks Press at the address above.

Quantity Sales. Special discounts are available on quantity purchases by corporations, associations, and others. For details, contact the " Special Sales Department " at the publisher's address above.

Printed in the United States of America.

Library of Congress Cataloging-in-Publication Data is available from the publisher.

ISBN 978-0-9893000-3-2

Interior Design: Fusion Creative Works, www.fusioncw.com
Cover Art: Kat Foley
Cover Design: Geoff Towel at Incubox

Disclaimer:
This book is a work of fiction. Any use of real names or places is done in a wholly fictitious manner and not to be taken literally. The cameos of people now deceased and portrayals of Bobby Rowels and Lee Marvin are also done in a fictitious manner. All other people and the events in this book are a product of imagination. Any resemblances to real people or events are matter of coincidence. The book was written with love and imagination.

For my mother
Norma Jean
She so loved her little
city by the sea.

Like Dreams,

As like everything

else in life,

Made of pieces.

— Paul Gauguin

1

I love dreams that last until morning. Nocturnal visions conjured by your subconscious mind creating a private world Carl Jung once described as a complicated dance with your shadow self, a secret garden full of archetypes, mysteries, and the unknown. Dreams often leave us searching for meaning, similar to life itself.

I was on a tropical beach watching a set of perfect waves march toward shore. It could have been Costa Rica or Bali or maybe even Hawaii, and the swell was building. I felt safe wrapped in my grandmother's quilt, a patchwork of old Hawaiian fabric and the softest white flannel she could find. It was the last quilt she made before she died and it always made me feel as if I was wrapped in unconditional love. But I was a little confused about why I needed a quilt in the tropics.

Ping.

The first pebble hit the window and the dream started to slip away as a beautiful girl walked toward me. She was blonde and tanned, her gait decisive and purposeful, and her figure gave new meaning to the words black bikini. The sun obscured her face but I knew she was the girl I longed for. A girl who loved me for who I am in spite of my flaws and who also loved her grandmother as much as I had loved mine.

Ping.

Another pebble hit the window hard as I drifted somewhere between the ethereal beauty of paradise and the reality of my life. Some people think that this is the best part of a dream. That indescribable moment when you are lost between two worlds where omens are revealed and many ancient civilizations believed you could glimpse the

future. I tried to hang on to the dream as twenty-five-foot waves suddenly appeared on the horizon, beckoning me to ride them.

Finally, there was banging, loud banging, and I bolted upright,
trying to adjust my eyes to the darkness. Then I realized it could only
mean one thing: Bobby was outside my window and the surf was up.

I reached over and pulled back the pockmarked aluminum frame
on the sliding glass window and stuck my head out. There stood Bobby,
and he had that smile on his face - a smile that lived somewhere between the Cheshire Cat and the Joker. A smile that said he knew something you didn't and was prepared to test the rules to prove it.

"The hurricane's here. Ten to twelve easily. The point will be going
off. I bet it's even breaking over the wedge into the harbor."

Compared to me, Bobby was nothing short of a stud. Six feet two
inches tall with muscles everywhere, he was easily the best athlete in
our high school, maybe even in the county. He had on a Wave Tools
baseball cap but I knew the hat was an affectation. He had just shaved
his head, a rite of passage for Newport Harbor football players. The
long black hair he'd worn before his senior year was gone, and with it,
part of his identity as a surfer.

I frowned at Bobby. "Don't you have practice this morning?"

"Yeah," Bobby replied sheepishly as he dug his hands into the pockets of his sweatshirt. "But a day like this doesn't happen very often."

The waves in question were being generated by a Category
5 hurricane called Liza. After butchering Cabo San Lucas, it was
now moving up the peninsula and sending huge south swells toward
California's south-facing beaches. Liza also happened to be the name
of Bobby's girlfriend. The fact that we often referred to her as The
Hurricane may have just been a coincidence but I wondered if the
waves generated by a real hurricane would give Bobby as much grief as
Liza did.

"Let me get my suit on," I yawned.

Through the darkness I made my way across the room to the closet
with the broken cantilever door hinges. It was always tricky, even in

the light of day, to slide the door out without the whole thing crashing down on my head. Sure enough, the door came down and smashed onto the nightstand beside my bed, knocking the small reading light onto the floor. The bulb shattered with a sound loud enough to wake the dead.

I ignored the disaster and grabbed my favorite Hang Ten trunks and slipped them on. Then I found a Frog House t-shirt that wasn't too dirty and threw that on, too. Leaving the mess for later, I headed toward the front room.

Maybe the cacophony of the closet door could have woken the dead, but my father was still passed out on the couch surrounded by what he affectionately called his dead soldiers, the empty red and white aluminum cans of his American birthright with the German name. A sandwich wrapper from the Tradewinds Liquor Store lay on the floor, indicating that he had at least eaten something. I guessed that the white noise from the television had muffled the racket of the closet door. I slipped over and shut the stupid thing off.

I looked closely at my father through the darkness: mouth open, unshaven, his gray chest hairs covered with pieces of lettuce from his dinner. It was comforting to know that he had been temporarily rescued from the many demons that seemed to be chasing him. I pulled the blanket up over his half-naked body and decided not to wake him to tell him I was going surfing.

I exited the trailer and found Bobby leaning against the side of his 1953 Chrysler Crown Imperial. It was Bobby's baby; a long black disaster of a car that Bobby loved because he could get his board in it, and there was plenty of room in the back seat for the nights when he wanted to steam up the windows. Bobby was always jiggling wires to get the car running after it had stalled out, usually on the freeway, and when it hit a speed of fifty miles an hour the Chrysler shimmied like an earthquake. Bobby had bought it from an old woman who lived in Newport Heights.

"What time is it?" I asked.

"Ten to five. It'll be light soon."

As if on cue, my neighbor's rooster squawked his spirited proclamation of the coming dawn. Bobby and I laughed. This trailer park was probably the only place in Newport Beach where your neighbors raised chickens to pare down the food bill.

"See," Bobby said. "Even the chickens know there's a swell. We better hurry."

We walked over to the box that Bobby and I built alongside the trailer to store our boards. I pulled out my 7'8 swallow tail. Bobby had two boards, a 6'7 egg and an 8'7 pintail. The latter board was for big waves and that was the board Bobby chose this morning.

"Wetsuits?" I asked.

"Nah," Bobby grunted. "The water's 73. We'll be sweating."

We piled our boards into the Chrysler and were pulling out when we saw my neighbor, Perry, walking into the park wearing a low-cut red top, a short black skirt and platform shoes. Perry was a pretty girl in her early twenties, blonde hair, and a smile that both attracted you and put you at ease. It was a perfect, imperfect smile.

For a moment, I wondered if she was the girl in my dream. I guess you could say I had developed a crush on her but I knew she was probably out of my league. She waved to us and we stopped. I rolled down the window.

"Hey, Perry," I said.

"Scotty, hi. Thanks again for helping me with my flat tire yesterday," Perry said with a Louisiana drawl that sounded like Southern Comfort - sweet and smooth.

"No worries," I replied a little too quickly. Fixing her tire had actually been a major pain in the ass. Still, I liked being around her even though she made me nervous.

"Where are you boys headed?"

"There's a hurricane," I said. "We're going to see how big the waves are."

"You know," Perry smiled, "if I wasn't so tired I'd come with y'all. Could I do that sometime?"

"Sure," I said. "Just let us know."

"I think I'd like that. Have fun."

"We will. Get some sleep."

I rolled up the window and Bobby pulled away. As we drove out of the park, Bobby looked over at me.

"What do you think?" He winked.

"I'd say hooker except I've only seen her with that one guy who always drops her off in the morning."

"That guy's old enough to be our grandfather."

"Yeah," I replied. "He is kind of a geezer."

"Lucky old goat."

"Maybe."

"What do you mean, maybe?"

"I don't know. What if the guy is married with a wife and kids or even grandkids?"

"So?"

"So he meets a girl like Perry and falls in love. Now he's screwed. He's forced to choose between his love for his kids and his love for Perry. What's more, he'll constantly live in fear that Perry will leave him for someone younger."

Bobby was quiet a moment. Then he looked over at me and smiled.

"Where do you get this shit? You are a born writer. If Stanford doesn't take you they'll be missing out on the next...what's that guy called? The Grapes of Wrath guy?"

"Steinbeck?"

"Yeah, John fucking Steinbeck. That's you."

As we rode on in the Chrysler, I smiled. It was possibly the nicest thing anyone had ever said to me. Steinbeck was my favorite writer and even the slightest, most removed comparison, was enough to inspire a hundred stories in me. I also thought about Perry. If she was the girl in my dream then she was rapidly becoming something beyond fantasy, and I quietly wondered what her story really was.

We turned right onto Balboa Boulevard, passing the brand new Jack in the Box, and headed for the Point.

2

Eighteenth Street on the Newport Beach peninsula is commonly known as the Point. Its location is about four blocks south of the Newport Pier and is also commonly known as Blackie's in honor of the dive bar fronting the parking lot. Like most places in the world, there are often nicknames for the spots that locals haunt.

As we pulled up, we spied the silhouettes of the dawn patrol through the darkness. There's something about the anticipation of a big swell that works its way through the surf community, and the rumor of big waves draws people to the beach like sharks to chum. It's sort of like little kids waking up on Christmas morning to find out if the reports of Santa's visit are actually true.

The surfers who had already arrived were standing wherever they could to get a good view of the surf. They stood on the roofs of their cars, on the city's large trash cans and on the lifeguard tower. More were standing on the walls of houses that lined the boardwalk. The owners of these oceanfront edifices hated this. They had paid enormous sums of money for their thirty by sixty-foot plots of paradise and figured they were entitled to some privacy and penniless surfers checking out the waves from "their" walls was a form of freeloading the owners just couldn't accept.

Some of the owners had banded together and resorted to placing two by fours on the tops of their walls with nails sticking up in an effort to deter us from invading their space. But one of the guys had come by in the middle of the night with a hammer and straightened things out.

Afterward, a brave property owner summoned the courage to confront us ocean-loving vagrants head on. He awoke in the wee hours to wash off his deck and walls with a garden hose. When a surfer jumped on the wall, the owner "accidentally" doused the young trespasser with water. Words were exchanged and the owner spent the next six months washing egg off the front of his expensive beach house. There were rumors of police reports and city council meetings, but the question of who owned this little strip of paradise was settled with a for sale sign. It had simply been a question of ownership, with the ultimate answer being that nobody really owns anything. We're all just borrowing what we think we own for a little while.

No homeowners were in sight when Bobby and I exited the Chrysler. However, there were several faces I had come to respect: Billy Pells, a goofy footer who owned this place, Jerrid Wooters, who always had a headache after surfing the Point because he challenged the lip like no other, and finally, Woody Schwarz, who could best be described by the phrase, "Now you see him and now you don't." There were also a couple of heavy hitters: David Nuuhiwa, with his signature white Jag, and Corky Carroll, a longtime Southern California legend. Both were stars of surf movies.

What surprised me was how quiet everyone was. Typically this group was anything but quiet. Surfers, for the most part, are irreverent, rebellious, and loud. At least half the reason these guys surf is because they love showing off for the girls. But this morning it was about something else, and I could feel everyone asking the same questions. Were the rumors and forecasts true, and if they were, would they be up to the challenge?

Bobby and I quietly walked to a wall and climbed up. I peered through the darkness toward the ocean. I could smell the sweet breath of the sea but could only make out the graffiti on the lifeguard tower, "Tourists go home but leave your daughters behind."

"Can't see anything," Bobby complained.

"The guys on the tower will let us know," I suggested.

We didn't have to wait long. The first hoot came from the tower just as I had predicted.

"Owwwwooo."

A lone voice drifted mysteriously across the beach. The hoot sounded like an Irish banshee luring us toward our demise. Several people looked at each other. Some smiled while others stood stone-faced like a band of Roman stoics preparing to meet an army of Huns, holding their ground with a grit that implied, I'll believe it when I see it.

The darkness was lifting now and the surf came into view. A huge set was lining up. They were the biggest waves I had ever seen that weren't in a surf movie and they had the kind of power that could break boards and mangle bodies.

"It's nothing short of epic," I whispered.

"Yeah," Bobby bellowed as a gaping grin spread across his face.

All around us people began emitting primitive sounds, the surfer's version of OM. Our sacred sound of hoots and yells that erupt from our guts when confronting the overwhelming power of the ocean. It's a language only a surfer can understand and represents respect and reverence, mixed with awe, fear, optimism and, of course, excitement, a lethal combination.

"It's gotta be fifteen feet," I heard someone mumble.

"No way," I heard another answer. "It's eighteen if it's an inch."

I stood, mesmerized, as a giant wave crested and fell in a crashing crescendo sending the power of the ocean rumbling across the beach.

"Yeah, bro," Bobby said. "Let's ride some waves!"

He leaped from the wall and headed toward the Chrysler. I followed, wondering why I was afraid, while Bobby just seemed excited. That was Bobby. He wasn't afraid of anything. Where I was cautious, circumspect, and limited, Bobby was courageous, adventurous, and expansive. I stood next to him as he grabbed his board like a five-year-old preparing for an Easter egg hunt.

"It's too big for me," I said. "I'll never get past the white water."

Bobby looked at me for a long moment.

"Why don't you paddle out down by the pier and then over into the lineup."

I shook my head. "Today is the biggest day I've ever seen. I'm not ready for it."

As I said these words, I wondered if I would ever be ready. Bobby looked at me again for a long moment.

"If I take you home, I won't have time to come back."

"No," I agreed. "You need to do this. I'll wait on the beach and watch."

Bobby nodded. "Thanks, bro. I hope I don't drown."

Before I could reply, Bobby turned and ran toward the water with his board.

3

I felt kind of useless watching Bobby run toward the ocean. Strike that. I felt inadequate, as if Bobby was on the verge of manhood and I was still a scared little boy. I took my time walking toward the shoreline to view the action.

A crowd of gapers had already gathered, and a lifeguard truck had appeared on the scene. The lifeguard was announcing through his loudspeaker that, "The surf is too dangerous," and asking for everyone to "please stay out of the water." Of course the surfers refused to heed any warning and were already paddling out. There were about fifteen courageous souls who had decided to challenge these waves.

Day was breaking in the clear morning sky and a light offshore wind was blowing. Conditions could not have been more perfect as a giant set of waves appeared on the horizon marching toward shore, the light of sunrise glistening off their crests. It was obvious that most of the surfers paddling out would not make it through to the lineup. The surfers who failed would be caught inside and crushed like Volkswagens at the scrap yard, repeatedly pounded by the oncoming waves.

Still, the surfers were optimistic and they dug in, heads down, and paddled for their lives. I could almost feel the adrenaline coursing through their veins, but to no avail. The set arrived with a fury punishing those who had not had the speed and strength to carry them out far enough. Almost all of the paddlers found themselves facing down a mountain of white water. They ditched their boards and swam for the bottom while the wave captured the boards and sent them bouncing like toothpicks toward shore.

Wave after wave arrived, persecuting the surfers who had ditched. I looked over at the lifeguard who was now pounding the steering wheel on his truck. He knew this break well and knew how dangerous it could be on a day like today. I was thankful that I was on the beach and not in the water.

When the cleanup set finally dissipated, I was surprised to see that only three surfers had made it. Two were the movie-star legends, the third was Bobby.

"Whoa," I whispered to myself knowing that this was a day when reputations would be made. Just being one of the first into the lineup is worthy of respect.

Another set appeared on the horizon that somehow looked even larger than the last. Like a rogue wave that comes out of nowhere, it was a mammoth mountain of water boiling toward shore. Bobby turned his board and began to paddle. He was in perfect position and the two legends were going to let him have the first wave. I'm sure they thought he was going to eat it.

Bobby paddled hard, having been taught that board speed was half the battle in catching waves. The swell rose behind him and began to crest. People on the beach, now a sizable crowd, hooted and yelled.

Bobby came to his feet and dropped down the huge face intending to go left with his back to the wave. He descended to the bottom, dug in hard and carved a perfect turn propelling him back up the face of the wave and into the pocket. The crowd on the beach grew louder as Bobby then trimmed his board on the face of the wave, trying to beat a large section starting to close out. He bent his knees and grabbed his rail just as the section broke over him. All appeared to be lost as the crowd moaned and I thought about Bobby's last words to me. I pictured him swimming for his life under a mountain of white water.

It seemed like forever as the wave closed out with Bobby completely covered under the white water. I expected his board to pop up at any moment and it was a nervous moment with the clock ticking.

Holding your breath is simply a matter of biology and time is your enemy. Bobby had disappeared for an eternity.

Then it happened. Bobby suddenly appeared from the bowels of the leviathan. It seemed unbelievable, almost impossible, maybe even miraculous. Bobby had disappeared for so long that common sense assured everyone on the beach that the power of the ocean, the power generated by a hurricane that had laid waste to Baja California, had struck again. But Bobby has always been a magician. He'd simply found a way to rise to the challenge and beat back that power, and harness the power for his own purpose.

The crowd erupted wildly as they watched Bobby literally shoot from the belly of the wave as if shot from a cannon. He surfed on, shredding the remaining sections of the wave. Finally, he kicked out on the eight-foot shoulder and flew ten feet into the air like an acrobat with an almost perfect somersault. Bobby had iced it.

The crowd cheered as if a promise had been fulfilled. From down the beach, I heard a photographer sitting behind a tripod with a long lens camera, yelling if anyone knew Bobby's name. It was obvious that with this wave, the first wave on an epic day in Newport Beach, Bobby had proven himself.

I knew my friend was stoked, and if there is a mythology associated with this feeling it is simply this: by mastering the power of the ocean, he had mastered something in himself. Bobby had tested his fear, his skill, and his courage in order to find the essence of his bliss, that deeply private place that whispers, "This is what it means to be alive." As I sat there on the beach, I could almost feel Bobby's voice whispering, "I am a surfer."

Bobby's session lasted just over an hour. He caught three more waves but they didn't compare with his first ride. Still, the crowd hooted and yelled for Bobby whenever he rode; his first wave was etched in their memories.

When he got out of the water. Bobby walked toward the beach and two little grommets raced toward him to ask if they could carry his board. The photographer left his position behind his tripod, rushed up to him and handed him his card. Bobby seemed oblivious to the attention as all eyes were focused on him. I imagined all the young surfers wanted to be him and I was betting that the girls, admiring his good looks, wished to know him better.

Instead of reveling in the moment, Bobby found me straight away.

"I gotta go," he said. "White is going to fry me."

"You've got that right," I nodded, and we headed for home.

As we drove down Balboa Boulevard, I couldn't help but ask him about the wave.

"What were you thinking when that section broke over you?"

"You mean on the first wave?"

"Yeah."

"I don't know. It was kind of weird. I knew that at any moment I could be going for the big swim. But when I felt the power of the wave engulfing me, I guess I was just humbled by it. I realized I wasn't in control. The wave was."

"It was an amazing ride," I offered.

"Yeah, thanks. But it could have gone either way. Pretty much, it just came down to luck."

4

Bobby dropped me at the trailer park and sped away. He was definitely going to be late and we both knew that Coach White was a fanatic about being punctual. Bobby had already decided that he would have to lie. Football and surfing were not compatible in White's eyes.

As I put our boards back in the box, I noticed that Perry's window shades were pulled down. She was probably out cold after her late night on the town. I headed to the trailer to find my dad still asleep on the couch. So I grabbed my journal and walked to Simonich Slough, a canal that runs behind Newport Shores and mixes salt water with fresh water from the Santa Ana River.

I frequently come to the slough to work on a story. The picnic bench at the water's edge always serves to inspire my writing. When searching for a line or a word, I watch the gulls, pipers, egrets, and the occasional crane, hunting for a meal. Usually, a line or word presents itself as if my subconscious mind had hunted down what I needed just like the birds hunt their prey.

I had a lot to write about. The words poured onto the paper as I recounted the events of the morning. I wanted to remember everything; the tang of the early morning salt air to the way the earth vibrated as the massive swells pounded the shoreline. But the words were mostly about Bobby. His courage, skill, and lack of pretense after what he had accomplished deserved my deepest respect. I imagined him as a mythic hero who, through some unknown power, had developed a will which enabled him to act in ways mere mortals only dream about. To ride an eighteen-foot wave at the age of seventeen took a will that was simply uncommon.

Finally, I got to the part where Bobby said it was "luck." I wrote down what I knew about luck. The Romans believed the goddess Fortuna dispensed luck and they were always blaming her for anything that went wrong. Lady Luck, the wheel of fortune, and the proverbial lucky streak can all be associated with the idea that there is a force in the universe that distributes good or bad luck according to laws we can't and don't understand. Sometimes people call this karma.

Then I wrote about fate and wondered if we are all destined to complete some sort of work with the lives we are given. Certainly, some seventeen years ago Bobby was born and all of his actions and decisions led him to those moments when he found himself underneath a mountain of water generated by a hurricane called Liza. Even his father's death was part of this moment. But Bobby was right. It could have gone either way. If the angle of the wave had been slightly different, or if the offshore wind had died down, or if the sandbar had shifted, he could have found himself in a very different situation. Even the moon, with its effect on the tides had played its part.

Was it luck or destiny? What the fool calls chance, the sage calls fate. I sat at the picnic table thinking for a long time about this question as it related to Bobby. Finally, I decided that the answer would be up to Bobby and how he deals with his newfound reputation. In other words, how will this day affect the journey of his life and the choices he makes from here? But even if it was fate, there was no denying that the goddess Fortuna had smiled upon a young surfer on a summer morning in Newport Beach.

5

"You're too dumb to play football," Coach Dale White yelled at the top of his lungs. "How stupid can you be that you can't even get out of bed to get to practice on time?"

"Yes, sir," Bobby replied sheepishly. He was well aware that the entire team and coaching staff were watching.

"What would your mother say?" White continued with a scream that caused the saliva to spew from his mouth.

This brought a laugh from the other players and Bobby grimaced. Anything to do with his mother was a sore subject between Bobby and Coach White. Bobby hated the idea that a divorced, survivalist freak football coach was dating his mother. Especially when that coach also happened to be his coach. It produced a whole set of emotions and feelings of rebellion that even Bobby couldn't understand.

"Now," White yelled. "I want you to start running. And don't stop until I tell you."

"Run where, sir?" Bobby asked.

White exploded. The veins on his forehead protruded like some kind of Frankenstein monster.

"Around the goddamn practice field, where do you think, stupid!"

"I just wanted to get it right, sir."

Bobby started running in the hot August sun, pads bouncing and sweat streaming down his face from under his helmet. But he had a smile on his face from the memories of eighteen-foot waves, that and the fact that he had made the veins appear on Coach White's forehead. For Bobby, it was always a good day when that happened.

6

After I finished writing about the morning and Bobby's wave, I decided I needed something to eat. I walked into the trailer to find my father awake and straightening up. He had picked up his beer cans and folded the blanket I had placed over him earlier. When I moved into my father's trailer, he had graciously given me the bedroom and taken the living room. The living room had been a wreck ever since.

"What's up?" I asked.

"Your mother called. She and your sister are coming to see you."

I had moved out of my mother's and stepfather's home a year before. They lived in an upscale neighborhood called Dover Shores, right on the bay. It was a mansion compared to the trailer, and my bedroom with its private bath had a view of the water. My friends all thought I was nuts for trading Dover Shores bayfront luxury for a shit-hole trailer park, but I have never thought twice about my decision. For me, it had been the right choice.

The reason was simple. My mother was married to an asshole. Dick, or rather, The Dick, was a financial geek who had made millions selling limited partnerships. He was an asshole because he thought his money bought him various entitlements, and he was hopelessly obsessed with how things appeared. In his mind, he wasn't keeping up with the Joneses, he *was* the Joneses.

My mother had met Dick just after she had a boob job, bleached her hair, and started working for his company. Shortly after, I came home from school unexpectedly. Horace Ensign Junior High was just a block and a half from our apartment. When I walked in the door, the first sound I heard was my mother moaning loudly in the bedroom.

"Mom?"

There was a long, terrible pause and then the door to her bedroom cracked opened.

"What are you doing home?" my mother asked. She seemed cross. No one was supposed to be home since my dad was in the hospital recovering from back surgery.

"I forgot my journal. What's going on? Who's here?"

The Dick walked out of the bedroom tucking in his shirt as if nothing had happened and introduced himself. It pissed me off that he thought I was some stupid kid who didn't realize he'd been screwing my mom. It was arrogance on his part, plain and simple. I hated him immediately, and this experience ranks at the top of my list for bad days.

Soon we were one big happy family. My mom quickly divorced my dad, flying to Las Vegas the day the divorce was finalized to marry Dick. She left her kids at home with Grandma.

But I guess my stepfather loved my mom or at least decided she looked the part of what his ideal wife should be, and accepted her with the baggage of two kids. For my mother's part, she was enamored of the idea of finally having money so she swallowed what Dick Sheperd was selling - hook, line and sinker. She became the quintessential Newport Beach hausfrau complete with cocktail parties at the yacht club, cotillion parties for my sister, and tennis lessons for me at the John Wayne Tennis Club.

But I hated every minute of being around The Dick and a cold war simmered between us. About a year after my mother and Dick were married everything came to a head. My eviction from The Dick's bay front house came after I had decided to quit tennis lessons.

"Suzanne," my stepfather yelled. "This son of yours is a quitter with a capital Q."

"I don't like tennis," I complained.

"What do you like?" The Dick retorted.

"Stuff," I said lamely.

"Stuff? You mean things? Things you can buy?"

"No. I don't know. I like Jack Kerouac and Camus."

"Who the hell are they?"

"Writers."

"Writers!" he shouted as he sipped his scotch. "Let me tell you something, writers don't know shit. They don't make any money and usually die in obscurity. They also smell. I talked to a writer once at a party. He was a Pulitzer Prize winner or some bullshit, and he was eating a sandwich. When he walked away, I looked down. The ham had fallen out of his sandwich and was sitting on my two-hundred-dollar Gucci loafers. You know what that told me?"

"What?"

"Writers are slobs."

I was quiet for a moment. A rage began to boil inside of me.

"Do you hear me?" my stepfather continued. "Writers don't know shit and they're all slobs!"

"Maybe he dropped the ham on purpose," I said and looked him straight in the eyes.

The Dick paused. It was a terrible pause as if his mind was trying to wrap itself around the meaning of my statement. Had I actually suggested that his opinion was worthless, or worse, that he was wrong?

"What?" His eyes narrowed and his nostrils flared.

"Maybe the writer dropped the ham on purpose. Maybe it was his way of making a statement that your two-hundred dollar shoes are obscene."

"What the...?"

I smiled and looked him straight in the eye again. "Dick, if the guy had a Pulitzer Prize, you can't assume he was an idiot. So I'm suggesting that the guy thought you were a pig and dropped the ham on purpose. The use of the ham was probably a metaphor."

My stepfather tried to say something but he was so angry that the words just wouldn't come out. He stood and stared at me with hatred for a long moment. Finally, he turned and went into the kitchen and I heard him yell at my mother.

"I'm finished. I want him to pack his bags and get the hell out of my house. He can go live with his dirt bag father. I never want to see him again."

My mother came into the dining room and glared at me.

"I want to go live with Dad," I said. "It's better than living with that asshole."

I got up from the table and headed for my room.

"Scott," I heard my stepfather call. I turned to face him.

"Don't take any of my cars. If you think my money is obscene then you will do fine on your bike."

I looked again to my mother. She was still glaring at me. Her eyes seemed to be saying "get out", too. Then I realized, she was relieved I'd be leaving. I was the one thing in her now perfect life that reminded her on a consistent basis that she had given up on a man who loved her because of his bad luck of getting hurt on a dangerous job, a job he had worked for years to provide for his family.

Finally, I looked at my sister. She had tears in her eyes. When I turned away, I felt a deep sadness knowing that I wouldn't be there to protect her against the twisted values of my stepfather, values that made materialism seem easy, glamorous and the answer to all your problems.

That was over a year ago. I hadn't spoken to my mother or sister in six months. I had tried to call my sister but the calls were never returned. Life with my father was far from perfect; he was on disability from the police department and had lost all sense of purpose and self-worth. His routine was to be drunk by five o'clock and passed out by nine.

Part of me wanted to blame my mother for his downfall. My dad had loved her and she had left him for a life of credit cards, yacht clubs, and Jaguars. But I realized that much of the responsibility was his. Yes, the person he had loved had given up on him. But that was no excuse for giving up on yourself.

Moving in with my dad was a small victory for him over my mother, especially because I did so well in school while living with him. It also gave my dad something to be responsible for other than himself. I was probably the only thing keeping him from completely falling through the cracks.

"Why are they coming here?" I asked.

My dad gathered his thoughts and tried to remember, the weight of his daily routine hanging over him like a cold wet rag.

"Your mother said that Dick is having a fiftieth birthday party and they wanted to extend the invitation in person."

"She needs to drive over here to ask me to come to Dick's birthday party?"

"I guess."

"Would you like to go with me?"

My dad looked at me and smiled. "That would go over big."

"I don't want to go either," I replied.

He nodded.

"I'll make some eggs."

We sat at the table with the broken leg, eating scrambled eggs in silence. I imagined that my father was wondering how everything had slipped away from him. For my part, I was wondering if Stanford was going to accept me, the college that would make me a writer and help me get out of Newport Beach. I also wondered how in the hell I was going to pay for it.

7

Bobby and I had not spoken for a couple of days. He had been at practice and I had been working as a dishwasher at Cappy's restaurant, trying to earn as much money as I could before the end of summer. I loved working at Cappy's because the owner, Pete, would let me eat whatever I wanted. I had also forged a friendship with the cook, Pineapple, and his daughter Pinaply. They were like my second family.

It was a warm evening and I felt like doing something. So when Bobby called and asked if I wanted to go over to the Lido Theater to see the surf movie, *Five Summer Stories*, I jumped all over it. I also told Bobby about my mom coming over and inviting me to The Dick's party and stressing, almost begging, that I bring him. I was sort of pissed about it because my mom and sister barely acknowledged my dad or the fact that we had not spoken in months. All they seemed to care about was that I bring Bobby to the party.

"Let's talk about it tonight," Bobby said.

I sat on the steps of my Dad's trailer and waited for him. To my surprise, my teenage fantasy in the person of Perry walked up.

"Hey, Scotty, what are you waiting for? A hot date?"

Perry made me feel nervous. I'm always a little shy around girls and Perry was not any girl. She was just so pretty, and tonight was a warm night, so she wore red cut-off shorts with a white tank top that accentuated her figure. Her blonde hair and blue eyes contrasted like a neon sign with her tanned face and chest. She could easily have been the inspiration for a Beach Boys song.

"Just waiting for Bobby."

"Is he the boy with the big black car?"

"Yeah," I said. "We're going to a surf movie."

"Really? I've never been to one of those. Could I come along with y'all?"

"Sure."

Just then the Chrysler pulled into the park, huffing and puffing like a three-pack-a-day smoker.

"I'll just grab my purse."

Bobby pulled up and rolled down his window. He watched Perry as she ran to her trailer. Then he looked at me.

"Why did she start running when I pulled up?"

"I told her she could come with us to the movie. She's grabbing her purse."

"Cool," Bobby grinned. "I hope she's up for an adventure."

For some reason that made me even more nervous. I had increasingly found myself thinking about Perry and now it was almost like a date. We looked up to see her running toward us.

"Hurry," Bobby whispered, "open the door for her."

I scrambled for the back door and opened it. Perry stopped and looked at me.

"Scotty, that's so nice. But do you think I could sit in front with both of you?"

I slammed the back door and scrambled for the front. When it was open, Perry looked at me and smiled.

"You're a gentleman. A woman appreciates that."

She climbed in. I slid in next to her on the bench seat and shut the door.

Bobby smiled at Perry.

"Hey, I'm Bobby."

"Perry." She offered her hand and Bobby shook it.

"Ever seen *Five Summer Stories*?" Bobby asked.

"No, I've never been to a surf movie."

"You're in for a treat."

Bobby hit the gas. We made our way out of the park and onto Pacific Coast Highway. Bobby snuck a look at Perry. He had a smile on his face and I knew he was up to something.

"So, Perry, Scotty and I have been trying to figure you out."

Perry returned the smile. "I'm glad I could be of interest."

"I would say it's more than interest. Scotty has all kinds of ideas. My bro's the best storyteller since Steinbeck."

Perry smiled at this, too, and turned to me.

"Tell me your ideas, Scotty."

I froze. It's hard when you come face to face with your fantasy, and your fantasy is asking you to explain yourself.

"Come on, Scotty," Bobby said. "Tell her what you think. Scotty's a writer and he makes up the best stories. Just pretend that you're telling us one of your stories."

Bobby winked at me and I just shook my head. I couldn't believe he was teasing me like this and I hated being put on the spot.

"Just trying to get the ball rolling," Bobby added.

"Yeah," Perry said. "Let's hear your story."

"Okay," I gulped. "But you gotta understand, it's only a story."

"Okay," Perry said. "Just a story."

"All right. I sort of think of you as a heroine in a story like *Vanity Fair*."

"You mean the book?"

"Yeah, by Thackery. Do you know it?"

"Not really. What's it about?"

"It's a story of a girl trying to find her way in the world of high society, and I think of you as a modern day heroine. Like Becky Sharp, you're an underdog."

"How so?" Perry asked.

"Maybe you are in love with a married man who's rich and part of Newport Beach high society. Right now you're his mistress but he's promising to make you his wife."

Suddenly serious, Perry's eyebrows narrowed and the smile faded from her face.

"Has someone talked to you about me?"

"No," I said. "I...I mean...we've just seen you being dropped off a few times. The guy with the Mercedes. But sometimes it's a Rolls. In the early morning."

Perry was dumbfounded. Now it was her turn to be silent, and she seemed deeply concerned. I knew what I said next would be the most important thing I ever said to this girl.

"I don't know anything. It's just observation, and my only wish, my only hope, is that the man you're in love with loves you, too."

Perry stared at me and I did not look away. Our eyes probed deep into each other's and I think she saw that I was sincere.

"Wow. You have quite the imagination and you are close. Bravo. But it's much more complicated."

"No," I replied, "society's complicated. But love never is. It's only true or it isn't."

"Yeah," Bobby said. "My boy's a born writer. You should read some of his stories."

Perry melted me with her perfect, imperfect smile.

"I'd like to." Then she took my hand and squeezed it. "Yeah, Scotty, I'd like to read your stories. Especially if I'm in them."

That's when I felt the blood running to my ears and I knew I was blushing. Perry sitting next to me and squeezing my hand was part of it, but the deeper part was the thought of her reading my stories.

8

"So you two are a couple of surfer boys?" Perry asked with a wink.

Bobby, Perry, and I stood together in a long line that wrapped itself around the theater and down the street of Via Lido. I found myself sneaking looks at Perry. I just couldn't believe she was here with Bobby and me.

"Yeah," Bobby said, "Scotty taught me three years ago, and I guess you could say I'd rather surf than do anything."

"How about you, Scotty?"

"I love surfing, but not like Bobby. He lives for it. But it is my favorite sport and I do it almost every day."

"Is that where you're going when I see you in the early morning?"

"Yeah," I answered.

"Oh, shit!" Bobby said.

I looked up to see Liza the raven haired Hurricane walking up. She looked pissed, and she had her posse with her, a group of three, sometimes four girls that always seemed to appear at her side. They were good-looking girls by Newport Beach standards, nice clothes, nice watches and perfect white orthodontic smiles. They were what you would call the "popular girls." I wasn't even on their radar screen, but Bobby, being the football star, was on everybody's.

Liza was, indeed, pissed.

"I thought you would be here," Liza said with an accusatory tone. "Your mom said you went to the movies." Liza looked at Perry, and her hazel eyes grew fierce. "Is she the reason you haven't called me in days?"

To my surprise, Perry grabbed my arm, snuggled up next to me and flashed her gorgeous smile at The Hurricane.

"Don't be silly," Perry said. "I'm with Scotty."

I saw the disbelief on Liza and the posse's faces. I could almost hear them asking..."She's with Scotty?"

"Oh," Liza said as a look of relief enveloped her face, "why haven't you called me back, Bobby?"

"It's White," Bobby said. "He keeps telling my mom that girls will screw me up for football. I didn't even know you called."

"Oh," Liza said. It was as if the sun had suddenly appeared, a smile blooming on her face. She looked toward the posse and they were all smiling, too, as if Bobby had been redeemed.

"Do you want to see the movie with us?" Bobby asked.

Liza turned to the other girls and they shook their heads no. She turned back to Bobby.

"I'm having a little party. My parents are in the desert so everybody is coming over. Why don't you come with us?"

"Nah," Bobby said. "We're in the Chrysler and I promised Scotty I'd see this movie with him. Maybe we'll come over afterward?"

Liza stepped up and gave Bobby a kiss on his cheek.

"I hope you do," Liza said with a playfulness that implied something more.

"We'll try, but White expects me early tomorrow. We're scrimmaging Mater Dei and they're supposedly pretty tough."

"Okay, I'll be looking for you."

Liza turned to Perry and me. Perry was still clinging to my arm.

"You should both come, too."

"Maybe," I replied.

"Scotty, she's so cute."

"Thanks."

With that, The Hurricane and the posse disappeared back into the night. Perry let go of my arm and turned to Bobby. She had a frown on her face.

"You've slept with her, haven't you?"

"Yeah," Bobby said. "A few times."

"Do you love her?"

"I'm not sure."

"Well, she loves you, so don't sleep with her again until you're sure. A broken heart is a hard thing, especially when you're young."

"Okay," Bobby said sheepishly. "But I can't guarantee it. Boys will be boys."

"I mean it, Bobby," Perry pressed. "It will not turn out good. Scotty, if you are Bobby's friend you see that he follows my advice."

I got what Perry was saying and in a way I understood. But our friendship was about support in spite of our dumb decisions. We usually weren't big on sage advice that kept us from making them.

"I'll try," I said.

Perry took my arm again and snuggled up to me. "It's fun being your date."

Then she grabbed Bobby's arm and pulled him close, too.

"This will be my first surf movie, y'all. Thanks for bringing me."

9

Five Summer Stories. What can be said about the greatest surf movie ever made? This was the fourth time I had seen it and somehow this time was different. I guess it was because of Perry. She sat between Bobby and me and grabbed both our hands and squeezed them several times. She even laughed out loud at the guy dressed as a girl for tandem surfing. It was as if I was seeing it, truly seeing it, for the first time, and Perry's approval and excitement made it even more meaningful. I was especially impressed that Perry hooted with the rest of the crowd as Jerry Lopez proved that surfing is often deeper and more passionate than competitive sports. It can be poetry or a dance with the sea. It can even touch your soul.

We talked about the movie the whole way home. Perry felt the stoke and her enthusiasm infected Bobby and me. Bobby had a cassette tape of the band Honk, a local band who had created the movie's soundtrack. Bobby cranked it up and we were bouncing, and reliving the movie with the music all over again. The song "Love You, Baby" is more than enough to make you want to move your feet.

"I want to learn to surf," Perry shouted.

"You should get Scotty to teach you," Bobby said. "He's the best teacher in Newport."

"Really?"

"He taught me. He had me standing up the first day."

"Will you teach me, Scotty?"

"Sure."

"I've always wanted to learn to surf." To my surprise, Perry grabbed my arm and snuggled next to me.

When we pulled into the park and stopped, Perry suddenly turned to Bobby.

"You're not going to run over and screw that poor little lovesick girl, are you?"

Bobby started laughing. Literally balled up. Then we all started laughing. It was a great moment. Bobby looked at me with that smile of his.

"What do you think, Scotty?" Should I go home to my lonely bed or should I go to the party and get laid?"

"I think you should follow Perry's advice. You know how Newport Beach is. You don't want the reputation of being a heartbreaker."

"You're right. Besides, Mater Dei is tough and everyone is expecting us to kick their ass."

"Bravo," Perry said. "There might be hope for you yet."

"Yeah," Bobby replied. "It's home to bed for me. I just hope White isn't there."

I opened the car door and Perry and I piled out. Bobby looked at me.

"Are you going to come watch the scrimmage?"

"Maybe, if the waves aren't good."

Bobby smiled.

"Dickhead."

"I'll be there." I nodded.

I closed the car door and Bobby pulled away. The Chrysler rattled off as if its next stop was the boneyard. I turned to Perry.

"Thanks for letting me come along tonight," she said.

"Sure," I replied lamely.

"Do you want to walk down to the canal?"

"Yeah. All right."

I couldn't believe my luck. I was going for a walk with the girl I was constantly daydreaming about. Daydreaming about a girl is something

I try not to do because I never want to get my hopes up. But Perry was special and the risk felt worth it. I also realized something else. Since I had met her, most of my stories had been in some way inspired by her, or at least the idea of her, and I quietly wondered if she was my muse. I was fascinated and curious to find out more.

We walked past the dilapidated trailers of people who had found a way to cling to a life near the beach. The residents had fixed up their yards and structures to reflect their image of a wayfarer's retreat.

There was Jim Zaltowski, who had once owned a construction company that ended up in ruins because of asbestos lawsuits. He spent his days painting coconuts, mostly with USC and UCLA logos and colors, and selling them at a local swap meet. His trailer was fixed up to look like the remnants of an abandoned boatyard.

Next to the boatyard was a trailer with a six-foot-high lighthouse at the entrance to its driveway. It belonged to Mary Curry who had once been mayor of Newport. Her life had gone to ruins when she got involved in some sex scandal with a judge that destroyed her career and marriage. I asked her once about the choice of a lighthouse in her front yard and she said, "It's a beacon of hope."

Everyone here had a story of loss and regret and had chosen to leave the world behind for a life inspired by Don the Beachcomber. Their visions of what that meant differed and they exercised their creative ideas in unique ways. Though at first glance it all appeared somewhat charming, it was actually just a sad facade. Try as they might, the residents couldn't conceal the fact that they were lost souls on a journey to nowhere.

I understood my place here. I was also a "nowhere man." I had nowhere else to go. For my dad and most of the others, however, this trailer park was about living simply, cheaply, and under the radar. It was also a place that didn't confront you on a daily basis with what you lost. It was a life of contraction, of pulling in as you wrote off your losses and licked your wounds.

I just couldn't figure out Perry's place. She was a beautiful girl and appeared so self-assured. Perry's life should be a life of expansion, surrounded by young people and fun. Besides Perry, I was the only other young person in the park.

"Perry, why did you choose to live here?" I asked.

"You mean, Newport?"

"Partially, but I actually mean here, in this park, The Seaside Estates. You just seem like someone who should be living in the Oakwood Apartments or maybe in a little place on Balboa Island."

"You sure assume a lot."

"I guess it's the writer in me. You don't have to tell me if you don't want to."

Perry was quiet.

"I'm going to tell you but first I want to establish something."

"What?"

"I want the truth. If I give you the truth, I expect you to give me the truth."

"Okay. That seems fair."

"No, this is serious. I've decided you're someone I can confide in and God knows I need someone to talk to. But unless you are honest with me, I'm not sure I can trust you."

"All right. All right," I said and placed my right hand over my heart and held up my left as if I was going to be sworn in. "Nothing but the truth."

Perry stopped and looked into my eyes.

"Promise?"

"I promise."

"Have you been peeping at me through your bedroom window?"

I was totally caught off guard. I thought I had been so smooth about it that there was no way she could have known. My cheeks turned red, my ears turned red and I felt the hormones in my blood rushing to places I never expected. I was being confronted with the actions of what Carl Jung would call "the shadow self", only it was my shadow self. My actions had been sneaky and voyeuristic, certainly taboo. I was the proverbial little kid caught with his hand in the cookie jar. I looked down. I looked past her. I tried to look anywhere but into her eyes.

"I...ah...guess...I look over sometimes."

Perry laughed. "Admit it, you've been peeping at me."

Perry reached out and grabbed my hands, forcing me to make eye contact. She bit her lip and grinned. It was an unusual smile. Her teeth weren't perfectly straight but they were brilliant white, and there was an openness that immediately melted me.

"Why do..." I started to stammer.

"No, Scotty, the truth."

I felt a bulge in my throat. I knew I had been caught. I was torn between the embarrassment of being a dirty little thief and the feeling of attraction. Again, I tried to look anywhere but into her eyes. But she squeezed my hands, forcing me to acknowledge her gaze.

"I...ah...yeah, I guess I have. It's hard because my bedroom window faces..."

"Have you seen me naked?"

I looked at her a long moment.

"The truth." she said. "And don't try and look away. Look me right in the eyes."

I paused for a moment and looked into the depths of Perry's blue eyes. Her eyes told me that I had no other choice but to tell the truth.

"Yes," I said. "I've seen you."

Perry smiled. "I thought so. There might be hope for you yet."

"I'm really sorry. I'll never do it again."

Perry smiled again.

"It's all right. Don't look so hangdog. As your friend Bobby says, boys will be boys. Besides, I've seen you too. You have a nice body."

"What!"

"Yeah, the other morning when you stripped off your shorts to put on your wetsuit outside the trailer. That place where you keep your surfboards."

I felt embarrassed again. It had been at dawn and I thought everyone was asleep.

"It's all right," Perry continued. "I don't think you're a pervert or anything. Just curious. But what this means is that we've both seen each other naked. That means that from this day forward, we can never lie to each other because the other one will know."

She stopped and put out her hand for me to shake.

"Is it a deal then?" she asked. "Pacts?"

"Pacts? You mean like in *Donovan's Reef*?"

"I don't know what that is."

"It's a movie with Lee Marvin and John Wayne. It's one of Bobby's favorites. He makes me watch it with him every time it's on."

"I don't know about *Donovan's Reef*, but pacts is the word I use with my close friends. It means a deal or a promise to never lie to each other and to keep each others' secrets. My dad said it to me when I was twelve and I've used it ever since."

"Pacts," I nodded.

"Pacts," she said and took my hand and shook it.

Perry and I walked on in silence, holding hands, and arrived at the strip of beach that lined Simonich Slough. We sat at my picnic table across from each other. She looked at me for a long moment. I met her gaze; she was the most beautiful girl I have ever known. Her blue eyes, glowing like phosphorescent jewels in the moonlight, seemed to speak of a wisdom that had seen much but still held on to a purity and innocence. She smiled a sad smile, as if the weight of the world had descended upon her shoulders.

"So you want to know how I came to find myself in this wreck of a trailer park?"

"Yeah, I'd like to know."

"The first thing is my name. Perry is short for Periwinkle."

"Really? Why did your parents name you that?"

"My parents didn't name me. My grandmother did. She said that I was going to need all the protection I could get and the Periwinkle flower was known as a form of protection against evil, the sorceress's flower."

"Why did you need protection?"

"Because growing up I never really had any parents, just my grandmother. But she was sick and knew she would die early. She died when I was eleven. After that I lived with my uncle and aunt for awhile, but their lives were wrecks. They had four kids and used me for free babysitting. I moved out at sixteen and I've really been alone ever since."

"That's how I've always felt since my grandmother died. But at least I had other people around. You had no one?"

"No one."

"So that's how the story begins. It's like something out of a Charles Dickens' novel. I was born. My grandmother died, and I was alone. Wow, can I hear the rest?"

"All right. But some of what I am going to tell you can't be repeated. At least for a while."

"How bad can it be?"

Perry took both my hands into hers and looked me deeply in the eyes again. Her eyes revealed a deep and kind soul with a will of iron. I knew she was serious and that my confidence was important to her.

"What I'm going to tell you, I haven't told anyone. Outside of a couple of lawyers, no one knows. You can't repeat my story. Not even to Bobby. Pacts?"

"Okay, I won't tell anyone. I promise. Not even Bobby."

"Pacts?"

"Pacts."

Perry nodded. She stood, took my hand and led me to the dry beach at the edge of Simonich Slough. We sat in the warm sand, and there, under the moonlight, I heard the most incredible story I had ever heard, a story about money and power, and how the innocent are sometimes caught in the middle. It took an hour to tell, and when she was finished there were tears in her eyes. So I put my arms around her and just held her.

"Pacts," I whispered and she began to cry.

10

Davidson Field is a large gray concrete monument on the east side of the Newport Harbor High School campus. Its size and mass, at least by high school standards, inspires the feeling that this is a special place. A lot of important games have been played here, and the legendary names of alumni who have spilt their blood and sweat under its Friday night lights echo like ghosts across a battlefield. People like Vince Mulroy, John Gust, Steve Richardson, Bucko Shaw, Jeff Balough, Mike Spratz, Marc Steverson, Dan Christy, Bob Unvert, and Andre Stewart. The names on the list are not just meaningful for their families and the community at large. It's also about giving meaning to a tradition that holds us together as a community, and serves to remind us that we belong to something larger than ourselves.

Of course, I have only been a spectator. I don't belong to the tradition of Newport football. Bobby tried several times to get me to go out for football. But I know what I am and I know my limitations. I'm a surfer and a writer, not a gladiator. Still, I've always admired the greater meaning of what happens on this field, for I know how it is connected to the past. It's part of the glue that holds the community of Newport together.

When I arrived, the stadium was not full. There was the usual group of older men that followed Newport Harbor football religiously. I suppose part of their interest is driven by the memories of their own personal experiences, although it is only a guess because high school football is an exciting form of entertainment. The more you know about the players, coaches, and dramas, the more exciting that entertainment becomes. I found a seat just to the left of this group.

The Newport Harbor Sailors were nowhere to be seen. Instead, the field was covered with the Mater Dei Monarchs who were warming up. They were big, there were a lot of them, and they acted with a precision that made them seem formidable.

Finally, Newport arrived on the field. I saw Bobby out front waving his arms and jumping up and down. That was Bobby. Everything he did, he did flat out. There was no holding back. Surfing or football, he was going to drive himself until there was nothing left. He lived entirely in the moment, without fear or doubt.

To say it was a hard day for Mater Dei would be an understatement. Bobby was playing the monster position which is essentially the middle linebacker. On the first play Bobby blitzed and sacked the quarterback. On the second play he hit the running back so hard that he coughed up the ball and the running back's helmet flew ten yards down the field. It took a few moments for the player to get to his feet. I imagined he was seeing stars because he wobbled to the sideline like a drunken sailor. On the third play, Bobby intercepted a pass and ran the ball back for a touchdown.

So the day went. It was the Bobby Rowels show. He ran the ball on offense for touchdowns, and on defense he single-handedly stuffed the ball down the throat of one of the major powers of the famed Angelus League. He was simply magnificent, and all around me people were talking about him. The legend of Bobby Rowels grew right before my eyes, and I was proud to call him my best friend.

11

After the scrimmage, Bobby and I went back to the trailer park to go surfing. We threw our wetsuits on, grabbed our boards and crossed Pacific Coast Highway by walking under the River Jetties Bridge.

The waves weren't very good. It was a little choppy and blown out. But we had fun and Bobby was happy to decompress.

Afterward, we stood together on the beach watching the sun drift toward the horizon. It was a large orange ball of light whose finger like rays reached out toward us, creating a golden, glittering swath of stepping stones across the surface of the ocean. Dorothy may have had the Yellow Brick Road that led her to the Emerald City but Bobby and I had this afternoon at sunset on the edge of our own Emerald City.

"You know, there's nothing better than surfing after football. I even love how the salt water stings my cuts and scratches."

"Maybe you're secretly a masochist."

Bobby laughed. "Maybe. But it just really makes me feel alive."

We went back to the trailer and showered in our outside shower. After I rinsed off, Bobby looked at me for a long moment.

"Tell me again why your mother and stepfather want me to come to this party?" he asked.

"Who knows? My mom said The Dick wanted me to bring a friend so I would have a good time. But she stressed it should be you and only you. It was like she was pleading."

He just looked at me with his expression that said, "You have to be kidding."

I nodded. One thing that Bobby and I were good at was seeing through the bullshit in each other's lives.

"You're right. When did they ever care about me? Something stinks."

"Yeah, I'm sorry. But let's have fun with it. We'll go and find out what it's about and split early. Then we'll know and they won't be able to screw with you. Speaking of screwing, how did things end up with Perry last night?"

"Good," I said and immediately blushed. I recovered quickly. "We stayed up all night and talked. She doesn't have a boyfriend and she isn't a hooker. But there are men in her life like some divorced millionaire that she doesn't exactly trust."

"Talked? Not a hooker?" Bobby gave me his "You're kidding" look again.

"Really," I protested.

"Bro, you're being played."

"No, really. Perry's had a really hard life. This guy she's with helped her so she feels like she has to stick with him."

Bobby looked at me for a long moment.

"You like her, don't you?"

"Yeah, she's really cool."

"How old is she?"

"Twenty one. Just turned. And she knows I was peeping at her."

Bobby looked at me in utter disbelief. Then he cracked up.

"You mean she knows you were watching her do her exercises in the nude?"

"I don't know if she knows that, but she knows I've seen her naked."

Bobby laughed even harder.

"Bro, she likes you. If she knows and didn't freak out on you, then you know she likes you."

I felt the embarrassment again.

"I just think she's cool."

"Scotty, into the older woman. I'm going to spread that around school, and Liza and the posse will back it up. You're going to have more girls chasing you than you know what to do with."

Bobby slugged me in the arm and laughed.

"Quit it," I said, pretending the slug actually hurt me.

Bobby smiled his mischievous Cheshire Cat smile.

"Dickhead. I'll quit when my boy gets laid. And I still think she's a hooker."

12

The Newport Balboa Club is one of the premier yacht clubs in the world. Established in 1947, it's been a hangout for Newport's wealthy and famous ever since. Dick Shepard considered his acceptance into the club one of the greatest achievements of his life. Membership meant he had arrived. That was the world according to The Dick.

When we went to our first dinner at the club he announced his philosophy of life. It was after three Mai Tais and he was feeling really good.

"The cream always rises to the top. Never forget that, Scott."

My mom looked at him with such admiration that it made me want to throw up.

"Isn't cream supposed to make you fat?" I replied.

It was a smartass remark and I knew it. The Dick looked at me with daggers, and I could tell that I had wounded him. It's just that it irked me that money was what he measured the world by. If you had money, you were worthy, and in his eyes if you didn't, you were a loser. It was this perspective, this materialistic consciousness that I objected to. It always made me think of my dad. I knew that The Dick felt superior to my father because of money. As much as anything, my remark was inspired by a sense of loyalty to my dad.

I was thinking of this moment as Bobby and I cruised down Pacific Coast Highway in the long black disaster of a Chrysler. My contemplation had a purpose: I was trying to understand the reasons I hated The Dick so much, and why I was still letting him jerk me around. I suppose it was because of my mother. Even though she seemed to be on Dick's side instead of mine, loyalty is always a tricky thing. She's my mother, and somewhere deep inside, I still wanted her approval and love. But it had been a long time since she had shown me either and I blamed The Dick for everything including my parents' divorce.

Bobby pulled into the long driveway that led to the club's entrance.

"So let's find out what this is and then get the hell out of here," Bobby said.

"Hey, bro."

Bobby turned to look at me.

"Thanks for coming."

Bobby smiled.

"I wouldn't miss it. I know you're going to mess with The Dick, and I want to be there to see it."

I smiled. "You're probably right. I just can't help myself."

"Hey, no worries. The only reason I came is to watch your back."

Bobby pulled up to the valet. Sitting right in front were The Dick's red Porsche, and a couple of Rolls-Royces.

"If you don't mind," Bobby said to the valet, "park it next to the Rolls. We're not staying long."

"Yeah," I added, "we're family."

"Sure," the valet replied.

We walked into the club and a receptionist met us at the door. She was a severe looking middle-aged woman big enough to be a bouncer or at least the keeper of the magic keys to a kingdom. Her name tag read Ingrid and I thought it was the appropriate name for a battle ax. She eyed us suspiciously, as if she was already angry at us.

"What can I do for you?" she asked.

"We're here for the birthday party," I said.

"You mean for the Shepard family?"

"Yes."

"Were you invited?"

"Yes."

"Names?"

"Ah, Scott Curtis and Bobby Rowels."

Her finger ran down a long list until she found our names.

"Follow me."

Bobby and I followed the large woman down a hall and we stepped into the world of wealth. Bobby and I looked at each other and smiled. It was a Ralph Lauren fashion show. The women were wearing floral dresses and skirts while the men had on polo shirts and seersucker jackets or navy blue blazers. Even the kids looked like little clones of their parents. Both Bobby and I knew how absurd we must look in the middle of this crowd. We had on faded jeans, flip flops and our favorite vintage Ellery Chun aloha shirts that we had scored from George the Magician down at the Frog House. Compared to the beautiful people wearing beautiful clothes, we were beach rats.

"Let's find the bar," Bobby suggested.

We made our way along the outskirts of the party. It seemed so surreal to be here. There was my mother talking to two other women who looked just like her: bleached blonde hair, huge diamond earrings, and fake breasts; typical Newport Beach trophy wives with the kind of beauty only money could buy.

I saw The Dick over in the corner talking to two other men. I wondered if they were talking about increasing productivity by working their sales people to death. I had visited The Dick's office a few times and it had a boiler room where sales sharks viciously tried to separate people from their hard earned money using every trick possible. My great economics teacher, Mr. Cochrane, had warned me about the promises these salespeople make. The idea of high returns with low risk was as old as capitalism itself, a "can't miss" opportunity that usually blows up in your face. "You can never trust them," Mr. Cochrane said. "All they want to do is make a sale. Before you hand over your money to someone, you have to do your homework."

"There's the bar," Bobby said.

We bellied up and Bobby wasted no time ordering our favorite drink.

"Two Peppermint Schnapps, please."

The bartender eyed us suspiciously. I guess he didn't like our looks.

"Were you invited?" he asked.

"Yes," I replied. "Dick is my stepfather."

The bartender poured two shots into two glasses. When he was finished, Bobby reached into his pocket and pulled out a dollar. He placed the bill in a Crystal bowl for tips. At the Newport Balboa Club, even the tip jars had class.

"Thanks," the bartender smiled.

"You're welcome," Bobby nodded. "But you should know, that was my last dollar."

Bobby and I clinked our glasses and we took a sip. Then the trouble started.

"Scott, Bobby, you came!"

We turned to see my little sister, Julie. Like everyone else, she had on a Ralph Lauren floral skirt and a white blouse. I knew it was Ralph Lauren because after my mom married The Dick it was the only place he would let them shop. There and Neiman's.

Julie had two friends with her and the three of them were staring at Bobby. I reached out and hugged Julie. She had just finished seventh grade and my only regret about graduating high school was that I wouldn't be there for her freshman year.

"Julie, I've missed you."

"I've missed you too, Scotty. When are you coming home?"

"Not for a while."

She pulled back and I noticed she was wearing too much makeup. Then she turned to Bobby.

"Dick told me to watch for you, Bobby. He'll want to know you're here."

"Really," Bobby said, "why is that?"

"He wants to introduce you to what he calls some heavy hitters. I'm going to tell him you're here."

She turned and headed straight toward my stepfather. Julie tugged on his sleeve and he looked over at us. Dick excused himself from his conversation, and he walked over to another man.

I felt Bobby lean into me and whisper, "This is the part that stinks. At least we didn't have to wait for it."

"He's never dropped a conversation for me before," I replied. "He thinks kids should be seen but not heard."

Dick walked to a second man and spoke to him. The man looked over at us and then whispered in Dick's ear. Dick turned and walked toward us. He was smiling and seemed excited we were there.

"Scott, Bobby. Thank you for coming to my little soiree."

"We wouldn't have missed it," I replied. "It's the party of the season."

As always, he was gracious and smooth, but I knew that what he valued here wasn't me. Still, it was his party.

"How's school going, Scott?" he asked.

"Good. Straight A's last year. I also took an economics course this summer. Got an A in that, too. If you want to know about supply and demand, I'm your man."

"That's good, Scott. I've always known you're a smart kid. You'll figure it out someday."

"Yeah, thanks," I said, wondering what I was supposed to figure out.

"How are your grades, Bobby?" The Dick asked.

"Not as good as Scotty's, but I passed."

Then my stepfather looked at me again.

"Could I borrow Bobby for a second. There's some people who would like to meet him."

"Sure. Borrow away. After all, it's your party."

"Thanks," Dick said. "Follow me, Bobby."

"All right." Bobby said and he looked at me and winked. "Bring on the contacts."

Bobby walked off with Dick, leaving me alone. I looked over at my mother. She was oblivious to the fact that I was even there. Then I looked over at my sister. She was talking to her two friends and they were still staring at Bobby. I turned to the bartender and asked for another Schnapps.

I took my drink and sat at a table overlooking the bay. Life appeared normal. People were coming and going with smiles. Men and women were attending to their boats and yachts. But life was anything but normal now. The realization that my family had used me to get to my best friend was a hard thing for me to understand. I sipped my drink. I was too young to drink, but no one seemed to care about that either. I wondered if life would be easier if I was a drunk like my father, and followed in the footsteps of such legendary writers as Jack London, F. Scott Fitzgerald, and Charles Bukowski. As Blake said, "The road to excess leads to the palace of wisdom."

I sat for a long moment thinking about Blake's assertion. I had been excessively drunk a few times. Like the time Bobby and I snuck into the Alley Bar. We got hammered and tried to ride our bikes back to the trailer park in the middle of the night. I didn't remember much the next day except crashing and throwing up the whole way home. I woke the next morning with my face skinned up and my head felt like someone had used it for a football. There wasn't much wisdom in that.

I set my drink aside and decided that would be it for tonight. My screwed-up family was not worth getting drunk over. I looked over at my mother. She looked toward me and then quickly looked away. I felt like she was ignoring me, or worse, avoiding me.

I gazed over at Bobby. The perfectly manicured Dick was standing next to two other men and they had Bobby surrounded. The men had intense expressions on their faces and seemed to be trying to tell Bobby something important. Bobby was nodding and smiling a lot.

I looked back out the window. An enormous yacht pulled up to the dock in front. I noticed a beautiful young woman jump off the yacht and start tying the massive boat to the dock. At first I was just admiring the yacht and how unusual it was for a young girl to be tying it up. Suddenly, I realized that the girl was Perry. She climbed back on the boat and disappeared inside.

"Hey, Bro."

I turned around to see Bobby standing with The Dick.

"Hey," I said.

"Thanks for letting me borrow Bobby," my stepfather said. "I think you helped your friend's future a lot by bringing him to my party."

"Dick," I said. "Do you know who owns that yacht?"

The Dick looked out at the boat.

"Yeah," he said. "That's old man Elliot's yacht. He's the richest old goat in Newport. Rumor has it that he only takes the boat out when he's bird dogging some young chick. I bet you boys can relate to that. The guy's in his eighties and I don't know how he still finds the energy. I mean look at that chicky helping him off the boat."

Bobby looked and saw that is was Perry. He looked at me and started to say something. I shook my head and he quickly closed his mouth

"Yeah," the Dick continued. "I bet old man Elliot has a lot of fun with that little beach bunny. Money does have its advantages."

"Dick, you really are an asshole, aren't you?" My statement was like an explosion that comes out nowhere. It was what Homer would call "lyssa", the wolf's rage.

"What?" The Dick stammered. "What did you call me?"

The Dick was so furious that he clenched his fists and took a step toward me. But Bobby stepped in front of him.

"Easy, Dick," Bobby said. "We're just here to pay our respects."

The Dick looked at Bobby and seemed to be at a loss for words.

"Come on, Bobby," I said. "Let's go. Happy Birthday, Dick." I stood and walked past him without saying another word.

Bobby smiled.

"Guess we're leaving. Thanks again for the contacts."

Bobby turned and followed me, leaving The Dick standing by himself on his birthday. I knew he would probably wonder what had inspired my outburst, but that was his problem. Still, it made me smile, his perfect life had once again been marred by his punk of a stepson. I doubted it would bother him for very long. In a few minutes he wouldn't even be thinking of me, grateful I was no longer part of his life. Nobody likes someone who constantly holds up a mirror that only reflects your imperfections.

By the time we got to the car, Bobby was laughing really hard.

"I couldn't believe the look on The Dick's face when you called him an asshole."

I didn't respond. I was really pissed. My mother had ignored me. I had been used because my best friend was Bobby Rowels. And The Dick, outstanding role model that he was, had decided Perry was a whore. Bobby sensed my anger and stopped.

"Sorry to laugh, bro. It's just that this was really fucked up and I'm glad The Dick didn't get away with it scot-free."

I was quiet for a moment. I knew Bobby was trying to lighten the situation by making a joke. But my stepfather and mother had used me to raise their social status and that fact hurt.

"Let's just get the hell out of here. I never want to see my stepfather again."

13

I like to think Bobby and I became friends three years ago because he liked what I wrote and it spoke to him. We met on the first day of our freshman year. It was during lunch, and I was sitting at a picnic table alone scribbling in one of the journals I always carried. I always write about my experiences and feelings and I have stacks of journals all dated and filed, a history of the life of Scott Curtis.

I was writing furiously when I looked up to find Bobby sitting across from me.

"Hey," he said.

I was surprised. I didn't have many friends. I was that guy you don't really notice: the proverbial fly on the wall, so easily forgettable I might as well have been a ghost. But this suited me fine because it enabled me to observe the world unnoticed. I had found it's better to observe than be observed.

"Hi," I replied.

"You're in my English class."

"Really?"

"Yeah, I liked the questions you asked about *The Pearl*. Whether we should view it as a true story or an allegory, whatever that means. The teacher looked a little surprised. I don't think he knew what to say."

"Yeah, I've read it a few times. It's a question I've asked myself."

"What's an allegory?"

"It's a story that has an idea or moral in it. It presents this idea in a dramatic way."

"Kind of like a Western?"

"Kind of."

Bobby nodded. "I'm Bobby. My dad said to me once, 'Bobby, find the smartest kid in the class and make friends with him. You can learn as much from him as you can from the teacher.'"

I didn't know it at the time, but whenever Bobby Rowels spoke of his father it was a really big deal. The summer before Bobby's freshman year, his father had been murdered. His dad had stopped at the neighborhood liquor store to buy a carton of milk for the family on the way home from his job as an estimator for an air conditioning company. He had stumbled upon a robbery. "The shooter didn't want a witness," the police report read.

That's how Bobby came to Newport. His mother sold the house, collected the life insurance, and moved Bobby to this shining little city by the sea. She wanted her son out of Anaheim, where the crime had taken place.

"I don't know if I'm the smartest kid in the class," I replied.

"Well, you're smarter than me," Bobby smiled.

Bobby took a bite of his sandwich and then looked at my journal. "What are you writing?"

"I'm writing about my life. My life is pretty screwed up so I guess I have a lot to write about."

"Why's your life screwed up?"

"My parents got a divorce last month and now my mom is marrying some rich asshole."

"That sucks."

"Tell me about it."

"But at least your parents are alive."

"Barely."

Bobby studied me for a moment. It was as if he was sizing me up, trying to decide if I was full of shit.

"Would you let me read something you've written?" he asked.

"You really want to?"

"Yeah."

When writers first start out they'll let anyone read their material. They don't care who, just so it gets read.

I reached in my backpack and pulled out a short story I'd just finished. I handed it to Bobby. He looked at me and smiled.

"Thanks," he said.

"Sure."

"Hey, do you surf?"

"Yeah."

"Would you teach me?"

"All right."

Bobby read my story, an allegory on loyalty, and he gave me great notes. I've grown to trust him completely with my writing and he is the first person I give my stuff to. In exchange, I taught Bobby to surf. Bobby was on the football team so Sunday became "our day" that first fall and winter our freshman year. The ocean was our church. Rain or shine, waves or no waves, we met every Sunday and I taught him what I knew. How to find the lineup and stay in it by using a landmark on the beach, what a roundhouse was or how you have to paddle hard, especially on smaller swells in offshore winds, to catch the wave early enough to stand up without being blown back.

Through September and October Bobby soaked up everything I said. By November he was under his own power and by December I was watching Bobby ride waves as well as I did. Maybe even better. That was the kind of athlete Bobby was. Any sport, any time, he was a natural.

That made being friends with Bobby hard at first. He was just so good at everything. He was also handsome and the girls were always chasing him. In fact, girls searched me out simply because I was Bobby's friend, and people began to know who I was because Bobby valued me, the reluctant sidekick.

I was struggling with this on Thanksgiving Day that first November freshman year when Bobby came to the beach. He was carrying a backpack and his new board I helped him pick out at the Frog House Surf Shop.

"Let's not surf right away," he said. "Let's just hang."

The wind was blowing offshore and the waves looked pretty good, three to four foot peaks.

"Let's surf," I said. "We can hang out in the water."

"No, let's talk first."

We sat on the beach next to our boards and Bobby was quiet for a long time. I imagined he was having a hard day thinking about his father. After all, Thanksgiving is really about family, and this was the first Thanksgiving without his father. For my part, I was exactly where I wanted to be because the last thing I wanted to think about was my family.

Then Bobby turned to me with a serious look on his face.

"I want to make a blood oath with you."

I wasn't sure what he meant.

"A blood oath?"

"Yeah, an agreement about being best friends."

"Are you asking me to be your best friend?"

"No," Bobby replied quickly. "I'm asking to be yours."

I was quiet. It struck me that I had never met anyone like Bobby Rowels before. One of his many passions was Western movies and by watching them he had built a code of sorts, a map that he lived his life by. He watched them whenever he could. On Sunday he would scan the newspaper's television schedule and circle when his favorite movies were playing. If *Red River* was on at 2 am he would set his alarm and wake up to watch it. If *Shane* was on in the afternoon, Bobby would drop everything to watch it. It was his fixation with Westerns that had compelled his mom to sell their house in Anaheim and move to Newport. After his dad was killed, Bobby had locked himself in the house and watched movies all day. His mother hoped the move would break his obsession. Instead, his connection to Westerns only grew stronger.

I've thought about Bobby's obsession with Westerns and I've decided it has to do with the simple integrity of the stories, a world filled with archetypal characters facing obstacles requiring courage, loyalty, and rugged resourcefulness to surmount their challenges. There are also themes of truth and honesty, values Bobby esteemed but that are seldom offered in the real world. Westerns, after his dad died, were something he could put his faith into, a mythic world where hopes and dreams are protected and fulfilled in meaningful ways.

I was in with both feet. Not because being Bobby's friend had brought me a modicum of popularity but because I thought Bobby had something to teach me. In a way, you could say, I was fascinated by him.

"Yeah, all right. But why me?" I asked.

"It's that story you gave me the first day of school. It's about loyalty to your father."

I was surprised. He said he had gotten it but now I knew he really understood it.

"Loyalty is so important," Bobby continued. "We just look at the world differently, Scotty. We see what's right and fair where most people couldn't give a shit."

Bobby reached into his backpack and pulled out an enormous butcher knife. For a moment, I thought he had lost his mind. Then he suddenly took the knife and sliced open his thumb. The blood began streaming out, and now I was certain he'd lost his mind.

"Give me your thumb." He had a smile on his face and looked maniacal with the huge knife in his hand. I knew this was a cliché, blood brothers created by some form of ceremony, but I was horrified.

"What?" I asked incredulously.

"Give me your thumb."

"No fucking way."

"Do you trust me?"

I looked at the knife and then at Bobby.

"I'm not sure."

Then Bobby looked at me hard.

"Do you trust me?"

I thought about our friendship. We had become surf buddies and our friendship had evolved. Sitting on our boards waiting for waves, the ocean had worked its magic on us and our conversations had grown deeper. We had talked about the hard things we were feeling, Bobby with the terrible loss of his father and my pain of dealing with the divorce of my parents. "Yes," I thought, "I trusted him." Slowly, almost reluctantly, I held out my thumb.

"You probably saw this in some stupid Western," I complained.

Bobby smiled

"I did. *The Sheriff of Fractured Jaw.*"

"Hawks or Ford?"

"Close. Raoul Walsh."

I closed my eyes as he sliced open my thumb.

"Shit, that hurt."

"Now you get to listen to something I wrote."

Bobby reached into his backpack and pulled out a piece of lined yellow paper with writing on it.

"With the ocean as our witness, we agree to a bond of friendship that no parent, girl, teacher, friend, coach, or anyone else can come between. We agree to always watch each other's back, win, lose or draw." Bobby looked at me for a long moment. "Agreed?"

"Agreed."

"Now give me your thumb again."

I held out my thumb to my friend and he pressed his bloody thumb into mine.

"We will never tell anyone about this moment," Bobby said. "It belongs only to us and represents the moment we became more than just friends. We became brothers."

For some reason the hair on the back of my neck stood up.

"Don't the good guys walk off into the sunset?" I laughed.

Bobby looked at me for another long moment. Then he smiled. Imitating his favorite character in his favorite Western, Ethan in John Ford's *The Searchers*, he said, "Goddamn right we will."

I smiled back. "Okay, Ethan, I'll be your brother."

"Then press your thumb on this paper with me."

I pressed my thumb on the yellow lined paper and Bobby pressed his. Two large blood stains appeared on the paper. Next, Bobby dug a deep hole, crumpled up the paper and placed it in the hole.

"Help me bury it," he said. Together we pushed sand into the hole. Bobby stood and looked down at me.

"This is about total loyalty, bro."

"Then I guess I'll have to start by lying to my mom," I smiled.

"Why?"

"She's going to want to know how I got all this blood on my shirt. I'll just tell her I got into a fight and she should see the other guy."

Bobby smiled, "Let's go surfing."

It was one of the best surf sessions I've ever had. With the cut on my thumb stinging from the salt water, I was enveloped in feelings of friendship and joy that only two teenage boys can know. Bobby became my best friend ever since that Thanksgiving Day freshman year, and the first call I made after The Dick kicked me out of his house was to Bobby. He had just gotten his license and he drove me to my dad's trailer in the Chrysler. The backseat was packed with only my clothes, books and typewriter. Win, lose or draw, we were on each other's side, desperately trying to hold onto our innocence in the face of an absurd world.

14

"My mother is such a bitch," I railed as we drove past Newport Harbor High School. "She's turned into a Newport Beach rich bitch. She's pathetic."

"Scotty, tell me what you really think."

"All right. She's a skunking whore that would sell her children if she thought it would help her with The Dick. What am I talking about? She did sell her children. She sold me out to get to my best friend. All for The Dick. Well, Happy-fucking-Birthday, Dick."

My diatribe had been inspired by what Bobby told me. The two men that my stepfather had introduced Bobby to were fat cat alumni from rival colleges, and they wanted Bobby for their teams.

Both men had started by trying to sell Bobby on their respective schools. Then the conversation escalated into something of a bidding war; job offers, use of their sailboats and cars, and access to their extensive networks of contacts. All Bobby had to do was sign a letter of intent to play football for their schools. Bobby was polite and thanked them. But he quickly realized that these men had no clue what would be the deciding reason if and when a choice came. They could only offer what they themselves valued.

"My family is so screwed up," I continued.

"Your family? What about mine?"

"Yours? You can't help what happened to your dad."

"Yeah, I know. But it was my mom's choice to date my football coach. You know what happened last night?"

"What?"

"I set the alarm to watch *High Noon* at midnight and awoke to the sounds of Coach White huffing and puffing on top of my mom."

"Don't tell me that, Bobby."

"I'm not kidding you. You know how thin those walls are."

Bobby lived next door to our high school in the Oakwood Apartments. A better name would be the Oakwood Sin Bin. It was known as the first stop after a divorce, a way station of sorts before you started a new life. The man who lived next door was in the middle of a messy divorce and brought home a different woman every night. Bobby and I once listened through the wall and we heard the guy commanding, "Come, sit, speak." Some woman was actually barking like a dog. That was bad enough, but it's worse when it's your mom. The idea of Bobby listening to that noise made me gag.

"Bro, that's just sick," I said, remembering the morning I walked into our apartment and heard my mother with The Dick.

"Yeah, it is," Bobby continued. "But here's my question. Why is my coach dating my mom?"

Bobby looked at me, waiting for my response. A smile crossed my face. I just couldn't help myself.

"What?" Bobby asked.

"Do you want the first thing that popped in my head or do you want me to think about it?"

"Give me your first thought."

"All right, I think White is dating your mom because he secretly wishes he was dating you."

Bobby's face showed utter surprise. "Have you read my mind?"

"What?"

"Have you become so close to me that you know my thoughts?"

"You mean to tell me that you think White is a closet pervert who's dating your mom to get close to you like some sort of predator with all kinds of planning and shit?"

Bobby turned pale.

"You're fucking sick. You know that. You're going to be writing some sick shit some day. Like those beat writers you talk about. Shit, now you've just given me something else to worry about."

"Hey, I'm sorry. You told me to say the first thing that popped into my head."

"I do think he's dating my mom because of me."

"You can't be serious. Why?"

"Because he thinks I might be his meal ticket."

"What?"

"Every high school coach longs to move up to the next level, and I'm getting a lot of interest from a bunch of colleges. What better way for White to get to know those coaches than to be part of my process? He thinks he should be the one to guide me, and I have the feeling that I'm what he talks about most with my mom. They're together because of me."

I was stunned. I didn't know what to say.

"Bobby, are you sure?"

"No, I'm not sure. I hope he really likes my mom. But let's face it. My mom isn't beautiful and she's kind of overweight. She's also older than White."

Bobby had a point there. It was a common cliché that divorced guys are looking for younger girls. Bobby saw it every day at the Oakwood Sin Bin.

"I've thought about it from every angle," Bobby continued. "The trouble is that I know my mom really likes him. He's the first man she's dated since my dad died. But White definitely thinks he's going to be part of my decision. He asks me every day about what letters I've gotten or who's contacted me. The guy wants to be involved and what better way to do that than to be part of the family?"

Bobby made a lot of sense but it was the most incredible thing I had ever heard. Still, I had just experienced my own family using me to get to Bobby because of football. He had made some kind of pre-season list for top prospects. Everybody was watching him.

"Shit," I said. "What are you going to do?"

"I'm going to move out."

"What?"

"I want to move in with you and your dad."

"Bobby, we live in a shit box. Why would you want to live with us?"

Bobby was quiet a moment. I could tell he was searching for the right way to explain it.

"Because I know I'll be safe. Safe from all the bullshit. Safe from people trying to use me to get what they want. People think my future is some kind of game. But it's my life and I'll be protecting my mom."

Now I knew how serious this was.

"But we don't have any money," I protested. "My dad's disability barely covers our rent. I have money because I wash dishes three nights a week and just added Sunday brunch. But that's not enough to cover both of us."

"I've got that part figured out. My dad left me his baseball card collection and I can sell it. It should be enough to cover me through the season. There's a lot of Mickey Mantles, and after the season I can get a job, too."

"What about your mom?"

"I love my mom, and she seems happy. For the first time in a long time, she seems happy. But I hate White. Always giving me some cliché on how to be a man like he's my dad or something. I can't stand being around him and I don't want to be the one to screw it up for my mom. I mean, it took everything I had to keep from going in my mom's bedroom and kicking his ass. If she's being used because of me I will never forgive myself."

We were quiet for a long moment.

"There's another thing," Bobby suddenly added. "I think this football season might be my last."

"What?" I was stunned. "You might be the best football player in the county. Everyone thinks you're going to the pros."

"It's just not fun anymore. I've been thinking I might move to Hawaii and just surf."

"What do you mean? Ever since I've known you, you've said football is your favorite sport."

"It was. But with White dating my mom, and people coming out of the woodwork trying to sell me on this college or that, it's taken the fun out of it. I want this to be my best season ever because it may be my last. If it's not fun at the end, I'm done."

I was quiet for a moment thinking about Bobby moving in with us. I already knew my answer, and it was really my decision to make. My dad would say yes. He didn't care who lived with him.

"Okay," I said. "But I love your mom. You have to tell her that this is your idea. I don't want her thinking I had any part in this."

Bobby looked at me and nodded.

"All right," he said with a seriousness I knew came from his heart. "But she must never know the reason. She must never know it was because of White."

"Agreed."

Bobby stuck out his hand and we shook like brothers - thumbs wrapped around thumbs.

"Welcome to the shit box," I said and added, "I guess we'll have to get some bunk beds."

15

Our destination was the outskirts of Newport's city limits where our friend, Jim Steiner, lived on a pond appropriately called Cherry Lake. There was a boathouse on the property detached and down the hill from the main house and it sat right on a large pond with a large wooden deck that extended out over the water. The boathouse came complete with a bar, couches, and a pool table.

The boathouse was a prized location for Harbor High kids since its privacy allowed for all kinds of shenanigans. Teenagers are naturally curious and there's nothing more interesting than a little danger. It was common knowledge at school that anything might happen at Steiner's boathouse. I couldn't count on both hands the number of guys and girls who lost their virginity there. Even the pool table had a nickname. Inspired by the movie *The Last Picture Show*, it was known as the Magic Carpet.

Jim Steiner himself was dangerous. Not because he was tough. Steiner was a kicker and kickers are usually anything but tough. No, Steiner's reputation was two-fold. First, he always had something on hand that would alter perception, like alcohol, pot, or ludes. Second, he was always the first to break the ice by getting naked in front of everyone and walking through his parties as if he were fully dressed. He was especially fond of shocking first-timers like freshmen or sophomore girls. As a result, both Steiner and the boathouse were infamous.

Oddly enough, for me Steiner's boathouse represented something else entirely: The feeling of innocence.

Bobby opened the gate revealing a plumeria tree with pretty pink flowers and the birds-of-paradise were in full bloom. A hummingbird danced above the giant ferns. In my mind, I was always immediately transported to the Fern Grotto on Kauai and those memories flooded in. My parents had brought me there when I was eight years old. It was before the war between them had erupted, before my mother had chosen a life of boob jobs and Porsches; a time when my father was still a hero in uniform and my parents put my sister and me first.

I felt a sharp pain in my chest as my heart pounded. It was like a panic attack. I stopped for a moment and thought of my mother while trying to catch my breath. She hadn't even searched me out to say goodbye. It was as if she was embarrassed by me, or worse, indifferent.

Then I felt Bobby at my side and he put his arm around my shoulder.

"Thinking of Kauai, bro?" he asked gently.

"Yeah." I croaked as my childhood memory held me in a stranglehold.

On Kauai, we had rented kayaks and paddled up the Wailua River and found ourselves alone in the middle of a tropical wonderland. We had played a game called "Searching for the Menehune," who are Kauai's leprechauns. We ran through the forest searching, screeching and yelling, wrapped in the warmth of the sweet Hawaiian air. My mother made my sister and me believe that we were surrounded by the Menehune who were whispering to us the secrets that would lead to a happy life of good luck and good fortune. All we had to do was listen.

"I don't know why this path always does this to me."

Bobby nodded. He knew what the memory conjured in my soul.

"Why doesn't my mother care about me anymore?"

"She cares about you," he said gently. "She just doesn't think about it. People get their priorities screwed up sometimes. Look at Coach White and my mom. Come on, forget it. Let's party."

But I hung back a moment as I remembered that special day when my mother loved me.

Bobby stopped and turned.

"Are you coming, bro?"

"Yeah." I smiled remembering another, more important reason why I think of the Fern Grotto as my secret garden. It was there that I first heard a little voice, the "faraway music" that Thoreau so eloquently describes. It was the Menehunes whispering softly, "You have a story to tell." The small voice that enables me to find my creative place of innocence and hope that enables me to write in spite of my pain. It's also the reason I never lost my virginity on Cherry Lake. I didn't want that experience to be part of that memory.

By the time Bobby and I reached the bottom of Steiner's path, the memory of the Fern Grotto had worked its magic once again and I felt my spirits lift.

16

"Drink, motherfucker, drink, motherfucker...." Jim Steiner was yelling at the top of his lungs as Led Zeppelin's "Misty Mountain Hop" blared through boathouse's giant speakers.

Bobby and I had walked in on a scene right out of page two of the teenage instruction manual on rebellion - the page that describes activities and rituals promoting depravity, our own private dance of ecstasy to Dionysus, the original party god.

Tommy Watts was on one end of a surgical tube that was inserted deep in his mouth. On the other end of the tube was a funnel into which Rickie Chandler poured a can of Old English 800. It was a potent concoction of malt liquor. Two cans, and I was buzzed, three cans and I was drunk. Four, I was passed out. It was the original blackout in a can. The cans were not only potent, they were large, and the speed at which the liquor ran through the surgical tube was nothing short of astonishing.

"Drink, motherfucker, drink...," Jim Steiner continued as Bobby and I stood watching.

Tommy Watts sucked it down, choking and burping as the malt liquor flowed like a deluge into his stomach. It always worried me to see Tommy Watts on the end of the beer bong. To say Old English fired Tommy up was an understatement, and after about three cans, Tommy would look at me with a maniacal grin and yell at the top of his lungs, "Time for some rug burns, Scotty." He was a big guy and a lineman on the football team. But his real love was wrestling. I can't count the number of times that I had been pinned to the floor after Tommy had slammed a few too many cans of Old English 800.

"Way to suck it down," Rickie Chandler screamed with glee. He was a thin wiry kid and Tommy's best friend. Rickie was also a ladies' man. With his button nose and blonde hair, he was just so cute, even with a shaved head, and the girls all loved him. According to Jim Steiner, who kept track of such things, Rickie was the record cherry buster of the boathouse.

When the can had been emptied into Tommy via the beer bong, the three hedonists finally noticed us.

"Shit, Rowels," Steiner shouted. "I thought you guys were never going to show. We're already on our second beer."

"I told you we had to make a stop," Bobby replied. "We're here, aren't we?"

"Hey, Rowels," Rickie Chandler said. "There's a rumor going around that you ditched practice that morning to go surfing."

"Yeah," Steiner added. "Rumor has it you rode a twenty-foot wave or something."

"He did," I said. "It was Homeric."

"What's that mean?" Tommy asked.

"Didn't you take an English class, Watts?" Steiner said. "It means that it happens once in a generation, it means that it was larger than life. In a word, it was mythic."

I liked Jim Steiner. He knew the value of a word, and he was the only other student to get an A in Mr. Wakeman's accelerated English class.

"What does mythic mean?" Tommy asked.

Steiner looked at me and laughed. Then he gently said to Tommy, "It means it was really good."

"Oh," Tommy said.

"It may have been good," Rickie Chandler added. "But the rumor is everywhere and if White finds out, it's going to be your ass."

"Fuck White," Steiner replied. "He's an asshole. But I do think we should make Rowels celebrate his wave with a beer."

The hedonists all yelled, "Yeah," and before you could question the wisdom of our choices, the end of the beer bong was inserted into Bobby's mouth as Led Zeppelin's "When the Levee Breaks" pounded our senses.

17

"Fuckin long-haired surfer pussy," Tommy Watts said.

On the surface, Tommy was referring to the fact that I didn't partake of the beer bong. But it also cut deeper. There was a divide between surfers and football players, especially after the players heads were shaved and surfer's got to keep their curls. It was another reason for the football players to hate the surfers and the surfers reciprocated by calling the football players jarheads. It had to do with what was cool, who had skills that were worthy of respect and, ultimately, how all that equated to getting girls. The surfers represented one idea and the football players another. For Tommy, this was a hard thing because it didn't matter what he was. He was never going to get a girl.

"Lay off, Tommy," Bobby said. "Scotty and I made a deal. He's going to drive."

"I could drive," Tommy said.

"Yeah," I said. "Right into a ditch."

"That's fuckin it," Tommy replied. "I'm going to pin your ass later."

We were all packed into the Chrysler. Watts, Chandler and Steiner in the backseat, Bobby and I upfront, heading down Galaxy in Dover Shores to the cruise spot. Once there, we would perform our reconnaissance and find out where the parties were.

"I wonder if Peek-a-boo Sue will be out, Tommy." Steiner said with a smile.

Peek-a-boo Sue was Tommy's nemesis. She was an older woman who lived at the central intersection for cruising. She would always peek through the window to see who was out there. She frequently called the police if we sat in our cars too long while trying to find out where the parties were.

We all laughed about her. But for Tommy it was different. Peek-a-boo Sue went to church with Tommy's mom and always reported to her on his activities. She once saw Tommy mooning some girls and when the report reached his mother, Tommy was grounded for weeks.

"I hate that bitch," Tommy said.

When we pulled up, another car was there. We recognized it immediately. It was a black Mercedes sedan and we knew it was occupied by Liza the Hurricane and her posse.

"Hey, Rowels," Rickie said, "your girlfriend's out looking for you."

Bobby smiled. He knew that Rickie always tried to compete with him in the girl department. But I knew Bobby was beyond Rickie and the idea of finding your self-worth in something as stupid as "who could get the chicks." Of course, Bobby liked hooking up with girls as much as the next guy. But it was for the actual experience of it, not how it made him look. Being a "chick-getter" was not on Bobby's radar.

I rolled down the window as we pulled alongside the Mercedes.

"Hey, girls," I called out, "where are you headed?"

Liza was driving with four of her usual friends in the car.

"There's a party in Bay Shores," Liza said. "We're on the list so you'll need to follow us to get through the guard gate."

"Who's party?" Jim Steiner called from the back.

"Cindy Stacker," Liza answered.

"Yeah, I forgot about that one," Steiner said. "I was invited. I think I'm on the list."

"We'll see you there," I said to Liza.

We pulled away and Bobby turned to Steiner.

"Why are you always invited to these parties?"

Steiner laughed. "I think it's because of who my parents are. When your dad is in the FBI parents think you're safe."

"I've always wondered what your dad would say if he knew what went on in his boathouse." I said.

"Please," Steiner replied. "He'd have a friggin' cow. Luckily he travels so much, he'll never know."

"Look," Tommy said. "There's Peek-a-boo. She's looking out the window again."

"You'd better hide," Steiner said. "She might tell your mom on you."

"Suck me," Tommy replied.

I shuttled the Chrysler down Dover Drive toward Pacific Coast Highway and into Bay Shores.

A guardhouse sits at the entrance complete with a gate, and as we pulled up, a tall, slender white-haired man stepped out. I rolled down the window as he walked toward us. He appeared smooth and confident.

"It's Jerry," Steiner called from the back.

"Can I help you?" the older man said.

"Hey, Jerry," Steiner said. "It's me, Jim Steiner."

"Oh, hi, Jim," Jerry said. "Are you boys going to the Stackers' house for the party?"

"Yeah," Steiner said.

"That's nice," Jerry replied. "Have a good time."

"Thanks."

Jerry turned to the guardhouse and motioned to someone to open the gate. The arm lifted and he waved us through.

Bobby turned to Steiner.

"What was that about?"

"Jerry isn't a security guard. He used to be my Dad's partner and was something of a legend with the FBI. Took down a Mafia kingpin. Now he works security for special situations. There must be someone important coming here tonight."

"That's Newport Beach," I said. "Nothing is what it appears. A security guard is actually an ex-FBI agent and the guy with a Ferrari and a mansion is millions of dollars in debt."

"That may be true in some places," Steiner countered. "But this is Bay Shores. The mansion, the money, and the Ferraris are real. You can't even live here unless they vote to approve you."

There was valet parking for the party. We pulled up and a pimply red-haired kid about our own age walked up to take our keys.

"Thanks," I said. He just grunted and handed me a ticket without making eye contact. I imagined he thought we were also rich kids whose parents could afford to hire a valet parking team for a high school birthday party. I could sense his anger, and I was pretty sure that envy of that kind of money would turn to bitter resentment by the end of the night. As he climbed in the Chrysler, I called to him.

"Hey!"

He turned to me.

"Just so you know, I work three nights a week as a dishwasher."

His eyes met mine and he nodded. He started the car and drove away. Then I realized my friends were all looking at me.

"Why'd you tell him that?" Rickie Chandler asked.

"Because that guy is going to be ignored by every girl here tonight, and by the end of the night he's going to be pissed. I don't want him screwing with the Chrysler because he thinks we're rich assholes."

Bobby put his hand on my shoulder.

"Thanks, bro," he said.

18

The Stackers' house was a five thousand square foot mansion centered on a huge chunk of bay front land. The Nantucket-style house even had a widow's walk, which I'm sure afforded a panoramic view of the bay and distant horizon.

I felt a little uneasy as we approached the front door. Cindy Stacker is a beautiful girl but it takes a little time to see it, her beauty sort of sneaks up on you like a slow-moving storm. But once it does, you are smitten. I had thought of asking her to a dance once but never found the courage and decided she was out of my league. Rickie Chandler took her and a rumor had it that she became another notch in his Cherry Lake legacy. I turned to Rickie.

"You think Cindy knows you're coming?"

Rickie smiled. "No, I'll just surprise her."

We knocked on the door and a nicely dressed Hispanic man wearing a dark pinstripe suit, red bow tie and pencil mustache appeared. He did not smile.

"Hi," Steiner said. "We're here for the party."

"They are in the ballroom," he said in perfect English. "Follow me."

Kids filled the ballroom, dancing to Van Morrison's "Moondance". The music reverberated off the room's twenty-foot ceilings as a band called King's Road blasted away. They were local guys who always played a great assortment of songs. From the Beach Boys to the Grateful Dead, King's Road could make the music come alive - especially after a couple of beers loosened up the party.

"Look at that," Chandler announced immediately, "Corona dick-heads. I heard Cindy's been dating the enemy."

The Corona del Mar Sea Kings are Newport's crosstown rivals. Newport Harbor players considered them rich kids and we usually beat the crap out of them in football. Still, the occasional win by Corona happened. For the Sea Kings, if they won only one game all year and it was against Newport, it made their entire season a success. That's because Newport, being a bigger school, is usually favored to win.

Several members from the Sea King football team danced right in front of us and not with just anyone. They were dancing with Liza and her posse. Liza saw us out of the corner of her eye and suddenly turned on the charm. She shimmied her breasts and bent forward so a handsome young Sea King could look down her low-cut top.

"Shit, Rowels," Rickie Chandler said. "Are you going to let Liza get away with that? This is our turf."

Bobby only smiled. It was obvious that Liza was trying to get a rise out of him.

"Come on," Rickie Chandler said. "Let's go fuck up some Corona guys."

Steiner, Rickie, and Tommy puffed out their chests and strutted toward the Sea Kings, intending to cut in. But Bobby turned to me and whispered, "Let's walk down to the bay."

I nodded and followed Bobby toward the open door that we guessed would lead us to the water. We stepped out onto an enormous patio. A huge pool was the central feature and beyond the pool was a large expanse of perfectly manicured grass that ran to the water's edge. The patio and lawn were empty of people and I think Bobby liked this.

"Let's walk out on the dock," Bobby suggested.

A brick walkway led to a large dock that extended far out into the bay. Alongside the dock, a white yacht glistened in the moonlight.

Bobby led the way and I followed. We walked in silence and I knew he was troubled. At first, I thought it was because of the Hurricane dancing with a rival.

"Are you pissed about Liza?" I asked.

"Nah," Bobby said. "You were the one who taught me about stuff like that."

"Me?"

"Yeah, one of your stories. You said that you can never control anyone. You can love them but never expect to control them. You can only control yourself and how you choose to react to their actions."

I was quiet remembering what I had written about my mother. I never knew it had touched Bobby this deeply, that he had found in my words a larger lesson than I had intended. He had taken a specific situation and projected it universally.

We continued out onto the dock and stood in the moonlight looking off across the bay toward Linda Isle. Sounds of the band playing The Grateful Dead's "Turn On Your Love Light" drifted to us from the ballroom.

But the party did not interest Bobby. He was trying to weigh something out in his mind and silence was the greatest gift I could give him. Friendship is more than the mere words you speak to each other. It is about understanding the rhythms of the feelings and emotions upon which the words are based. Silence often allows these rhythms to unfold. We stood at the end of the dock looking out at the lights of Linda Isle. Finally, Bobby spoke.

"You know, it's just all so screwed up. My dad gets blown away and now my coach is dating my mom. Why couldn't I just have a normal childhood?"

"Normal? I don't even know what that means. Is anybody's childhood really normal?"

"Yeah, like in your story. We often lose perspective of our feelings. I mean half of the entire world is walking around feeling the same way. I just wish that I was the other half."

"Trust me, Bobby, there is no other half."

We heard footsteps and turned to see the silhouette of a lone man walking along the dock connected to the house next door. He appeared to be headed toward the yacht that was tied up to the end of the dock.

"Damn," Bobby said. "I know that walk," and he yelled, "Ahoy!"

"Go fuck yourself," came the reply.

Bobby looked at me and laughed.

"You must be Liberty Valance," Bobby called.

"Who the hell wants to know?" the silhouette stopped to stare at us through the darkness.

"Bobby Rowels."

"And who is Bobby Rowels?"

"Just someone who thinks that *The Man Who Shot Liberty Valance* is one of the greatest movies ever made."

It was true that Bobby thought this. Many nights we had holed up at his mom's apartment watching John Ford's great psychological Western. We were especially impressed with the performance of Lee Marvin as the villain Liberty Valance. He simply fleshed out the idea that "If you're going to be a bear, be a grizzly."

"When you told me to go fuck myself," Bobby added, "I knew it was something Liberty Valance would say. Sorry to have bothered you, sir."

There was a long pause, and I could feel the eyes of Lee Marvin peering at us hard, trying to size us up.

"Who's that with you?"

Bobby elbowed me.

"I'm his best friend, Scotty."

There was another long pause.

"How old are you?"

"Seventeen, sir."

"What the hell does a snot-nosed kid know about friendship?"

"Enough to know that it matters, and that it isn't easy to find. True friendship, that is."

There was another long pause.

"Do you believe that too, Bobby fuckin' Rowels?"

"Goddamn right I do, sir."

Again, there was a silent pause from the actor. Then a laugh started. It began as a giggle and grew until it was an outright belly laugh. The laugh was so infectious that soon both Bobby and I were laughing, too.

"I want you boys to swim over here."

"What?" Bobby asked.

"I want you to swim over here."

Bobby looked at me and smiled.

"Can we swim over naked?" I called.

"Suit yourselves. There's probably some towels around here somewhere."

I looked at Bobby.

"Let's do it," he said.

"What?"

"Let's do it. Let's swim over and pay a visit to Lee Marvin. You gotta admit, it would be something worth writing about."

"Yeah," I agreed. "Let's do it."

We quickly stripped off our clothes and soon found ourselves standing in our birthday suits on the edge of a dock in Bay Shores. Bobby looked over at me and smiled.

"I'll race you."

"All right," I was prepared to meet his challenge: "On three One... two...three!"

We dove into the water. It was cool but not cold, and after my streamline I was slightly ahead. I had the benefit of years of summer swim team, and instinctively knew to come up swimming hard in my freestyle. The yacht, moored about thirty yards away, still gave Bobby enough distance to catch me and I knew that breathing is the kiss of death in a short sprint like this. So I put my head down and dug in hard. I was pulling away from Bobby when it suddenly occurred to me that we would have no idea when we were close to the boat. I lifted my head for a look and saw we were less than fifteen feet away. Next to me, Bobby was still driving hard with everything he had. I reached over and grabbed his legs. Bobby pulled up, too.

"You're such a pussy cheater."

I pointed to the boat and he saw how close we were.

"Oh," he said. "Thanks."

"So? Who won?" Lee Marvin called from the deck. There was a twinkle in his voice.

"We both did," I replied. "Neither of us smashed our heads on the side of your yacht."

"This isn't a yacht," the actor replied. "This is a boat. Yachts are for assholes."

That was the moment I realized I liked this man. He had a genuine lack of pretension.

"How do we climb up?" Bobby asked.

"There's a ladder over here. I'll find some towels."

The actor disappeared inside the cabin as Bobby and I climbed up the ladder. Once on deck, we looked at each other, naked as jaybirds and cracked up laughing. It was like something out of a dream as we stood there in the moonlight waiting for a man that had entertained us in so many different ways. *Liberty Valance, Donovan's Reef, Cat Ballou.* Like the characters Lee Marvin portrayed, our meeting seemed mischievous, like we were somehow breaking the rules.

Marvin appeared from the cabin and walked toward us. It was the man himself, the great American actor, an icon, winner of an Academy Award. I had no idea what to expect. He had played so many different roles, played them so well, that the man himself was a mystery.

When he saw us he smiled. Not a simple smile, but a smile that seemed to capture the entire universe. It was obvious he was enjoying this, too.

"Here's some towels, boys," Marvin said. "Follow me."

We took the towels and wrapped them around us. He led us through a passageway and we entered something of a salon with a giant painting of a sea battle between ancient ships. There was a bar set up at one end of the room and the actor walked behind it.

"I'm having Irish whiskey, but I think there's some Cokes around here," Marvin announced.

He rummaged through the cupboards and looked in the small refrigerator. He seemed uncertain where anything was.

"Is this your boat, Mr. Marvin?" I asked.

"Nah. Belongs to a friend of mine. Another actor. He's inside getting ready for the party."

He looked in another cupboard, finally finding three tumblers.

"How long have you two been best friends?" he asked.

"Thanksgiving Day, 1972," Bobby said.

This gave the actor pause and he looked at us for a long moment. "You remember the day?"

"Yeah," I said. "We made a pact."

"A pact? What kind of pact?"

"That's between us," Bobby said.

The actor broke into another big grin. He had a way of smiling that made you think of everything from Socrates to Keith Richards.

"That's good," he said. "The best friendships are based on secrets."

"That's actually really good," I said. "Bobby and I have a lot of secrets."

Marvin smiled at this too as he found three tumblers and placed them on the bar. Next, he opened a can of Coke he had found and filled our glasses. Then, he opened his bottle of Irish whiskey and filled his glass. Bobby snuck a look at me and smiled. The actor noticed.

"Age does have its privileges."

Once he filled his glass and put the bottle away, he looked at us for a long moment.

"Do you know who John Ford is?" he asked.

"Sure," Bobby said. "He was the director of *The Man Who Shot Liberty Valance*. Not to mention *The Searchers, Fort Apache, Wagon*

Master, She Wore a Yellow Ribbon, Donavon's Reef, and about twenty other great movies."

Lee Marvin was surprised at the breadth of Bobby's knowledge.

"Bravo, kid. You know your movies. Most people don't realize how important the director is. When they hear Western they think of John Wayne. But there never would have been a John Wayne without John Ford. Like a magician, Ford conjured him, with help from Hawks."

"I love Westerns," Bobby said. "Especially John Ford Westerns."

"Well, Ford was my friend, and the man knew the value of friendship. Maybe that's why his movies were so damn good. I remember when he called me to do *Donovan's Reef.* I wasn't sure I wanted to do it and he said, 'goddamn it, Lee, don't you want to spend the summer in Hawaii and get paid for it? It's going to be a helluva good time?' And as usual he was right."

The actor looked down and was quiet for a long moment.

"Anyway," he continued. "I remembered that tonight is August 31st, the anniversary of his death. That's why I'm down here on this tub of shit drinking a shot of Irish whiskey in honor of Ford. You boys reminded me of why. Boys, to friendship."

Marvin raised his glass and we raised ours in response. The actor threw down his shot and we slammed our Cokes. Then he closed his eyes as if remembering a faraway moment in his life.

From somewhere outside, we heard a woman's voice call out.

"Lee?"

The actor put his finger to his lips indicating that we were to remain quiet. He walked from behind the bar to the door and opened it.

"I'm here," he said.

"You're not down here drinking alone, are you?" the woman called.

"Just wanted a few moments to think about Ford," he replied.

"Well, don't be too long. The guests are arriving. The governor's here and he's asking for you."

"Okay, I'll just be another few minutes. I'll meet you in the house."

He closed the door and returned to us.

"Goddamn Hollywood. I spent the first twenty years of my life trying to break in and the next twenty trying to get out. There's a party or social event I must attend every night."

I could feel his resentment from the pressure of being a movie star. Fame is a double-edged sword that can cut deeply in many directions as the people around you change. Bobby and I had been willing to rip off our clothes and swim across the bay just to meet him. It reminded me of a line I had once expanded on - "Be careful of what you wish for, that crown may be too heavy to wear."

"At least the governor's here," the actor continued. "There's a couple of things I want to talk to him about. I'm probably the only democrat for miles around so I have to defend the underdog. Come on, you boys have to swim back now."

We walked out to the deck of the boat. Bobby and I handed the actor our towels.

"Thanks for sharing a memory with me. You boys appeared out of nowhere and I always trust that. The surprise of the moment. That's why Ford was such a good director. He trusted it, too. Hell, he probably staged this whole thing."

We stepped to the edge preparing to dive in.

"Hey," the actor said suddenly.

We turned to face him.

"I want to give you two some advice. When the big decisions come, and they will, you will find that this is the time friendship really matters. Having someone who will tell you the truth, a truth you can trust. It is possibly the greatest gift you will ever give each other."

"Thanks," we said in unison.

"And thank you for reminding me of what true friendship is all about."

We nodded, turned, and dove into the black water of Newport Bay.

19

We took our time swimming back to the Stackers' dock. A slow breaststroke seemed best since we were talking nonstop about what had just transpired. Actually, Bobby did most of the jabbering and the cool water did nothing to dampen his exuberance or mine.

"Bro," Bobby exclaimed. "We just met Lee Marvin."

"Yeah, we did."

"Liberty Valance himself and he talked to us about movies. And John Ford. He talked to us about John Ford. We even made a toast to John Ford with Lee Marvin."

"Hey," someone suddenly screamed. "It's Bobby Rowels out for a midnight swim with his fag lover."

We looked up to see a group of Corona football players holding up our clothes and laughing. Liza the Hurricane and the posse were with them.

This was not good, especially for Bobby. Part of the edge in football is your street value or reputation for being tough. There wasn't much street value in being caught swimming naked at a party with another guy.

The value of friends and a clan can't always be measured but their importance becomes evident in a situation like this. For once, I appreciated the Neanderthal spirit of Tommy Watts. Like a blur, he suddenly raced down the dock and slammed into the back of the Corona guy who had yelled at us. The blow was devastating and even from the water we could see the snot fly out of our crosstown rival's nose. His body followed and he flew through the air. He hit the water hard and Watts landed on top of him.

Next, Rickie Chandler and Steiner descended upon the Corona guys and fists flew. An errant punch accidentally hit one of the posse, knocking her into the bay. She screamed bloody murder as she swam for her life in her Ann Taylor silk skirt and high-heeled shoes.

All the girls began to scream and this ignited a firestorm. A ton more kids swarmed from the house and the fight grew exponentially. Punching, kicking, headlocks, bloody noses, a fierce battle of cross-town rivals raged. Even girls were fighting. Bobby and I watched in disbelief as girls grabbed each other's hair and threw each other into the water. When adults arrived on the scene, I knew it was time to make our escape.

"Come on," I said and motioned toward the shore. Bobby nodded and we swam to safety. The situation on the dock was so out of control that no one noticed a couple of naked teenaged boys climbing out of the bay.

We crept along the fence separating the neighbor's house from the Stackers' and hid behind the bushes to watch. A couple of adults had joined the twenty or so kids in the water as the screams of panic echoed across the bay. Still, more kids arrived, along with two security guards.

"What about our clothes?" Bobby whispered.

"We have to leave them."

"Damn," Bobby said. "I really love that shirt."

I looked over the fence into the neighbor's yard. There were some towels lying on a chaise lounge next to the pool.

"Let's grab those towels and get the hell out of here."

"That'll work," Bobby agreed.

We jumped the fence and ran for the towels like a couple of hungry squirrels. Just as we arrived at the chaise, the sliding glass door of the house opened and Lee Marvin stepped out onto the patio with another man. It was the governor.

Both men looked at us. The governor's mouth fell open while Marvin's face lit up with that huge grin of his.

"Had a little trouble on the other dock," I called out. "We'll return these."

We grabbed the towels and ran for the side of the house. As we passed the two men, I heard Marvin call out,

"See what I mean, Ron. Teenagers by definition aren't fit for society."

We sprinted along the neighbor's fence to where it met the street. From there we ran to the valet who parked the Chrysler.

"What's going on?," he asked. "I heard all this screaming and something like ten security guards ran into the house."

"We can't explain," I said. "We just need to get our car and get the hell out of here."

The guy gave us the keys and we ran to the our car. I could imagine the look on his face watching two guys wrapped in towels running through the streets of Bay Shores. We got to the Chrysler just in time as sirens screamed all around us. We drove slowly down the street toward freedom, passing people who had come out of their houses to see what the commotion was about. As we waited at the light to exit Bay Shores onto Pacific Coast Highway, police cars arrived from every direction and entered this small enclave by the bay. When the light turned green, we turned left and slipped away down the highway.

By the time we reached Cliff Drive, we knew we were safe. That's when we started laughing. We laughed so hard Bobby had to pull over because tears were running down his face and he couldn't see.

"I couldn't believe it when Watts sent that Corona guy flying through air," I said.

"And how about the looks on Lee Marvin's and the governor's faces. Those were priceless."

"Are you sure that was the governor?" I asked.

"Yeah, it was him all right. He was in the movie *The Santa Fe Trail.* Played a young General George Custer."

"Hawks or Ford?"

"Curtiz."

When we got to the trailer park we sat in the car for a half hour talking about the night. It was like magic the way it had taken Bobby out of his funk.

"Big changes tomorrow, bro," he said.

"Are you sure you want to do this?"

"Yeah, I don't want to ever come home to find White sitting on our couch until I know he really cares about my mom."

"All right. Let's meet about ten."

Wrapping the towel around me, I started to get out.

"Hey, bro."

I turned back to Bobby and he stuck out his hand. We wrapped thumbs around thumbs like the brothers we were.

"To friendship," he said. "Just like Liberty Valance said."

"Yeah, to friendship," I grinned.

20

The next morning, I woke and the first thing I did was laugh out loud thinking about the previous night's escapade. Not meaning to break the rules, we had inadvertently broken several. The events on the dock seemed funny but also surreal, like when you were a kid and you set up a long line of dominos. You accidentally hit one and knock all the others down. Last night struck me as a metaphor for life. Every action leads to a reaction as way leads to way on your journey and sometimes things happen you never intended. The last thing we wanted was for Cindy Stacker's party to end up in the bay.

I rose from my bed and stumbled to the living room. I was still laughing. To my surprise, I found my father sitting at the table. He looked at me gravely.

"Sit down," he said and handed me the *Daily Pilot*, our hometown newspaper. The headline read:

"Riot Disrupts Governor's Party."

I gulped and quietly read the article. No names were mentioned, but the article pretty much had the facts correct. It had been total chaos. When I finished the article, I looked at my father.

"I got a call last night from one of my buddies at the department. It seems the police think you and Bobby caused the whole thing. They were getting ready to come here and arrest you. But for some reason Lee Marvin and the governor intervened. There's not going to be any charges. Why?"

I told my dad the whole story. At the end he just smiled. Then I dropped the next bomb.

"Oh ...and Bobby's moving in with us."

"What?"

"Bobby's moving in."

"When?"

"Today or tomorrow."

"Why?"

I told my dad about Bobby's trouble with White. He listened carefully and thoughtfully. When I was finished he was quiet for a long moment. Then he grew serious.

"Okay," he said "But you guys need to be careful. What happened last night could have ruined your lives. Indecent exposure can be a really big deal. Once that's on your record people think you're sick or something. People are watching Bobby, and because you're with him so much they're watching you, too. So I expect you guys to work hard and stay out of trouble."

"Okay, dad, we'll be careful."

"And one other thing," my father continued.

"What's that?"

"You are not to set foot inside Bay Shores again."

It was funny. When he said that I thought of Cindy Stacker and guessed that we'll never be dating. I knew my dad was right. The community of Bay Shores and the Cindy Stackers were way out of my league. I was really just trailer park trash. A kid from the wrong side of the tracks trying find his way in a city of dreams. But the adventure had sure given me something to write about.

But as this was sinking in my father added something else.

"Scotty, it's important to be careful but it's also important to know that you can't make everyone like you. Everyone's got an opinion. They're sort of like assholes, and they are usually full of shit."

21

After talking with my dad, I took my journal and walked to the picnic bench beside Simonich Slough to write before Bobby arrived. It was Sunday, a day when most people go to church for their spiritual connection. I have always found my connection through writing or surfing.

Head down, my pen racing, I was totally absorbed in my thoughts and words. Any time I work through a first draft of a story, I write in my journal as fast as I can. This way I don't waste a lot of time over-thinking my words and choices. It usually works out and I find that when my first draft is finished, the bones of the story are there. Mistakes are fixed later if and when I decide to type it out. Only my most inspired stories make it to the typewriter.

But something crept into my consciousness, a presence or warm feeling, causing me to look up.

"Hi." It was Perry.

She giggled at the surprise on my face.

"How long have you been sitting there?" I managed to stammer.

"About five minutes."

"And you were just watching me?"

"Yeah, don't stop. I like watching you."

"Why?"

"I don't know. There's something in your face and the way your mouth seems to frame the words in a sort of whisper. You're just so focused. I wish I was creative like that."

"Everyone's creative."

"Not me."

"Yes you are. You just have to learn how to tap into it. It's a craft."

"Maybe you can teach me sometime?"

"All right. Close your eyes."

"Right now?"

"Yeah, why not."

Perry closed her eyes and I let her sit for a long moment.

"What do you hear?"

"I hear the traffic of PCH and a bird just sang out."

"What do you feel?"

"I'm not sure."

"Not emotionally. I mean physically. Do you feel the breeze rubbing against your skin and the ground under your feet?"

"Yes."

I allowed for another long moment of silence. Finally, I posed another question.

"What do you see in your mind's eye?"

"Hmm. I guess I see you sitting in front of me."

"And what am I doing?"

"You're looking at my face."

"And what am I thinking?"

A smile crossed Perry's face.

"Just tell me and always trust your first instinct."

"I'm embarrassed."

I smiled. "Are you thinking I would like to kiss you?"

Perry opened her eyes and blushed. "Yes," she said, looking away.

"Look at me," I said.

Perry's eyes returned to mine and I held her gaze for a moment.

"Now you have the basis for a story called *The First Kiss*."

"Really? How do you mean?"

"Well, you begin the story at this moment. Then you could have us get into a fight or we could turn our lives upside down by falling in love. The most important part is how your imagination made you feel."

"Explain that to me."

"You start with the physical feeling of the world around you. The sound of the gulls over the canal or the soft cool breeze you felt brushing your skin. Then you move inside to the emotions you feel. Were you simply embarrassed by the thought of me kissing you, or did it scare you into feeling vulnerable?

"I don't scare very easily."

"I expect you don't. But in examining your emotions and being brutally honest with your feelings, your characters will come to life and be truthful. They will never lie to you."

"What were you thinking?" Perry asked while flashing her perfect, imperfect smile.

"Whatever you wanted me to think. It's your story. I'm just a character."

"That's good. That's really good."

"Hey, Scotty, let's go," another voice rang out.

It was Bobby calling from the end of the road.

"I'm sorry, Perry. But I promised Bobby I'd do this thing with him."

"Great, run out on me while I'm in the middle of my imagination."

"A promise is a promise."

Perry looked at me for a long moment. Then she said, "I like that you keep your promises, Scotty."

22

Bobby and I had made an appointment with Newport Collectibles in the Lido Village shopping center. The owner, Ward Hailey, had set aside time to give us his undivided attention. It had to do with how Bobby had described the collection, a lot of Mickey Mantles, including several rookies.

Mr. Hailey loved his work. He was in his sixties with short white hair and had been in the memorabilia business for years. But he wasn't in it only for the money. He was a huge fan of anything that had to do with sports and the memories sports created for him. He was an aficionado of sports history. It was the love of sports history that guided him, and there was a reverence to it all.

As Hailey thumbed through the cards in Bobby's cardboard box, his face registered his excitement. The cards were in plastic sheets, and each sheet contained nine cards.

"These are very good cards," Hailey said. "A very nice collection, indeed."

"Yes," Bobby affirmed.

Hailey held up a sheet of cards to the light. He was practically drooling.

"Very nice cards, and in wonderful condition."

"Thanks," Bobby replied.

"Did you put this collection together?"

"No, my dad did."

"Does he know you want to sell them?"

"My father died," Bobby said. "He left them to me."

Mr. Hailey looked at Bobby closely. Then he held up another sheet.

"A whole sheet of Mantle rookies. Mantle was something. I saw him play once. Hit two home runs. If it hadn't been for that stupid sprinkler he might still be playing."

Mr. Hailey held up another sheet of nine cards. They were all Nolan Ryan rookies. He was an Orange County favorite currently pitching for the Angels.

"This is a very good collection. Your father was a smart collector. Why would you want to sell these?"

"I need the money."

"Why?"

"Look," Bobby said. "Do you want to buy the collection or not?"

"Oh, I want to buy the collection. I'm just trying to figure out why the son of a dead father would want to sell something that his father cared so deeply about. A collection like this doesn't happen by accident. It's obvious it was put together with care so it could be passed on to his son."

Suddenly, the gates of heaven opened as tears streamed down Bobby's face. He stood looking at Mr. Hailey. He tried to speak but couldn't. Then he turned and walked outside. When Bobby was gone, Mr. Hailey's attention turned to me.

"What's going on?" he asked.

"It's like this. Bobby and his father shared something much deeper than these cards. Bobby wants to sell the cards so he can completely focus on his senior football season. Trust me, his father would approve."

"What's his last name?"

"Rowels."

Mr. Hailey's eyes opened wide.

"You mean Bobby Rowels of the Newport Harbor football team?"

"Yeah."

"I was at the scrimmage against Mater Dei. He has quite a future."

"That's why he wants to sell these cards. There's a lot going on in his life and he wants to protect his future."

Mr. Hailey was quiet for a moment.

"Ask him to come back in," he said gently.

I walked out of the store and found Bobby sitting on the curb still crying.

"Mr. Hailey wants to talk to you." Bobby nodded and stood. His eyes were red. He followed me back into the store where Mr. Hailey stood smiling.

"How much do you need?" he asked.

It was an odd question. Bobby and I had not talked about it. Bobby turned to me.

"What do you think?"

"I'm not sure." I said. "I make a little under a hundred a week. That seems to work for me."

"How long is the season?" Mr. Hailey asked.

"Fourteen weeks," Bobby said. "That's the time it takes to win a CIF championship.

"That's $1400," Mr. Hailey said.

Bobby's eyes narrowed.

"My dad's collection is worth more than that."

"I'd say so. The Mantle rookie sheet alone is worth three thousand."

"Then why do you think I'd sell the whole collection for fourteen-hundred dollar's?"

"Oh," Mr. Hailey smiled. "I'm not buying the whole collection. I'm giving you an interest-free loan."

"A loan?" Bobby asked.

"Yes, a loan. Of course, I'm going to keep the cards in my safe until you pay the loan back."

"Why?" Bobby asked.

"Because someday you will be rolling in dough and will be able to afford whatever you want."

"So?"

"So the thing you'll be wishing you could buy is this baseball card collection, your dad's baseball card collection. You may even have a son of your own to give it to, and you'll realize that this collection is worth more, much more, than the money it represents now."

"Thank you." Bobby choked on the words.

Mr. Hailey nodded and reached into his pocket. He pulled out the biggest wad of cash I had ever seen. He also counted money faster than anyone I had ever seen. In mere seconds fourteen one-hundred dollar bills were lying on the counter.

Bobby looked at the pile of cash. I knew it was the most money he had ever seen. Mr. Hailey pulled out a drawer and found a receipt book and scribbled the words "loan against collateral." Next, he wrote on the cardboard box "Property of Bobby Rowels." When he was finished, Mr. Hailey stuck out his hand and Bobby shook it.

"Are you sure?" Bobby asked.

"Ah, hell," Hailey said. "I specialize in USC memorabilia. I've got every millionaire in Newport Beach breathing down my neck. The last thing I need to do is to make money off of you."

"You're a nice man," I said.

"Nice doesn't have anything to do with it. Once you've made enough money you realize that what matters most in life are your relationships. I now have a relationship with you, Bobby Rowels, so I expect you to live up to your end of the bargain. That goes for you, too, Scott."

"How's that?" I asked.

"By achieving your goals. When I see you succeed I will feel like I've shared in it in some small way. Money can't buy that. Now get out of here and go win a championship, and I don't care if it takes twenty years. The cards will be waiting for you."

Bobby nodded and picked up the money. We started for the door. Then Mr. Hailey called out to us.

"Boys, one more thing. Don't tell anyone about our agreement. I don't want my rich customers to think I'm getting soft. I have a nasty reputation for being a tough negotiator that serves me well, and Bobby, it's important to stick to your budget. Cash has a way of disappearing faster than you think. This money has bought you the freedom to pursue your dreams. Protect it."

"I will," Bobby promised.

23

Flush with cash, we headed straight to Terrie's Waterbeds and Unfinished Furniture store on Newport Boulevard to buy some bunk beds. A tall blonde kid named Nate helped us pick them out. He said things had been slow so he gave us ten percent off because we were paying cash. Cash does make a difference.

We loaded the frames into the Chrysler so that part of them stuck out the windows, and tied the mattresses onto the roof. We stood back to admire our creation.

"Now I know how Tom Joad felt," I said.

"Is that the guy from *The Grapes of Wrath*?"

"Yeah, Steinbeck's great anti-hero, arrived home from jail for killing some guy with a shovel just in time to watch his family disintegrate right before his eyes."

Bobby looked at me. "Well, at least I don't have a shovel."

Bobby's words struck me. To me, Bobby was just moving in with us. But to Bobby it meant so much more, and in that moment I realized the courage of his choice. I had moved away from my mom because I was running away from something and I had a place to go. Bobby was moving toward something, toward meeting the world on his own terms, and he was breaking up his family, or what was left of it, to do so. I knew how much he loved his mom. It might be the hardest choice he'd ever made.

We rolled down Newport Boulevard into Newport. It was funny because the whole way people were pointing at us and laughing.

"You know," I said. "People move to Newport to get away from people like us."

Bobby laughed. "Yeah, but we're just what this place needs, a little color. Without us, Newport would just be filled with Mercedes Benzes and Topsider look-alikes."

We pulled in front of my dad's trailer and started to unload.

Perry walked up. "What's going on, y'all?"

"Bobby's moving in," I said. "We have to rearrange the room a bit."

Perry placed her hands on her hips and winked at me. "I guess I'll have to double check my blinds. No telling what you boys will be up to."

"Maybe we better check ours, too," I replied.

Perry smiled. "Hey, what are you doing later?"

"Nothing, I guess."

"You want to come over and listen to the new Bruce Springsteen album? I could make some dinner?"

"Okay, sure. That would be great."

"Good. Dinner'll be ready at six."

She walked away. I looked up and saw Bobby standing at the door of the trailer. He had heard the whole conversation. He gave me a thumbs up and then smiled.

"What?" I asked.

"Don't give me 'what'. You and Perry are getting ready to do the wild thing."

"We're just friends."

"Sure. Just friends. That's how it always starts."

"No, really." I protested. "She's turned me on to this Springsteen guy. I've got one of his albums inside that she loaned me. I'll play it for you."

I played Bobby "The Wild, The Innocent and The E Street Shuffle" while we put the bunk beds together. By the time the beds were up, the album was finished.

"Great album, bro," Bobby said. "I really like that song about that girl Sandy."

"Yeah, it's kind of cool how he celebrates life."

Bobby was quiet, thinking deeply about something. I gave him his space and started making the beds. Finally, he spoke.

"You know, I just don't get it sometimes," he said.

"Don't get what?"

"Newport. I mean, you meet guys like Hailey and Lee Marvin who would give you the shirts off their backs. Then you've got guys like your stepfather and White that just want to use you or screw with you."

"Yeah," I stopped to think. "I guess I'm pretty much ready to hate everybody around here. But I suppose it's like anywhere else, only more so."

Bobby nodded and then leaped to the top bunk.

"I get the top."

"Why do you get the top?"

"Because you'll want the bottom so you can stare out the window at your girlfriend all night."

"Quit it."

"I'll quit when you get laid."

24

Bobby left my house to spend the evening with his mom. They were going to make some dinner and watch *Butch Cassidy and the Sundance Kid,* a movie Bobby said reminded him of us.

The real reason he chose to spend the evening with his mom on a potential party night was to help her come to terms with the idea of him moving out. Bobby knew his mom would be in shock. He desperately wanted to make it easy on her.

At six I walked over to Perry's. When I knocked on the door, Perry answered. She had on a white backless sundress. The white material against her tanned skin made her look fresh and vibrant.

"I've got to play this song for you," she squealed as she ran to the record player. "I've listened to it at least twelve times."

The song was "Thunder Road." She played it for me once, and that was all it took. I was now officially a Bruce Springsteen fan. When Bruce sang, I got goose bumps. I wanted to throw my head back and feel the wind blow through my hair, too. I felt the desperation it takes to live in the moment, the quiet courage that it takes to live in this world at all.

When the song ended Perry looked at me expectantly.

"It's a great song," I said. "I'm going to go out and buy it."

"Let's play it again," she suggested.

"Okay."

"And I want you to dance with me."

This surprised me and scared me too. I wasn't much of a dancer.

"What?"

She walked to the record player and started the song again. She turned to me, took both of my hands and put my arms around her. She pressed in close. I could feel her breasts pushing into my chest as we swayed to the music and every fiber of my being exploded.

"Close your eyes," Perry said. "I want you to feel the music with me."

"What?"

"Silly," she replied. "Close your eyes. I trusted you, now it's your turn to trust me."

I closed my eyes and we swayed for a while to the words and haunting and immortal piano of the E Street band's Roy Bittan. Then I felt Perry's lips touch mine. Like a good pupil, I followed instructions and kept my eyes closed. My mouth opened and I felt the fullness of Perry's tongue wrap around mine. It was a long kiss, lasting until the end of the song, and the sweetest kiss I have ever known.

Perry pulled away from me and stood looking into my eyes. I was speechless. Did this girl, this woman, actually feel what I was feeling? I was exhilarated, joyful, lustful, hopeful, and confused. It was like wishing for the moon on your birthday. I had never felt this way before.

I wanted more and pulled her to me, but she took my arms, pried them away and smiled.

"Not yet, Scotty...someday, maybe."

"Really?"

"Don't sound so sad. Your time will come but you need to learn to be patient. There's power in patience."

"I don't feel very powerful."

"Of course not. Patience is about allowing yourself to be weak. That's where the power is found."

I wasn't sure what to say. "Well, thank you for kissing me," I blurted and felt silly and stupid for saying something so dumb.

"You're welcome. Now sit down. I've made us a steak dinner and we're going to talk about writing."

"My favorite subject," I smiled.

"That's right, and that's why I kissed you. Someday you're going to realize that through your writing, you can do anything. Even get the girl."

25

After dinner Perry said she had to go out. I sulked. She had not mentioned that our dinner would end early.

"Where are you going?"

Perry didn't answer. Instead, she led me to the door and gave me a kiss on the cheek.

"Remember, you have a purpose, Scotty. And with a purpose and patience you can achieve anything. That's what makes you so darn attractive."

"Thanks, I guess."

Perry smiled her perfect, imperfect smile.

"Scotty, I'm sorry, but I've really got to go. I'm late. I'll see you tomorrow. Okay?"

"Okay."

Perry disappeared. I stood looking at the door as emotions swept through me. Where did she have to go? When would I see her again?

As I started to step down the stairs, the door opened and Perry reappeared.

"Hey, just so you know, I had a really good time."

"I did, too."

"Good," she said with another smile that suggested she had accomplished something, and then she was gone like the goddess in my dream.

I was totally confused. Patience, purpose, what is this shit and what was I to make of it all? I was just a seventeen-year-old kid. Perry was twenty-one. She had more life experience than I ever dreamed of.

Instead of going home, I walked down to Simonich Slough. Magic hour had descended upon my small corner of the earth, and the full moon, already risen, bathed the world around me in a soft glow.

I stood looking out across the Slough. The silhouette of a large heron stalked the far bank for a meal while bats swooped around me in an acrobatic dance. Beyond the canal, the lights of the houses built on the distant bluff twinkled like stars. It was as if the world around me was suddenly filled with magic.

Not the magic of card tricks or the hocus pocus found in books like *The Lord of the Rings*, but those simple magical moments that change your life; that change your consciousness and enable you to see the world in a whole new way. The kiss I had shared with Perry had changed me. It struck me as I stood on the edge of this canal, with the sounds of cars speeding by on Pacific Coast Highway, that I might have found out what it means to fall in love.

A tingle, almost like an electric shock, shot up my spine and my head suddenly felt light, almost woozy. I sat down at my favorite picnic table. When the feeling passed, I asked myself a simple question. Was I falling in love with Perry? For the first time in my young life, was I feeling the emotion that had inspired Shakespeare to write Sonnet 116, the emotion that had inspired Shelly and Voltaire, the feelings that had inspired poets and writers for centuries? Is this that ever-fixed mark that makes you feel more alive than you ever thought you could? Almost desperately alive?

I knew that elsewhere in the world people were sleeping and waking or playing and working, going about their lives experiencing every emotion possible: love, anger, envy, hope, grief, fear. People were even dying and being born. Yes, I thought, the earth keeps turning but in my small corner of the world I was falling in love.

I looked out across the canal. In what seemed like an instant, night had fallen and I could no longer see the heron, and the bats were gone. The world had suddenly turned black and the darkness brought back fear and doubt. Again I asked myself, what am I compared to Perry?

She is a woman really and I'm just a seventeen-year-old fool stepping off a cliff, enamored of a vision of what I want to become.

Why did I love her? Was it the kiss or the fact she took my love of writing seriously? Did the thought of loving Perry bring me closer to my vision of being a writer? Or was I turning into a love-sick puppy terrified by my own shadow? Maybe Bobby was right. I could almost hear his voice, "Don't be a dickhead. She's way out of your league. Sleep with her. Don't fall in love."

Still, I was feeling something I had never felt before, and that, for me, is something worth writing about.

I laughed. Perry had taken our conversation about creativity and turned it on its head by kissing me. I was a goner. I decided there was nothing left to do but head back to the trailer to find my journal and typewriter. Perry had inspired me and only by writing my words down could I make sense of it all. I didn't write because I wanted to. I wrote because I had to.

26

Soft knocking on my window woke me up from my daze. I had stayed up until after three writing a story, dedicated to Perry, and now my sleep pattern was upside down. I looked at the clock. It was seven a.m.

I slid the window back to find Bobby standing there with a smile on his face. But this smile was different from the morning of the epic waves. There was sadness in his smile, and I will never forget Bobby's smile on this Labor Day morning.

"How are the waves?" Bobby asked.

"I don't know. I was up all night writing a story."

"Let's walk down to the beach and check it out," he said.

"Okay."

I stumbled out of bed, made my way to the closet with the door that always falls off the track, and pulled it back carefully. Grateful it didn't fall, I found my favorite shorts and a yellow, long sleeved t-shirt with the words "inner visions" on it.

I tiptoed past my father, who was passed out on the couch, and opened the front door. The first thing I saw was the Chrysler packed to the gills with Bobby's things. Next, I saw Bobby slouched against the hood, head down and shoulders slumped, hands in his pockets, the weight of his world crushing his spirit.

"Hey, bro," I said. "Just so you know, this is your place now. You don't have to knock on the window."

Bobby nodded and we started walking to the beach. As usual we took the path from the trailer park under the River Jetties Bridge.

Sometimes there were bums in the early morning, especially on a rainy day, as the bridge afforded the homeless a place to stay dry. Today, with the sun beating down, the path was bum-free.

We walked in silence. I knew it had been hard informing his mom about his decision to move out, but I didn't ask. Bobby would talk to me when he was ready.

Perry was still fresh in my mind and I wanted to tell my friend what I was feeling. But I decided to keep quiet about that, too. Somehow, my feelings weren't what mattered here. Bobby had made one of the biggest decisions of his young life. I had, at least in my mind, merely fallen in love and that seemed kind of juvenile compared to the upheaval in Bobby's life. Bobby had affected other people with his decision, especially his mom. My feelings affected only me.

When we got to the beach, the sea looked more like a lake than an ocean. Even the shore break slid up the beach like milk spilt on the floor. A week ago the waves had been the size of skyscrapers pounding these south-facing beaches. It always amazes me that the ocean never remains the same, and I suddenly realized what I had spent the previous night trying to convey in words: Perry was like the ocean. Every time I saw her she seemed different and unfathomable, a mystery I found extremely attractive.

"Shit, ankle snappers," Bobby said.

"Yeah."

"Our last day of summer," he continued. "And the waves suck."

"So?"

"What do you mean, so? Tomorrow we start our senior year."

"So let's not waste it," I offered.

"What?"

"Let's not waste it by thinking about anything. Tomorrow we can start worrying about our futures."

Bobby cracked a smile. "Yeah. Let's make this the best summer day of our lives."

"Right on. Let's unload the Chrysler and get the room organized. After that, there will be no labor on Labor Day. We'll just be boys of summer."

The Boys of Summer had been Bobby's father's favorite book. It was about his father's favorite sport, baseball, and I knew this would inspire Bobby. To live like there was no tomorrow, to live in the moment the whole day, this Labor Day, on the eve of our senior year. To just throw it all up for grabs.

Bobby held out his hand and I shook it, wrapping thumbs around thumbs.

"Boys of summer," Bobby said. "That's what this day will mean."

And as we walked back to the trailer, Bobby's spirits lightened considerably.

27

Even with the bunk beds, our quarters were cramped. We had organized the room as best we could but we were presented with a dilemma. Where would we study? The front room was usually inhabited by my dad whose routine was to drink a couple of six packs while staring blankly at some inane show on TV. The distraction of television is the kiss of death for getting homework done.

However, I had an idea on how to establish a routine that would work for us. We would simply study at the diner. That way we would only have to use the small bedroom for sleeping. But we made a deal with each other that we would keep the room as neat as possible.

When we were close to finished, Bobby suddenly turned to me.

"My mom was crying when I left."

I nodded. I knew how painful that moment must have been for him.

"Consider yourself lucky," I replied. "I think my mom threw a party when I split."

Bobby looked at me for a long moment. Then he started to laugh, which made me crack up. Before we knew it, we were both laughing so hard that we fell onto the lower bunk, and laughed until it hurt. It was the kind of laughter that can only be shared with someone you know completely and trust on a very deep level. Someone who knows how much pain is actually behind the remark.

Slowly, the laughter subsided to a giggle. Finally we looked at each other with smiles on our faces.

"That was funny," Bobby said.

"Yeah, someone once wrote that finding humor in our dark moments may be the most elegant of human experiences. It serves as a kind of revolt."

"A revolt?"

"Yeah, our greatest expression of courage and hope in the face of an absurd world."

Bobby picked himself up off the bed and turned to me. He still had a smile on his face.

"I think you're right. This whole day should be one big revolt."

"Maybe we should call Steiner and take out his dad's boat. Do some wakeboarding."

"No," Bobby said thoughtfully. "Bike ride. I think today demands a bike ride. Let's ride and swim, let's try to get into Blackie's, let's hit the Fun Zone and play some baseball, let's check out the girls in their bikinis, let's give the wannabes at Thirty-Second Street shit, let's..."

"Yeah, let's just be."

"Exactly. Screw everything. Screw school, screw White and football..."

"Yeah, screw it all. College, our futures, everything. Bring it on. Boys of summer."

"Yeah," Bobby said with a grin that could light up a carnival.

28

Newport Beach is filled with stories that are both large and small, some heroic and some tragic, and it's the perfect place for someone like me who sees the world through story. A ride down Newport's boardwalk is a story in itself, an adventure where anything can and does happen.

The boardwalk stretches from Thirty-sixth Street to just beyond the Balboa Pier, an approximately two and a half mile stretch running right along the ocean. Anyone who has ever lived in Newport has cruised it and it takes a special kind of bike for a peak experience - one speed, fat tires with a seat so wide you'd think you were riding on a cloud. The beach cruiser is Newport's answer to East L.A.'s low rider; more style than performance, and the words that best describe it are smooth, deliberate, and cool.

Bobby and I had great cruisers. We had bought them from Tom the fisherman, a longtime trailer park resident whose diabetes had settled in his legs. He couldn't ride anymore but he could still fish. Tom hit Davey's Locker half-day fishing boat every weekend, and he had needed the bike money to pay for his habit. The bikes were both 1959 Schwinn Rat Rods and they were in great condition. We loved these bikes almost as much as we loved the Chrysler, and Tom always smiled when he saw us on them. Today was no exception, and as we rode past his trailer, we waved our hellos.

"Hey, Tom."

"You boys going for a ride?"

"Yeah, we have a date with the boardwalk."

Tom had failed to put in his teeth but he flashed his gums in a wide smile as we rode by.

"Why don't you come with us?" I called. "There'll be lots of bikinis."

"Yeah, if I was fifty years younger. Better just stick to fishing. It's cheaper."

I had written a short story based on my neighbor Tom. It was simply called *The Fisherman* and it had to do with the large sub-group of people in Newport that live for fishing. I tried to write in the style of Hemingway's *The Old Man and the Sea* and compared the fishermen to the golfers who live in Big Canyon. My conclusion was that Hemingway preferred fishermen.

We headed out of the park and onto Pacific Coast Highway. The highway was a massive traffic jam, the beach being a prime destination for the hordes trying to escape the inland heat. From Italy to Southern California, from Australia to Brazil, summer has always driven people to the beach.

There were people on bikes everywhere, and because the sun was beating down hard at this late morning hour, people wore a minimal amount of clothing. Half-naked people swarmed the streets and beach.

I love these crowds and I take people-watching a step further with what I like to call subjective projection. Every person I see has a story to tell and the storylines range from Raymond Chandler to L. Frank Baum. The images of the people and their interactions with each other are like stars that produce rays of light which extend out in a million different directions, sometimes bouncing off each other and at other times connecting or colliding. This light twists and molds itself in a myriad of ways through the connections of emotions, thoughts and actions. It forms the basis of the stories that roll around in my head. If the light is strong enough then the characters start speaking to me. When their words begin to shout, I know the story is ready to be told.

We stopped at the traffic light at Pacific Coast Highway and Orange Street. People crowded the corner to cross, their arms filled with beach chairs and coolers.

My dad was among this throng and he stumbled across the street toward us. He had a paper bag under his arm that I knew contained a couple of six packs from Tradewinds Liquor Store for his own private celebration of Labor Day.

"It's my boy," he slurred. "And my new housemate."

It was obvious that this wasn't his first trip to Tradewinds this day.

"Hey, dad."

"Hey, Mr. Curtis."

My father frowned at Bobby. "Don't ever call me Mr. Curtis again. The name's Ed."

Bobby smiled. "Okay, Ed."

"Dad, I'm not sure when we'll be back."

"Okay, but did I ever tell you that I love you?"

I looked at Bobby and rolled my eyes.

"Yeah, pop, you've told me."

"Good. Don't ever forget it. And if you see that son-of-a-bitch Dirty John, tell him I'll be stopping by."

Dirty John was my dad's hero. My dad told me he was called Dirty John because he had been the toughest football player to ever come out of Benjamin Franklin High School in Highland Park, a blue collar town where being tough actually meant something. I also admired him. He had been a cop with the Los Angeles Police Department for thirty years. Through grit and luck, he had found the money to live on the oceanfront. Captains, police chiefs or fire chiefs lived on the oceanfront. Not simple everyday cops. Dirty John was a simple cop's hero because he proved you could be a good cop and still achieve your dreams. I liked Dirty John because he was always supportive and kind to my dad.

"Yeah, dad, if I see Dirty John I'll tell him."

My dad swung his fist and gave me a light punch in the arm. He almost lost his balance. "You're a good kid," he added.

"I love you, dad."

"Yeah, I know you do, shit bird. Go have fun and don't break too many hearts."

He turned and walked off toward the trailer park. I was glad he wasn't on his bike because he was weaving like a ko'd boxer.

"Even when he's drunk, your dad is the coolest," Bobby said.

I looked at Bobby and realized he saw what I saw in my dad: a noble, good, ruffian spirit who was in a fight to the death with his demons. I just didn't know if he was going to win.

29

We crossed Pacific Coast Highway and turned the corner off Orange Street heading due south on Sea Shore Drive, probably the only street in Newport that was made one-way for cars so bikes could have a two-lane path.

One of the best parts of a bike ride in Newport are the girls. Today they were everywhere, and they came in all shapes, sizes, and colors. They were on bikes, on foot, on roller skates and skateboards and riding in cars with the tops down. It was a feast for the eyes. For this reason, a pair of sunglasses is a necessity. I have no doubt that the girls, wearing next to nothing, expect to be checked out. But you've gotta be cool or they think you're a pervert or something, and sun glasses help keep girl-watching on the sly, what Bobby and I call "the sweet down low". We wore Wayfarers.

The traffic of cars and bikes was heavy but people didn't seem to care. It was the final weekend of the summer, and you could feel the joy and see it in people's faces. We were simply living in the right now surrounded by sunshine and cool ocean breezes. It felt as if summer, this summer, could last forever.

When we got to Sixty-Second Street and Sea Shore, we ran into the man himself. The one and only Dirty John. He was an enormous man walking to the mailbox with letters. His gait alone gobbled up large sections of real estate.

"Well...damn it...Butch," Dirty John said. "Where's that old man of yours been hiding himself?"

"My dad said to tell you he was going to stop by."

"Tell him I've got a cold one waiting for him."

"I will."

"Good, and stay out of trouble, Butch."

Dirty John continued his walk to the mailbox and Bobby looked at me.

"Who's Butch?"

"That's just Dirty John. He calls every kid Butch."

And as we rode away, I was reminded of another story. When I was twelve and my family was still together, we went to Dirty John's house for a Fourth of July party. It was a festive event, with the adults drinking and the kids totally running amok. The next thing you know, Dirty John's cousin and his friends show up with the biggest box of firecrackers you ever saw. They were firemen and the firecrackers were the accumulation of their firehouse's confiscations for the year. Suddenly, firecrackers were going off everywhere as the men began throwing them at each other - the cops against the firemen in a fierce battle. I mean, the bottle rockets were flying on Dirty John's beach front patio. Women screamed, children ran for cover and my dad was in the middle of the fray standing shoulder-to-shoulder with Dirty John - throwing firecrackers at the firemen.

"Dirty John and his friends are the biggest assholes I've ever seen," my mother railed on the drive home. Evidently, a bottle rocket had blown up causing her to spill a glass of red wine down the front of her white dress.

My dad didn't say a word and my sister and I were silent as well. We were listening from the backseat of our Chevy Nova as Johnny Cash's "Sunday Morning Coming Down" played on the radio.

"Did you hear me?" my mother continued. "Dirty John is an asshole and so are his friends. This dress is ruined."

Finally my dad had heard enough. "Well, I'm Dirty John's friend and he is the kind of man I've always hoped to be. Sorry about your dress."

"And you're an asshole, too."

My dad looked at my mom for a long moment. Then his eyes returned to the road and he remained silent the rest of the way home. I sat there wondering how anyone could think that Dirty John was an asshole. It was one of the best parties I had ever been to.

"Bro, did you see that crash?" Bobby exclaimed. "That guy just ran right into those chicks."

I was shocked from my memory and looked at Bobby blankly. Then I saw up ahead of us a drunk guy trying to pick himself up from the street. Two girls were screaming at him. I looked at Bobby.

"Dude," Bobby said. "Where is your head? It's Labor Day. Nothing else matters."

"I'm cool."

"No," Bobby replied. "You're the coolest. Stay with me."

Yes, I thought, Newport is alive with stories both present and past. Every corner, every street, every house has a story to tell with characters that can not only entertain you but also give meaning to an insane world.

30

Our journey led us to the area in Newport known as "The Zoo." Large duplexes lined the street and their balconies and patios were packed with college-aged kids. Practically every house had a kegger going.

At Fifty-Fourth Street, Jethro Tull's "Locomotive Breath" blasted from one house as several people danced right in the middle of Sea Shore Drive. Maneuvering our way through the crowd was tricky, and it suddenly became dangerous when someone from a balcony threw a pack of firecrackers into the crowd of dancers. Girls and guys scrambled to save their toes from getting blown off, and a big blonde guy blindsided Bobby, knocking him from his bike. He hit the street hard.

"Hey, Dude, I'm sorry man," the blonde guy said.

He picked Bobby up and I saw Bobby had skinned his elbow.

"Are you all right?" I asked.

Bobby looked at his arm and shrugged. "Yeah, I'm fine."

"Hey, I'm really sorry," the blonde guy said again.

"No worries," Bobby replied. "It's Labor Day."

Bobby got back on his bike and our journey continued down Sea Shore.

"Hey," Bobby suddenly announced, "let's watch some volleyball."

Fifty-Second Street was known for having the best volleyball in Newport and players from all around Southern California came to test themselves and hone their skills.

Bobby and I have always liked to stop and watch a match or two. Beach volleyball players are close cousins to surfers. They value freedom and are deeply suspicious of rules, too.

Bobby and I walked our bikes toward the courts to watch. A crowd of people had gathered around the winner's court. We arrived just in time to see a muscular player drive the ball straight down. The spike was so hard that the ball left a crater in the sand. It always amazed us how hard these guys could hit the ball. But what was more surprising today was that one team had a girl on it. It is rare that a team with a girl could make it to the winners' court at Fifty-second Street.

She was cute, young, and not very tall, and as the game unfolded, she began sacrificing her body in front of the spikes and coming up with incredible defensive plays. She electrified the crowd, and with each play people yelled.

"Great dig, girl."

"Better watch out, Martin, she's got your lips."

The girl was really pissing off the hitter and after her third dig, he took off his sunglasses and set them down, an acknowledgment that the girl had earned his respect.

The young girl had courage and grit. The opposing team would hit the ball as hard as they could and by some instinct or intuition, the girl seemed to find a way to pop the ball up to her teammate. Many times the force of the spikes knocked her to the ground.

The team with the girl didn't win. But when the match was over, it was obviously a victory of sorts for the girl. The crowd began teasing the players that had played against her.

"Hey, Hall," someone in the crowd yelled at a winning team member, "you almost got beat by a girl."

"She's good," Bobby said.

"Yeah, she is," I replied.

"Let's go," he said. "I don't think another match would be half as good."

We grabbed our bikes and headed back to Sea Shore. When we got to the street, Bobby turned to me.

"You know, if I didn't play football and surf, I think I would play volleyball. It's a cool sport."

31

At the intersection of Thirty-Sixth Street and Seashore, Bobby heard someone call his name.

"Hey, Rowels, aren't you supposed to be doing wind sprints or something?"

It was Bucko Shaw and Steve Richardson, two Newport legends who had graduated the year before. They were legends because, among other things, they seemed to always have the most fun. Even the biggest choices in their lives were about having fun. Instead of going to college, they both took jobs as bartenders and in construction so they could do what they did best, have fun, boatloads of fun, and they were creative about it. Their entire lives were like a happy-go-lucky Labor Day weekend.

"I've given up on football," Bobby answered with a smile. "I want to emulate you guys."

Both Shaw and Richardson had been outstanding athletes at Harbor. Richardson was what you would call a man-child. Shaving at the age of twelve, he had been the strongest guy in the school. Shaw had been an all-county linebacker, his football sense and intuition was uncanny always enabling him to make the "big play". Bobby had backed them up last year. Shaw had held down the monster, and Richardson had been the outside linebacker while they played Bobby sporadically at five other positions. But Shaw was only five-foot-nine and his opportunities to play beyond high school were limited. Richardson's problem had been foot speed, although teams found that running at him was like running into the side of a cliff. He just didn't give any ground.

Shaw and Richardson helped create one of the best defenses Newport Harbor has ever known.

"We've earned our right to party," Shaw interjected. "All-county, remember? You've got some big shoes to fill."

Bobby chuckled at Shaw's attack. It was a well-known fact that Shaw had the smallest feet and hands on the team. He had the feet and hands of a little kid, and he was always teased about it.

"We both know that your size sevens will be easy to fill. In fact, they won't even fit."

Shaw shot right back. "I'm talking about legend, Rowels. My size sevens have gone places you're only dreaming about. Where will your shoes take you?"

"Mine will be what they will be."

"Hey," Richardson said. "There's no waves so we're going over to jump off the Lido Bridge to cool off. Want to come?"

Richardson could be a hell-raiser. Once on the Balboa Ferry some neo-nazi skinheads were giving some old people a hard time, asking them for money with the implied threat that if the old people didn't comply, there would be violence. Richardson simply got out of his car and punched them all out, then threw their bikes into the bay.

Bobby and I looked at each other and nodded.

"Yeah," Bobby said. "A little bridge-jumping is just what we need."

"Last one to jump is a pussy," Shaw said.

We peddled off in the direction of the Lido Bridge at high speed. This is what happens to you on an unscripted adventure. You start in one direction and end up heading in another direction entirely. It's a little like life in general. It's supposed to be an adventure and sometimes you just have to throw it up for grabs.

32

We stashed our bikes, shirts and sunglasses behind some bushes in the small park at Thirty-Second Street and Via Lido. We left the bikes unlocked because a quick getaway can be as important as the jump itself. The city fathers frown on bridge jumping, inspiring the police to enforce strict laws against it.

We stood in the park surveying the bridge. It's a good bridge for jumping. It was built high enough for small boats to pass beneath and the twenty-foot fall is exhilarating. The bay was clear of any sign of the Harbor Patrol.

"Let's do it," Richardson said.

Everyone nodded and we surreptitiously slipped onto the bridge, watching closely for any sign of authority. At the top, I peered over the side. It was a long way down to the water. Then I looked off across the bay, spying the Harbor Patrol just nearing the Rusty Pelican Restaurant.

"Shit," I said.

"Screw them," Richardson countered. "They're too far away to catch us."

With that said, Richardson climbed the railing and jumped. You could hear his scream all the way down, silenced only by the enormous splash he made. In similar fashion, Shaw followed.

"Yeeeowwww."

"Come on," Bobby said. "It's our turn."

"But," I stammered.

"No buts. The only but I want to hear is when our butts hit the water. I'm not going to listen to Richardson and Shaw calling us pussies the rest of our lives. Come on."

Bobby and I climbed the railing and jumped. On the way down I stole a look toward the Harbor Patrol. They had seen us, and with lights flashing, the patrol boat raced toward us.

The force of my fall caused me to sink deep into the channel. Wasting no time enjoying the sensation, I fought my way back to the surface, swimming to shore with the adrenaline flowing, and the Harbor Patrol's siren ringing in my ears. Bobby, next to me, matched my strokes. We reached dry land and gave new meaning to the phrase "hit the ground running." The patrol boat's loudspeaker screamed, "Halt, Halt." And as we reached the seawall, I stole a look back at the patrol boat. An officer had leaped from the boat and was rushing up the beach in his hip-high waders like a floundering walrus. We scaled the seawall just in time and ran toward our bikes. Richardson and Shaw were already on their bikes making their break for freedom.

"Leave the bikes," I shouted.

"What?"

"Leave the bikes," I pointed toward the sky. The police helicopter was making its way toward us from the beach. We sprinted down Via Lido, crossing Thirty-Second Street and onto Lafayette. The pavement, baked by the hot sun, barely registered; our feet were moving too fast. The Cannery Restaurant loomed ahead of us.

"Maybe Cristy's working," Bobby shouted.

Dan Cristy was another friend who played football and parked cars there. He worked every chance he got, almost as much as me, to save money for college.

"We can hide in a car," I shouted.

When we reached the parking lot, we did in fact see Christy.

"Dan," Bobby yelled. "The cops are after us. Can we hide in one of the cars?"

Dan ran up to us.

"Here," he yelled. "Hide in the Rolls. They just got here."

He opened the door and we scrambled into the backseat of a brand-new Silver Shadow, our wet swim suits staining the tan leather upholstery.

"What did you guys do?" Dan asked.

"We jumped off the Lido bridge," Bobby answered.

We lay down, hiding from view, the steaming upholstery frying our skin. But it was hotter outside. Through the open window, we could hear the helicopter buzz the area and a police car roll into the parking lot.

"Hey," the policeman yelled to Dan. "Did you see a couple of kids run through here?"

"No," he replied. "Haven't seen anyone."

After that, all was quiet. Although they were out in force, the police had too many headaches on Labor Day to waste much time on a couple of bridge jumpers. But we hid in the car for nearly a half hour, melting like popsicles in the sun. Finally, Dan walked up to the car.

"I think you're safe," he said. "The police are gone."

"Thanks," Bobby sighed with relief.

"Yeah, thanks, Dan," I added. "You saved our asses."

"No problem," he said with a smile. "But were Shaw and Richardson with you?"

"Yeah," Bobby said.

"Well, their Labor Day's over."

"Why?"

"I saw them in the back of a police car."

"Shit," Bobby said. "The helicopter got them."

Bobby and I split up and headed back for our bikes. We weren't taking any chances and we expected the worst, a long walk home on Labor Day. But to our surprise, we found our bikes safely tucked away behind the bushes.

"Shaw and Richardson covered our butts," I said.

"What do you mean?" Bobby asked.

"If they had talked, the cops would have found our bikes. Maybe we should call my dad to see if he can help."

Bobby was thoughtful. "Better not. The cops know there were four of us who jumped. If your dad calls they might put two and two together. Cops aren't dumb."

"Yeah, you're right," I replied. "Better to let sleeping dogs lie. I guess I just hate the idea of Shaw and Richardson in jail on Labor Day.

"They'll get out. I mean, it's not like we robbed a bank or something."

"But there's no doubt about it. Richardson and Shaw are studs."

"Yeah, and I guess we owe them." Bobby was quiet a moment and then broke into a big grin. "At least we weren't pussies."

33

Bobby and I pedaled our cruisers through the back alleys of Newport's Cannery Row, an area that had once been home to businesses canning everything from tuna to sardines. The area always reminded me of John Steinbeck's novel, *Cannery Row*, where men and women worked long shifts canning the fish for America's cities. The area is now full of boutiques and restaurants. The evolution of our hamlet from blue collar working town to playground for the rich and famous has been astonishing. I'm sure the McFadden brothers are still kicking themselves in their graves for having sold their new port.

We crossed at the corner of Newport Boulevard and Thirty-Second Street and made our way into the Market Basket shopping center.

"I think we're safe," I called to Bobby.

"Why don't we stop and grab a burger? I'm hungry."

"Yeah," I affirmed. "And I could use something to drink. I must have sweated out twenty pounds in the back of that Rolls."

"Why don't we sneak into Woody's Wharf," Bobby suggested.

I paused. Woody's was one of Newport's favorite watering holes. A fisherman named Woody had used the property for storing his boats. One day he decided to build a bar for himself and his fishing buddies. The bar was an instant hit.

"Why not," I said. "We've broken about twenty laws today. What will another matter."

"That's us. The Werewolves of Newport, and we have cash. I'm buying."

We rode down Newport Boulevard to the parking lot of Woody's Wharf. The lot was full of cars and about twenty bikes were locked to the railing on the edge of the lot. We found an opening and locked our bikes. Then we made our way to the entrance and stood in the line. There were three girls in front of us pleading to get in.

"There's only three of us. We won't take up much room," an attractive blonde girl said.

"No can do, little girlie. Can't let you in until someone comes out," the bouncer replied. He had a foreign accent and I thought he seemed a little small for a bouncer. But as if on cue, a large group of people walked out. They were older, 50s, nicely dressed. They reminded me of my mom and The Dick.

"Thanks Jean," one man said as he passed. The bouncer nodded and then turned to the girls.

"Okay," the bouncer said. "You can go in now."

Two of the girls slipped in but the blonde girl lagged behind. She had on a low-cut white denim vest, revealing a good portion of cleavage, which seemed to be distracting the bouncer.

"You're really cute," she said to the bouncer. "What time do you get off?"

This was our chance. Bobby grabbed my shirt and nudged me forward. The bouncer, distracted by the blonde, just nodded to us as we walked past. We were in.

People lined the bar three deep but we found a side bar that had an opening. I surveyed the room. I don't much like drinking but I actually like Woody's. It is filled with characters, and stories never fail to present themselves. Like the older guy with about a pound of gold chains hanging around his neck hitting on a girl half his age or the group of guys who had just arrived on their small boat called a Duffy, which was the optimal transportation for Newport Beach bar-hopping. They all had on USC shirts and looked like fraternity brothers.

"How did you boys get in here?" It was the waitress and she was staring directly at me. Bobby, being taller, was not as obvious.

"What?" Bobby quickly lied. "They checked our IDs at the door."

She was a pretty girl, about five-three, with sparkling blue eyes and it was obvious she was swamped. She looked at Bobby for a long moment.

"Okay," she said. "It's not my job to check IDs. What do you want?"

"Two tall drafts," Bobby said. "Budweiser."

She nodded.

"And two burgers," I added, "with grilled mushrooms."

"One beer each and then you guys are out of here," the waitress said.

"What about the burgers?" I pleaded.

For the first time our waitress smiled. "Okay," she said, "after the burgers. But only one beer."

With that news, she was gone. Bobby and I turned to each other and cracked up.

"Scotty, we are having an adventure. This will definitely be a day to remember."

"Or regret."

Bobby frowned. "No, bro. No regrets. Never. Whatever happens."

"Yeah," I nodded. "It's all just part of the journey."

"That's right. It's just part of the journey, and the trick is like you said, you just have to be open to it."

Bobby was quoting from a paper I had written for Mr. Wakeman's accelerated English class. We had to pick a philosopher and write a paper about what he taught us. Most people picked Socrates or Aristotle, but I picked an obscure philosopher named Joseph Campbell who had written a book called *The Hero with a Thousand Faces*. I was interested in finding out what his study of mythology had to teach me. A writer always searches out those nooks and crannies in life that will help hone his craft.

Instead, Campbell himself was the real teacher. My paper began with his words, "We must let go of the life we planned so as to accept the life that is waiting for us." It ended with, "Follow your bliss and the universe will open doors where there were only walls." Bobby loves this paper, and for me, Campbell's philosophy has become something of a map that guides my life. The great philosopher also started me on the road to accepting the pain I felt because of my mother. Campbell felt that in order to grow, we must suffer, and that we should embrace our suffering, even be grateful for it. "The only true wisdom lies far from mankind out in the great loneliness and can only be reached through suffering." I think it helped Bobby, too, in dealing with the loss of his father.

"Like in your story," Bobby added, "life is an adventure, a mystery to be lived."

This line was borrowed from Campbell, too. All writers borrow, but wisdom holds that a good writer only borrows from the best.

Our burgers and cold beers arrived. We gobbled the food, drank our drafts and then paid our waitress. We gave her a good tip. In return, she escorted us to the door. As we walked to our bikes, we heard her say, "Jean, you got to be more careful. You let in a couple of babies."

34

With fuel in our stomachs, we headed to Thirty-Second Street on the beach. I'm sure every Newport generation defines itself by the street they decide to call their own, that place where they gather every summer. Even Tom Wolfe wrote about this territorial beach phenomenon in his story *The Pump House Gang*.

My generation had chosen Thirty-Second Street as their spot and most of the surfers we knew hung there. They were mostly grommets and wannabes, but a couple were the genuine article, like Bobby. After Bobby's ride at the Point, he'd become something of a legend; his name was on everyone's lips. The riot in Bay Shores probably inspired a lot of tongue -wagging, too.

"Damn," Bobby said, "it's the posse."

The posse was surrounded by a group of guys we knew, including Rickie Chandler. Even though he was technically a football player, Rickie lived close and would often stop by to eyeball the chicks. But Rickie was also a good athlete and could handle himself on a board, so the surfers accepted him. Rickie's interest in Thirty-Second Street was the girls. The hottest chicks at Harbor hung out there. He was always trying to figure out a way to get in their pants or, in this case, their bathing suits. Rickie's plan seemed to be that he would see them at the beach, charm them, and nail them later that night.

Liza saw us and jumped up from her chair and ran toward us.

"Hey," she called as she approached. There was no doubt about it, she was a beautiful girl, and her bathing suit was a cliché: too small with yellow polka dots.

"Hey, yourself," Bobby said as she drew close.

"I called your house. Your mom said you moved out."

"Yeah, I moved in with Scotty."

"Really? Into the trailer park?"

"Yeah."

"Now you'll really be on your own. Just like Scotty."

"That's the general idea."

I had to crack a smile when Bobby said that. He sounded just like the character Ethan from John Ford's *The Searchers*.

Liza frowned. "Are you guys going to hang out for a while?"

"No," Bobby said. "We're headed for the Fun Zone."

"Are you avoiding me, Bobby Rowels?"

"No," Bobby replied.

"Then why won't you hang out with me?"

"Do you want the truth?"

"Yeah, I think I'm entitled."

"You see those guys on the beach hangin' with you?"

"Yeah."

"They've got no concept of the meaning of today."

"Which is?"

"Tomorrow we start our senior year but all they're thinking about is how to get you naked."

Liza blushed. "No, they're just friends."

"Trust me, Liza," Bobby said firmly. "I'm a guy and I know how those guys think. But I'm thinking that I will never be seventeen again. I will never be this free again. There's no room for a girlfriend today. I don't want to be waiting around until I get you alone. I want to spend this day living in total freedom."

I looked at Liza. She was about to start crying, but before the tears began to fall, Bobby came to her rescue.

"But I will also tell you this. If I did want a girlfriend today it would be you, and only you, and if you meet me at Scotty's trailer around seven, I'll walk you to the beach so we can watch the sunset."

Liza's face suddenly brightened,

"But on one condition," Bobby added.

"What's that?"

"Leave the posse home."

"Deal," she said with a huge smile on her face. She moved close to Bobby and gave him a kiss on his cheek.

"Don't even mention that we have a date."

"All right." Liza turned to me. "Make sure he doesn't stand me up, Scotty. He can be slippery."

"I will, Liza."

Then she turned and walked back to the group on the beach. As we watched her walk away, I noticed there was a bounce in her step, like she was walking on a rainbow. Liza was definitely a beautiful girl, and I was certain that Bobby's opinion of the guys in the group was accurate. Bobby turned to me.

"Are you ready for an ass-kicking?"

I smiled.

"Bring it on."

35

The boardwalk was alive with activity. Barbecues were smoking away on almost every patio, along with groups of people enjoying the sun, drinking beers with their friends and saying their own personal goodbyes to summer. Songs by the Eagles, Doobie Brothers and Lynrd Skynrd spilled out of the houses onto the boardwalk as we passed by. "The Best of My Love," "Black Water," and, of course, "Free Bird" filled our ears, leaving us with an easy, gentle feeling.

At about Twenty-Eighth Street, I heard someone call out "Scotty!" I turned to see my friend Wizard, a tall slender blonde guy whom I often ran into on the boardwalk. He loved to get stoned or eat mushrooms, sometimes acid, and march up and down the boardwalk in just his bathing suit playing his electric bass guitar, pounding away on the strings like a madman across the water. He was amazing on that bass. But no matter how well he played, he was too much of a head case for any band to accept.

"Hey, Wizard," I said.

"Man, isn't it beautiful?"

As usual, he was stoned.

"Yeah, Wizard, it's a beautiful day."

Wizard was my friend because I got my first hit in baseball off him. It was one of the most important moments of my life. He was twelve and I was seven and I popped the ball over the second baseman's head. I can still hear my mom and dad cheering wildly for my success.

I was able to get a hit because I trusted Wizard. He was too nice to ever intentionally hit anyone, and for that reason alone I had the courage to swing at the ball. I was never sure what had happened to make him such a nut job. Maybe it was his parents' fault. I mean, who would be stupid enough to name their kid Wizard. They were aging beatniks who owned a tie-dye clothing shop on Balboa Island.

Wizard suddenly started playing his bass. Even though he didn't have an amp, it still gave off a lot of sound, probably because it had six strings, and his fingers moved like the speed of light up and down the neck.

People stopped to watch Wizard, who was completely rocking out for my amusement. Whipping his shoulder length blonde hair into a frenzy, hips gyrating, spinning in circles, he created sounds you never thought possible on a bass. Then suddenly he stopped.

"Hey man, have you seen Lupe?"

"I don't know who Lupe is."

"You'll know her when you see her. She's beautiful."

I looked at Bobby, who rolled his eyes at me.

"Ah, Wizard, we're on our way to the Fun Zone."

"Okay, man, but if you see Lupe tell her I'm looking for her."

"All right, Wizard, I will."

"Yeah, tell her I'm writing a song for her that will make Emerson, Lake, and Palmer sound like three-year-olds. She'll love me when I'm famous. Then I'll be a lucky man."

"All right, Wizard. I'll keep my eye out for Lupe."

"Thanks, man."

As we rode away, Bobby turned to me.

"Think he's on acid?"

"No telling," I replied.

"Every time we see that guy he's flipped out of his mind."

But it was not without a little sadness that I rode away from Wizard. He was a gentle soul who deserved the best that life could offer. Still, life often isn't fair and gentle souls are sometimes crushed by the sheer weight of the world's insanity. I knew that one day I would write a story about the Wizard of the Boardwalk. I just wasn't sure if it would be tragic or humorous. I suppose it depends on where I choose to end it. Or maybe the choice is up to Wizard himself.

36

The Newport Pier parking lot was backed up with the traffic snarled. In order to avoid the cars and other bikes, we had to ride onto the sidewalk. It was packed too so we got off our bikes and walked. The last thing we wanted to do was hit someone.

Our path took us past a head shop with its posters of Woodstock, Jimmy Hendrix, The Grateful Dead, and a huge assortment of pot pipes, items that represented the youthful rebellion of the sixties still spilling over into the seventies. We also passed various tourist shops that supplied everything from beach towels to heavy-duty blowup rafts. Anything a great day at the beach could require.

We continued on until we reached Blackie's, a dive bar inhabited by young and old, where people shoot pool and drink pitchers of cold tap beer. You couldn't really understand Newport until you had visited Blackie's. It is the most local of local hangouts where millionaires mix with construction workers and cops, and you never know who's who. In a word, Blackie's is an everyman's bar.

It was a packed house, and the crowd trying to get in was so large that people overflowed onto the sidewalk. They were an unruly lot with a guy singing at the top of his lungs the words from the Beach Boys song, "Help Me, Rhonda" while ogling a couple of girls in skimpy bathing suits racing by on roller skates. The guy was obviously drunk on beer, sunshine, and Newport-inspired optimism.

"Do you want to try to sneak in?" Bobby asked.

"Nah," I replied. "We already hit Woody's. Let's head for the Fun Zone. Besides, there might be someone inside who knows us and you don't want White thinking you were out bar-hopping on your day off."

"You're right," Bobby nodded.

We got back on our bikes and rode past the Dory fishermen. Another memory struck. My parents used to bring my sister and me here to see these fading craftsmen at work.

The Dory fishermen are as old as Newport itself, even older, for the first homes built in the area over a hundred years ago were by the first Dory fishermen. To this day, they go out before dawn in small, weather-beaten boats to catch fresh fish.

I still sometimes come here in the morning to watch them work. The way they use their knives to filet the fish in just seconds is inspiring. Like all great craftsmen, their work often rises to the level of artistry. There's also a story here somewhere in their history and work: a tale of tradition and craft colliding with the incredible changes taking place all around them.

37

We traveled past Eighteenth Street and the Point where two weeks earlier Bobby had ridden his wave. Beyond the Point, the boardwalk sliced through Newport Beach Elementary school, probably the most valuable public property, per square foot, in the United States. It's a whole block sitting right on the oceanfront in Newport Beach with the blacktop playground and grass field extending to the ocean.

The first acknowledgment of my writing happened here. I was in sixth grade and they had a short story contest. I wrote a yarn about a policeman who tracks down the devil and arrests him. The whole time the policeman is driving the devil to jail, Satan negotiates for his soul. The policeman thinks he's arrested a nut. To get him to shut up, the policeman accepts his offer of becoming Chief of Police in exchange for his soul. There is finally silence from the backseat and the policeman is pleased. But when he gets to jail, the devil has disappeared. He looks in the back of the car and it's empty. A year later, he suddenly finds he's been selected as police chief and as he takes his oath he remembers the lunatic that wanted his soul. My story was inspired by Washington Irving's *The Devil and Tom Walker.* I won the contest and still remember how good it felt.

Just past the school we came upon an enormous crowd, mostly guys. They were gathered on the sand and it was obvious something was happening.

Bobby looked at me. "Come on, let's find out what's going on."

"Absolutely."

We parked and locked our bikes alongside the dozens of other bikes. Then we proceeded toward the crowd that was about fifty yards from the boardwalk.

I'm not sure how you would describe this crowd. Testosterone-fueled insanity may be the proper words, but utter stupidity is a close second. The guys, mostly in their early to mid twenties, were chanting and throwing their fists into the air.

"Show us your tits, show us your tits…"

As we drew closer, we saw the crowd was shaped like a donut with a circle in the middle. Inside the open space were five girls. Young and attractive, they wore t-shirts with the logo of Mama's Pizza Palace. At first, the girls were smiling in an embarrassed way, but their smiles evaporated as the aggressiveness of the crowd escalated. Next to the girls were pitchers of water.

A skinny guy wearing sunglasses and trying to look cool raised his hands and silenced the crowd.

"You've all been to Mama's, and today we are here to prove that we have the hottest mamas in town!"

The guys all cheered loudly as the skinny guy picked up a pitcher of water and poured it on a blonde girl's breasts. It was quickly apparent that she wasn't wearing a bra or bathing suit top underneath the t-shirt. The white material clung tightly and became transparent, displaying her breasts to the world.

It always amazes me how excited guys get when they view a pair of breasts. This mob was no exception. They went wild, completely insane. A fight broke out between three or four guys who started punching each other. Then, in just a matter of moments, the crowd became a mob with punches flying around us like a school of piranha in a feeding frenzy.

"Shit," I said. "This thing has no planning."

The crowd began to collapse in on the girls who screamed in fear. I turned to Bobby but he was gone. I whipped back around and saw that Bobby had entered the crowd and grabbed a tall brown-haired beauty, easily the most attractive of the bunch, and was trying to drag her through the crowd.

But two guys grabbed the girl from Bobby and ripped the T-shirt from her body exposing her naked breasts. Other guys appeared around her, reaching in and groping the girl. Bobby started swinging and a couple guys quickly went down. He was trying to rescue the defenseless girl.

A guy jumped on Bobby's back. I ran and punched the guy and tore him away from Bobby. Then someone punched me and my sunglasses flew off as I fell to the ground.

When I picked myself up, I saw Bobby had made his way out of the center of the crowd but three more guys had surrounded him and the girl. Bobby placed the girl behind him and was trying to fight the guys off. He was swinging for all he was worth as the young brunette cowered behind him.

I picked myself up, ran as fast as I could, and plowed into the group of men confronting Bobby. A couple of guys went down, and Bobby punched another guy hard in the face sending him to the ground. They all jumped up and turned on me. They began swinging and a shot landed on my jaw. I found myself eating sand as they tried to kick me in the face. But the guys soon lost interest in me, probably because I didn't have mammary glands, and returned to the mob now surrounding the remaining girls. I stood to look for Bobby. But Bobby was gone. He and the girl had escaped.

I surveyed the crowd. A couple of the other girls had been knocked to the ground and lost their t-shirts as well, surrounded by men who were groping their bodies while the girls tried in vain to protect themselves. I thought about trying to help them, but before I could do anything, the police arrived from all directions. The maulers were no match for the police and they began running in all directions as the police swung their batons wildly at anything that moved. It was a mess with guys slumping to the ground from the blows of the batons.

I peered around the beach and spied Bobby about a block away. He was holding the girl he had saved as she sobbed. Two other girls dressed in shorts and t-shirts were there too, trying to console the young brunette. Bobby released the girl into their care and the three girls slipped away, leaving him standing alone. I headed toward him.

By now the crowd had dispersed and the police were helping the half-naked girls to their feet. They were crying hysterically. When I joined Bobby, he was shaking his head in disbelief. We stood for a moment watching the remains of the frenzy as more police arrived.

"You want to explain that?" I asked.

"I went to grammar school in Anaheim with her," Bobby offered. "I had to protect her. She was my first crush."

"I just wish we could have helped them all. This was fucked up. These girls didn't deserve this."

"Dog-dick-daddies. Nothing but a bunch of dog-dicks."

I knew this was Bobby's worst insult, and I nodded. We were silent as the police escorted the women off the beach. The skinny guy that was in charge along with four other guys were being handcuffed. I noticed the skinny guy no longer had on his sunglasses, and I suddenly realized I didn't have mine either.

"Fucking dog-dick-daddies," Bobby said again.

"Yeah, and I lost my sunglasses. That's forty dollars down the drain."

"Yeah, I lost mine, too."

"Come on," I said. "Let's get our bikes and get the hell out of here."

"Are you okay?"

"Yeah, it kind of reminded me of that Irish proverb. Is this a private fight or can anyone join in?"

"It was a free-for-all.""

"Yeah."

"Thanks for watching my back, Scotty."

"Always."

38

We rode down the boardwalk in silence. It had been an ugly scene and I found it ironic that a mob had gone berserk just a few short blocks from Eighth Street, an enclave of Newport's old wealth. These first families, and others scattered throughout Newport, were the bedrock of a city that has become something of a dream for countless people, an idea that with a little luck and hard work, anyone can make something of themselves. But man is also very close to being an animal, and without police and authority, civilization quickly disintegrates.

Finally, the Balboa Pier came into view. The area, known simply as Balboa, was for years the final destination of Henry Huntington's fabled red car, an electric train that traveled from Los Angeles to Balboa. During World War II, the Rendezvous Ballroom drew thousands. My grandmother, Norma Jean, told me stories of how young soldiers, facing the prospect of going to war, came here to enjoy the music and beauty of the bay, a final celebration in the face of a dangerous and uncertain future.

It's easy to imagine hundreds of servicemen in uniform strolling this boardwalk with their dates before taking in the music of Tommy Dorsey or Glenn Miller. Many of these men, not much older than Bobby and me, never came home, and it sometimes feels to me as if their spirits have returned to the place where they last experienced joy and hope. If Newport has a sacred ground, Balboa may be it.

Largely due to the work and sacrifice of many of these men, I had the luxury of arriving on my bike. My challenges are trivial compared to what many young men faced in 1942 or in Korea and Vietnam, and I suppose what I feel is a profound sense of gratitude.

We turned off the boardwalk and headed east. We crossed Balboa Boulevard, passing the Balboa Theater now playing *Deep Throat*, and rode straight into the Fun Zone, a tiny amusement park on Newport's beautiful bay.

"I'm going to whip your butt," Bobby suddenly shouted as we zipped past the bumper cars, the memory of our boardwalk fight fading from our minds. He was definitely fired up.

"You can dream," I replied "Newport's the land of dreams."

"I just hope you're ready to lick your wounds."

Families crowded the Fun Zone, trying their luck at the various booths with games of skill like Punk Rack or Spill-the-Milk. We rode carefully through this maze and arrived at The Bay Arcade.

This was our favorite arcade because they had a game called Batter Up, an ancient form of pinball. Instead of using a plunger, the game pitches the ball to you from a pitcher's mound. You hit the ball with a bat that swings like a flipper.

There are holes in the infield designated as singles or outs. In the outfield are holes designated as doubles, triples or outs and, at the fence, there are mostly outs, except for a couple of places designated as home runs. But the most difficult shot of all is in the center of the fence. It's called "double-your-runs." There, the ball has to roll up a narrow ramp without sides. If the ball falls off the ramp you are out, and ninety-nine times out of a hundred, your attempt proves disastrous.

Bobby and I had been playing this game since freshman year. It was our game, and a great competition had developed between us. We spent hours competing against each other as if locked in mortal combat, arguing and accusing each other of cheating. When that didn't work, we resorted to name calling, anything to unsettle the other and gain the upper hand. I guess it was because it was a game of skill, where Bobby's superior athletic ability was not an advantage that we were close to being tied in wins.

But there was something deeper going on between us. It had to do with who we essentially were and what strategy we deployed. Bobby was "go-for-broke" and "swing-for-the-fences" while I was strictly a safe player who went for singles and consistency. On any given day, either strategy could prevail, and we would always bet money. A dollar an inning, five dollars to the winner and the overall loser would have to supply the quarters the next time we played. That was big money for us.

"Do you have the quarters?" Bobby asked, since he had beat me the last time we played.

"Yeah," I replied. "Do you have the dollars you're going to lose?"

"I didn't bring any because I'm going to be taking yours."

Bobby batted first, homers versus singles, back and forth, yelling and screaming.

"Oh, you pussy."

"You suck at this game. You always have."

"Fuck a duck, you are the luckiest bag of shit to ever swing a bat."

Our dialogue was growing increasingly colorful; we were having way too much fun. But, as often happens when you are having big fun, you attract a crowd. It's as if the fun you're having makes people think that you know something they don't, and they want to find out your secret. Today was no exception. Three girls surrounded us and peppered us with questions.

"Are you from Newport?"

"Do you go to Newport Harbor?"

"What kind of car do you drive?"

We were focused on the game, and answered their questions with some annoyance.

"Screw it," Bobby shouted as he made his last out in the bottom of the ninth. The score was 39 to 36, with the home run strategy of Bobby's slightly ahead.

It was my turn to bat. I made an out and then a single. I made another out, then two more singles. The bases were loaded, with two outs in the bottom of the ninth.

"Do you play football too, Scotty?" one girl asked.

"No," I replied. "I'm...ah...a surfer."

"Yeah," Bobby said, "Scotty's too cool for football."

Then something happened that I can't explain. I suddenly changed my whole strategy, a strategy I had used against Bobby since freshman year, and swung for the whole enchilada. Why? I will never know for sure. Maybe it was because three pretty girls were watching. But I did, and not just for the easier homerun at the fence. But for the double-your-runs homer that almost guarantees failure. Even Bobby seldom tried this shot.

Surprised at what I had done, I watched the ball roll up the ramp, expecting it to fall off to the side for my final out. But by some miracle it continued up the ramp and fell into the homerun hole.

The game went crazy as the runs on my scoreboard began flipping like pancakes at the diner during breakfast rush. I looked at Bobby who had a stunned look on his face.

"Shit," he said. Bobby hated to lose at anything.

The girls cheered as Bobby tried to say something more. Finally, he just shook his head and grinned.

"Scotty, you beat me at my own game."

I jumped up and down and threw my arms in the air as if I had just scored a touchdown. It was like I had broken some sacred rule inside myself; the rule that says play it safe, don't take chances. I suppose it's really the fear of failure, a defense mechanism of sorts. Bobby was never afraid to fail at anything, and part of me, through this silly game, was always trying to prove him wrong. But now I realized the joy that comes from feeling the fear and doing it anyway. It brings a sense of freedom. Of course, it helped that it had worked.

"Yeah, it only took three years," I offered.

"Better late than never, dickhead," Bobby countered.

He reached into his pocket and pulled out a five-dollar-bill and handed it to me with a smile.

"You're the luckiest son-of-a-bitch I know."

We turned our attention to the girls. They were pretty and dressed only in bikinis. We had been so focused on the game that they could have been gorgeous and naked and we wouldn't have noticed. They were from Long Beach and had rented a room at the Balboa Inn for the weekend. Like us, they were preparing to embark upon their senior year at Long Beach Wilson. This weekend was a celebration of sorts to mark the beginning of their journey.

"What are your names?" Bobby asked.

"I'm Shelly," the tallest girl said. She had long black hair with the body of a model.

"Shelly," the next girl said with a giggle. She had long blonde hair that fell halfway down her back and dark brown eyes.

"I'm Shelly, too," the shortest girl said. She could have been a gymnast and her hair was fiery red.

They laughed. Obviously, it had been a running gag all weekend and, the way they had each taken turns telling us their names seemed rehearsed.

"The three Shellys from Long Beach?" I asked.

"Yeah," they said in unison.

Bobby and I looked at each other and cracked up.

"Would you like to come back to our room?" The tall Shelly asked. "We have some beers."

Bobby cocked his head at me and lifted one eyebrow up and down in a sly sort of way. I knew what he was thinking. Maybe I can finally get my boy laid.

"Nah," I said quickly before Bobby could respond. "But I would like to buy each of you a Balboa Bar with my winnings."

"What's a Balboa Bar?" short Shelly asked. The question was directed to me.

"You've never had a Balboa Bar? You're in for a treat."

"That wasn't the treat I had in mind," tall Shelly said. She was staring at Bobby.

Bobby looked at me grinning mischievously.

"After you've had a Balboa Bar," I said, "you won't need another treat. Come on."

The three Shellys looked at each other, shrugged, and followed me out the door. I could feel Bobby trailing behind me. I was sure he was grinning and making plans for my future.

39

The world famous Balboa Bar, a solid block of vanilla, strawberry, or chocolate ice cream, dipped in fudge and rolled in either sprinkles or nuts, is simply the best ice cream concoction ever created. To Bobby and me, the Fun Zone meant Batter Up and Balboa Bars. The two went together like bikinis and suntan oil.

We treated the girls and ourselves to Balboa Bars and walked to a place between the arcade and the Ferris wheel that afforded a stunning view of the bay. Bobby and I sat on a bench while the girls leaned against the railing licking their ice cream.

It was a perfect spot. To our right sat the Pavilion, Newport's famous landmark, and we could watch the boats pulling up to Davey's Locker to fill their bait tanks. To our left, the Ferris wheel, commonly known as The Bird Cage, spun the people in a circle while they looked out over Balboa from the best seat in the house. Beyond the Ferris wheel, the old ferryboats transported cars and people from the peninsula to Balboa Island. The boats were crowded.

The Shellys enjoyed their Balboa Bars. Then a competition broke out. They put on quite a show as their tongues sensually traversed their ice creams up and down. The tallest Shelly intended to outshine them all when she opened her mouth and literally inhaled the entire bar. It was obvious that she was trying to shock us. But in a moment she was choking and short Shelly had to help her pull the large ice cream out of her mouth. We all nearly died laughing.

"That was funny," Bobby said. "You gave new meaning to the word gag."

"I'm glad you laughed," tall Shelly said, "but you weren't the one choking."

The girls had worked all summer at an El Taco drive-thru earning money for college. They were blue-collar girls, their fathers were mechanics and truck drivers, and there was a refreshing lack of pretension among them. A stark contrast to the sense of entitlement many Newport girls possessed. The Shellys had come to Newport on this Labor Day weekend to remind themselves of why they had worked so hard.

"Are you guys from rich families?" medium Shelly asked.

Bobby and I looked at each other and laughed.

"Sure they are," tall Shelly said. "Everyone in Newport is rich. At least richer than us."

I was sure tall Shelly was smitten with Bobby. I noticed that she stole glances at him when he wasn't looking.

"Why don't we have some beer?" short Shelly suggested again. The question was directed at me and I wondered if she had been stealing glances at me, too. I must admit, I found her extremely attractive.

"No, Bobby's got a sunset date and I promised to have him back in one piece."

"Our weekend has been a bust," medium Shelly revealed. "All we've met are bozos from Westminster and Garden Grove."

"We wanted to come to Newport and meet some rich guys and party," tall Shelly explained.

Bobby and I laughed again.

"Well, Scotty's not rich but his mother is," Bobby said.

The girls' eyes all brightened at this news and they began to look me up and down. Bobby smiled at me, and I knew what he was after. It's time for Scotty to become a man.

"Do you have a sunset date?" short Shelly asked me.

"No," I replied. "I've got a date with my journal. I need to write about today. Perfection is hard to find and when you find it, you never want to forget it."

"Why was it perfect?" medium Shelly asked.

"Because I rode in the sunshine with my best friend who almost got me arrested on Lido Island. Or maybe it was because I rode with my best friend who got me into a fight on the boardwalk. But probably it was because I swung for the fences and I had the privilege of watching three girls from Long Beach eat their Balboa Bars with utter abandon."

I looked at Bobby. He had a big grin on his face. I knew it had been a near-perfect day for him as well.

"I like the way you talk," short Shelly said.

"If you like the way he talks," Bobby said. "Then you'll love the way he writes."

"You're a writer," short Shelly squealed.

"How cool," medium Shelly seconded.

Bobby was elbowing me. He wanted me to make my move. But I didn't want it this way. Not from three girls who thought money somehow made people different. I agreed with Hemingway, "The rich aren't different, they just have more money." These girls had put money on a pedestal and that had clouded their perspective. It could wreck them, the same way it wrecked Fitzgerald or my mom.

"Thanks," I said. "But I've got to get Bobby home. I made someone a promise."

The girls' faces grew sad and they pouted like little girls being told they couldn't have what they wanted. They walked us to our bikes and we hugged each of them.

"Maybe we'll hook up again," Bobby offered. "We might see you guys in the playoffs."

"Really?" tall Shelly said hopefully. There was a story here, I could feel it and I could almost hear tall Shelly saying this was a great weekend because she had met Bobby Rowels. But Bobby was someplace else.

"Yeah," he smiled, "if your team is good enough."

As Bobby and I rode away, I stole a glance back. The three Shellys from Long Beach stood on the curb watching us disappear like forlorn kids at the end of a day at Disneyland, holding on tight to the dream that money could buy a fairy tale.

40

Instead of heading toward the beach, Bobby and I rode on the boardwalk that ran along the bay, past Bay Island, and onto the quiet side street of Bay Avenue.

It was just after five, and the day was starting its long fade toward evening. The air was warm, and the long shadows and golden shafts of afternoon light made for a very pleasant ride.

Bobby and I always took this route home from the Fun Zone. There was never a discussion about which route we would choose. We just always chose this one, along Bay Avenue, and a conversation always broke out as the street's width afforded the opportunity to ride side by side. The boardwalk, with its traffic of pedestrians and other bikes, was often too narrow for a decent conversation.

"Tomorrow we start school," Bobby lamented. "And next Friday I have my first game."

"The summer sure went by fast."

"Kind of like today."

"Yeah," I agreed. "Time seems to melt away when you're having big fun."

"I think this was the best bike ride ever. I'll never forget it."

"Me, too."

We rode along for another block in silence. The clickety-clack of our bike chains kept a tempo that has always reminded me of summer.

"Do you ever wonder where you'll be in twenty years?" Bobby asked.

"I don't know. Sometimes I can guess. I see my dad lying passed out on the couch and say to myself, 'That will never be me.' Then I see myself in some really cool space, writing away."

"I've tried to picture myself twenty years from now and I can't. Maybe if my dad hadn't been killed I would have his life to guide me. Even if it's just a guide for what I don't want."

"Yeah, seeing what you don't want can be as helpful as seeing what you do want."

"Yeah."

The clickety-clack of the chains took over again for another block. Then Bobby turned to me with a huge smile on his face.

"My boy, Scotty, swung for the fences and nailed it!"

The way Bobby said it caused the elation of that moment to fill me again.

"It's been a great day," I said.

"Yeah, because you beat me at my own game, dickhead."

"Well, if I did, it's because I was taught by the best fence-swinger in Newport."

Bobby smiled again. I could tell he liked that.

"Why didn't you go off with the Shellys from Long Beach? I could tell that short one really liked you."

I was quiet for a moment. "I don't know. I thought she was really cute."

"Was it because of Perry?" Bobby asked.

"Maybe, I guess."

"Scotty, Perry might be a whore. We see her with an old guy almost every morning. And when she's not with him, she's with some other guy. She's way out of your league. She's a player. If you just hooked up, okay. But don't start liking her."

I was quiet again. I did like Perry. In fact, I was pretty much smitten.

"I just don't want you to get hurt," Bobby continued. "You're not like me. I don't want you falling in love with the first girl you screw."

"I'm not sure I even have to sleep with her."

Bobby looked at me and then shook his head.

"Dude, you're in way over your head. Trust me, you're screwed. Perry's probably a whore and she's using you to feel better about herself. 'Pick up the young dude and play with him.'"

"It's a little more complicated than that."

"More complicated than that? How?"

Still side by side, we rode in silence for another block. But the tempo of the clickety-clack sounded different. There was an uneasiness to it. I didn't like Bobby calling Perry a whore. There was also something else, the promise I had made to Perry. For the first time since we had become best friends I couldn't tell Bobby a secret. I wasn't exactly lying but I was keeping something from him, something that might be important. Bobby's final words about the situation made my dilemma worse.

"Dude, I'm your best friend and that means total truth. Total honesty. Just like Lee Marvin said. Perry might be a whore, and that means you better be careful."

Bobby and I looked at each other for a long moment.

"Hey," he said. "I'm just trying to watch your back. I know you'd do the same for me."

41

We got home to the trailer park just after six, sweaty and sticky from riding the final mile hard. Bobby always said that the final mile was like smelling the goal line and he always rode flat out. I always had to work to keep up with him.

"I'm going to take a shower," Bobby announced.

My dad wasn't home; probably he had made his way to Dirty John's. So I wandered over to the worn-out deck that extended off the side of our trailer and sat in the old rusted lawn chair with my journal, intending to record my memories while they were fresh.

"Hey."

I looked up from my journal to find Perry standing in front of me. She had on cut-off blue jeans and a skimpy bathing suit top. The waning afternoon sun glinted in her blonde hair. One look at her and I was glad I hadn't gone off with the red-haired Shelly.

"Hey, yourself," I answered.

"What'd you do all day?" she asked.

"Bike ride, boardwalk, Fun Zone, and we jumped off the Lido Bridge."

"Oh," she said. I detected a note of sadness in her voice.

"What did you do?"

"Went sailing."

"Was it fun?"

"Not exactly. There was supposed to be a group. But no one else showed up."

"So you went by yourself?"

She bit her lip. "No, there was someone else. But his idea of fun wasn't mine."

I nodded. I wasn't sure how to respond to that. It was obvious that she'd had a date and it didn't turn out as she hoped.

"Well, we had fun," I said.

"I bet you did. You and Bobby always have fun."

"Yeah, it was a great day. One for the record books."

"I should have hung out with you guys. Where's Bobby now?"

"Taking a shower. He has a date to see the sunset."

Perry smiled. "Would you like to walk to the beach and see the sunset with me?"

"Sure, I'd like that."

"Just let me put my purse away."

She walked toward her trailer as I sat there for a moment thinking, it was going to be the perfect finish to a perfect day. Then I headed to the front of the trailer to put my journal away. Just as I was about to enter I heard a sound; a sound that could only be created with the kind of engineering that has the money and time to seek perfection. I turned to see a Ferrari pulling into the trailer park. It was red as only a Ferrari could be, and the car still had paper plates. The top was off and a young dark-haired girl was driving. Even a couple of neighbors turned to gawk.

To my surprise, the car pulled up in front of our trailer and I saw it was Monica. She was one of Liza the Hurricane's best friends, a girl I always shied away from. She worked hard at being wild and loved having a "bad girl" reputation.

"Is Bobby around?" Monica asked.

David Bowie's "Diamond Dogs" blared through the car's speakers.

"Monica, what are you doing here?"

"I don't know, I guess I just decided to pop by. Thought maybe Bobby would want to go for a drive."

Just then, I looked over and saw Liza the Hurricane pulling into the park in her Mercedes.

"Does Liza know you're here?" I asked quickly.

"No, Liza went to her grandmother's house."

"No, she didn't. She's pulling in right now to walk with Bobby to the beach."

"Oh, shit," Monica said, then she began to plead. "Scotty, please don't say I asked for Bobby. Say I came to see you."

Before I could answer, Liza pulled up and rolled down her window. David Bowie's "Fame" blared from her speakers. I knew Liza and the posse were big Bowie fans but I never expected to have a concert in my front yard.

"Whose Ferrari?" Liza called.

I looked toward Monica who mouthed the word, "Please?" I looked back over at Liza. She had a smile on her face.

"It's Monica's," I said. "Or at least her father's."

Liza's face registered confusion. "Monica?   You mean Monica Keller?"

"Yeah."

Liza frowned. She shut off her car and got out. She walked up to the Ferrari like she was ready to punch someone.

"Monica, what are you doing here?"

"I came by to see Scotty," Monica said quickly. "I thought he might like to drive a Ferrari."

Liza looked relieved and then she turned to me.

"Every guy in the world dreams of driving a Ferrari."

Out of the corner of my eye, I saw Perry. She stood thirty feet away staring at me in disbelief. I was sure she had heard Monica's invitation.

"Come on, Scotty," Monica giggled. "Let me take you for a test drive."

Monica got out of the car. To my surprise she was wearing the shortest dress I had ever seen a girl wear. She had attractive, long legs, and the dress was low-cut, revealing a good portion of her other attractions. It was obvious she had put some planning into this visit.

"Just a minute," I said.

I turned to walk toward Perry to explain what was happening. But Perry was gone. Then the door to our trailer opened and there stood Bobby with a frown on his face.

"Liza, I told you not to bring the posse."

"I didn't," Liza protested. "Monica came to see Scotty all on her own."

"Is that true?" Bobby asked. His question was directed at me, but Monica answered quickly.

"Yeah, I thought Scotty might like to drive a Ferrari."

Bobby's face softened, and then he cracked a smile.

"Who wouldn't like to drive a Ferrari?" Bobby said.

"Come on, Scotty," Monica called. "Let me take you for a ride."

She walked around the car and slid into the passenger seat. Both Liza and Bobby were looking at me, waiting for me to get into the Ferrari and drive away. But I didn't want to drive away. I wanted to walk to the beach with Perry.

Then I looked at Liza and realized I was already in too deep. I got in, and knew the moment I did it was a mistake.

"Have fun, bro," Bobby said.

"Yeah, don't do anything we wouldn't do," Liza added.

It was a mistake that just grew worse, exponentially. As we pulled away, Monica reached over and kissed me on the cheek.

"Today's the last day of summer," she said. "I want to get laid, and if Bobby's not available, you'll do just fine. Let's find some place and fuck like rabbits in this Ferrari."

I looked at Monica, who had a lascivious smile on her face. She licked her lips with her tongue like a rattlesnake about to devour a mouse. I was mortified.

42

I'm not sure if girls in Newport are faster than girls in other towns. But Monica was about as fast as they come, almost as fast as her dad's Ferrari. When we got to the driveway that led onto Pacific Coast Highway, Monica's hand slid between my legs, rubbing the inside of my thigh. I suppose a lot of guys would have been flattered. A lot of guys would probably feel like they had been dealt a royal flush in a poker game. A hot girl in a Ferrari shows up on your doorstep, out of the blue, ready to give it to you, and all you have to say is yes. But not me. I wasn't interested in being another notch on her lipstick case. I was pissed.

We pulled out of the trailer park and turned right onto the highway heading toward Huntington Beach. I wasn't about to head toward Newport. I hit the gas and felt the acceleration thrust my head and body back into the seat like a F-4 Phantom charging the runway. I had to admit, it was an exceptional car, the hottest car I had ever driven. We flew over the River Jetties Bridge in just seconds.

"You know, Scotty," Monica purred. "You get cuter every time I see you. And I hear you're into older women. They must have taught you some tricks."

She reached over and turned up the cassette player. Bowie's "Rebel Rebel" was now playing on the Ferrari's stereo.

"I love Bowie. His music makes me want to have wild sex on the last day of summer."

She leaned over and stuck her tongue in my ear.

"Fuck," I yelled.

"Dirty words. I like that."

I turned right on Brookhurst, headed up to Hamilton and pulled into a gas station. Monica looked around, surprised.

"We can't do it here, Scotty. Someone will see us."

I just shook my head, got out of the car, shut the door and looked down at her. Her dress had slipped down her chest and a portion of her breast was exposed. Monica had definitely come loaded for bear.

"Monica, you don't get it. I had a date too. Now my date's pissed."

"You mean you don't want to do it in a Ferrari?"

"No, and if you ever think twice about it, you'll realize that I think you're a pretty shitty friend. The only reason I covered for you was for Liza's sake. See you at school tomorrow."

I turned and walked away. I wasn't twenty feet from the Ferrari when a carload of guys pulled up alongside in a beat-up dark blue Volkswagen bug. There must have been five guys in it, probably from Anaheim or Garden Grove.

"Are you out of gas?" one guy called.

"No," Monica replied. "I've got plenty."

"Maybe you need a driver?" another guy called.

"Maybe I do."

Who could blame these guys, a pretty girl in a Ferrari? It's a can't-fail combination that sends young men's libidos on a collision course with their fantasies, and if Monica was dead set on finding trouble, there wasn't much I could do about that. I just kept walking.

43

As I was hoofing my way down Pacific Coast Highway, back toward the trailer park, Monica passed by in the Ferrari with the Volkswagen in hot pursuit. The guys in the Volkswagen honked at me and I was pretty sure I heard them laughing.

This pissed me off even more. In the short time I had driven the Ferrari we had covered a lot of ground. Nearly two miles, I estimated. It took a fat half-hour to get back to the trailer park. By the time I arrived, I was fuming.

I went straight to Perry's trailer and knocked on the door. But there wasn't any answer. So I knocked again and called her name. It became clear she wasn't home.

For a moment, I was hopeful she had just walked to the beach on her own and that I would be able to find her. But my hopes were dashed when I checked the other side of her trailer and found that her car was gone.

I was so pissed. How could I have ever been so stupid? I should have cut Monica loose immediately. But that's what you get for being a nice guy. It sometimes blows up in your face.

I walked back to my trailer and found a pen and a pad of paper. I sat down and wrote out an explanation about what had happened with Monica and the Ferrari. Then I took the explanation and the story I had written the night before and walked to Perry's trailer. I set them on her doorstep.

It was now dark, and tomorrow was the first day of school. I gathered up all my supplies and books for the next day and put them in my backpack. Then I took a shower. Afterward, I checked Perry's trailer from my bedroom window. She had not returned.

It was after nine when Bobby walked in with a smile on his face and some story about finding a hidden place between the rocks at the River Jetties.

I told him about what had happened with Monica and he was pissed, too.

"Those stupid girls she hangs with," Bobby said.

"Liza can be nice but she sure has some shitty friends."

"Yeah," Bobby said. "If they're not scratching out each other's eyes, then they're stabbing each other in the back."

"With friends like that, who needs enemies." I was still angry.

"Speaking of friends," Bobby said. He still had a smile on his face from his perfect day. *My Darling Clementine* is on television tonight. Do you think your dad would want to watch it?"

"Maybe, let's ask."

We found my dad sipping his beer while watching the news. It was something about Patty Hearst and the Symbionese Liberation Army.

"A movie?" my dad asked.

"Not just any movie," Bobby said. "It's *My Darling Clementine*."

"Trust me, dad," I said. "It's a great movie."

I can't remember the last time I had sat with my father watching a movie and, what's more, he loved the movie. But I think it was more than that. I think what he really loved was watching the movie with Bobby and me. It's a man's movie, a story about loyalty and honor and everything a policeman believes in. The fact that he was sharing it with us made it even more meaningful.

It was after eleven when Bobby and I stood to head for the bedroom. But something funny happened. My dad changed the channel to the Johnny Carson show. Carson was interviewing Lee Marvin. Bobby and I sat back down to watch.

"Lee," Johnny said. "A lot of people are unaware that you were a Marine in the initial landing on Iwo Jima."

"Yeah, yeah," Lee replied.

"And during the course of that action you earned the Navy Cross and were severely wounded."

"Yeah. Yeah. I got shot square in the ass and they gave me the cross for securing a hot spot halfway up Suribachi. Bad thing about getting shot on a mountain is guys getting shot hauling you down. But Johnny, at Iwo I served under the bravest man I ever knew. We both got the cross that same day but what he did for his cross made mine look cheap in comparison. The dumb bastard actually stood up on Red Beach and directed his troops to move forward and get the hell off the beach. That sergeant and I have been life-long friends. When they brought me off Suribachi we passed the sergeant and he lit a smoke and he passed it to me lying on my belly on the litter and asked, 'Where'd they get you, Lee?' 'Well, Bob,' I said. 'If you make it home before me, tell mom to sell the outhouse.' I'm not lying Sergeant Keeshan was the bravest man I ever knew. Bob Keeshan. You and the world know him as Captain Kangaroo."

Johnny said a few more words, followed by a commercial. We looked at each other.

"Do you think it's true?" Bobby asked. "That funny little man, Captain Kangaroo?"

"I've never heard that before," my dad said.

"Maybe it doesn't matter," I said. "Maybe what's important is the legend. Like in *The Man Who Shot Liberty Valance*. 'When the legend becomes fact, print the legend.'"

"Yeah," Bobby said. "But who decides the legend?"

We climbed into bed and Bobby and I talked for a while about how cool Lee Marvin was and what an adventure our bike ride had been. It was our first night as roommates.

"Today was one of the best days of my life," Bobby said. "Thanks, bro."

"Yeah, it was great," I offered but I was disappointed about Perry and I didn't want to talk to Bobby about it. I knew how he felt, and I couldn't tell him why he was wrong.

Finally, Bobby drifted off to sleep. I looked out the window and saw that Perry still wasn't home. My story and explanation were leaning against her front door like a yellow ribbon tied around an oak tree. I fell back into my bed staring at the bunk above me for a long time. How could a day that started out so great, end so badly? But that was life. It was often unpredictable, just like a bike ride on a summer's day or the fact that a goofy actor on a kids' TV show was actually one of the bravest men in the world.

44

I woke early and sat up in bed, my first day of being a senior. I also thought of Perry. I looked out the window toward her trailer and saw my story still sitting on her front doorstep. Perry had stayed away all night.

I climbed out of bed and peered at Bobby. He was snoring away, still out cold on the top bunk. I nudged him gently.

"What...?" Bobby asked as if still lost in a dream.

"First day of school, bro."

We dressed and sat at the kitchen table with the broken leg eating a bowl of cereal. My dad was passed out on the couch.

"Perry didn't come home last night," I said.

Bobby looked at me and shook his head.

"What do you expect? You know she has a lot of boyfriends. When she thought you were busy she moved on to someone else."

"No, I think I really hurt her."

"Come on, dude. It's Newport. Stuff like this happens all the time. She's a big girl."

We gathered our stuff for school and headed out the door. One of the major perks of Bobby living with us was that I didn't have to try to negotiate the school bus. We had the Chrysler. Before, I would have been walking six blocks to Orange Street and Newport Shores Drive to catch the transportation provided by the Newport-Mesa school district, as a senior that would have been a real drag.

But the first day could have been interesting, watching the freshmen, scared of their own shadows and embarking on this journey we call high school. If I had the chance, I would have told them to relax and enjoy the ride. Four years will fly by so fast, you'll wonder what happened.

I thought that high school had sort of been like a surf safari. I remember George the magician at the Frog House Surf Shop once saying to me, "Any safari to find waves seems like it takes forever because the anticipation of what you are going to find makes it that way. But once you get there it seems like the trip passed too quickly and you realize that half the fun is the safari itself. Of course, the memory is all the sweeter if the universe smiles on you and you find good waves." This was after his recent trip to South Africa to surf Jeffreys Bay. I had asked if the trip was worth it.

But this was true of any journey, and also of life itself. Thinking of the freshmen made it seem almost surreal that I had awakened this morning a senior. It also reminded me that in a few short months I would be graduating, and I had to wonder where the time went. It seemed like the days and weeks of the last three years had dragged on, but the years had flown by. The real meaning of this moment had been in the journey, and what I had learned.

I was a senior and I couldn't help but smile when we passed the school bus in the Chrysler. I realized that my interest in the freshmen would have probably lasted about thirty seconds. After that, I would have just been annoyed.

45

The first day of school is always a bigger deal for girls than it is for boys. Dressed in outfits that had probably taken several trips to the mall to find and excited by social expectations, they are filled with hope. As one silly girl put it, "I just have to find a boyfriend this year. If I do nothing else, I have to find a boyfriend." This plan begins with looking good on the first day of school.

The guys, on the other hand, could care less. Most of us hate the idea of being back at school, and wish we were still hanging out at the beach, soaking up the sun, surfing, and ogling the girls in their bikinis. The girls' new clothes were something of a letdown after weeks of watching what the summer revealed.

Then there are the serious students who know how important it is to prove yourself in order to move on to college. Either from advice or self-awareness, these students realize early on that the choices they make today could affect the rest of their lives.

Bobby and I fell into a gray area. We took the hard classes but we were so laid-back that the serious students didn't understand us. They often wondered why Bobby was even in the class as he often struggled. But Bobby, since freshman year, always matched his schedule to mine, and with my help, he always managed to get passing grades. Still, we were outcasts with the serious students who thought an exciting evening was spent with a slide rule and that party time involved "Dungeons and Dragons."

In the social scene we were outcasts, too. This was largely due to me because I found this scene filled with mostly trivial romantic pursuits to gain popularity and acceptance. Popularity took way too much work, and I believed that high school sweethearts never work out. If you did marry this person, you would most likely end up divorced, like my parents, who fell in love in high school.

Instead, I always disappeared to the library at lunchtime and Bobby usually came with me. We would find a quiet cubicle and study. This is where the gray area came in. The social set would have called us nerds except Bobby was the football star and I was his best friend. So the nerd label just didn't fit. But because we weren't hanging out at lunch with either the surfers or the football players, those social labels didn't fit either. I suppose in some strange way this lent an air of mystery to Bobby and, by extension, me. As a result, rumors often circulated about what we were up to. We laughed when we heard them. Some people speculated that we were plotting some diabolical scheme like mad scientists and some said that we were antisocial because we felt superior while another group speculated that we were laying low because we were drug dealers. This particular speculation intensified when Bobby moved in with me. The question on everyone's mind was, where were we getting our money?

We weren't up to anything. We were just trying to get a head start on our work. But we did have a larger plan, a simple plan. Take the hard classes, take summer school, talk to the teachers about extra credit when needed, meet often with our guidance counselors, and graduate six months early. At the end of this semester, Bobby and I would officially have enough credits to graduate. Then we would have an entire semester to do whatever we wanted; surf safari to Mexico, sleep in, take a ceramics class, it didn't matter. The time and freedom would be ours because we had earned it. That first day of school in the library was sweet because we could almost taste the freedom.

"I'm thinking Costa Rica, Scotty."

"How?"

"The Chrysler, dickhead. How else? We'll throw our boards on the top and pack it to the gills with food."

I laughed. "We'd be lucky to reach Oceanside."

"No, I'll give her a tune-up. We'll make it. You have to have faith."

"You'd better give calculus a tune-up. I don't think Mr. Manly likes football players very much."

"It's not football players. It's me. I've seen him hanging with White. That's what sucks about high school. The teachers and coaches think they can decide your life."

"Just do the work and play your best. Then they can't say shit."

Bobby looked at me and smiled.

"Yeah, that's right. Bring it on, and you know why?"

"Why?"

"Because I've got you, Scotty. I've got a secret weapon, and they can screw with me all they want. But I've got you. Just like Butch Cassidy. He had the Sundance Kid."

I smiled.

"That's right. We're in this together. Now let's get to work. The first quiz is on Friday."

46

After school Bobby went to practice, and I rode home on the bus. I would have taken the Chrysler and come back to pick Bobby up after practice but I had to get to my job as a dishwasher at Cappy's, a popular local diner that always hired cute young girls who wore short skirts and tight t-shirts. But Pete the owner was smart enough to know that cute girls weren't enough for a going concern. He also hired the best cook he could find, a black man named Pineapple.

Pineapple and I were great friends and he had a story to tell. Most of his youth was spent in jail because he had belonged to a notorious street gang called The Crips. But it was in jail that he learned to cook. Even though he never graduated high school, when it came to cooking, Pineapple knew how to make food sing.

He was still a gangster when he got out of jail with his cooking degree and he returned to his gangster ways. Then something happened to change his life. A girl he was dating got pregnant and decided to have the baby. It was a girl. But after she had the baby, she didn't want to keep it. Pineapple woke one morning to find the baby sleeping in a basket outside his door with a note from the girlfriend saying she was on her way to Chicago.

"The first thing I felt was fear," Pineapple said. "The kind of overwhelming fear that paralyzes you. Shit, I had stared down guns, I had stared down knives, and I had even stared down The Man. But I had never stared down something I had to protect. It was the scariest moment of my life."

He realized that his decisions would affect this girl for the rest of her life. He brought the baby into his studio apartment and just sat staring at her, wondering what he was going to do. He thought about dropping the baby at his mom's, but she had six other kids. At twenty, Pineapple was the oldest, and his mother had just had twins. His mother also didn't have any means of support other than welfare. Since this child wasn't hers, it would just be a burden, not a source of income.

"Then the baby began to cry. That shocked me into reality. The first thing I did was run to the store to get some formula and diapers. Then I began taking care of her and one thing led to another. At first, it was for a day. Then it became a week. After a month, my friends thought I was crazy."

"What the hell are you doing, Pineapple?" his gangster friends asked.

"What does it look like? I'm taking care of my daughter."

He named the little girl Pinaply and when she was a year old he loaded her in the car and went for a drive. He had heard that Orange County was safe, and he drove the county looking for a place to land. He wanted his daughter far away from gunshots and helicopters, and away from the gangs and drug wars he had known.

"I wanted to raise her right," he said. "To have a chance."

As luck would have it he found himself on Pacific Coast Highway in front of Cappy's. There was a sign on the window that read: Cook Wanted.

Pinaply is ten now and, as far as I know, the only black child at Newport Elementary. In fact, I would say that other than Reggie Jackson, Pinaply and her father are the only black people in Newport Beach. They live in the apartment house directly behind Cappy's and have been there for nine years. Pete would do anything for Pineapple. He's the best cook the diner has ever known.

That's where I come in. Pete loves me, too, because Pineapple loves me. For Pineapple, the sun rises and sets on his daughter and for three years I have helped her with her school work, an area of her life that

Pineapple doesn't feel qualified to help with. Because his daughter has been getting the best marks in her class, Pineapple thinks I walk on water. But, as I tell her father, the reason she's getting great marks is because Pinaply is the smartest kid in her class.

Pinaply and Pineapple are the reason I love my job. I look forward to sitting down at the little card table in the diner's kitchen with Pinaply every night at work. We go over her lessons while eating a great dinner prepared by her father. My relationship with Pineapple and his daughter is also the reason Pete agreed to my request to let Bobby and me use a booth every night to study.

Bobby arrives after practice at seven. We work for three, sometimes four hours in a booth at Cappy's Diner. Often, we are the last to leave and Pete has given me a key to lock up. What's more, Pete always comps Bobby a free meal and, thanks to Pinaply, the meal is always excellent. Like every other girl in Newport, Pinaply has had a crush on Bobby since the first time she met him, so she constantly pesters her father to cook him something special. As a result, Bobby often eats better than I do, and I must admit, I'm a little jealous.

Pete just smiles at it all. He's a nice man, generous and fair. But he also knows he's got something very special going on and his business couldn't be better. Magic: those experiences that touch your life in profound and life-affirming ways, don't happen very often. At Cappy's Diner, magic is all around us.

47

Since Bobby moved out of his mother's apartment, Coach Dale White had been on the warpath. Every day at practice, he was harder on Bobby, and Bobby's reaction was to grow distant. The rift widened and fed on itself.

On Thursday the war escalated. White called for the first team defense. Of course, Bobby ran onto the field. But when he got out there, White yelled, "Blackburn!"

Blackburn was a junior who played behind Bobby. He was a good player but nowhere close to the player Bobby was.

"Rowels," White barked. "You can have a seat."

Bobby walked to the sideline and stood by himself for the remainder of the practice. When practice was over White gathered the team around him.

"Men, tomorrow night is our first game against Costa Mesa. We are a better team than the Mustangs. But I'm worried some of us are over-confident. So I'm going to make a few changes. People who think they can be late to practice because the waves are good are just too over-confident for our team."

Most of the players stole looks at Bobby. His wave at the Point was just too big a deal and the word had gotten out. Someone had gone to White about it. But instead of talking to Bobby directly like an adult who truly cares about his welfare and future, his coach chose to humiliate him.

"So we'll play those people who know that winning is about hard work. Dismissed."

As the team ran off the field, Jim Steiner searched Bobby out.

"What's White fucking doing?" Steiner asked Bobby.

"He's benching me because he can. He doesn't need me to beat Costa Mesa."

"White is such a dick," Steiner said and ran off the field toward the locker room.

Bobby smiled. Steiner was right. There was a dishonesty about White. Bobby sensed it, and he saw White as an enemy, not as a stable adult who could help guide him through the maze he was facing. What Bobby valued above all else was honesty. People with hidden agendas like White were not worthy of his respect. In Bobby's mind, his coach lacked integrity and courage. Anyone can be a dick. It takes courage and a deep moral compass to be a great teacher. Bobby knew he had made the right decision to move out.

Bobby found a strange form of liberation in White's actions. He was now free to rebel against his coach's expectations. White assumed that by position or rank he had some sort of power over Bobby and that Bobby wouldn't dare challenge him.

But White had miscalculated. In Bobby's case, the way to reach him was by being honest and direct. It was the only way to reach him. Once Bobby became suspicious of you he would never trust you again. The reason was obvious. How could he trust a world that lets a father get murdered for buying a carton of milk?

On Friday, under the lights at Davidson Field, the Newport Harbor Sailors defeated the Costa Mesa Mustangs, 21-7, and Bobby Rowels spent the first game of his senior year on the bench.

48

After the game, Bobby just wanted to get drunk. It had been a hard thing watching his teammates win a game without him and he was in a foul mood. For a player like Bobby, who truly loves playing the game, being forced to watch is like torture. But that was football. The game is destined to break your heart in big and small ways. Even players who find success beyond their wildest dreams face a huge letdown, for your days as a player are numbered. It ends for everyone, and all you are left with are the memories. Tonight was a memory Bobby wanted to forget.

"Are you sure you want to do this?" I asked

"Yeah," Bobby replied. "I want to get blasted."

We blew off Liza and the posse and decided to join Steiner, Rickie Chandler and Tommy Watts at an unusual place: O'Malley's Funeral Home on Seventeenth Street in Costa Mesa. Steiner's boathouse was being used by his parents. They were throwing a party for the Boosters Club, an organization of players' parents who get together after each game to dissect the highlights. It was Tommy Watts who suggested the funeral home. He worked as a delivery boy for a flower shop and had a key.

"That's pure genius, Watts," Steiner said.

"Yeah," said Bobby. "We can get dead drunk and feel right at home."

It was another half-baked idea and we found ourselves caravanning over to the funeral home. Bobby, Rickie Chandler and I rode in the Chrysler and Steiner and Tommy Watts drove in Steiner's white

Datsun truck. Chandler had caught two touchdown passes in the win over Costa Mesa and he was elated.

"Man," Chandler crowed. "What a great fucking game. We kicked their ass!"

"Yeah," Bobby said. "I'm glad we won."

Bobby's mood was darkening and I immediately wished we had chosen another way to finish the evening. I also wished Chandler had ridden with Steiner and Watts.

We parked in the lot behind the building so our cars would be hidden from passersbys on Seventeenth Street. All we needed was the posse tracking us down in a funeral home. Steiner got out of the truck holding the infamous beer bong and Watts got out carrying a case of Old English 800.

"It's party time!" Chandler shouted and jumped out of the backseat.

Bobby looked at me and smiled. "Like Chandler said, it's party time."

"I'll drive." I reached over and took the car keys out of the ignition.

"Thanks," he said and hopped out of the car. I followed reluctantly, thinking this had disaster written all over it. Watts produced his key and we stepped into an old and respected family business.

The reception room was large enough to hold twenty people and the walls had dark oak paneling that gave you a solid feeling of being in a place you could trust. A large oak desk sat at the far end of the room. There was a heavy oak door behind the desk. To our right were two double doors, also oak, and Watts walked over and opened them.

"This is where I bring the flowers," he announced. "I put them around the coffin."

We looked into the room and saw it was a chapel with large stained-glass windows. The figures in the windows were Jesus, Mary and various saints. It was obviously a Catholic establishment. I was struck by the beauty of one window and saw that it was St. Jude. I remembered my grandmother telling me he was the patron saint of hopeless causes. If you prayed to him and your prayers were answered you were supposed to publicly thank him. Slamming beers in a funeral home seemed pretty hopeless.

Two rows of pews lined either side of the chapel with an aisle down the center. A large oak podium stood at the end of the aisle. It struck me that the building felt bigger on the inside than it did on the outside.

"Let's break out the beers," Bobby suggested.

"Yeah," Chandler seconded. "Let's drink to victory."

In seconds, the tube was in Bobby's mouth and he was engulfing a tall can of the potent beer.

"Hey," Watts said. "Don't spill any."

The ritual had begun and I was not really part of it. I wasn't drinking and I was not on the team that had just won their first game. In a way, Bobby wasn't part of it either, and as Steiner, Chandler and Watts celebrated and boasted of their exploits in the game, Bobby grew angry.

"Two sacks," Watts recounted. "Mesa's quarterback had my number tattooed on his forehead."

"Fuck White!" Bobby said several times as they each took turns with the funnel. In a matter of twenty minutes, half the case was gone and my friends were obviously drunk. I could almost feel the saints inside O'Malley's Funeral Home looking down disapprovingly on our actions. Especially after Watts himself dropped an open can of Old English 800 onto the carpeted floor. A good portion of its contents spilled out before Watts could pick it up and the room soon smelled of beer.

"Shit," Watts said. "Scotty, give me your shirt."

"My shirt?"

"Yeah, I got to mop up this beer."

"Fuck that noise."

Watts glared at me. "You want some rug burns?"

The drunk football player took a step toward me. Bobby, sitting in a pew with the end of the beer bong stuck in his mouth, had just finished his turn. He pulled the surgical tube out of his mouth, stood, burping like a sputtering well pump, and walked unsteadily toward Watts.

"Shit, Tommy. You can't expect Scotty to give up his shirt."

Watts paused and looked hard at Bobby. For a moment I thought they were going to come to blows. This was not good. Bobby was by far the drunker of the two. It had been his fourth beer and he was staggering. I was prepared to jump in but Watts was a big guy. Finally, Steiner came to the rescue.

"Hey, Tommy. Are there any dead bodies in here?"

Forcing Watts's mind to think distracted him from the heat of the moment. The Neanderthal looked at Steiner.

"Yeah, I guess."

"Can we see one?" Steiner asked.

"Dead bodies?" Bobby said. "I haven't seen a dead body since my dad's funeral."

Bobby's father had been shot in the face but the mortician had filled the hole with wax and had used make-up to cover the bruising. Bobby told me his father had looked peaceful. Still, Bobby often awoke at night after seeing this final image of his father in his dreams.

"I don't know," Watts said.

"Don't be a pussy," Steiner admonished. "Let's look for the bodies."

"Yeah," Chandler echoed.

"All right," Watts agreed. "I think they're behind the door in the reception office."

We left the saints in the chapel and piled into the reception office. The heavy oak door behind the desk was locked.

"What do we do?" Bobby asked. He had grabbed another beer from the case and was now sipping on it.

"Leave it to me," Steiner said.

The kicker pulled out his wallet and produced his plastic student ID card. He slipped the card between the door and the jam where the dead bolt stood. Steiner smiled.

"They forgot to lock the dead bolt."

In a flash, Steiner slipped the card down to the door handle. We heard a click and the door popped open.

"Cool!" Watts said, completely forgetting his initial reservations. "Dead bodies. I've never seen one."

We stumbled down a short hallway with a couple of doors on either side. Steiner opened the first door. It was an office with two wooden desks. There were phones on both desks and one desk had a stack of paperwork on it.

"No bodies in here," Steiner said.

"Guys, maybe we shouldn't be doing this." Alarm bells were ringing in my ears.

"Don't be a pussy, Scotty," Steiner scolded.

"Yeah, I want to see a body," Chandler said.

Bobby looked at me and shrugged. Then he took another big swig from his can. His balance was suffering.

Like a flock of turkeys, we followed Steiner to the second door. He tried the door handle but this door was locked, too. However, the door did not have a dead bolt. Steiner produced his ID card again and in mere seconds we heard another click. He pushed open the door and we smelled a tangy iron odor.

"Shit," Watts said. "Is that smell from the bodies?"

Steiner flipped on the light. Two eight-foot fluorescent lights flickered and then drenched the room with harsh bright light. We all stood for a silent moment.

"What's this?" Chandler asked.

Two white marble tables, as stiff as the corpses they served, stood in the middle of the room. Above the tables, a large metal showerhead hung on a flexible hose which enabled it to reach either table. The windowless room had white ceramic tile flooring with two large metal drains under each table, and white cabinets on one wall. Between the cabinets was a gray Formica-top counter with a white porcelain sink in the center. It was an uncomfortable room, stark and cold in its cleanliness.

"It's the Embalming Room," I said. "The last stop before they bury you."

"Why do they embalm people?" Chandler asked and added, "it seems kind of weird."

"The Egyptians," I answered, "believed it empowered the soul which would one day return to the body."

"That's creepy," Watts said.

I stole a look at Bobby. He was as pale as a ghost and as quiet as a cemetery. I was also going to say that it preserves the corpse so it looks good at the funeral but decided against it.

"Maybe we should just go," I suggested again.

The remark was prompted by the look on Bobby's face and the earlier warning from my dad, "Scotty, you need to be careful."

"Nah," Steiner directed. "We've come this far, let's see a body."

"Yeah," Chandler clucked. "I want to see a dead guy."

"This feels creepy," Watts added gleefully. "I like feeling creepy."

Bobby was silent and I was outnumbered.

"Where do you think the bodies are?" Chandler asked.

"My guess," I said. "They're behind that door."

I pointed to a large gray metal door on the far wall. I could tell by its weight and unusual handle that it was the door to a refrigeration room. We had a similar refrigerator at the diner that served to keep the vegetables and meat cold so they wouldn't spoil.

We stared at the door for a long moment. Then Steiner walked over, pulled the handle, and the door opened. A puff of cold air hit the warmer air of the room and vaporized like a steam cloud, lending a feeling of mystery.

"Cool!" Watts slurred loudly.

The refrigerator was like a dark black hole and we stood for a long moment staring into nothingness. The night had turned surreal. What started out as a drunken beer fest in a chapel had turned into the search for a dead body.

Steiner flipped on the light switch. A large room was revealed, big enough for several bodies. Three gurneys with wheels were lined up side by side in the center. Two of the gurneys were empty but one gurney did carry what appeared to be a body covered with a white sheet.

"Cool," Watts said again. "A dead guy."

But there was nervousness in his remark, In fact, I think we were all a little bit nervous. The thought of death, the ultimate end, makes most people a little nervous.

We piled into the frigid room, gathering around the body like a band of ghouls. The body was obviously an adult for we could make out the bumps of the head and the feet. It was too large to be a child.

"I've never seen a dead guy," Watts said again, his hot breath pouring out like smoke in the cold room.

"I have," Chandler boasted. "I saw my uncle at his funeral last year. He ran into the back of a truck on his motorcycle."

"It could be a woman," I suggested.

This gave everyone pause. Their eyes shot around to each other and then settled on me. The idea of the body being a woman had not entered their minds. Their eyes returned to the body under the sheet.

"Who's going to pull the sheet off?" Watts asked.

Our eyes again darted to each other. Finally, Bobby stepped forward.

"I will," he growled.

He grabbed hold of the sheet and yanked it off with such force that it startled us. Bobby threw the sheet on the ground and our eyes settled on the body.

It was an old man. He was lying naked on his back, mouth open and eyes staring blankly at the ceiling. He almost looked surprised. His head was bald, maybe even shaved, and the body was skinny, almost emaciated. His chest hairs were as white as snow and his pale body was as wrinkled as a naked mole rat.

We stared for a long moment at the body before us, almost in reverence, for death does demand respect. Finally, Steiner broke the silence.

"So this is what death looks like."

We were quiet again. Then Bobby exploded.

"No, fuckheads, this is what life looks like! Take a good look at it. You live and then you're fucking dead. It's what we're all going to look like after life's beaten the crap out of us and kicked our asses. After your coach throws you away just because he can."

Bobby's anger took us by surprise as tears ran down his cheeks. This surprised us, too. I knew part of it was the memory of his father and another part was his deep disappointment over sitting on the bench. The beer helped, too.

Bobby quickly regained his composure. With the back of his hand, he roughly wiped away the tears.

"Screw it," he said.

"Hey, bro," I said gently. "It only matters if you let it."

"Like it doesn't matter? Scotty, you know how much it matters."

"White's an asshole, Bobby," Steiner said. "Scotty's right. He's not worth it."

"Yeah," Watts said. "I hate that asshole."

"We should fuck White up," Chandler said.

We were quiet a moment as Bobby pulled himself together. He straightened up and stood looking at us.

"Screw it," Bobby said again. "It's only a football game. Let's have another beer."

"No," Steiner said. "Chandler's right. We should fuck White up."

I knew that Steiner hated White almost as much as Bobby did. White was always yelling at Steiner, "you should wear a dress because you kick like a girl."

I looked into the kicker's eyes. I could see the wheels of his inebriated brain turning. Steiner was a smart guy and a little diabolical. His eyes left mine and settled on the body.

"Bobby's right. Life is short and White should be reminded that he isn't God." Then he smiled. "I say we take this old guy out for one last party and have him pay a visit to White's doorstep."

"What?" I asked incredulously.

Everyone started laughing, even Bobby.

"We can't steal a body," I protested.

"We're not stealing it. We're just borrowing it. Besides, once we deliver it to White it will technically belong to him. Can you imagine the look on his face when he finds it?"

Everyone started laughing again and I saw that this crazy idea was taking hold.

"Steiner," Bobby said. "You're a genius. It'll be the best revenge since *Stagecoach*."

After Bobby had invoked one of his favorite Westerns, I knew we were headed for trouble... big trouble. The Ringo Kid was unstoppable in his pursuit of revenge.

"We can't do this," I protested. "There will be an investigation. There will be police. Shit, we could all go to jail."

"Not if we stick together," Steiner countered. "We'll take Tommy home to watch TV with his sister."

Watts's older sister weighed two hundred and fifty pounds and it was common knowledge that she sat watching television day and night with a Coke and a bag of potato chips.

"I don't want to go home," Watts said.

"No, Tommy. You have to sit this one out. You are the only person who connects us to the funeral home. You need an alibi."

"All right," Watts said. He trusted Steiner and always agreed to whatever he suggested.

"After we drop Tommy off," Steiner continued, "we'll come back, get the body and deliver it to White's house. But the main thing is we make a deal. We were never here. We were never together. This night never happened."

"That won't matter," I said. "Our fingerprints are everywhere."

"Right," Steiner said. "Your job will be to get some towels and Windex and wipe the whole place down. Bobby, Chandler, and I will take care of grandpa here."

I decided right then and there that Steiner's upbringing in an FBI family made him dangerous. I looked at Bobby.

"Are you really going to do this?" I asked.

"Scotty, I need to do this. It's like the Ringo Kid going back for his revenge. He had to do it."

"What if White catches you guys?"

"He's at my house," Steiner said. "The Boosters Club party, remember?"

"Yeah," Bobby added. "He was taking my mom."

"Okay," Steiner said. He stuck out his hand, palm down, and we each placed a hand on top of his.

"We'll take this secret to our graves," Steiner said. "We will never talk about it. Even amongst ourselves. When we think about it we will just smile and the others will know and smile back. Agreed?"

We all agreed and once again I was outnumbered. But mostly, I was outnumbered by the empty cans of Old English 800.

49

Bobby, Chandler and Watts took off with Steiner in his Datsun pickup to drop Watts at his house and I drove the Chrysler to Hi-Time Cellars Liquor Store at Seventeenth Street and Irvine, the closest store to the funeral home. The parking lot was relatively empty and I parked right in front of the store.

But for a moment, I had second thoughts. La Cave restaurant, a well-known hangout for Newport Harbor High teachers, stood right next door. Our friend Brian Tremor worked there as a salad boy and always regaled us with stories of the teachers who came in and had a little too much fun. La Cave had great food and was close to the school.

The situation warranted cautiousness since Newport had just played their first game a couple of blocks down the street. I was involved in something crazy that could lead to calamity and I didn't want to have to explain my late-night purchase of Windex and paper towels to an intoxicated teacher.

I sat in the car for a long moment casing the area. When I was satisfied that the store was empty, I stepped out of the Chrysler and went in. The clerk eyeballed me as I searched the aisles for cleaning supplies. They were low on paper towels, only three rolls, and entirely out of Windex. But they did have a product called Mr. Clean. I thought the name sounded appropriate so I grabbed two bottles.

I took a quick look around the store and it was still empty except for the clerk. With my arms filled with cleaning supplies, I walked to the clerk and deposited my horde on the counter. But as I was preparing to pay, I heard a voice.

"Hey, Scotty."

I turned quickly. It was Jan Brousard, a lovely girl with blue-green eyes that reminded you of the lagoons of an island paradise, and also a sweetheart, one of the nicest people in our school.

"Oh, Jan, hi," I stammered.

"Where's Bobby? I saw his car."

"Ah, home in bed."

Jan looked suspiciously at the paper towels and Mr. Clean.

"It's cleaning day tomorrow," I said too quickly, and added, "we'll need this stuff in the morning. Are you picking up Brian?"

Like every guy at school, I once had a huge crush on Jan. But Tremor had stolen her heart. He was a track star destined to be a Newport legend, he was that good, and it's hard to compete with a legend.

"Yes, he gets off at twelve. We're meeting some other people at Squeezems."

Squeezems was a parking lot on a Dover Shores bluff that afforded one of the best public views of the bay. Kids from Harbor usually went there to make-out.

"You should come," Jan added.

"Ah, thanks Jan, but tomorrow's cleaning day so I'm off to bed." I gathered up my cleaning supplies. "Say hi to Brian."

"I will," Jan said. "See you at school on Monday."

I walked to the car thinking, "what the hell am I doing?" On the drive, I asked myself "why?" By the time I got to the funeral home I knew. I was doing this for Bobby. When Bobby Rowels made up his mind to do something, there was no stopping him. It was lead, follow, or get out of the way. The best thing I could do was to watch his back as best I could. I parked behind the funeral home, gathered up my cleaning supplies and entered the building. I started in the chapel, wiping down every inch of the pews and doors that could have a fingerprint on them. The room also reeked of beer, thanks to Tommy Watts, and I spent a half-hour trying to mop up the spill.

I was just finishing the chapel when Steiner, Chandler, and Bobby came in, laughing their heads off. They were carrying a couple of large cardboard boxes.

"We hit the training room," Bobby said. "Got some athletic tape."

Great, I thought, we can add burglary to our list of crimes. I followed them into the embalming room and watched as they entered the refrigerator. I walked over and stood at the door.

Bobby picked up the sheet and threw it over the old man's body while Steiner broke open the box of athletic tape.

"Scotty," Steiner said. "Look for another sheet."

I began searching through the cupboards which were filled with various bottles of chemicals and instruments of destruction necessary for the journey's end.

From the refrigerator came the sound of athletic tape being unrolled and torn.

"This is fucking great," Steiner shouted "White's going to shit his pants."

"Yeah," Bobby replied. "Revenge is sweet."

The next cupboard had a stack of sheets. I grabbed one and returned to the refrigerator. They had managed to wrap the sheet around the old man and were now taping the entire body. It was beginning to look like a mummy.

"Do you still need the sheet?" I asked.

"No," Steiner replied. "The tape is working better than I thought."

I returned the sheet to the cupboard and made a mental note to wipe down all the places I had touched.

"That should do it," Steiner said. "Bobby, grab the shoulders, Chandler, you take the middle, and I'll take the feet."

"Shit," Chandler said. "He's heavier than I thought."

"Of course," Steiner replied. "He's dead weight."

The thieves laughed hysterically as they carried the corpse from the refrigerator. The entire body had tape around it. Only the old man's face was visible, mouth and eyes still open.

"Hey," I said. "Why don't you roll it out on the gurney?"

A look of confusion crossed their faces for a moment.

"Scotty," Steiner said. "Your name should be Einstein. Why didn't I think of that?"

It was obvious the alcohol was still affecting their judgment and this worried me. If these guys do something stupid and get caught, our lives will be severely affected. Maybe even ruined.

"No," I replied. "I'm the only one not shit-faced. You guys will have a tough time explaining to a cop why you have a body in the back of your truck."

"We'll just tell the cop grandpa's sleeping," Steiner replied, cracking them all up again.

"Yeah, just don't get stopped or crash."

They muscled the corpse back into the refrigeration room and returned pushing the gurney. I followed them out of the room and down the hall.

"I hope White's wearing brown pants," Steiner said.

"Yeah, he's going to shit his pants, all right,

Bobby affirmed. "Best rat-fuck ever."

We entered the parking lot and they pushed the gurney over to Steiner's pickup. The truck had a shell on it and they opened the gate and window.

"Time to go for a little joy ride, grandpa," Steiner said.

They slid the body off the gurney, which was higher than the truck bed and the corpse's head made a loud thump on the steel bed.

"Oops," Steiner said. "Sorry, Gramps."

This caused more laughter as they slid the rest of the body in and closed the gate and window.

"Next stop," Chandler said. "White's residence."

Bobby turned to me. "Are you going to come?"

"Nah, it'll take me an hour to wipe this place down. I'll see you at home."

"Okay," Bobby said.

"If you get caught, call me."

"We're not going to get caught," Steiner replied.

"Just be careful," I answered.

"Remember, Scotty," Steiner said. "This night never happened."

I nodded. "See you at home, Bobby. Good luck."

"Let's roll," Steiner said.

The three grave robbers climbed in the pickup and I waved to them as they drove away. I returned to the building with the gurney and wiped down every inch of the embalming room and freezer. Afterward, I worked my way down the hall and into the reception room. Finally, I made sure all the lights were out and the doors were locked. As I drove home, I decided I never wanted to see the inside of a funeral home again.

50

It was late when I arrived at the trailer park. But instead of going to bed, I walked over to Perry's trailer and stood outside for a long time. The trailer, black as the night itself, seemed lonely and sad with no sign of life, my story and explanation still leaning against her door. She had been gone nearly a week and I had no idea where she was. I felt lonely. Maybe it was being in the presence of death or maybe the feeling that I had blown it badly that caused me to feel low.

"Perry," I whispered. "I need someone to trust, too."

Digging my hands into my pockets, I shuffled to my trailer as a deep wave of depression washed over me. Perry had chosen to trust me and in her eyes I had broken that trust.

The phone rang when I stepped inside the door. I knew this was not a good thing. My dad was snoring away on the couch so I picked the phone up as quickly as I could.

"Hello?"

"Bro, it's me. You've got to come get me."

"Where are you?"

"Dick Church's on Newport Boulevard. Hurry, the cops are out in force."

I ran out of the trailer and jumped in the Chrysler as fast as I could. But I drove the speed limit. It took about fifteen minutes to get to Dick Church's restaurant. I pulled into the parking lot and Bobby appeared from behind the dumpster. He sprinted to the Chrysler and jumped in quick as a lizard.

"What happened?" I asked, as I hit the gas and pulled away.

Bobby laughed hysterically. "Dude, he was home."

"What?"

"Steiner and I carried the body up to the doorstep and leaned it against the door. Next thing you know, we hear him screaming from inside the house, "You fucking Mustangs, I'm going to kill you!"

"He thought you were the Mustangs?"

"Yeah, it was priceless. Steiner and I ran for our lives. He went one way and I went the other."

"Where was Chandler?"

"He was parked around the corner waiting for us in Steiner's truck. But it gets better. I heard the front door fly open and then I heard a pop, pop, pop and Steiner yelling "Ow, ow, ow!" So I ducked behind a parked car to see what was going on. White was on his front lawn with a BB gun, firing shots at Steiner running down the street."

"A BB gun?"

"Yeah, he must have been waiting up for trouble. My mom told me some Mustangs had TPed his house last week."

White lived in College Park, a modest Costa Mesa neighborhood and some Costa Mesa High School football players lived on his street.

"Since we beat them," Bobby continued, "he probably thought they were going to seek revenge."

"Did he see you guys?"

"He had no idea it was us. Watts gave us some ski masks that completely covered our faces."

"Good thinking. Then what happened?"

"So after Steiner disappeared around the corner, White's sort of milling around the front yard and the neighbor came out in his pajamas and asks, 'Did you get them, Dale?' 'Yeah!' White shouts, like he's boasting how tough he is. 'I got one of the little punks real good. They won't be back.' Then he finally looks over at his doorstep and sees grandpa lying there. He must have come out of the house so fast he didn't notice him."

Bobby starts laughing so hard he can't talk.

"Dude, what happened next?"

"Okay, okay. So White walks over to the body real slow, like he's sneaking up on it and stands there for awhile looking down at it. Then he pokes it with his BB gun a couple of times. All the while, the neighbor is calling to him, 'What is it, Dale? What is it, Dale?' And he's just stands there trying to think."

Bobby starts laughing again, really hard.

"Then what happened?"

"Dude, it was priceless. I wish you would have been there to see it with me." Bobby just shakes his head as if relishing the memory.

"Come on, bro," I pleaded. "Don't make me wait."

"Okay, okay. Finally, White reaches down and turns the body over and sees the old man's face. He jumps about ten feet in the air, throws down his BB gun and starts running around the yard screaming, "what the fuck is this?" I mean he's panicked, literally pissing his pants, and he's running around like a chicken with its head cut off screaming, "What the fuck is this? What the fuck is this?" Then the neighbor runs into the yard and looks and starts screaming, "It's a dead guy, Dale. It's a dead guy."

We laughed hysterically at the idea of White getting his comeuppance. I hated White, too. He was sneaky and unfair and I hated what he stood for: an archetype asshole, the tough football coach who equated his power with his masculinity, and I hated him for what he had done to Bobby.

"That's when I split. The whole neighborhood was waking up. I took off my ski mask and just started walking. White and the neighbor were still screaming like lunatics when I reached the corner. When I got to Fairview and Wilson, two police cars sped by with their lights on. Someone must have called the cops."

"What about Steiner and Chandler?"

"Who knows. I didn't see them again."

"I hope they didn't get caught."

"Yeah, but they won't squeal. We talked about it on the way over to White's. Anybody gets caught, they acted alone."

Bobby and I drove the rest of the way home laughing. It was late when we climbed into bed. I stole one last look at Perry's empty trailer as Bobby burst out laughing again. Then he drifted off to sleep. Bobby had gotten his revenge and I was happy for him. But I remembered a Latin proverb, "Revenge is only a confession of your pain," and part of me felt bad that Bobby had needed to seek his revenge at all.

51

Saturday we chose to sleep in because it had been a late night. We finally started moving around eleven. Bobby had to get to films at noon. The team always ran films of the previous night's game. Awards, in the form of stars for your helmet, were given out for outstanding plays, which Bobby wouldn't be receiving.

I took my journal and walked to the picnic bench. It was a bright, sunny day and the canal was alive with birds. I watched the birds for a while until I felt ready to write about the previous night's escapade. The story took a couple of hours to get down on paper because I had to write in a code I use for things that are only meant for me. This story could be used as evidence. When I was finished, I walked back to the trailer laughing about the thought of someone reading about the body thirty years from now. It was going to make a great story someday, one that I would neither confirm nor deny.

My dad was sitting at the table reading the *Daily Pilot* when I walked in. I sat down at the table.

"Anything in the paper, Dad?"

"Just reading about the game. It's a shame that Bobby didn't play. Even the reporter is asking why. Oh, and Scott, that little girl from next door called."

"What?" I asked jumping up. "Did she leave a number?"

"No, she just said she would call later."

"Did she say where she was?"

"Nope. Just said to tell you she called."

I went to the window in my room and looked out. My story was still leaning against her door. Perry wasn't home. Then I thought I better check to make sure in case she was calling to tell me she didn't want to read my story. I walked over and knocked. There was no answer and I looked through the windows. As far as I could tell, she had not come home.

I walked back just as Bobby pulled up and parked. I waited for him to get out of the car.

"So?" I asked.

Bobby laughed. "Everything was normal. White acted as though nothing had happened. But I couldn't look him in the eye. I was afraid I would start laughing."

"And Steiner and Chandler didn't get caught?"

"Nope. They drove home to Steiner's without a problem."

"What do you think happened to the body?"

"No telling. It's a mystery."

Bobby looked at me with a huge smile and I couldn't help but crack up. Bobby laughed, too.

"Let's go surfing," Bobby said.

We threw on our wetsuits and headed to the beach. The River Jetties was head high peaks and glassy. Bobby tore it up: head dips, roundhouses, lip-crashers. Bobby's crazy act of rebellion seemed to liberate him from the pain White had caused him. I didn't know how our actions were going to play out, whether there would be an investigation by the police or some other consequence I couldn't foresee, but for the moment, Bobby's spirit had returned, and I was happy to have helped in the effort to screw with White. We surfed until the sun set over Catalina and walked home in the dark.

We decided to stay home Saturday night, much to Liza's disappointment. She called three times trying to convince Bobby to come out and meet her. There were some parties happening but Bobby wanted to watch Howard Hawks' *Rio Bravo* and I hoped that Perry would call back. My dad was out, probably over at Dirty John's place. Bobby and I sat on the couch eating pizza and watching the movie. When the movie was over, Bobby turned to me.

"Dean Martin's character sort of reminds me of your dad."

I hadn't really thought about it but Bobby was right. In the movie, Martin's character has a huge heart, is a loyal friend, and is competent when sober. Alcohol had gotten the best of him but he comes through in the end.

"It's a great movie," Bobby added.

I had to work the next day so I went to bed. Bobby wanted to stay up to watch Howard Hawks' *Eldorado* which was followed by Hawks' *Rio Lobo*.

52

The Sunday brunch crowd was heavy at the diner, with people waiting an hour for a table. Pineapple and I worked our tails off. It finally quieted down around two, enabling me to finish off the dishes, clean the floors and empty the trash. The diner always closed after brunch on Sunday, and by three, Pete was ready to lock up for the day. I called Bobby to bring our books. We had some work for our calculus class and I wanted to get it finished early so I would be home in case Perry called.

When Bobby arrived, he was famished from surfing all morning so Pineapple found him some leftovers from brunch and made him something to eat. Pinaply sat with us at the card table in the kitchen while Bobby ate. I was trying to help her with her homework, but she was distracted by Bobby.

"Pinaply," I pointed out. "Looking at Bobby won't get your work done."

Pinaply blushed and Bobby smiled.

"Pinaply, I wish I was back in fifth grade. You'd be the first girl I'd ask on a date."

"Really?" Pinaply squealed.

"Really," Bobby replied.

Then we heard Pineapple laughing. He had heard the exchange between Bobby and his daughter.

"Bobby Rowels," Pineapple said. "Are you trying to steal my daughter's heart?"

"No, sir," Bobby replied. "But if I was in fifth grade, you might be in trouble."

After Bobby finished eating, Pineapple and his daughter left us to our work. But something seemed to be weighing on Bobby's mind. Finally, I asked him about it.

"It's my mom," he said. "White never met my mom at the party. That's why he was home."

"He stood her up?"

"Yeah, he called her today and said that after the game he had checked his house and found he had a break-in."

"He lied to her?"

Bobby nodded. "Never mentioned anything about the body. White's a liar. He's using my mom."

"I'm glad you dumped the body on his doorstep." I was pissed. "And if he doesn't treat your mom right, we'll think of some other ways to screw with him."

"Thanks, bro."

The school week started with little fanfare. There was no mention of dead bodies and we held fast to Steiner's pledge. When we passed each other in the halls we smiled and nodded.

At practice everything seemed normal on the body front, too. But Bobby was still second team and he sat out most of the drills. Bobby took it in stride as White ignored him.

"Every time I get bummed," Bobby said. "I just picture White running around his front lawn screaming his head off and I smile."

But on Wednesday, things started to heat up. Principal Doyle found Bobby and me in the library at lunch.

"Scotty, could I have a word with you?"

Principal Doyle had spent his life at Newport Harbor, starting in the fifties as a student. He was a kind and honest man and I had a great deal of respect for him. A friendship of sorts had developed between us and I trusted him. We stepped outside the library.

"Scotty, where were you after the game Friday night?"

His question took me by surprise. "I was home," I stammered. I immediately thought of Hi Time Liquor Store and Jan Brusard. I prayed they hadn't spoken to her.

"And Bobby?'

"He was home, too. He lives with us now."

He nodded. "Yes, I know. Just thought I'd check." He stuck out his hand and I shook it. "Scotty, be careful," he said and walked away.

I watched Principal Doyle fade into the crowd, hating myself for having lied to him. I also sensed he was trying to warn me. When I returned to the library, Bobby looked at me expectantly.

"They're investigating," I said.

There wasn't any more news for a couple of days and Bobby and I followed our routine. We met at Cappy's for dinner and homework both Wednesday and Thursday. But Principal Doyle's warning was weighing heavily on my mind. On Thursday Bobby told me something that added to my concern.

"White won't even look at me or speak to me. After practice today I went up to him to ask if I could at least be on the kickoff team and he turned and walked away."

"I wonder if he's figured it out?"

"I don't know but it's like I don't exist."

The dead body escapade was even crowding out my concern about Perry, but I finally heard from her Thursday night. The phone was ringing when we got home from the diner.

"Hello," I answered.

"Hey, it's me."

"Where are you?"

"New Mexico."

There was a long pause. Finally I said, "Perry, I'm sorry."

"What's there to be sorry about? It's not like I'm your girlfriend." There was another long pause, then she said, "I'm just trying to figure out why I chose you to confide in."

"It wasn't what you thought."

"You mean the girl in the Ferrari?"

"Yeah, it was a mistake and a misunderstanding."

"No, Scotty, the mistake was mine for thinking that you were someone I could depend on. But you're just a kid. We'll talk when I get back. Say hi to Bobby."

Before I could say anything else, Perry hung up and I went to bed worrying. I was worried about Perry. I was worried about Bobby. I was worried that we were all going to jail. It was like an elephant sitting on my chest.

On Friday, my worries intensified. We arrived at school to find out that Tommy Watts had been fired from his job at the florist and asked to turn in his key. I knew the people conducting the investigation were close. At lunch, instead of going to the library, Steiner, Chandler, Watts, Bobby, and I met on the bleachers of Davidson Field.

"I hated that job," Watts boasted. "I'm glad they fired me. I don't care."

"Yeah, so we had a few beers and borrowed a body," Steiner laughed. "Nobody got hurt and if we just stick to our story that we were all at home, they won't be able to prove shit."

"The only thing I'm worried about," Chandler said, "is whether or not we're going to kick the Sea Kings' ass tonight."

"Yeah," Watts said. "I've been fired before. Who cares? We got a game tonight."

Steiner, Watts and Chandler began high-fiving each other but Bobby just sat there. They looked at him.

"Hey, I'm not even playing tonight."

Bobby was right. He sat on the bench while an overflow crowd looked on. But White did pay a price for it. The Corona Del Mar Sea Kings came ready to play and rose to the challenge the Sailors presented. It was a close game and late in the fourth quarter Newport was trailing Corona 14 to 10. That's when the student body of Newport Harbor erupted to test White's resolve. They began chanting, "Bobby, Bobby, Bobby." Soon the entire stands were chanting.

Newport drove the ball inside the Sea Kings' ten yard line with less than two minutes left on the clock, and the stands were screaming for White to put Bobby in the game. Even some of the players took up the chant. But White didn't even look at Bobby and that's where the game ended. The Sea Kings' defense exploded and hammered Newport's offense until Corona took over on downs with only seconds left. When time ran out, Corona had won and their entire school poured out of the stands and onto the field to celebrate. It was a big win for Corona and they were the Kings of Newport. Our stands exploded into boos. Some people may have thought we were booing the Sea Kings but I'm pretty sure the boos were for Coach Dale White.

I waited for Bobby after the game outside the locker room. I was standing with Liza and everywhere around us people were complaining that White had not put Bobby in the game. Since Bobby had not played, he didn't have to shower and was one of the first to walk out. People actually cheered when they saw him and yelled things like, "White's an idiot!" and "what a jerk!" and "if White had put you in we would have won!"

Bobby ignored the fans and found his mother straightaway, giving her a hug. They spoke for a few minutes and then Bobby drifted over to us. He gave Liza a hug and handed me the keys to the Chrysler.

"I'm going to walk home. I need to decide some things."

"Are you sure?" I asked.

"Yeah," he replied. "We lost to Corona. It doesn't get any worse than that."

"I could walk with you," Liza said.

He looked at Liza for a long moment. "Thanks, Liza. But this is something I've got to figure out alone."

Bobby reached out and hugged Liza tightly for a long moment. Then we watched him walk away down Irvine Avenue, his hopes for a perfect senior season crushed.

53

Bobby climbed on my bunk and woke me well before dawn the following Saturday morning. I sat up and peered at him through the darkness. He was smiling.

"Hey, birthday boy. Let's go surfing."

It was the morning of my eighteenth birthday, September 23rd, the start of autumn, the season Keats called a time of "mellow fruitfulness." I hadn't talked about my birthday but somehow Bobby remembered. I was now officially able to vote and kill for my country.

"Where?"

"Old Man's."

We put our boards onto the top of the Chrysler and headed to San Onofre. We cruised along Pacific Coast Highway, the route we always took south because the Chrysler sometimes died on the freeway. It was a major hassle and dangerous to pull over onto the shoulder with cars bearing down on you at seventy miles an hour.

I enjoyed the drive down PCH. The road wound its way through the sleepy little towns of Laguna, Dana Point, and San Clemente, towns that weren't yet awake and so empty it seemed as though Bobby and I were the only people in the world.

"Are you bummed about last night?" I asked.

"Nah, screw White. If he wants to lose, let him. But I sure hate it that we lost to Corona."

We rode on a little further.

"Perry hasn't been home in nearly two weeks," I said.

I had checked before we left. My story was still sitting on her doorstep.

"Maybe she moved in with some guy or hopped a private jet to Mazatlan. Pretty girls in Newport have lots of opportunities."

"She's in New Mexico."

"Mazatlan, New Mexico, what's the difference?"

"You know I really like her."

Bobby looked at me and nodded.

"I know you do. That's why I'm being so hard on her. I wouldn't care except I know how much you like her, and I don't want to see you get hurt."

We arrived at Old Man's in time to catch the sunrise. The sky exploded into a brilliant salmon red lighting the buttermilk clouds on fire. My first thought was of the sailor's warning about a red sky, but I decided it was a gift to me on my eighteenth birthday. The waves were also really good - five to six, peaks, and the crowd was thin. It was the kind of morning any surfer would cherish.

It's a long paddle to get to the lineup at San Onofre. Bobby and I wasted no time pounding our way through the whitewater. Once in the lineup, Bobby literally tore it up. He drove hard, slashing huge and ungodly turns, ripping and lacerating the faces of these forgiving and gently rolling waves. At many breaks like the Point or the Wedge, the wave itself is the challenge. But the challenge at Old Man's was not the waves but the rider's own ability. The waves allowed you to push your limits in whatever direction you chose.

At one point I paddled over to Bobby.

"Shit, bro, you're surfing like it's your birthday."

"Yeah, it feels good," he said. "After last night and being so pumped, I have to put it somewhere."

We surfed for almost three hours. Then I remembered it was Saturday and Bobby had films. I paddled over to Bobby.

"Don't you have a meeting?"

Bobby shrugged. "Yeah. But I think I'll blow it off. The waves are good and besides, it's your birthday."

"No way," I said. "Don't give White any more excuses."

"Maybe I should just quit."

"Screw that noise. One more wave, that's it."

We both caught our last wave and headed home in time for Bobby to go to his meeting. After Bobby left, I sat with my dad at the table while he drank his coffee.

"Do you know what today is, Dad?"

"No."

"I'm eighteen."

He looked at me for a long moment.

"Eighteen? I had no idea."

Then he looked down, and I thought he was going to cry.

"Scott, I'm sorry I haven't been a better father."

"That's okay, Dad. You've done the best you could, and I know you love me. Will you let me know if Mom calls?"

My father nodded. "Sure, kid."

I picked up my journal and walked to the canal.

54

I started writing and lost all track of time. It was a story about a girl whose family had forgotten her birthday. I wasn't sure why I decided the protagonist would be a girl, but changing gender sometimes makes me feel as if I could write more freely about my own feelings.

The story was a metaphor about birthdays being like signposts, reminding you to think about the journey that has led you to where you are and also serving as a guide to where you may be headed. Only four more years until you arrive to where you want to be. Or, maybe the question is, "who" you want to be.

As I was writing, head down, driving hard, with my trusted Rolling Writer pouring forth words, I felt something. I looked up to see Perry staring at me. She had her hands on her hips as her eyes focused hard on me. Her mouth was serious, almost defiant.

"Is it true?" she demanded.

"Is what true?"

I put my pen down and shook out the cramps in my fingers as some gulls squabbled over garbage on the canal bank.

"About the girl in the Ferrari?"

"Absolutely, and I am so sorry."

Perry looked away.

"No, Perry. I was so stupid. But everything happened so fast. I was just thinking of Liza and how I didn't want her last day of summer to be ruined. I had made her a promise. I'm really sorry that you were hurt in the process."

Perry looked at me hard again

"I was ready to give up on you."

"Please don't."

She was silent for a long moment, her blue eyes looking into mine. It was as if she was studying me, trying to reach out with intuition or something to feel more than what my words were revealing. Finally, she sat down on the bench across from me and looked at me again for a long moment. I waited for her to speak.

"I really liked your story," she finally said.

It was the story of a Hawaiian maiden who saves her village from a warring tribe by seducing the god Lono with just one kiss. One kiss was all it took and Lono was a goner, and the maiden's village was saved and protected. It was obviously inspired by our first kiss.

"Thanks. It's been sitting on your doorstep for almost two weeks. Were you really in New Mexico?"

"Only passing through. I went to see my grandmother's grave. I needed to be near her."

"You drove all the way to Louisiana?"

"Yes."

"By yourself?"

"Yes. Everything is just getting so complicated."

"Why?"

"Well, for starters, there's all this stuff with my dad. Lawyers and private detectives. It's just so nuts. I needed some time to clear my head."

"I wish there was something I could do to help."

"That's funny. Because you're as big a problem as the other things."

"Me?"

"I really like you, Scotty. But I'm twenty-one and you're seventeen. You're not even legal. My dad went berserk when I mentioned you. He even called his lawyer."

I smiled.

"I'm legal."

"What?"

"I'm legal. Today's my birthday. I'm eighteen."

"Today's your birthday?"

"Yeah."

Perry suddenly seemed relieved. For the first time today, she broke into her perfect, imperfect smile.

"Scotty, what are you going to do? You need to celebrate."

"Can I wish for anything?"

"Sure, why not. It's your eighteenth birthday."

"Okay, then I'd like to hang out with you today."

Perry smiled.

"Okay, hot-shot eighteen-year-old. Get your board. You can teach me to surf."

"Deal."

"And bring your journal. I want to watch you write."

"You mean you want to watch me suffer?"

"I make you suffer?"

"All writers suffer, and it usually has to do with a girl. But don't worry too much about it. It's good for a writer to suffer. It deepens the perspective."

Perry laughed.

"That's good. That's really good."

I smiled.

"I'll get my board."

Perry acted like a little kid getting a puppy. She jumped up from the table and did a little dance.

"I'm going to learn to surf," she giggled. "I'll pack a lunch, meet me at my trailer."

She ran off in the direction of her trailer, and I gathered up my journal and pens. I felt like a little kid, too, getting my wish on my birthday.

55

Don't let anyone tell you otherwise. The best month in Newport is September. The weather's great, the beaches are relatively empty, and the waves are generally good. September in Newport is like a George Benson song - easy, smooth, and cool

Perry and I spent the afternoon on the beach, and I valued every moment. I've had a few dates, to the movies, dances, or double dating with Bobby. The experience always felt awkward and a little forced. Maybe I relaxed because Perry was older and more confident so the conversation and closeness seemed easy and natural.

I had an extra wetsuit. It was a little big on Perry but it kept her warm and we splashed in the white water for a couple of hours. She listened to my every word about surfing, reminding me of the day I first taught Bobby, and Perry was standing up almost from her first attempt. Like Bobby, she was a natural athlete.

After the surf session, it was fun watching Perry squirm out of the wetsuit, revealing a black bikini. As we sat on a blanket eating cheese, bread, and a seafood salad, Perry asked me to write in my journal.

"Why?'

"I want to watch you. I want to see how you just invent a story that makes me feel something so deeply."

I smiled and started to write. I felt a little self-conscious, but after a paragraph, I forgot Perry was watching. The story was about a girl who is scared to love because she is juggling the whole world in her hands and fears that if she lets someone into her world everything will collapse around her. The story ends when she faces her fear, accepts it, and realizes that her power to hold the world is strong enough to trust in love.

When I finished, Perry snatched the journal from my hands. I watched as she read. A smile slowly spread across her face telling me that she understood my intention. In the story I told her that I loved her.

"How do you do it?" Perry asked.

"What do you mean?"

"Your words. They make me feel things I've never felt before."

"Probably because I've never felt it before either."

Perry's eyes held mine for a long moment.

"Can I keep this?"

I had brought an empty journal so if I wrote, the composition book would only have the memories of this day.

"Sure."

"Can I cook you dinner tonight?"

"No, I promised Bobby I would go out with him."

Perry looked disappointed.

"Do you always keep your promises?"

"Hey," I said. "It's a guy thing. When you turn eighteen, you're supposed to go out with your bros and get good and drunk."

"And chase girls in Ferraris?"

I smiled.

"I am really sorry about that, Perry. There won't be any Ferraris, I promise. Just Bobby in the Chrysler. And I do keep my promises."

Smiling mischievously, Perry reached over and squeezed my knee.

"Good," she said. "Try to get home early and don't get too drunk."

56

Bobby had tried to keep it secret, but Liza spilled the beans when she called looking for Bobby.

"See you at the boathouse," she said.

Bobby had organized a surprise party for me at Steiner's boathouse. Of course, there had been other hints along the way, but Liza confirmed it. I was deeply touched that Bobby would go to the effort and I never let on that I knew.

As we tooled along Irvine Avenue past the high school and Davidson Field, I told Bobby about my perfect day with Perry. Bobby could easily see that I was officially smitten, head over heels, deliriously and hopelessly in love with the girl next door.

"Does she know you're a virgin?" Bobby asked.

"Yeah. But what does that matter?"

"Because she's had experiences. She'll probably sleep with you once and drop your sorry ass."

"It's not like that, and I really think she likes me too."

"Bro, she's a player. She's not the sweet little girl next door. She's probably the whore next door."

"Will you lay off."

"Lay off? Come on, how many different guys have we seen her with? And she disappears for weeks and expects you to come running?"

"There's more to it than that."

"What?"

"Stuff."

"What stuff? Like in *Stagecoach*? She's a hooker with a heart of gold?"

"I can't tell you right now. Just lay off."

Bobby looked at me hard. I thought I saw something in his eyes as they flared at me. Anger, mistrust, hurt, I wasn't quite sure. Maybe it was all of those.

"Hey, what was our deal?" Bobby exploded. "Total honesty. Like Lee Marvin said. And no bitch, no whore, no fucking anything comes between that."

"Man, you're getting really fired up about this."

"Goddamn right I am. No whore comes between us."

This was hard for me. My best friend was calling the girl I was in love with the worst things you can call a girl and I couldn't do anything about it. I had made a promise to Perry.

"I know our deal, and I intend to tell you why Perry's not what you think she is. I just can't tell you now."

"Why?'

"Because... it might be dangerous."

Bobby looked at me and laughed. I could tell he was really pissed.

"The only one in danger here is you, dickhead."

We rode the rest of the way in silence.

57

The street outside Steiner's house appeared empty as we entered the side gate in silence. The tension between Bobby and me was so thick it felt as if the walk down Steiner's tropical path was encased in fog. When we reached the boathouse and walked through the door, about twenty people yelled "Surprise!" Of course I acted duly surprised and turned to Bobby and shook his hand.

"Thanks, bro."

Bobby nodded and walked straight to where Steiner and Watts stood with the beer bong. They raised the funnel and a full can of Old English 800 flowed straight into Bobby's stomach. It didn't pass go, it didn't collect two hundred dollars, and I was certain he would be burping for a week. Then he asked to hit it again.

"What's got into you?" Steiner asked with a laugh. "You're acting like it's your birthday."

"Nah, it's my boy's eighteenth birthday. I'm just greasing the wheels."

I hit the beer bong with everyone cheering and yelling, "Happy birthday!" But when Bobby hit the beer bong a third time, I decided I better not drink anymore.

Liza the Hurricane arrived with the posse, and Liza found me straight away.

"Scotty," she said. "I'm so sorry I wasn't here for the surprise but Monica screwed everything up. It was like she didn't want to come and then she decided at the last second to drive herself. The Ferrari, of course, the big showoff. But maybe she'll let you drive it again and give you a present for your birthday."

"It's all right, Liza. Once was enough. I'm just glad you came."

Bobby, with Liza's help, hit the beer bong a fourth time. He was officially shit-faced. Liza and the posse quickly followed suit, slugging down their favorite drink - Sloe Gin. Soon, Monica was three sheets to the wind and hanging all over Rickie Chandler and Bobby and Liza were making out on the pool table. It was obvious they didn't care who watched.

More people arrived. The beer bong was in steady use and people were dancing to the sound of Elton John's "Benny and the Jets." From somewhere on the deck, the pungent smell of a joint floated into the boathouse.

The next thing we knew, Steiner started shedding his clothes. He was soon naked and walking around the party. There were a couple of sophomore girls who had never been to the boathouse before. Steiner walked up to them and talked as if nothing was amiss. There was no doubt about it, my eighteenth birthday party had become a debauched night of revelry.

Then the lights went out. Girls screamed, guys laughed, and a birthday cake, complete with lit candles, appeared. A naked Steiner delivered the cake to me while the party sang, "Happy Birthday."

When you're in a room with thirty drunk and stoned people singing to you and you are reasonably sober, the only word to describe it is surreal. I closed my eyes, thought of Perry, and blew out my candles.

Bobby had stayed away from me the whole night. But after I blew out my candles, he walked up to me and gave me a hug.

"We need to talk later," he slurred. "But right now I'm going to leave for a while with Liza."

I looked at Liza. She was clearly drunk too, though not as drunk as Bobby, who needed her help to keep from falling down.

"Here's the keys," he tossed them to me. "I love you, bro."

"All right. See you at home."

Bobby and Liza stumbled away and out the door, leaving me alone.

I looked around the room. The naked Steiner was dancing with two girls as Alice Cooper's "I'm Eighteen" raged through the speakers in my honor. Over in the corner, Rickie Chandler pressed Monica up against the wall and his hand was reaching under her skirt. There were other couples, too, on the couch and in the corners, groping and slobbering on each other. But it wasn't until Tommy Watts walked up that I knew it was time to leave.

"Shit, Scotty," Watts mumbled. "I've been waiting all night to pin your ass. It'll be my birthday present."

The loutish lineman was clearly suffering from his relationship with the beer bong. I knew I had to think quickly. Otherwise my birthday would end with me lying on the floor in a half nelson.

"Ah, great Tommy. Let's do it. But first I gotta take a leak."

"A what?"

"A leak. You know, water the lawn, bleed a lizard."

"Do it later. I want to wrestle now."

"Come on, you don't want me peeing on you, do you?"

The drunk wrestler paused. His alcohol consumption had reduced his already feeble mind to a soggy bog. It was actually funny watching him trying to puzzle out a response.

"Nah," he finally said. "You're right. I don't want to get wet when I knock the piss out of you."

I nodded.

"Wait here. I'll be right back."

But instead of heading for the bathroom, I went out the back door, up the rain forest path that reminded me of Kauai, and headed for home. My eighteenth birthday party had come to a fizzling close.

58

The lights to Perry's trailer were off when I passed by in the Chrysler. I assumed she was out on the town. I hoped she was having some fun but it did make me sad and a little jealous. Part of this was due to the fact that my birthday night had pretty much been a bust. I had argued with Bobby and barely escaped the clutches of Tommy Watts. The whole event had been kind of a fiasco. Instead of celebrating, I had felt bad about Bobby the whole night. I knew I had hurt him by not being completely forthcoming. But I had made a promise to Perry and the less Bobby knew about Perry right now, the better.

When I walked into the trailer I was surprised to find that my dad was still awake. He was watching *The Archie Bunker Show* and sipping a Budweiser.

"Hey, Dad."

"Hey, kid. How was your big night out?"

"Lugubrious. Did Mom ever call?"

"Nope. Why don't you call her?"

For a moment I was stunned by the suggestion. It was my birthday and I thought my mother, of all people in my life, should remember this day. Then I decided, "what the hell?"

I picked up the phone and dialed. There were a few rings before the machine came on. It was my sister's voice announcing they were out of town. In that moment I realized just how much I missed my sister, how much I missed my mother and how much I hated the Dick.

"Hi, Mom. It's me. I just wanted to say thank you for having me."

I stood there for a moment after I hung up. I felt a sharp sting in my stomach that rose into my chest. I closed my eyes for a long moment before the feeling went away. I walked to the worn-out red and brown plaid couch and sat next to my dad.

"Where's Bobby?" he asked.

"Out with his girlfriend. We sort of had a fight."

"You want a beer, Mr. Eighteen-year-old? The first beer in honor of your birthday?"

I looked at the beers sitting at his feet. There was an entire case with about five already gone. I shrugged.

"Sure, why not?"

He reached down, tore a beer from the case and handed it to me. I opened it and took a huge slug.

"Easy there, tiger."

"Heck, Dad. Maybe I'll have ten of these."

"No, you won't. You'll have one. This is my life, not yours"

I took another sip. My old man looked at me and smiled.

"I hate to tell you, Dad. But this isn't my first beer."

"I know. But humor me anyway."

We sat for a few minutes more, sipping our beers.

"By the way," he said. "That pretty little girl from next door stopped by with a card."

"Where is it?"

"I think she put it on your bed."

I jumped up, ran to my room, and turned on the light. Sure enough there was a card sitting on my pillow. I tore open the envelope. The card was handmade. There was a surfboard on the front with words that read:

May the waves be really good
And the ocean, a clear blue
May the wind be offshore
And all your birthday wishes come true.

I opened the card. In beautiful handwriting Perry had simply written, "Look out your window."

I looked toward my window but realized I couldn't see anything because the reflection of the light in my room prevented me from seeing out. I quickly flicked off the light and peered through the darkness.

The windows of Perry's trailer glowed a soft warm light. I looked closer at one window where a stronger light flickered. I looked closer still, and saw that a person was holding a candle. Then I really focused, and though I couldn't actually see anything, it looked as if the person was naked.

I paused, wondering what it all meant. Was it a test? Was it a suggestion? Was it an invitation? For a moment I didn't know what to think.

Then by some force, I was overwhelmed. Call it nature, call it passion, call it whatever you want, but I tore out of the trailer so fast I'm surprised the hinges stayed on the door. I'm sure my dad was wondering what was going on.

Perry opened the door before I could knock. She was, in fact, naked. She looked at me, smiling her perfect, imperfect smile.

"What took you so long? I must have been standing there for an hour."

She threw her arms around me and kissed me. It was a deep, powerful kiss that could have lasted forever.

59

"Liza," Bobby said. "I have something I need to talk to you about."

Bobby and Liza were in the backseat of her father's Mercedes. Liza's blouse was unbuttoned revealing a low-cut red bra, her breasts spilling out of its top.

"Bobby Rowels, you're not going break up with me, are you? Because if you are I'm going to screw every one of your friends. Including Scotty."

"And Watt's too."

"Maybe. If I'm drunk enough."

Bobby laughed at this and held Liza tight. She was lying on top of him.

"No, I'm not going to break up with you. I'm actually thinking that we should be really together. Not this hook-up when we see each other."

"You mean, like boyfriend and girlfriend."

"Yeah, I'm asking you to be my girl."

"Oh, Bobby, I love you so much."

She kissed him deeply and drove her hand down his pants, but the moment was rudely interrupted by a loud tapping on the window. Bobby and Liza sat up and peered out the window. A drunken Tommy Watts stared back at them through the glass. Bobby opened the door and stepped out as Liza buttoned her blouse.

"What's up, Watts?"

"Where's Scotty?" the wrestler slurred.

"I don't know," Bobby replied. "Isn't he at the party."

"No. He snuck out like the fucking surfer pussy he is. I'm going to find him and rip his ears off. Then I'm going to stuff my fist down his throat. Nobody sneaks out on Tommy Watts."

"You're not going to touch him," Bobby said with annoyance.

Bobby reached out to grab Watts but the wrestler knocked his arms away and threw Bobby to the ground, hard. Before Bobby could get to his feet, Tommy Watts had run toward a car. Not just any car. It was Monica's dad's Ferrari.

Bobby turned to Liza.

"Come on. We have to follow him. He might hurt Scotty."

"Okay."

Liza jumped over the seat and was behind the steering wheel in seconds. Bobby slid into the passenger seat. Liza started the car as the Ferrari pulled away.

"Where do you think Scotty is?" Liza asked.

"Probably, he went home. I was such a jerk tonight."

Liza pulled out quickly and was about a block behind the Ferrari. Watts turned right at the corner to head down Irvine Avenue.

"Hurry," Bobby said. "There's no telling what this jackass will do."

Bobby and Liza turned right at the corner onto Irvine and saw the Ferrari about a block up. Watts had intended to race away but he had missed second gear and the car stalled. Bobby jumped out of the Mercedes and ran toward the Ferrari. But just as he got there, Watts pulled away. Bobby ran back to the Mercedes.

The Mercedes tore down Irvine Boulevard through the S curves in hot pursuit of the Ferrari. But Tommy Watts threw them a curveball. Instead of continuing down Irvine, he tuned left onto Santiago, running a red light, and headed into the community of Dover Shores.

The two cars raced through the streets of Dover Shores, taking corners at forty miles an hour. Tommy Watts drove the Ferrari onto front lawns and through a couple of mailbox stands erected on the sidewalk. He even knocked down a stop sign. Then, suddenly, Watts slammed on the brakes. The tires screeched and smoke evaporated into the air like a giant mushroom cloud. He pulled into a driveway honking the horn.

"Shit," Bobby said. "It's Peekaboo Sue's house."

With tires screeching again, Tommy backed out of the driveway and into the street. He hit the horn again and the windows of the Ferarri came down.

"How do you like me now, Peek-a-boo." Tommy's screams could be heard up and down the block.

"Fucking idiot," Bobby said. "His life is over. His mom is going to fry his ass. I gotta put a stop to this now."

Bobby leaped from the Mercedes and ran toward Tommy. The window was still down and Tommy was yelling all kinds of profanity toward Peek-a-boo Sue's house. Bobby arrived just as Tommy began to gun the motor.

"Come on, Watts, let's shut this down," Bobby yelled.

"No fuckin' way," Tommy screamed back, spit flying from his mouth. "Scotty's a pussy. I'm the powerful one. You get that Rowels? I'm the powerful one. Nobody runs out on Tommy Watts. I'm a fucking legend."

Tommy gunned the engine again and popped the clutch. The Ferrari took off. Bobby dove out of the way as the Ferrari bounced over the curb and onto the lawn where Tommy began spinning donuts. Bobby lay there until he saw Peek-a-boo Sue standing at her living room window watching her sod fly twenty feet into the air.

Bobby jumped to his feet and ran toward Watts, waving his arms for him to stop. But he was not in time. Tommy Watts suddenly lost control of the powerful car. It raced directly toward the front picture window of the living room, and the crash caused the earth to shake beneath Bobby's feet.

60

The morning light streamed in the window from a crystal-clear blue sky reflecting my optimism. Perry lay next to me still asleep. I looked at her for the longest time, the memory of the night just spent fresh in my mind. Perry had pulled the mattress from her bedroom into the living room and lit the room with about a dozen candles. It was more than romantic, it was as if the universe had burst forth and showered me with blessings by giving me an angel who had shared her most generous gift, herself.

I could watch her forever, her face, her hands, her breasts. For years I had imagined what the first time would be like. But every time an opportunity presented itself, I made an excuse because it never felt right. Still, nothing in my imagination could have prepared me for last night. The moment had been more than right. It had been perfect. Perry was the most beautiful girl I had ever known. Her lips, her smile, her spirit enchanted me, maybe even bewitched me. Bobby's words proved true. I'd fallen head-over-heels for the first girl I slept with. I was grateful it was Perry and deep and powerful emotions arose inside me. I felt anything was possible.

I suddenly realized it was Sunday morning and I had a job to get to. As much as I would have preferred to sit and watch Perry while she slept, I knew there were people who depended on me. I nudged Perry gently and she stirred from her dreams, opening her eyes. Then she broke into her smile.

"Hey," she whispered.

"Hey, yourself."

"What time is it?"

"I'm not sure. But I've got to get ready for work."

She reached out and pulled me close, kissing me gently on the lips.

I stood and began searching for my clothes. Perry watched as I dressed, and the smile never left her face.

"Do I need to tell you how great last night was?" I said.

Perry had been patient with me in my awkward and embarrassing attempts to figure it all out, just as I had been patient during her first surfing lesson.

"Yes," she replied. "A woman always wants to be told how great it was. Did the earth move?"

I smiled.

"Something moved."

Perry laughed at this. Then she stood, naked, and walked over to give me another kiss, her confidence overwhelming me again.

"Thank you for making my birthday really special. I'll never forget last night."

"Come over when you get home."

I took one last look at Perry's smiling face and felt like I was the luckiest guy on earth.

As I walked to my trailer, I wanted to shout my joy to the world. My life had changed. There are milestones in life: the day your parents tell you that they are separating, the day you get an acceptance letter from a college you want to attend or the first day of high school. Losing your virginity has to stack right up there. I know some people run into the act without much thought as if they just want to get it over with. I was glad I had waited. Sharing the experience with someone I loved made it feel sacred.

My dad wasn't home. I was surprised because he usually slept until nine or ten. Then I walked to the bedroom and found that Bobby wasn't home, either. For a moment I wondered what was going on. Part of me was disappointed but another part was relieved from not being

confronted with having to tell Bobby I had finally been laid. I decided
he must have spent the night at Liza's and I quickly dressed for work.

I thought about Bobby as I rode my bike down Pacific Coast
Highway. We had quarreled over Perry and I was worried he would
ridicule my feelings about last night, driving another wedge between
us. I didn't want that and thought about keeping my experience private. But Bobby had taken a keen interest in my sex life, and keeping a
secret like this could damage our friendship. It was a question of trust,
a trust we shared and a trust I valued. I was torn.

The usual pile of dishes awaited me at work. Cappy's stayed open
on Saturday nights until two. We knew Pete wanted to catch the people
who were leaving bars like Malarkey's Irish Pub, the Goat Hill Tavern,
and the Villa Nova who wanted a late night snack. But he didn't want
to pay a full staff because this business was often unpredictable. Also,
his best cook, Pineapple, always took the night off, so the food wasn't
as good. Pete used one waitress and a cook and let the dishes pile up.

As I worked through the pile I could feel Pineapple watching me.
It was as if he was inspecting me. I continued washing dishes, slowly
working my way through the massive pile. The work seemed easy with
the memories of last night filling my heart and mind. All the while,
Pineapple was watching me. Finally he said, "Scotty, I don't know what
it is, but you seem different."

"Different? How?"

"I don't know. Older or somethin'."

"Well, I did turn eighteen yesterday."

Pineapple, with a lifetime of street smarts, sensed something in my
demeanor.

"Nah, it's more than a birthday. It's like you've suddenly grown up
right before my eyes."

I smiled. Pineapple was right. In a way, I was older. I had finally
lost my sexual innocence. I would no longer have to wonder what it's
like to share my body with another person and Bobby's incessant teas-

ing would end. I'd given up something in the process but I had also gained something. I had grown.

At two, we slowed down enough from the Sunday brunch rush that I was able to empty the trash and mop the floor.

"I'll finish the rest," Pineapple said. "There shouldn't be too many."

I pedaled home to find my dad asleep on the couch. That was curious because my dad's best hours were between ten and three during the day. He was usually up and feeling productive by now. Then I went in the bedroom to find Bobby asleep in his bunk. I nudged him and he woke.

"Jesus," he mumbled. "I am hung over. I've been twitching and slobbering for an hour. Why'd you let me drink so much?"

"Me?" I laughed. "There was no stopping you. You were a wild man."

Bobby shook his head as if he could shake away a heavy fog.

"Yeah," he said. "I acted like an asshole. I'm sorry."

"No worries."

"You know the shit really hit the fan last night."

"What happened?"

"Liza and I were groveling in the car when we heard knocking on the window."

"The police?"

"No, they came later. It was Watts. He was looking for you."

I laughed. "The asshole wanted to wrestle me so I sorta snuck out on him."

"Yeah, Watts said something about that and it really pissed him off. Anyway, he had the keys to Monica's Ferrari."

"How did he get those?"

"Evidently, after you left, Watts had gone to Chandler in a rage about you skipping out on him. Monica had given Chandler the keys to the Ferrari and Chandler gave Watts the keys to go find you."

"What is it with that guy?"

"Who knows? But he was screaming he's going to kick your ass and I stepped out of the car. He runs for it and takes off in the Ferrari before I could stop him. I ran back to Liza's car and told her we had to follow him. I thought he was headed here."

"As far as I know, he never came here."

"No, he didn't. He drove straight to Peek-a-boo Sue's house."

"What! Why'd he go there?"

"I have no idea. The guy's messed up. So he gets to the house and starts racing the Ferrari up and down the street in front of the old lady's house. Forward then backward, grinding the gears and slamming on the brakes. Then he drove the car onto the lawn, spinning donuts."

"Monica's dad's going to kill him."

"Dude, you have no idea."

Bobby rubbed his face hard as if to erase the memory. Finally, he looked at me and just shook his head.

"What?"

"Watts lost control and plowed the car through the front window of the house."

"No. Peek-a-boo Sue's?"

Bobby looked at me gravely and nodded his head.

"Was anyone killed?" I asked.

Bobby shook his head no.

"That was the weirdest part. I thought for sure someone was dead. Smoke billowing and the house and car all smashed. Horn blaring. I mean, the sound alone was enough to make you start praying. But the old woman had been quick. She somehow got out of the way. All she did was pee her pants."

"What about Tommy?"

"Dude, not a scratch. After I had checked on the old woman. I ran to Tommy. He was sitting in the Ferrari just mumbling crazy shit. 'Scotty's a pussy. I'm the powerful one. I'm a legend.' Like a broken record."

I was stunned. What did it mean? Why was he so obsessed with me that he would crash a Ferrari into an old woman's house?

"Man, poor Tommy," I said.

"Screw, Tommy. The old woman didn't deserve this. But she turned out to be really cool. She just kept saying, 'Is Tommy hurt? Is Tommy hurt?' She wasn't even mad."

Then Bobby went on to tell me the aftermath. The police had arrived and arrested both Bobby and Tommy Watts. Bobby had spent the night in jail. But before they had taken him away, Bobby had sent Liza to pick up my dad and bring him to the police station. Because my dad knew people, the police quickly determined the facts of the case and decided not to press charges against Bobby. When they released him to my dad, the police even patted Bobby on the back and promised to keep his name out of the papers.

Tommy Watts, on the other hand, had ruined his life. He was charged with grand theft of the Ferrari, reckless driving, drunken driving and attempted murder.

"Your dad really came through for me," Bobby said.

"Yeah. My dad's life is a mess. But he always comes through when the chips are down."

Bobby and I were quiet for a moment.

"And where were you last night?" Bobby suddenly asked.

I looked at Bobby for a long moment. Then I decided to tell him everything. His friendship was that important to me. I told him about the card, the candles, and the mattress. I even told him about how good it felt to be in Perry's arms.

"That's cool she did that for you," Bobby said.

"But I think you were right about one thing," I responded.

"What's that?"

"I think I love her."

Bobby smiled at me. Then he jumped off his bunk and threw his arms around me.

"I'm sorry for last night, bro," he said. "I'm going to trust that you know what you're doing and there's a reason. But if she hurts you, if she starts screwing with your head, then she's going to have to deal with me. Until that happens, I'll support you."

"Thanks, bro."

After our talk, I went over to Perry's. We spent the afternoon and evening mostly talking about Bobby, and why Tommy Watts would smash a Ferrari into Peek-a-boo Sue's house. Perry thought it had to do with girls.

61

On Monday morning, we arrived at school to find a crisis had enveloped Harbor High. Tommy Watts' fiasco started an uprising among various parents and Steiner's boathouse became the focus of their wrath. As a result, there was an investigation into my party.

Since it had been my birthday party, I had to meet with the principal. Principal Doyle obviously hated this part of his job and clearly felt uncomfortable asking me the required questions. I told him I didn't drink anything and went home early to help my dad.

"If something went on after I left, I wouldn't know."

"How about drugs?"

"No, not that I know of."

For my part, I hated lying to this man whom I considered my friend as well as my principal. But the less I said the better, especially for Bobby. If White found out the truth, he could kick Bobby off the team.

The boathouse was another story. Once Steiner's parents were contacted, our little secret spot was officially closed. When we heard the news, Bobby and I looked at each other and shrugged.

"I guess Steiner will have to find some other place to get naked," Bobby said.

By Thursday, the whole thing had blown over and Tommy Watts was gone from our lives. Life simply moved on. The big event at lunch was the pep rally for the football game against Loara High School, our first Sunset League game. Bobby starred in the rally by getting up and leading a cheer with the girls. He acted with class and excitement, bringing the whole crowd to their feet. Everyone knew Bobby was the best player on the team, but according to White, he was still second team at four positions.

On Friday night Perry met me at the game. I told her where I would be sitting, with Pineapple, his daughter, and my dad. She found me straight away in the overflow crowd.

Bobby did not play in the first half, and the score sorely reflected it. It was 17-0 in favor of the Loara Saxons. Tommy Watts was missed. He wasn't a great player, but he was solid and the defensive line simply fell apart without him. The Saxons ran the ball like it was an outing in the park.

When Loara received the kickoff to open the second half, they began driving again. After Loara crossed the fifty yard line into Newport Sailor territory, White threw in the towel.

"Rowels!" he yelled.

Bobby sprinted to stand in front of him.

"Yes, sir!" Bobby yelled.

White looked at him for a long moment.

"Monster, now!"

Bobby sprinted onto the field, and the Newport crowd erupted into an enormous cheer. In one play the ball was back in Newport's hands thanks to Bobby's jarring tackle that knocked the ball loose from the running back's hands. Then White got smart.

"Rowels!" he yelled.

"Yes, sir!"

"Tailback!"

In two plays Newport found the end zone. Bobby had carried the ball twice. It was at this moment that Perry turned to me.

"Bobby's a really good player."

I looked at her. "No, he's more than good. He might be the best."

The rest of the night was all Bobby. He ran for two touchdowns and threw for a third, a tailback pass to Chandler. At the end of the night, the Loara Saxons walked off the field wondering what happened. The Newport Harbor Sailors had won by a score of 28 to 17.

After the game, Liza, Perry and I waited outside the locker room for Bobby. A crowd gathered and cheered when Bobby walked out. But the first person he found was his mother. He hugged her, they talked and he hugged her again. Then Bobby found us and we headed for Me and Ed's, a Costa Mesa pizza joint.

We celebrated over a pitcher of root beer and a large sausage and mushroom pizza. Bobby filled our glasses and immediately raised his glass for a toast.

"Here's to victory," Bobby beamed. We clinked our glasses and he added, "Damn, it feels good to win."

Bobby was clearly happy. It was like he finally fulfilled himself. I envied his experience while at the same time I felt proud.

"Well, one down, six to go," Bobby said. "Now it gets tough."

"Not if you play like you did tonight," Liza replied.

"No, it's different now. It's the Sunset League. Every game will be a dogfight."

"Why's that?" Perry asked.

"The players are bigger and faster," Bobby said. "And there's a lot more of them. Now that we beat Loara they'll all be gunning for us."

"Happy you didn't quit?" I asked.

Bobby looked at me and smiled.

"Why are you always right? I really hate that about you. You're such a dickhead."

I reached across the table and extended my hand. Bobby shook it like a brother, thumb wrapped around thumb.

"I'm not always right. But it's pretty clear that tonight made all the White bullshit worth it."

62

After the win against Loara, life improved dramatically for both Bobby and me. We fell into our routine and found it was solid. For me, work, study and sometimes evenings spent with Perry after being at the diner while Bobby concentrated on football and school. Bobby stopped wanting to party, and spent a lot of time with Liza.

Of course, Bobby and I still found time to surf. We chose Saturday mornings for our ritual that fall. Starting out before dawn and ending in time for Bobby to get to his game film meeting, we'd load up the Chrysler and hit distant spots like Salt Creek, Trestles, and the Redondo Breakwater. Once we got really ambitious and ran the Chrysler on the freeway through Camp Pendleton all the way to Oceanside. We didn't always find the best waves but the trip itself was worth it.

It was our way of connecting with each other. We would talk over everything and our friendship grew even deeper.

On the football field, Bobby excelled. Newport continued to win. Marina, Edison, and Huntington Beach all bowed to the Sailor warriors. The games were close but because Newport had the stronger defense they always prevailed. Letters began to pour in from various colleges. USC, UCLA, Notre Dame, Alabama, Ohio State, the list was long, and Bobby found it distracting to answer them all. He asked my dad to take over the letters and reply as needed. You would have thought my dad had been given a Christmas present. It was like he suddenly had a purpose.

"Bobby, why'd you ask my dad to help?"

Bobby thought about it.

"Because I don't have time and I wanted someone I could trust. Your dad's a really smart guy."

Bobby gave my dad a new lease on life. Every day, Bobby brought home a stack of letters from all around the country, and dad organized and answered them. Then he started doing research on the schools, and would talk with Bobby about his various choices. He also did research for my college choices. Almost overnight, Big Ed Curtis became something of an expert on the merits of various colleges around the country. He read books, made phone calls and talked to guidance counselors at the junior college. He knew the requirements and SAT standards both for Bobby and me. I was totally amazed by the change that came over my father and appreciated that Bobby had asked my dad for his help. Sometimes asking someone to help is the greatest gift we can give them.

Toward the end of October, a problem arose for Bobby in our calculus class and I could see that it was because the teacher, Mr. Andy Manly, clearly disliked Bobby.

"Why do you think he has it in for you?" I asked.

"He's friends with White," Bobby replied. "He comes out to practice and I see them talking."

Bobby's problems with White were still simmering. But his play had been outstanding, and even White couldn't argue with that. Still, White rode his back like a monkey, and the harder Bobby tried, the harder White rode him.

"When I intercepted the pass that iced the game, all White did was scream that I was out of position and could have cost us the game. He didn't even give me a star for my helmet."

I counseled Bobby not to give White any excuse to bench him and Bobby heeded my advice. He never complained and never talked back, and Bobby's play painted White into a corner. It's hard to bench a player who's leading the league in tackles and interceptions.

But in calculus, Bobby continued to struggle. When his grade fell below a C, I began going over his tests. It was obvious that the teacher had graded Bobby's work unfairly. Math is not subjective like English or history. There's truth in it, and lies are easily found out. Bobby didn't deserve an A, but he definitely didn't deserve a D.

Then Manly gave a pop quiz on material Bobby had missed because of football. They had a Thursday night away game and Bobby had to miss class. He did so poorly that he failed the test. The next day Mr. Manly was all smiles.

"Rowels, you are officially getting an F in the class now. I think that means you're going to be ineligible."

Bobby started to say something, but I put my hand on his shoulder and shook my head.

"Let me talk to him," I whispered.

Bobby nodded.

After class, I lagged behind. When the classroom was empty, I approached Mr. Manly's desk. He peered at me from behind his wire-rim glasses.

"I know what you're doing," I said.

"What?" Mr. Manly looked at me sternly as if he thought he could intimidate me.

"I've gone over Bobby's tests. You graded him wrong when he actually had the right answer on several questions."

"You can't prove that."

"I can prove it."

"No you can't."

"Teaching is a privilege, Mr. Manly. It means you have to give the best you have to give."

"I can do whatever I like. I've earned the right. I'm not going to pass a kid just because he's the football star."

"You don't know Bobby. You never even tried to know him. You just formed an opinion which makes you think you have some kind of right to screw up his life."

Mr. Manly just smiled.

"So sue me."

"All right," I replied and walked out of the classroom.

Instead of going to the library at lunch, I went straight to Principal Doyle's office. I caught him in the hall outside his office and quickly explained the problem. He rubbed his chin in a thoughtful way for a long moment.

"I can't interfere with a teacher's grading. This sounds like a problem for the district office. Have Bobby check there. I think there's a Mr. Robinson who can help you."

"Okay."

I started to walk away.

"Scotty."

I turned to face Mr. Doyle.

"This isn't the first time I've heard complaints from students about Andy Manly."

That afternoon I went to the district office on Bear Street in Costa Mesa. I told the nice receptionist about my problem and asked her advice.

"You can file a complaint," she said.

"We need to hurry," I replied. "There's no telling what this guy will do."

"It's a problem that happens all too often. I'm glad you're doing something about it. But you do need a parent's signature."

I drove to Bobby's old apartment. His mother, Ellen, had just gotten home from work. I explained the situation to her and she signed the complaint immediately. I returned to Bear Street just before closing and filed the complaint.

Then we waited. A couple of days later an ancient man, Mr. Robinson, was assigned to the case. Fortunately, he had also been a math teacher at one time. Ellen, Bobby, and I went over Bobby's tests with Mr. Robinson and he agreed that I was right. The tests had been graded unfairly. A meeting took place between Mr. Robinson and Andy Manly. The next thing we knew, Bobby's grade was changed to a C, and the grade on the pop quiz was thrown out. I guess job security was more important to Mr. Manly than being a jerk. He was also very careful around Bobby and me for the remainder of the semester.

63

At the end of October, the day that I had lived in total fear of arrived. It wasn't Halloween, it wasn't an appointment for a root canal, it was a day that would have an enormous impact on my future, a day that might very well live on in infamy if I blew it. It was the day of the SAT test.

The night before, Newport, had dismantled Anaheim. The wheels had come off the Anaheim offense early when Bobby intercepted a pass in the first quarter and ran it back for a touchdown. After that, it was all Newport. Actually, it was all Bobby with a little help from Newport.

It had been a big game for Bobby. A lot of guys whom he had gone to grammar school and junior high with were on the Anaheim team. This made the win even sweeter, and the coach of Anaheim acknowledged Bobby's performance. He searched Bobby out and found him in the middle of the field hugging Liza. Perry and I were there as well.

"Rowels," the coach said, "I knew when you moved away we had lost someone special."

But instead of celebrating, Bobby followed my lead. We both went home early for a good night's rest. Bobby knew how important the SATs were too.

The test started at eight and I knew it would be torture in various forms. We woke early and my dad fixed us some eggs. My dad and Bobby talked while I ate in silence. Finally, Bobby noticed.

"I've never seen you worried about a test."

"I'm not worried about the test. I'm worried about getting into Stanford."

As we drove up Cliff Drive in the Chrysler, Bobby turned to me.

"I hope I do well."

"Why are you even worried? You'll have your choice of a dozen colleges."

"I might want to go to Stanford, too. Your dad said they've been sending me letters asking me to come visit after the season."

"Really?"

"Yeah, I think it might be great to go to the same college."

"It would be cool. But I'm not sure they're even going to accept me."

"Sure they will. You're the smartest guy in our school."

"Just do your best," I said. "If Stanford doesn't accept me, maybe I'll go to the same school as you."

"Really?"

"Yeah, I don't really have a second choice."

"Scotty, why Stanford? Why have you always wanted to go there?"

"It's simple. Steinbeck went there. He didn't graduate but I think that's where it all started for him."

As we drove toward what I thought was my destiny, it struck me that dreams are funny things. They often start in obscure ways. I had read *Cannery Row* and *Tortilla Flats* and decided that Steinbeck was my favorite writer. That led to a period when I read all his other books and everything I could about the man. I found out he had gone to Stanford. From that moment on, Stanford became the college of my dreams.

64

In the second week of November, the weather turned cold. An early storm clobbered Southern California and Bobby played his heart out against Westminster in a freezing downpour. Westminster was otherside-of-the-tracks-tough and a big bruising running back gave Bobby fits. Newport lost their first Sunset League game by one point, 7 to 6. Steiner missed three field goals, and everyone was pissed.

Ensconced under our umbrellas, Perry, Liza and I waited at our usual spot outside the locker room. We had become something of a foursome and always had dinner at Me and Ed's after the game. When Bobby came out he walked straight to his mom and gave her a hug. It was their routine, too, along with Sunday dinners and talking on the phone every day. For some reason his mom was crying.

There was something about my friend tonight that seemed sad. Head down, hands stuffed in his pockets, he appeared dejected. I knew how much Bobby hated to lose.

After he said good-bye to his mom, Bobby walked over to us. He was limping slightly from an injury sustained in the game. Liza gave him a kiss, Perry gave him a hug, and I shook his hand.

"Hey," I said. "That was a tough one."

"Yeah," Bobby looked down.

"Do you want to get something to eat?"

"No, I think I'm just going to walk home."

"Walk? It's raining, and you're limping."

"Yeah, I'm all right. I'll catch you at home."

"Do you want me to walk with you?" Liza asked.

"No, I just need some time."

He shuffled away through the crowd. People expressed their condolences for the loss as Bobby passed but he didn't react. He just pulled the hood of his sweatshirt over his head. The girls looked at me.

"Something's happened," I said. "He'll tell me when he's ready."

Perry and I went back to her trailer. A driving rain pounded the metal roof with a deafening roar.

"Want to listen to some music?" Perry asked.

"I guess," I said.

All I could think about was Bobby.

"Maybe I should go look for him."

"Maybe you should," Perry agreed

Then I saw the light go on in our room.

"He's home," I said. "I need to go talk to him."

I ran back to the trailer. Dad was sitting at the table reading some of Bobby's letters.

"What's happened?" he asked.

"I'm not sure."

I went into the bedroom. Bobby, sitting on my bunk with his hood still up, stared numbly at the floor. He was completely soaked, water dripping from his clothes and face. His eyes rose to meet mine and he began to cry.

"Fucking White," he said. "I was standing naked in the shower and he just starts screaming that we lost because of me. Right in front of everyone. Telling me I was a piece of shit as a football player. There was nothing I could do but take it."

He sat sobbing as I walked over, sat next to him and put my arm around him. He shivered.

"White's an asshole. There's a lot of other players on the team. I mean, Steiner missed three field goals."

"No... it was like... he raped me." Bobby whimpered.

"Come on, bro. Let's get you out of those wet clothes."

I stood him up, peeled off his clothes and threw them in the tub in the bathroom. When I returned, Bobby stood naked, shivering and still crying. It broke my heart to see my friend so vulnerable and in pain. I quickly found some sweatpants and a sweatshirt in the closet. As I dressed him, Bobby revealed something else.

"He fucking dumped my mom."

"He dumped your mom?"

But Bobby didn't respond to my question. I helped him climb into my lower bunk and he crawled under the covers. He rolled over and faced the wall below the window as his shivering grew into shaking. I pulled the heavy blanket off his bed and threw it over him. Then I pulled my grandmother's quilt up off the end of my bed and covered him with it as well.

"Hey, bro. Can I get you anything? Water?"

I was met with only silence and I felt that it would be a long time before Bobby recovered from this. I wondered if maybe Bobby was right. It just wasn't worth it.

65

The next morning Bobby was sick. He had a fever and was coughing his brains out. Outside, a cold damp fog as thick as yogurt engulfed the city of Newport. With the fog came a gloom that seemed to have settled upon the earth.

"I have to go to films," Bobby said.

"Absolutely not," I replied. "You're staying in bed."

"White will bench me. We're not going to win the championship now, so he doesn't need me."

"I'll deal with White."

Perry made Bobby some soup and he went back to sleep. I spent the morning composing a letter. Then I drove the Chrysler to school and found my way to the Newport Harbor Varsity locker room.

I had never set foot in this room before. On the walls were slogans such as "When the going gets tough, the tough get going," and "Sailor Pride." It struck me that my best friend had spent an important part of his life in this room. A room filled with passion, dreams and hopes. A kind of a sanctuary where glory is celebrated and failure is shared as a team. But thanks to White, the loss to Westminster had not been shared.

White walked out of the coach's room in the back. Newport has had a long line of great coaches: Pizzica, Lent, Johnson, Giddings. They were tough, hard-nosed men but they embodied a fairness and honesty that inspired their players with their solid character. White was a sneaky, dishonest coach who placed his personal ambitions above the welfare of his players. His presence made the room feel like a crime scene. I walked directly up to him.

"Coach White."

He stared at me blankly as his mind tried to puzzle out who I was.

"I know who you are. You're Rowels' little surfer friend."

"Yeah. Bobby won't be coming to films because he's sick."

"What's wrong with him?"

"Fever, cough."

"Are you sure he's not surfing?"

"No, he walked home in the rain because some asshole said it was his fault we lost the game last night. Can you imagine that? And the asshole didn't even have the decency to let him get dressed."

"What did you call me?"

"Here's a letter that spells out our grievances. I'm prepared to go to the school district with them."

It had worked with Manly. Why not White. But White didn't take the letter.

"It was his fault we lost," White answered.

"That's funny. I thought the game was played by twenty-two players and coaches who knew what they were doing."

I tried to hand White the letter again. It was a passionate letter written in anger. First, the letter spelled out Bobby's success in the season using all the stats my dad had compiled. Next, I wrote the facts as I knew them, specifically White's unfair treatment of Bobby. From there I got into the personal stuff and how White began dating his mom, forcing Bobby to move out of the house. Finally, I wrote about the previous night in the shower. I closed with a statement that summed up my whole idea about coaches and teachers in general.

"Your work is eternal, it is passed on through the generations, and there's no more important profession, for it's through education that the world evolves. But with this comes a profound responsibility, the responsibility of service to your students. Not just to the student's athletic abilities or intellectual capacity, but to the whole person, for your service must include their spirit. It's a moral responsibility, not a political one, and a responsibility that requires deep thinking. Every decision, every choice, every grade, every word spoken to a young person will live with them forever, and these students and athletes will carry these things out into the world."

I closed the letter with this statement. "The problem with you, Coach White, is that you are filled with hidden agendas that put your needs before those of your student-athletes."

Again White refused the letter. Instead, he grabbed me by the collar and dragged me out of the room. When we got to the door leading out to the front lawn, he threw me and I fell to the ground, skinning my elbow.

"Don't you ever set foot in this locker room again," he growled. "This room is for men, not little sissies."

66

Bobby was still sick on Sunday. He burned with fever and complained of sharp pains in his back and stomach. He couldn't even get out of bed to see his mom. I called Ellen and she came over and spent an hour or so with him in our room. It was the first time she had been to our trailer. When she saw the bulletin boards my dad had set up outlining the various college choices for Bobby and me, her eyes filled with tears.

"Thank you so much," she said.

My dad smiled. "No need to thank me. This is the most fun I've had in years."

On Monday, Bobby had not improved and we decided he should stay home from school.

"I'll make sure he has everything he needs," my dad said as I left the trailer.

"Thanks, Dad."

Bobby wasn't much better on Tuesday and I grew alarmed.

"Maybe we should go to the emergency room," I suggested.

"It's just the flu," he croaked. "I'll be better tomorrow."

For four days Bobby lay in bed staring at the wall and when I spoke to him he mostly grunted or remained silent. I knew he was sick but I had never seen him this way. It was more than the flu. I felt his spirit was sick, too.

"The waves are looking good," I offered.

Bobby just nodded.

On Wednesday, my dad took Bobby to the emergency room. A doctor saw him and said, "it's the flu."

"There's a lot of influenza going around. Drink plenty of water and stay in bed," the doctor instructed.

I was at work at the diner and my dad and Bobby stopped by for something to eat on the way home. Pinaply was overjoyed to see Bobby and told her father to make something really special. It had been a slow night so I went into the kitchen to mop the floor. The next thing I knew a waitress rushed in.

"Bobby's yelling at some old man and a girl."

Sure enough I could hear yelling. Then the cashier rushed in.

"Bobby's in a fight."

Pineapple and I looked at each other and then we rushed through the doors to find an enormous bodybuilder of a man had wrestled Bobby to the ground. He was holding a gun to Bobby's head.

"Don't move a muscle," the big man yelled.

But the bodyguard had miscalculated and the arrival of my dad changed things. Being a retired policemen, he was allowed him to carry a gun, which he often did. My dad pulled his gun and put it to the big man's head.

"Let him up or I'll blow your brains all over this floor."

There was something in my dad's voice, calm and certain, that made me believe him.

"Yeah, motherfucker," Pineapple yelled. "And I'm going to cut your head off."

Pineapple had a meat clever in his hand. It was a standoff.

"All right, all right," the big man finally said. "I'll release him."

He let go of Bobby. My best friend slowly got to his feet and turned toward the booth. I saw what had created the problem. It was Perry sitting with Old Man Elliot

"You're a whore," Bobby said. "How could you do this to Scotty?"

"Everybody stop," I yelled. "Bobby, the old man's not her lover, he's her father."

Bobby looked at me.

"What?"

"He's her father. That's what I couldn't tell you."

Elliot looked at his daughter.

"He knows?"

"Yes," Perry said. "I told you I love him."

"Yes, I know about your plan," I said.

The tycoon shrugged his shoulders. Then he looked out the window at a nondescript navy blue sedan with two men inside. Elliot laughed.

"The dumb shits are reading the paper."

"This doesn't change anything," I said. "Your plan is safe."

Elliot looked me in the eye and I found myself staring back into the eyes of one of the most powerful men in the world. His glare was almost enough to make a super-hero shudder.

"How so?" he asked.

"Well, I assume this thug is your bodyguard." I pointed to the bodybuilder.

"Yes," he said. "Go on."

"Everyone else I have a relationship with. You've met Bobby, and he's my best friend. This is my dad, and Pineapple loves me. So if I ask them to keep quiet they will. No one will ever know since the detectives in the car missed their opportunity."

The tycoon looked at me carefully, sizing me up.

"You know my plan?"

"Yes, sir."

"Are you an opportunist?"

"I'm eighteen years old. I don't even know what I want from life yet. All I know is that I love your daughter."

Elliot shrugged.

"All right," he said. "You seem like a smart kid. You know there's a lot at stake so you know that I won't be kind if this spills out."

"Yes, sir," I said.

"What's going on?" Bobby asked.

"I'll tell you later, bro," I said.

"No," Perry interrupted. "Let me tell him."

I looked at Perry. She knew how much I loved Bobby and she wanted to do this for us because she loved me.

"Let me drive you home, Bobby," Perry said.

Perry stood, took Bobby by the arm and started for the door.

"Go out the back way so the dumb shits don't see you," Elliot said.

Perry led Bobby through the kitchen and I turned to the old man.

"I'm sorry for the disturbance, sir," I said. "Let me buy your dinner."

67

Perry drove Bobby back to the trailer park in her little white Rabbit. It was the appropriate car, almost poetic, because Bobby was about to fall down the rabbit hole, just as I had.

As they sat in Perry's trailer on the brown leather couch, Bobby finally heard the tale: a story of money, power, and revenge. Perry's father had been married four times, and had seven children with these wives, all of whom hated him. His children were given law degrees, MBAs, and PHDs. They were smart kids who had banded together to overthrow their father. It was a mythic tale almost like Cronus being overthrown by Zeus and his brothers and sisters. Except that it was so sordid, even by the standards of Greek mythology.

Old Man Elliot was being accused of incompetence and an inability to handle his affairs because of a lifestyle of debauchery. The kids all thought he was going to give his enormous fortune to a gold-digging hooker. Perry, for the last year, was the apparent gold-digger.

The stakes were enormous. Elliot and his companies owned oil wells in Signal Hill, Huntington Beach, West Texas, Bakersfield and Louisiana. With the profits from oil, he had bought companies, lots of them. He had also bought real estate, lots of it. His fortune was massive and well diversified. Elliot was probably the richest man in Newport, maybe even in California.

Elliot had met Perry's mother in New Orleans. He was sixty and she was twenty. He had come there to look at oil leases. They never married, but they did have a child. The child was named Periwinkle.

The last thing Old Man Elliot wanted was another child, so his intention was to throw money at the problem. Perry's mother, a stripper, died of a drug overdose when Perry was three and her grandmother took on the job of raising her. She died when Perry was eleven. At the age of twelve, Perry hopped a Greyhound bus and headed to Newport Beach to find her father.

Old Man Elliot had never laid eyes on her, so when she presented herself on his doorstep, he was stunned.

"You took a bus all the way from Louisiana?" the old man asked.

"I wanted to meet my father."

"You look like a drowned kitten."

Twelve-year-old Perry smiled.

"That's good. I like kittens."

No one had ever been so relaxed with the old man or so willing to stand up to him. Elliot found himself amused by the young girl. Currently between girlfriends, he invited her to stay the summer and began spending time with her. They sailed, rode bikes, and went fishing. They even watched the fireworks from the top of the Ferris wheel at the Fun Zone on the Fourth of July.

The old man found he loved this upstart little girl and began canceling meetings to spend time with her.

"But we might lose the deal," his vice president protested.

"So?" Elliot replied. "Then we lose the deal. There will be another one."

Elliot was smitten. For the first time in his life he felt the power and meaning of being a father. It's not the power you hold but the power that's held over you. The power that creates in you a passion to protect those whom you love and the desire to nurture those you care for.

When the summer ended, Elliot was heartbroken when he chose to put Perry on a plane to New Orleans, first class, to return to an aunt and uncle she hardly knew. The Old Man had a company to run and didn't want to be a single father. He knew that being a father was not something he was good at.

He stayed in contact with her secretly. He didn't want it public or the rest of his family to know that Perry existed. He paid for her college at Tulane and always made sure she had whatever she needed. If there was anything she wanted, all she had to do was ask. She seldom asked. When she called, it was only to talk about life and the memories of that summer when she was twelve, memories both she and her father cherished.

In his personal life, Elliot fell back into his old ways, and the reputation of the old goat grew. At eighty one he found a girlfriend who was twenty-six, and the family was alarmed. They hired a team of lawyers to question his judgment in an attempt to take over his affairs.

Elliot, not one to be too concerned over such things, was struck another blow. He was diagnosed with the early stages of ALS, commonly known as Lou Gehrig's disease. It is a degenerative and fatal nerve disease, a death sentence.

It was like a lightning-struck tower, his empire was going to be toppled. Not by some lawsuit, his lawyers were too good, but by the vicissitudes of life. His days were numbered and facing his own mortality turned everything he ever thought or believed in upside down.

He began to seriously think about his fortune and what he intended to do with it. Who was going to receive his legacy and the benefits of a lifetime of work? He was also scared of dying alone in some sterile hospital room. Richard C. Elliot had never been scared of anything in his life.

Thoughts of the twelve-year-old girl entered his mind, the daughter that no one knew about, his only child who had simply loved him and who had never really asked him for anything. The more he thought about it, the more obsessed he became.

He also realized how much he hated his other kids. The only time they called was for money. He was always generous with his kids but they never said, "Thank you." Instead, they grew up hating and resenting him, largely because of their mothers, who, like a flock of parrots, had joined together in saying, "Richard C. Elliot is a terrible father." As a result, his kids grew up feeling entitled and ungrateful and now they were actually suing him. When he was called in for an exhausting and humiliating deposition, he made his decision, and during the ride home from the deposition, Old Man Elliot hatched his plan.

Bring Perry to California, make everyone think she's his girlfriend, and at the competency hearing, reveal that Perry is actually his daughter. Then he will also announce that he's suffering from ALS. Finally, he intended to inform the world that he's leaving most of his estate, his considerable fortune spread out across the world, to his youngest daughter, Perry. Though he made provisions for his other children in the form of trusts so that they would be comfortable, the power and control of the fortune would be Perry's. It was nothing short of a major rat-fuck.

Bobby was floored.

"So you're going to be really rich?"

"Yes, and it scares me," Perry replied. "I've read books about a lot of people who have come into sudden wealth. Doris Duke, for example, or Barbara Hutton. The money ruined their lives."

"I really can't relate," Bobby said. "I've never had much money."

"Trust me, it does. The problem is that you can never really be sure that you are loved for yourself. The idea always creeps in that you are loved for your money."

"Yeah," Bobby replied. "I wonder if girls sometimes love me because I'm supposed to have a football career."

"Exactly," Perry said. "And that's why I chose to give Scotty and me a chance. I saw how much he loved you, and if he loved you, then he could love me."

Bobby smiled.

"I get it now."

Bobby was quiet a moment. Then he looked at Perry.

"I'm sorry. I was wrong. You really do love Scotty."

"Yes, and that's why I brought my dad to the diner. I want him to love Scotty, too."

Bobby reached out and gave Perry a hug.

"Welcome to the family," he said.

68

When I arrived home from the diner, I went straight to Perry's trailer

"Bobby gets it. He understands everything," she said. "I think he approves now."

I reached out and pulled her to me. I squeezed her tight.

"Thank you," I whispered.

Perry had healed everything. She knew the knowledge of her situation had weighed heavily on my mind. Not because of its potential impact on me or Newport Beach high society; I could care less about that. But because I had, at Perry's request, kept it from Bobby.

When I got back to my room, Bobby woke. He seemed better. He looked at me and smiled.

"Hey, Perry's cool."

"Yeah."

"You hit the jackpot, dickhead. And not because she's going to be richer than sin. I think she really loves you."

"Yeah. She's one of a kind."

"That's good. Now you'll have someone to take care of your sorry ass when I'm not around."

Bobby rolled over and went back to sleep.

69

On Thursday morning, Bobby was still not well enough to go to school. His fever had broken, but his stomach and back ached and he said he felt a heaviness inside, like there was a balloon growing in his chest.

"One more day," Bobby said. "I'll be better tomorrow."

He had missed almost the entire week of school. I collected his homework for him but it was starting to pile up. I also made it a point to keep his teachers well informed about his condition. They all seemed genuinely concerned except for Mr. Manly. He just said, "Thank you."

On Friday, Bobby stayed home again. He looked terrible. The blood had drained from his face as if he were a vampire in need of a feeding. My dad had made some eggs and bacon and we all sat at the table together.

"Your dad's been so great," Bobby said. "My mom has been stopping by on her lunch hour, and even she's seen how your dad has taken care of me."

I looked at my dad.

"Hey," he offered. "If it hadn't been me then it would have been you."

"Thanks, dad."

I went to school and the first thing I heard was that Westminster had played the night before and lost to Edison. That meant that Newport could still be sole champion since Westminster had one loss and one tie. All we had to do was beat Fountain Hills, which had one tie. This would leave Newport standing alone as champion with one loss and no ties. Steiner and Chandler cornered me outside Beek Hall.

"How's Bobby?" Steiner asked.

"A little better."

"Can he play tonight?" Chandler asked.

"No," I replied. "Today was his first day out of bed."

I went on with my day and didn't think much about it. It was just a football game. Bobby would have other football games.

But when I got home in the afternoon, I found Bobby dressed and his sports bag packed.

"What's up?" I asked.

"White came by and asked me to play."

"Screw that noise."

"Yeah, I know. He had all kinds of bullshit going. Said he knows it was me that put the body on his doorstep. Said he protected me and I owed him. Then he said he wouldn't tell the recruiters that I flaked out of practice to go surfing if I played and we won the championship."

"So you're not playing, right?"

Bobby looked at me. When I looked in his eyes I knew. There would be no stopping him. His mind was made up, and he had his game face on.

"Bobby, why? White's an asshole. All he cares about is winning a championship. He doesn't care about you."

"I know. But I'm not doing this for White. I'm doing it for my team and myself. I want us to win the championship."

Bobby had been in bed for a week and now he wanted to play in a football game. And not just any game. Fountain Hills was tough, they had two German linebackers, 6-3, 250 pounds and they were twins. Rumor had it that they were aspiring skinheads and when they got angry in the games they would start yelling at people in German. The only thing that stood between them and all-county recognition was Bobby, and there was no doubt in my mind they would be gunning for him.

"Come on," Bobby said. "Drive me to school. I've got a date with the Titans."

We climbed in the Chrysler and the whole way I kept trying to talk Bobby out of this madness.

"It's one game," he assured me. "Then I can rest."

"Did White say anything about your mom?"

Bobby was quiet for a long moment.

"He said he was sorry. It just didn't work out."

I pulled up to the front of the school. Steiner and Rickie Chandler were there and when they saw Bobby it became a circus. They started jumping up and down like cheerleaders.

"Yeah," Chandler yelled. "Now we're going to kick their ass."

As I watched Bobby walk to the locker room high-fiving Steiner and Chandler, I had a terrible premonition. It was what my grandmother called a brush with the eternal, causing a shiver to run down my spine. I wanted to jump out of the car and drag Bobby home. But other players appeared and he was surrounded by his team. There was no turning back.

I drove home with a heavy heart. Football is a dangerous game, and that was part of the reason Bobby loved it. But Bobby was weak from being sick and people get hurt all the time. Being surrounded by your team does not make you safe.

70

Because Fountain Hills is a giant school with a huge student body, the game was being played at Orange Coast College, whose stadium was much larger than Newport's. But we still needed to get there early to get a good seat. Perry and I drove to the apartment building behind Cappy's to pick up Pineapple and Pinaply. Pineapple got into the car complaining about not having had a shower.

"A pipe blew under the slab," he said. "The landlord's been there all afternoon with a jackhammer trying to find the leak."

"That's a bummer," Perry said.

"Yeah," Pineapple replied. "It's surprising all the things we take for granted. Hot water and electricity, for example. When they're gone it kind of throws everything off. That's why you always have to be grateful for the little things."

On the ride to the stadium, Pineapple regaled us with stories about his apartment building. There was the drunk girl who climbed onto the roof and jumped thirty feet into the shallow pool, and the dentist who smoked pot morning, noon and night, or the rabble-rouser who was always trying to enlist the other tenants in a lawsuit against the landlord.

"I tell you, the landlord's got his hands full with that place. Wouldn't want to be him. No, sir."

I was happy to listen to Pineapple's stories because it took my mind off Bobby. My grandmother, Norma Jean, could be superstitious and she once told me that if a bird flies into a house it is an omen that someone was going to die. I hadn't been able to shake the uneasy feeling that a black swan had just flown through the window.

We made our way into the stadium and found some decent seats. I saw my dad arrive with Bobby's mom, Ellen. At first I was surprised. Then I realized it sort of made sense and I smiled. They made a cute couple.

The night air felt crisp and electricity filled the stadium. Newport's band was next to us blasting the sounds of Chicago's "Twenty-Five or Six to Four" and you could sense the anticipation in the crowd as the stadium filled to capacity. You could also see the big-game anticipation as the players warmed up and the adrenaline kicked in. Their steps were a little higher and their hits a lot harder. There is nothing like a big-game, a game where everything is on the line and nothing will be left for those who lose. Those who prevail will have a lifetime to remember these shining moments of glory under the lights on a cool autumn evening in late November. Football weather, a perfect night for a big game.

"We just talked to Bobby," my dad said as he and Ellen joined us. "He's only playing defense tonight."

"That's good," said Pineapple. "He'll be doing the hitting instead of getting hit."

"How's he feel?" I asked.

"Pretty good, I think," Dad answered. "He says he's ready."

"See," said Perry and she pulled me close. "Bobby knows what he's doing."

From the start of the game, I could tell Bobby wasn't himself. He got up from the piles slowly and seemed to drag himself back to the huddle. When he wasn't on the field, he usually stood on the sidelines yelling for his teammates. But tonight he huddled on the bench. Still, he was on the field more than he wasn't, but at the end of the first half the score was 3 to 0 in favor of Fountain Hills.

When the players returned to the field for the second half, the Newport Harbor Sailors burst through a banner held by the cheerleaders. Bobby usually led this charge. Instead, Bobby walked slowly onto the field. I watched closely as he approached the trainer who had him lie on the bench and lift his jersey. The trainer felt his stomach and then gave Bobby a thumbs up.

The third quarter was scoreless. Newport, without Bobby, was miserable on offense. Three plays and out. But Fountain Hills wasn't finding much success either until the end of the third quarter when the Titans started to move the ball by wearing Newport down with their massive offensive line.

At the start of the fourth quarter, Fountain Hills found themselves just shy of the fifty-yard line and began to inch their way toward Newport's goal line. They ground it out in the proverbial three yards and a cloud of dust, running play after running play. Twice they went for it on fourth down and succeeded in securing a first down.

That's when magic struck. Fountain Hills made their way inside Newport's ten-yard line and a Titan score appeared inevitable. But Bobby began blitzing and he guessed right every time. On three consecutive plays he dropped the Fountain Hills' running backs for losses. On the fourth down, the Titans lined up for a field goal. It was a fake and they tried a pass. Bobby stopped that too. He knocked the pass down in the end zone.

There were six minutes left and Newport still trailed 3 to 0. The ball stood on their own twelve-yard line.

Bobby walked slowly off the field and headed straight for the bench. He did not sit. Instead, he lay down on it. The trainer came over to check on him. Bobby gave the trainer thumbs up and the trainer walked straight to White. White turned.

"Rowels."

Bobby sat up slowly and walked to his coach.

"Tailback, now!"

Bobby turned and jogged onto the field. He lined up in the backfield and was handed the ball. Bobby ripped through the Titan line for a gain of nine yards. It was Newport's first gain in the second half.

On the field the twins yelled at their teammates. The linebackers were pointing at Bobby, and I was pretty sure that they were yelling in German.

But that didn't stop White from giving the ball to Bobby. They gave him the ball on every play, and Bobby delivered. Five yards, seven yards, three yards, twelve yards, soon Newport was in Fountain Hills' territory while using up the clock.

The crowd began to chant "Bobby, Bobby, Bobby!" His name rang out through the stadium like a church bell. Every play Bobby ran the ball, and he pounded his way through the Fountain Hills' defense. With thirty seconds remaining on the clock, Newport called time out. They were inside the Fountain Hills' ten-yard line, the mythic red zone, God's country, the place where character is tested and measured both for the offense and the defense, first down for Newport.

It was obvious that Bobby was tired and in pain. At one point I saw him wobble and he took a knee. Play resumed and, of course, they gave the ball to Bobby. The linebackers came after Bobby, but somehow he managed to slip away to the three-yard line.

The next play Newport tried to get cute. They faked to Bobby and threw a pass. But the tight end, Blackburn, dropped it in the end zone. It was third down and three with 17 seconds on the clock.

The crowd was now on its feet yelling, "Bobby, Bobby, Bobby!" Everyone in the stands and on the field knew that Bobby was going to get the ball, and the linebackers, all 6'3, 250 pounds of them, knew it, too. When Bobby was handed the ball, they blitzed and both linebackers hit him at the same time. The hit was so hard I could hear it in the stands.

The twins celebrated. They jumped up and down giving each other high fives. But Bobby didn't move. It was obvious that something was wrong, and when the crowd realized it, the stadium turned into a church, so quiet you could hear your own breath as Bobby lay motionless.

The trainer ran onto the field and took off Bobby's helmet. He began waving his arms. The trainer from the other team ran onto the field and a paramedic also appeared. I turned to Perry.

"I have to go down there."

I rocketed from my seat and flew down the concrete stairs, taking them three at a time. As I climbed through the bars and down the wall, an assistant coach tried to stop me from going on the field.

"No way," I screamed. "Bobby's in trouble."

I sprinted onto the field just as an ambulance arrived. A small crowd gathered around Bobby and a stretcher was being moved in. The players from both teams had taken a knee.

"Stand back," the paramedic said.

The men lifted Bobby's limp body onto the stretcher. I could see blood running from his nose and down his chin. Then the men hurried Bobby into the ambulance.

"Where are you taking him?" I yelled.

The trainer turned to me.

"Hoag. They're taking him to Hoag."

71

I scrambled back to our group who had moved to the railing along the field. Everyone looked to me for an answer, but I had none to give and I wasn't about to say anything about blood in front of Bobby's mother.

"They're taking him to Hoag Hospital," I shouted.

Bobby's mother looked stricken. She leaned against my dad for support.

"We should go there," I yelled as I scaled the wall into the stands.

We all ran to our cars while the game on the field resumed. There were still eight seconds left and Newport had the ball on the six with fourth down. White sent out the field goal team.

The Chrysler is not a fast car, but Perry, Pineapple, Pinaply and I were the first to arrive at the emergency room. Pinaply cried the whole way.

We barged through the double doors, finding ourselves in a big open room with rows of chairs against the wall and down the center. There were a few people waiting for treatment who eyed us curiously. Against the far wall was a counter with a long line of reception desks. I walked up to a receptionist as the others waited. She was young, with a sweet round face, and she had just hung up the phone.

"I need to inquire about Bobby Rowels."

"The football player?" The look on her face registered deep concern.

"Yes," I said as a feeling of anxiousness took hold of me.

"Are you related?"

"Kind of, he lives with us."

"We can only give out information to his relatives."

"Can you tell me if it's serious?"

I looked into the young woman's eyes. Tears were forming.

"Yes. It's serious."

Ellen and my dad walked in.

"There's Bobby's mom now."

"I better call the chaplain."

"What?" A piercing fear sliced through my body as my mind raced, trying to think of the reasons we would need a priest. I staggered backward a couple of steps.

The room was starting to fill now. Liza and the posse arrived along with several other parents. I stood in a daze as I heard someone call my name.

"What?" I asked the receptionist again.

Suddenly agitated, the young woman jumped up from her desk. "Just wait here. I'll be right back."

In this moment, I knew. A low, fierce growl erupted as I tried to form my words. But I couldn't talk. Everyone was looking at me. Liza walked up to me.

"What's happening? Is Bobby all right?" she asked nervously.

I couldn't answer her. The room was suddenly spinning like a roller coaster at the Orange County fair. Instead, I hugged her and walked straight to Perry. I couldn't face Bobby's mom.

"Follow me."

She stood and followed. As we walked through what was quickly becoming a crowd. People were asking, "How's Bobby, how's Bobby?"

Perry and I stepped outside. I turned to her and hugged her. Then I pulled back and looked at her. The tears were streaming down my face.

"He's dead."

"What?"

I handed her the keys to the Chrysler, turned, and started running. I didn't know where I was going. I just started running. Running from the terrible truth that Bobby was dead.

72

Into the night, heart pounding, blinded by my tears, I ran. I didn't have a plan, but I knew where I needed to go, to the ocean. The only place that could help me make sense of this horrible tragedy.

I stumbled and fell on the steep grade of Superior Avenue and found myself splayed out on the concrete sidewalk face first. The concrete ripped the skin from my face and hands, but I picked myself up and ran on.

At Pacific Coast Highway, with my eyes blinded by tears, I sprinted straight through the intersection without waiting for a green light. Traffic, traveling at high rates speed, swerved to avoid me. A Mercedes horn blared and I heard tires screeching as I dodged the car.

Onward, down Balboa Boulevard, I crossed on the red again. Then up Forty-Seventh Street, careening into a couple walking hand-in-hand on the narrow street. I nearly knocked the guy to the ground.

"Hey, asshole! Watch where you're going!" he yelled after me.

I didn't stop. I couldn't stop. I sprinted across Sea Shore and onto the beach. The full moon glistened low in the sky with its light shining across the ocean like a shimmering white path to heaven itself. A wild idea arose in my mind. This path would lead me back to Bobby.

Suddenly, I found myself diving into the cold, dark sea and swimming toward the light of the moon. An incoming wave swept over me while pain, powerful and fierce, shot through my entire body, leaving me helpless in its wake. It wrenched my stomach, my heart, my very soul.

I threw up several times. Curling into a ball, choking and coughing. I shuddered as spasms of nausea swept through me while slowly sinking beneath the waves. I was only released from my pain when the urge to breathe grew stronger than my agony. Swimming for the surface, I broke through to find myself beyond the breakers.

The lights of the houses along the shore sparkled, and above the shoreline, the lights of Hoag Hospital blazed brightly on the bluff. I imagined that one of those lights was the room that held Bobby's body, his strong, athletic body, that would never walk this earth again.

Then, out of nowhere, I heard Bobby's voice inside my head.

"Stay safe. You still have work to do."

Maybe it was my subconscious or maybe it was madness, but it shocked me into my senses. I was in trouble, serious trouble. A rip current held me in its grasp and was pulling me out to sea. I was also growing tired and my clothes were dragging me down and constricting my movements. Suddenly, my feelings of grief gave way to fear and panic. I kicked off my tennis shoes and unzipped my hoody sweatshirt and tore it off. My t-shirt was next. The real struggle was getting out of my jeans. I fell beneath the surface struggling and shimmying out of my Levi's, losing my briefs with them.

Freed from my clothes, I swam, paralleling the shore to get away from the force that held me. But I was exhausted and quickly losing the strength to make it back to shore. Then Bobby's voice came to me again.

"Swim for the groin."

I stopped and looked around. The moonlight revealed the outline of a rock groin that extended out into the ocean from the shore. The Forty-Eighth Street groin or possibly Fifty-Fourth Street, I wasn't sure, but it was about fifty yards away. I knew it was my best chance to live.

But the current was strong, stronger than I, and I began to lose. I stopped swimming, sinking into the ocean.

"Don't stop," came Bobby's voice again.

A large swell rose up behind me and pushed me toward shore. Then another and another. I swam toward the groin using the power of the swells to push me along. But as I grew closer, I could hear the sounds of the waves crashing against the rocks. The hope that buoyed me deflated. The groin stood only twenty yards away now but I knew I would never have the strength to climb the rocks with the waves pounding me into the jagged boulders.

Like a freight train, thoughts of Bobby lying dead in the hospital rattled my mind and I started to give up again. I saw my mother and sister as the pain of my entire life engulfed me. My best friend dead, a mother who wants nothing to do with me, and a world that could care less if I lived or died were all that waited for me.

Bobby's voice came to me again. "Don't be a dickhead. Fight. Fight like I taught you."

"I can't," I said. "I'm sorry."

The frigid ocean swallowed me, and a kind of peace washed over me, a letting go of sorts. But Bobby was not going to allow me to give up.

"Fight. Think of Perry. Swing for the fences, dickhead."

Something happened. I found a burst of energy and swam for the surface. When I broke through, the sea was silent and the stars and moon shone brightly as they have for a million years. It was beautiful. I wanted to live.

Then I realized it was a lull between sets. The groin was only a short distance now and I swam with everything I had left. I slowly pulled myself out of the water and onto the boulders. Rock by rock, I climbed as the lull held. I made it to the top just as a mighty swell arrived and exploded against the groin. I could feel the vibration of the ocean's fury all around me.

Panting and totally spent, I collapsed onto the rocks as the waves continued their mighty assault. I had been lucky, and I felt an overpowering sense of gratitude.

"Thank you, Bobby," I whispered.

I rested for a long time pondering the experience of nearly drowning. Call it my subconscious or call it luck, call it my guardian angel or call it the universe, maybe even call it God, but the spirit of Bobby had come to my aid, and without his help I would be dead. His voice, so real to me, had spoken the right words at the right moments, inspiring me to save my life.

But it was more than just Bobby's words. I was helped by the swells that had arrived seemingly out of nowhere to push me out of the riptide, and the lull that lasted long enough for me to climb to safety. Some people would call it dumb luck but I believe there are no accidents or coincidences. There are deeper reasons all around us for the things that happen and coincidences only serve to remind us that everything is connected.

I sat on that groin for a long time while the spray from the waves showered my naked body with cold water. I was deep in thought but my thoughts began to fold in on themselves until I arrived at a simple question. Why had I been spared? Why was Bobby dead while I had, by some miracle, been allowed to live? Suddenly, I understood what I had to do. I needed to go home. The people who loved Bobby needed me and I had to be strong. This is what Bobby would want. Like he said, I had work to do.

I picked myself up and started toward the beach. My face and hands were stinging from the salt entering the wounds I had received from climbing the rocks and my naked body felt cold in the crisp night air. Even the soles of feet hurt as I made my way over the boulders. These were my first steps back to the people who loved Bobby, and who loved me, and the pain, both physical and emotional, served to remind me I was alive.

73

As I made my way along the ocean, the waves rushing the shoreline lapped at my ankles with a rhythm as old as the earth itself. The cold water caused me to shiver but taking this path meant I wouldn't be confronted by people. I planned to walk to the River Jetties and cross under Pacific Coast Highway at the bridge. The only people who might see me would be the residents of the trailer park and I was fairly certain they had seen much worse than a naked body in their lifetimes.

The beach at this late hour was relatively empty, but I passed by a lifeguard stand where a couple of guys sat smoking a joint. The tangy aroma of the weed fifty feet away drifted toward me.

"What happened to your clothes, dude?" one guy yelled. The pair giggled like a couple of school girls. It was obvious they were stoned.

"Shit happens," I called back.

The potheads yelled something else but I wasn't listening. I was lost in the past, working backwards through the memories of Bobby from the present to the first day of school, freshmen year. Even though the exercise proved painful, several memories brought a smile, especially the day we became blood brothers under the shadow of the Orange Street lifeguard stand. There was no doubt about it. I would miss him forever.

A few blocks later, another problem arose. Headlights appeared on the beach in front of me. It was the police patrolling the beach.

At first, I wondered if I should try to hide by lying down in the sand, because my nakedness could easily result in a charge of indecent exposure. But from somewhere deep inside, the words "screw it" arose.

If I end up in jail for nearly drowning after the loss of my best friend, who's going to really care?

The Blazer pulled up slowly and the police turned their spotlight on me.

"Stop where you are," the loudspeaker commanded.

I stopped as two cops exited the vehicle and walked toward me. They shined their flashlights in my face and over my body. One cop was a giant of a man, well over six-and-a-half feet tall, while the other was short and stocky.

"Well, look what we have here. A naked shit-bird out for an evening stroll," the big cop said. Both cops had smiles on their faces.

"Yeah, it's a rare species," the short cop added. "You don't see one of these every day."

"Where are your clothes?" the big cop asked.

"The ocean took them," I answered.

"What do you mean, the ocean took them?"

"I swam in the ocean and got caught in a rip. I had to lose them to keep from drowning."

"Do you have any ID?" the big cop asked.

I smiled and shook my head no.

"Look, sir, my best friend died tonight and I went a little crazy and swam out into the ocean. I nearly drowned and now I'm on my way home."

"Was your friend the football player?" the big cop asked.

"Yeah."

"Are you Scotty?"

"Yeah."

"I know your dad. Everyone's been looking for you."

The two cops exchanged looks.

"Let me get you a blanket," the short cop said. "We'll drive you home."

The stocky cop hustled back to the Blazer while the big cop looked at me sadly.

"I'm really sorry about your friend. Why did they let him play with an aneurysm?"

"What?"

"Yeah, the word is he played the entire game with an aortic aneurysm the size of a grapefruit. It finally ruptured. There wasn't anything anyone could do."

Newport is basically one big small town. Word travels fast. The word tonight was about Bobby's death; the story of the football player who had died was on everyone's lips.

"Your friend must have been one tough son-of-a-bitch," the big cop said. "I heard he was playing one helluva game."

"We just came from the hospital," the stocky cop said while wrapping a blanket around me. "Someone took a swing at the coach. I wish they had knocked his teeth out."

As they escorted me to the Blazer, I wondered if it had been my dad.

We drove across the beach, passing the lifeguard stand at Orange Street where Bobby and I had made our pact freshman year. But there were no tears. I couldn't cry. I just felt numb.

The trailer park was empty and dark when we arrived.

"What time is it?" I asked.

"Nearly two," the big cop said.

"Turn right," I directed. "It's just up the row."

He turned and we slowly made our way up the narrow street.

"There, it's that one," I pointed. We pulled to a stop.

"Who's that on the steps?"

The cop shined his spotlight onto the steps of my trailer. It was Perry. She was just waking up.

"That's my girlfriend."

"I wish I had a girlfriend who loved me that much," the short cop said.

"Girlfriend?" the big cop replied. "I wish my wife loved me that much."

I stepped out of the Blazer and Perry saw that it was me. She ran and threw her arms around me. She was crying, and through her tears, she whispered, "You're safe."

74

The next morning I awoke in Perry's arms. We were in her trailer because I couldn't bear the idea of sleeping in the room Bobby and I had shared. Being with Perry also made me realize how affected she was by Bobby's death. I held her in my arms all night as she cried and dozed, twitched and jumped.

"Why?" she pleaded. "Why do things like this happen? It's not fair."

"I know, babe."

"People are always dying; my mother, my grandmother. Now my dad. But Bobby was so young."

For my part there were no tears. The ocean had swallowed them. Like the good soldier I knew Bobby would have wanted, I shed no tears. I summoned the strength for the people who needed it most.

I called my dad. He had spent the night with Bobby's mom at the Oakwood Apartments.

"When can you come?" my father asked.

"When do you want me?"

"Now."

I had Perry drive me over. We went up the elevator and down the hall to the door of Bobby's old apartment. My dad answered the door and seemed relieved to see me.

"You're the only person Ellen wanted to see."

Even with Bobby's mother there were no tears from me. She had me sit next to her in the living room. She just wanted to talk about Bobby's life. She shared stories about Bobby growing up and how much he had loved his father. But I already knew that. In return, I shared with her stories about Bobby's life with me. This included his epic ride at the Point this past summer.

"I had no idea," Ellen said. "An eighteen-foot wave. Imagine that."

I knew why Bobby had kept it from her but I didn't say it. Coach White went berserk when he found out and Bobby didn't want to put his mom in the middle of it.

"Bobby loved you so much," Ellen said.

"And I loved him."

Then I told everyone about my near death experience the night before, and how I believed Bobby had come to my aid. Everyone was shocked, especially Perry.

"I think my experience goes much deeper and speaks to all of us. It means that Bobby will always be with us. All we have to do is think of him and know that if we need him, he'll be there."

Ellen started to cry. My father sat next to her on the couch. He put his arms around her and held her as she sobbed. There was a tenderness in him I had never seen, and it was obvious that something very deep and profound was taking place between him and Ellen. Perry noticed it too. I wouldn't dare to say that everything happens for a reason. Bobby's death was too devastating for that. But my father had found something in himself, or at least the best part of himself, and it was all because of Bobby. Way leads to way, and every action has a reaction.

Ellen turned to me.

"Thank you, Scotty, for sharing what happened to you and how you think of it."

I nodded.

"Will you write something for Bobby's funeral?"

"I would be honored."

"Something fearless."

"Fearless?"

"Yes, Bobby always said that when you wrote you were fearless."

I paused to think about the meaning of the word fearless. Free from fear. Brave. I shook my head.

"It wasn't me. It was Bobby who was fearless. That's what he taught me."

75

The coroner performed an autopsy. The cause of death was the rupture of an aortic aneurysm. The heart doctor told Ellen that these types of aneurysms are usually the result of a genetic weakness in the lining of the arteries.

"It could have ruptured at any time but the trauma from the football game obviously aggravated it. He shouldn't have been playing."

The next few days were a blur. I stayed home from school reading my favorite book, *The Art of Wondering*. In it are stories about the lives of great philosophers, Aurelius, Spinoza, Thoreau, Camus, the list is long, and the stories reveal how other men have attempted to negotiate the labyrinth we call life. Through struggle, pain, and perseverance, they created maps that can give us clues for finding our own way through the maze.

I had found the book on a bus stop bench in Costa Mesa when I was fourteen years old. I opened it and thought I had found a map to buried treasure. This proved true as it helped me come to terms with my parents' divorce. That's the strange thing about books that change your life. They often come to you by accident and you read them at the precise moment you need them, when you're ready for their wisdom. But even my most trusted book was not helpful to me in understanding or accepting Bobby's death. The words just left me numb.

I spent my days alone in Perry's trailer. She was staying with her father preparing for the court trial, and my dad was at Ellen's making arrangements for the funeral. Some wealthy Newport Beach citizens had made a large donation to pay for the costs and my father intended to send Bobby off in style.

"Ellen will always remember this," he said. "The memory will help ease her pain."

Thanksgiving Day arrived and I took a walk along the ocean. It was a beautiful day, warm, with offshore breezes and good waves. But I didn't feel like surfing.

Instead, I walked to the spot where Bobby and I had become blood brothers. It seemed like a dream that three years ago I sat looking at Bobby holding a ten-inch butcher knife with a maniacal look on his face.

I climbed the tower and stood looking out toward the ocean with the past pouring into my heart. The sun was setting over Catalina in a fiery crescendo as day surrendered to dusk, and I knew I was beginning a ritual of sorts. I would return to this spot, to this Orange Street lifeguard stand, every Thanksgiving, to remember my friend with gratitude.

"Bobby," I whispered. "Your heart was just too big for this world."

76

The funeral for Bobby Rowels was held at Pacific View Memorial Cemetery. The weather had turned miserable, foggy and wet. But that didn't stop a thousand people from showing up. The small chapel couldn't accommodate everyone so speakers were set up on the front lawn where people stood quietly listening to the eulogies. Everyone I knew put in an appearance, including my mom and the Dick. Coach White and Mr. Andy Manly were there as well. I didn't talk to any of them but I wasn't really angry, either. Bobby was gone and the people that had screwed with him and betrayed him just didn't matter.

People got up and said some amazing things about Bobby. For me, it was the moment I dreaded. Ellen had asked me to write something fearless but my words had gone dry. I had even driven over to Steiner's house in the Chrysler to walk his path to the boathouse. I thought memories of my sacred garden in Kauai might inspire the words to flow. Nothing. I couldn't even write in my journal.

When it was my turn to speak, I got up and simply said, "Bobby was my friend. I loved him. I will miss him forever."

I looked out through the crowd. To my surprise, the face I picked out was Lee Marvin's. He looked me in the eye, smiled sadly, and nodded his head. Then I saw another face. It was Mr. Hailey, the owner of the memorabilia store who had given Bobby the money to live on his own. He smiled sadly, too. Later, my father told me that it had been Lee Marvin and Mr. Hailey who had donated the money for the funeral. Mr. Hailey's donation came when he delivered the baseball cards back to Bobby's mom.

When the service ended, people stood in line to view the body. It took over an hour for everyone to say their last goodbyes to Bobby. Many people cried. Liza completely broke down and fell to the ground. The posse had to help her to her feet. When it was my turn, I bent down and kissed him on the forehead and placed a photograph of a perfect wave in the casket.

It had been my job to choose the pallbearers and I had chosen Pineapple, Steiner, Chandler, Shaw, Richardson and myself. Pineapple, Steiner and Chandler had been easy choices but I chose Richardson and Shaw because they had been part of the Labor Day adventure Bobby and I had shared. It was the last time I remembered Bobby being, in the words of Jane Austin, "completely and incandescently happy."

We carried the casket from the chapel to the grave site across the street. Bagpipes played "Danny Boy" and there wasn't a dry eye in the cemetery. Even the funeral director cried.

Fortunately, this part of the funeral was short. After all the speeches in the chapel, people were worn out. A priest closed with, "God, our Father, Your power brings us birth. Your providence guides our lives and by Your command we return to dust. Into Your hands, we deliver the soul of Bobby Rowels. May he rest in peace."

People left the cemetery but I waited with Ellen, my dad, and Perry for the men to come and lower the casket. Two Mexican men arrived and took hold of the straps, slowly lowering Bobby into the damp ground. A cold, biting wind blew across the hills of Newport and I shivered. A backhoe arrived next and picked up dirt, dropping it into the grave. In minutes, the hole was filled. Bobby was gone, along with the magic of his spirit. It was finished. All that was left was a gaping hole in our hearts. It would take much more than a backhoe to fill that.

I did not write in my journal so I don't remember much else. Like everything in my life, it all became a blur, as if the sun had been blotted from the sky. But people said it was a grand affair, a parting from the world that would make an Irishman jealous.

77

I returned to school the next Monday. People were in shock, and all sorts of chaos had broken out over Bobby's death. White and his staff were fired and the athletic director's job also appeared to be on the chopping block. One thing that really drove people insane was the fact that White had settled for a tie with Fountain Hills instead of going for the win. Steiner had made the field goal but the tie gave Fountain Hills the championship.

"Can you believe White?" Steiner said. "Bobby gives his life for us and he goes for the tie."

I didn't care anymore. Instead of rehashing the events surrounding Bobby's death, I put my head down and concentrated on my school work. Freedom was less than two months away and I wanted to get the hell away from it all.

When I went to the library, I had a surprise waiting for me. It was Liza. She said she wanted to study with me to feel close to Bobby.

"Okay," I said. "But expect to work. I always made Bobby work."

She worked hard and as I had with Bobby, I helped her with her work. Together, in a strange way, we both felt closer to Bobby.

"Thank you so much," Liza said one day with a sad smile.

"No, thank you, and I want you to know something."

"What?"

"I know why Bobby loved you."

"Really? Why?"

"Because he could trust you with his heart."

"Really? Do you really think he loved me?"

"I know he did."

Liza started to cry. She completely broke down. I reached out and hugged her.

"I needed that so much, Scotty" she sobbed, "to hear it from you. Thank you so much."

She pulled back and wiped her eyes.

"Now I know why the two of you always disappeared to the library. It was because of you."

Three weeks before our Christmas break, Newport Beach buzzed with gossip. It wasn't about the Newport to Ensenada race or a debutante ball. It wasn't even "Irrelevant Week." The big event on everyone's radar was the trial for Old Man Elliot's millions.

The trial was really a preliminary competency hearing. It took place in the Santa Ana Courthouse over the course of one week. Ellen gave me the Chrysler and I sat in the courtroom every afternoon to support Perry. I held up my end of the bargain, never approaching Perry or giving any indication that I knew her. In a way, I felt like I didn't. I hadn't spent time with her in nearly two weeks. Perry had temporarily moved from the trailer park to a hotel for her own protection. Old Man Elliot didn't trust his other children.

The room was packed with reporters, lawyers, bailiffs and the curious, and they were spellbound by the sordid details of Elliot's life. Testimony from his progeny, ex-wives, and various call girls with whom he'd had relations painted a dark picture of reckless behavior spinning out of control. The defense countered with canceled checks for college tuition and pictures of the old man with his children in happier moments.

His seven estranged children sat with their seven lawyers on one side as a united front. Behind the lawyers and children sat the four ex-wives and their lawyers.

It was a murderer's row of sorts, an emotional and moral lynching by the mob called society because a man had chosen to live his life in a way that deviated from the expected norm of social behavior.

But the way Richard C. Elliot lived his life would probably not have mattered except that his children and ex-wives wanted something they felt entitled to, namely, the old man's money, and with that, his power.

Elliot, in contrast, sat with one lawyer. I didn't pay close attention to the trial because I was only there for Perry, and the only reason that I got a seat in the afternoon was that I got a special pass from one of Elliot's security guards, the same guard who had tackled Bobby in the diner. Still, it appeared to me that the old man was on the ropes. He was losing, and losing badly.

Finally, on Friday, Old Man Elliot took the stand in his own defense. At this point, I was certain that the judge was on the side of his seven estranged children and the ex-wives. In fact, the judge appeared to be only moments away from ordering the old man to a retirement home.

"What do you have to say for yourself, Mr. Elliot?" the judge asked.

"About what?"

"About the accusations."

"Which ones?"

"Well, let's start with the young girls."

"Which young girls?"

The judge reached into the pile of photographs. Since Perry had been the only girl seen with the old man these last few months, the pictures mostly involved her. It was contended that the old man was casting aside his family for her. As a result, the judge pulled one of Perry and her dad. They were hugging at the bow of the old man's yacht.

"This one," the judge said.

"Oh, her?"

"Yes, her."

"I'm just wondering. When did it become a crime to hug your own daughter?"

The courtroom fell silent. You could have heard a pin drop. I looked over at his children with their lawyers who all broke into huge grins. They assumed that the old man had finally cracked and his millions would soon be theirs. But the trap was about to slam shut.

"No, sir," the judge said. "I think you're confused."

"About what?"

"About who your children are."

"I'm not confused. Dennis," the old man turned to his lawyer, "give the judge a copy of Perry's birth certificate and the paternity test."

The courtroom went berserk. Reporters leaped from their seats and rushed out of the room. Ex-wives screamed and shook their fists at the old man. The seven lawyers leaped to their feet shouting objections like a Greek chorus. But it was his seven estranged children who really caught my attention. They cried like four-year-olds who just had their toys snatched away. I stole a look at Old Man Elliot. He sat quietly watching the whole scene unfold. I wasn't quite sure but I think I detected something of a smile on his lips, like the cat who swallowed the family canary.

78

In the aftermath, a bailiff removed Elliot from the stand and led him out of the courtroom. People, still scrambling, ran into each other as the judge pounded his gavel on his bench.

"Order! Order!" the judge shouted.

Once Elliot disappeared through a side door, the courtroom did quiet down. I watched the family huddling together like a football team trying to figure out if they had a Hail Mary in their playbook.

A few moments later, I felt someone touch me on the shoulder. I turned and saw it was Perry.

"Come with me."

I followed her and we exited through the same side door as Elliot. There was a hallway with several offices off to each side. Perry turned to me and kissed me on the lips.

"I've missed you so much."

She took my hand and led me into an office. I found myself standing in front of the old man and his lawyer. Richard C. Elliot, with a full head of silver hair, handsome face and tanned complexion, looked at me for a long moment.

"Hello, Scotty," he said. "I'm sorry about your friend."

"Thank you, sir."

"I'd like you to come to the house for dinner tonight."

"Tonight?"

"Yes, around six. Will that work?"

"I guess."

The old man nodded.

"Good. See you at six."

Old Man Elliot turned to his lawyer and they began talking. Perry grabbed my hand and led me from the room. When we got into the hall, she turned and hugged me.

"It's almost over. Thank you for being there for me."

"When can I see you?"

"Soon."

"Will you be there for dinner tonight?"

"No. My father wants to meet with you alone."

"Why?'

"He wants to ask you something."

I had just seen the old man set up his whole family. I wondered if I was next.

We walked hand in hand to the end of the hall and we stopped at the door.

"Don't worry," she said. "Everything's going to be all right now. I'll see you tonight after you talk to my dad."

She kissed me lightly on the lips, smiled and opened the door. Outside were about ten reporters. When they saw it was Perry they all rushed toward her.

"It's her! It's the Elliot girl!" They cackled like a pack of hyenas.

I stepped through the door and Perry quickly closed it behind me as flash bulbs exploded and reporters surrounded me.

"Who are you?" someone asked.

"I'm nobody."

I turned and walked away from the hyenas as fast as I could. But one reporter decided to follow me. I exited the courthouse and she followed me across the lawn and out into the parking lot. Finally, she approached me as I was getting into the Chrysler.

"Excuse me, sir. But how do you know the Elliot girl?"

"Who?"

"The Elliot girl. If your story is good we can pay you."

"I don't know what you're talking about."

I closed the door and started the car. Through the rearview mirror I saw the reporter writing down my license plate number.

79

I wasn't sure why Elliot had invited me to his house for dinner. Perry said he wanted to ask me something. It seemed to me now that the court case was concluded the old man wanted to settle something else. It had to do with Perry and me, and he wanted to do it quickly.

The house stood at the very end of the peninsula, an area with some of largest bay front lots, some even larger than the ones in Bay Shores.

Elliot's property was the largest by far. Through the years he had bought the houses on either side of his, which he tore down. On one side he built a magnificent rock pool and lovely gardens. On the other side he built a giant garage for his many cars. He also built four small cottages for guests. The cottages sat right on the bay, each with its own patio and yard.

I pulled up in front. The buildings were all done in the craftsman style with dark wood shingles and it looked as though the brilliant white trim on the houses had been painted yesterday. The striking contrast between the white trim and dark shingles created a stunning house, massive and substantial.

I parked the Chrysler on the street. I wasn't about to park in Elliot's driveway, which was a mosaic of stone bordered by incredible landscaping of ferns and flowers. The Chrysler leaked oil like a punctured water balloon, and his stone driveway would be ruined.

I got out of the car and made my way self-consciously to the front door. Even in my nicest jeans and best Hawaiian shirt, I felt underdressed. I rang the bell and waited. The door opened slowly and an ancient Filipino man peered out at me.

"Are you Mr. Curtis?"

"Yes, sir."

"Follow me."

I stepped into the foyer. The ceilings were very high with hand-hewn dark beams and moldings. The floors were also dark, made of distressed hickory and the beams, trim, and floors contrasted dramatically with the walls that were covered in light-colored grass wallpaper.

I followed the diminutive man through the foyer, stepping into a room that reminded me of a basketball court, longer than it was wide. Again, the ceilings were crossed by heavy dark beams and against one wall stood a massive stone fireplace. Three sitting areas with elegant Koa wood furniture gave the room a comfortable feel despite its size.

But the room was dominated by the view. There were fifteen glass doors, all open, which looked out across the bay to the picturesque boulders and cliffs of China Cove. To the left, a huge sailboat rested majestically in its berth. With its two wooden masts, it was a boat right out of a wayfarer's dream.

"How do you like my boat?"

As if on cue, something I had completely missed stole my attention. In the far corner of the room was a large wrought iron cage that contained a gray parrot. The bird began singing at the top of his lungs.

"Yo, ho, yo, ho, and a pirate's life for me."

Elliot stood at the door, also dressed casually in shorts and a Hawaiian shirt. He smiled.

"Shut up, Belfry."

The parrot was immediately silent as the industrialist strode confidently across the room.

"You'll have to excuse my parrot. He's an African Gray. I bought him because they're considered the most vocal of all parrots. One of the few times I wish I hadn't gotten my money's worth. He picks up a word and it sets him off. I'll show you." The old man turned to his parrot. "Belfry, this is Scotty."

"But I love him, Daddy," the parrot screamed. "I love him."

"My daughter and I had a conversation about you in this room. Now you can see what I'm up against. Even my parrot is on your side. Would you like a drink? I'm told you like Peppermint Schnapps."

"No, thank you. A Coke would be fine," I said hesitantly.

The whole situation made me nervous. I didn't know if this meeting was going to be some sort of a test or maybe another trial like I witnessed today. My father once told me that anytime you find yourself around massive power, money or weight, it's always a little dangerous. Based on what I had witnessed at the trial, Richard C. Elliot could be a very dangerous man indeed.

Elliot turned to his Filipino man who had been standing quietly in the corner.

"Rodolfo, a scotch and a Coke." He turned to me. "Over ice?"

"Sure."

"Over ice, please," he told Rodolfo. "And we'll take them out on the terrace."

The old man turned back to me.

"Come on, I want to show you my new boat."

We walked through one of the glass doors. A soft Santa Ana breeze had kicked up, making the evening unseasonably warm. It felt pleasant as we stood on the terrace admiring the boat.

"Isn't she something? She was built in 1923 by Fife and Son Farlie in Scotland. Teak planks over English Oak frames and bronze rivets. She's a hundred feet if she's an inch and seventy-three tons. I've renamed her The Periwinkle."

"She's something," I said, thinking of Perry.

Rodolfo arrived with our drinks on a simple silver tray. We took our drinks. Then the old man looked at me.

"You know I'm dying?"

"Yes, sir. Perry told me you had ALS."

"The doctors said I might have six months, maybe a year. But what do they know?"

The old man was quiet a long moment as he looked out toward his boat, and I supposed he was contemplating the meaning of his last words.

"Let's eat," was all he said.

Dinner was served on a stone patio near the pool. Plumeria trees with large pink and white blooms were everywhere, their fragrance engulfing us like a tropical, aromatic quilt. There were also towering ferns and other exotic-looking plants and flowers. A stream ran from the top of a rock formation and made its way down until it poured into the pool like a waterfall. Elliot's yard reminded me of Kauai, even more than the path to Steiner's boathouse.

"So tell me about your friend," Elliot said.

"Bobby?"

"Yes, Bobby."

"He was my best friend."

"It's hard to lose a friend. I know. At my age, I've lost a few."

"Yeah."

"Why was he your best friend?"

"There's a thousand reasons."

"Give me a couple."

I told him about Bobby's wave at the Point and how I had been too afraid to join him.

"Bobby never brought it up to make me feel bad nor did he ever brag about his accomplishment. He just respected my decision."

I also told him about Bobby losing his dad in a violent way, how it led to his search for meaning and eventually finding something in Western movies.

"I can tell you loved him."

"Yes, sir. I did. Bobby was special."

Rudolfo unobtrusively served dinner. Everything appeared as if by magic; the bread, the Caesar salad, the mushroom risotto and Key Lime pie for dessert. Our water glasses were filled unnoticed. In a word, it was elegant. What's more, I can't remember one request Elliot made to the small, quiet man.

It made me think of my dad, how this graceful meal contrasted with my dad's deli sandwich from the Tradewinds Liquor Store washed down with a case of beer. I wondered if maybe Hemingway was wrong and Fitzgerald had it right: the rich are actually different.

"So what are your plans?" Elliot asked.

"Plans?"

"You know, college, career, future?"

"I don't have any."

He looked surprised.

"My daughter said you want to be a writer, maybe go to Stanford?"

I shrugged.

"I haven't written a word since Bobby died, and I don't really care about college anymore. About the only thing I can focus on is graduating next month."

"Then what will you do?"

"I don't know. Bobby and I had plans to travel. He thought we could drive the Chrysler down to Costa Rica. I'm thinking I might go anyway."

"By yourself?"

"Not really. I sorta like to think that Bobby will be with me."

Throughout the night I noticed the old man's hands twitching - the ravages of ALS. I wondered why a dying man, a man who could have anything he wanted, would choose to spend an evening with me. After all, time was his most precious commodity.

Elliot was quiet a long moment staring into his wine glass. Then he turned and looked at me closely.

"How would you like to sail to Hawaii?"

"Hawaii?"

"Yeah, it's one dream I've never fulfilled. I want to do it while I still have my sea legs."

I was surprised for a moment. and then I realized this was the reason he had invited me to dinner. The old man wanted something from me and it involved his daughter.

"Is Perry going?"

The old man paused.

"I don't know. It depends."

"On what?"

"On you."

"Me?"

"My daughter won't come unless you come. She thinks you need her."

I wasn't sure how to respond so I said nothing. Perry had been so wrapped up in the trial that I hadn't really felt connected to her. I loved her. There was no doubt about that. But I didn't feel connected to anything. It was like I lived in the middle of the Rolling Stone's song "Paint It Black", the color had been drained from my life and the world felt like a big black hole. The only thing keeping me from completely falling through the cracks was the idea of getting out of high school. After that, I felt there were no guarantees about anything. All bets were off.

"You know," Elliot said. "In contemplating the time I have left, I've decided I want to do something that captures the spirit and beauty of this world. But I also realize that if I have no one to share it with, the experience will be empty. I want to share it with my daughter."

It struck me like a thunderbolt. This man could have anything he wanted. His money and power had controlled the world around him for most of his life. But his money and power had not bought Perry. She had given the old man authentic, genuine love for one reason, because she had grown to love him. And the old man, now nearing the end of his days, knew that this was possibly the most important gift he had ever been given, the love of his daughter. But love can be a tricky thing. It is the most powerful force on the planet. Our greatest achievements in art and science are in no small measure connected to its power. Yet it is as fragile and fleeting as the memory of a summer's day that dissipates the very moment we attempt to grasp it.

I looked into the eyes of the dying man and knew he would have said yes if I had asked for a million dollars.

"Thank you, sir. I am honored by your offer. But I can't give you an answer now. The trouble is I don't know what I want. But I will try to see that Perry goes with you even if I don't come."

The old man smiled.

"Thank you, Scotty. I deeply appreciate your understanding."

80

Since Bobby's death my dad had not really come home. He was spending all his time with Ellen. In fact, he never seemed to leave her side and I admired him for it. He had risen to the occasion and pulled himself together because she needed him. Ellen and my father were two very damaged people who seemed to be healing each other.

But tonight I wished he was home. I came home and found walking into an empty trailer with the lights out incredibly depressing. Through the darkness, I could see piles of dishes and half-eaten food stacked on the counter. The table with the broken leg was covered with newspapers and mail. Most of the letters were for Bobby, offering hope and opportunity from the various colleges he would never attend. The letters would eventually be thrown in the trash, like so many of the hopes, dreams and promises people hold dear.

A letter waited for me as well. It was from Stanford, an application to attend the university. I looked at it for a long moment. Then I threw it onto the pile of Bobby's letters. Like Bobby's dreams and hopes, mine were destined for the trash heap as well.

I sat on our broken-down couch realizing how dark I felt. What Churchill referred to as "his little black dog," the name he had given to his bouts of depression, had lifted his leg and peed all over me. The strength I had summoned for those who loved Bobby was spent. I felt frozen, numb, and scared, the kind of fear that comes from knowing how alone we are in this troubled world. My world was in tatters. Bobby was dead, and Perry, because of her father, was slipping away too. It would only be a matter of time, and I had no idea where I was going or where I would end up. Like the trailer, everywhere I looked there was nothing but a dark, ugly mess.

I wasn't sure how long I had been sitting there in the dark. It could have been an hour or it could have been ten minutes. My mind was drifting, scattered like the leaves in a cold autumn wind. A knock on the door brought me back to the present.

"Scotty?" Perry called.

I didn't answer. I knew she was anxious to find out how it went with her father. But I couldn't move. I couldn't see or talk to her.

"Scotty, I know you're there."

Still, I didn't answer.

"Scotty, I love you. We don't have to go to Hawaii. We can go to Costa Rica in the Chrysler. Please, Scotty, don't shut me out."

But I felt that she had let me be blindsided by her father with his offer to sail to Hawaii. How could I deny the man his dying wish? Perry should have warned me of his intentions and I also felt the old man had spun it into a request that I release Perry to go. I couldn't tell her she was going to Hawaii and I wasn't. Not tonight.

Perry began crying and part of me wanted to hug her, but I realized it wouldn't solve anything. I was a drowning man, drowning in my despair and grief. I didn't want to take her down with me. It was a journey I had to take alone.

"Just go away!" I screamed. Where the words had come from or why I reacted that way, I will never know. Again, it was Homer's "lyssa", the wolf's rage.

There was a long silence followed by a whimper and I heard the sound of her footsteps walking away. It was the loneliest sound I have ever heard. My wish had been granted. I was now completely alone to wallow in my pain. Be careful what you wish for.

81

Saturday arrived. I still hadn't moved from the couch. It wasn't a day that inspired much movement. I hadn't eaten, either. The only time I was motivated to move was to visit the bathroom. I was a goner but not that gone.

A storm was blowing hard with pouring rain. The sound of the deluge pounding on the metal roof drowned out everything except my pain.

At around ten a.m. the phone started ringing. I let it ring. But whoever it was kept calling. Somebody was trying to reach us and they weren't giving up. After half an hour I finally answered, thinking it was Perry.

"Scotty, hi."

"Oh, hi, Mom."

"How are you?"

"All right, I guess."

"Listen, the reason I'm calling is that we just saw your picture in the paper with the Elliot girl. It was on the cover of the *L.A. Times*. You were standing with her in the courtroom."

"What do you want, Mom?"

"Well, we didn't know you knew the Elliot girl."

"So?"

"So Dick and I would like to invite you both to the Club for dinner and..."

I hung up the phone and unplugged it.

For the rest of the day, I sat on the couch. After a while I turned on the television. To my surprise, John Ford's *The Searchers* was playing, and Ethan's journey took on a whole new meaning. When the door closes at the end of the movie, I realized Ethan is destined to be alone forever. I felt his sadness in such a profound way that I curled into a ball for hours while the storm outside raged. Its fury was matched only by the turmoil I was feeling, angry, ugly, and unrelenting. I missed Bobby and I felt Perry slipping away, too.

Night arrived and with it the loss of electricity. The winds must have blown some wires down and West Newport went black. I sat in the darkness staring at nothing, still unable to move or eat. Eventually, I drifted off to sleep.

82

Bang, bang, bang.

Someone was pounding hard on the front door. Startled, I looked around trying to get my bearings. It was early Sunday morning and for a second night, I had slept on the couch in my clothes. I just couldn't enter the room that Bobby and I had shared. I lay there for a long moment as the pounding continued.

"Open the goddamn door, Scotty."

It was Pineapple, and his pounding grew even harder, almost violent. He sounded pissed.

"Either open the fucking door or I'm going to kick it in!"

His words startled me. I had no doubt that he was going to break the door down. I rose slowly and walked to the front door and unlocked it. Pineapple ripped it open. He was indeed angry. I looked past Pineapple and saw Perry standing on the drive. She looked as if she had been crying for days.

"What the hell is going on?'

"Nothing."

"You didn't show up for work!"

"I don't feel like working."

Pineapple's eyes narrowed.

"You're coming to work!"

He grabbed me and dragged me into the bathroom. He began ripping the clothes from my body.

"You think you're the only one who's ever lost something?"

My shirt came off and was thrown into the giant pile of dirty clothes in the hall.

"It hurts!" Pineapple yelled. "It fucking hurts. I know how it hurts. But you don't give up. You never give up."

I felt like a zombie, a numb, sleep walking zombie. Pineapple yanked me out of my pants. I stood naked in front of my angry friend. He turned the water on in the shower and literally threw me in. It was cold and the water shocked me.

"Shit!" I yelled.

"That's it," Pineapple yelled. "Get mad. Get pissed. That's the first step back."

I quickly turned on the hot water. For the first time in days something felt really good.

"This place is a pigsty," Pineapple said as he searched the bathroom for a razor. He finally found one and handed it to me. I took it and started shaving, wondering if Bobby had used this razor too.

"I don't want to go to work!" I yelled.

"You're coming and that's final. I'm not washing all your fucking dishes again."

He left the bathroom and I heard him enter the bedroom. The room I had shared with Bobby.

"This place stinks!" he yelled.

Pineapple began slamming drawers and throwing stuff around. Suddenly, there was a crashing noise and I knew the closet door had fallen off its hinges.

"Shit!" Pineapple yelled.

The absurdity of it made me laugh. Not a soft, easy laugh, but a hard belly laugh, the kind of laugh that brings tears to your eyes.

Pineapple walked back into the bathroom to find me laughing hysterically. He eyed me suspiciously.

"What's so funny?"

This made me laugh even harder.

"You're coming to work," he said and he threw down some clothes. "Don't think you're getting out of it."

83

There was no doubt about it, Pete was a smart businessman. He had, some time ago, purchased and installed a generator. He knew that when the power went down he needed to keep the lights on and the kitchen open. During the storm, Cappy's diner had been the only game in town. Consequently, they had been packed all night, and the mountain of dishes waiting for me was gigantic.

I set to work, and to my surprise, as I worked my way through the pile, I began to feel a little better. Not good, but better.

Pineapple kept saying things to me all morning as if to remind me of what I was about to give up.

"That girl loves you. Why are you going to screw everything up? Bobby wouldn't have wanted that.

"Where's Pinaply?"

"She's with Perry helping your sorry ass out."

"What do you mean?"

"You'll find out. And when you do you'd better say thank you and mean it, or I'm going to spank your sorry ass."

At around ten Pineapple presented me with some breakfast. My favorite, a BLT with avocado. It was the breakfast my grandmother had always made for me. Pineapple knew it was my comfort food.

"I'm not hungry."

"I made it and you're going to eat it."

I sat at the card table and ate. It was my first meal in thirty-six hours and the food also helped me feel a little better.

As the morning rush began to wind down, Pineapple came over and put his arm around me.

"A lot of people love you, Scotty, and sometimes it's important to let people love you. Not just for you but for them."

When I got home I was floored. The trailer was spotless. Perry and Pinaply had cleaned it from top to bottom. What's more they had hauled the huge pile of laundry to the laundromat behind the Out Post Liquor Store. My clothes were in neat piles on the floor of my room and my Hawaiian shirts were hung in the closet. Bobby's were too, and the door was back on its hinges.

I walked over to Perry's trailer and knocked on the door. She answered dressed in an old sweatshirt and jeans. I could tell she had worked hard.

"Thank you, and I'm sorry."

Perry began to cry. I reached out and hugged her. It felt good to hold her in my arms.

"I love you, Perry. But I don't know if I can go to Hawaii with you and your dad."

"Then I'm not going either."

"You have to go. Your dad is dying and if I stopped you from going, you would never forgive me."

"Then come."

"I have to think about it. I need to do something to say goodbye to Bobby. I just don't know what that is yet."

"I'm afraid, Scotty. I'm afraid if I go, then we'll drift apart."

"Let's not talk about it tonight. Let's just be together. We'll figure it out later."

Perry sucked back her tears and managed a small perfect, imperfect smile.

"Okay, but you better talk to me. Never tell me to go away again. Pacts?"

"Pacts," I agreed.

84

Perry and I worked out an agreement. We wouldn't talk about Hawaii until after Christmas. We would just be together as much as we could. But I quietly gathered some maps of Mexico. The idea of fulfilling Bobby's dream of driving to Costa Rica in the Chrysler was taking on power. The adventure would be a tribute to my friend, a way for me to honor his memory in my own private way.

One evening while Perry and I were making dinner in her trailer, the phone rang. Perry answered it. She quickly turned to me.

"It's my dad. He wants to talk to you," she handed me the phone. "Hello."

"Hi, Scotty. I was wondering if you could help me with something?"

"What's that?"

"I've decided to put the Periwinkle in the boat parade and I need help decorating it. I thought you might like to earn some extra money for Christmas."

I wasn't sure what to say.

"It would really help me out," he continued. "I want to do this myself and for obvious reasons I can't do it alone."

I paused for a moment, wondering what this meant. But then he said the word. The word that immediately disarms the person to which it's directed. It's a simple word, but possibly one of the most powerful words in our human language.

"Please, Scotty."

"Sure... all right."

"What time do you get out of school?"

"One-thirty."

"Good. Be here at two, and we'll get our hands dirty."

When I hung up Perry looked at me expectantly.

"Your dad wants me to help him decorate his boat for the parade."

"That's good," was all she said.

85

The next day I arrived at Elliot's home to decorate his boat for the 68th Annual Newport Boat Parade, Newport's Christmas card to the world.

The Newport Boat Parade began in 1907 when a crazy old Italian named John Scarpa decorated his gondola with some Christmas lights, probably to attract business. The idea caught on and by the seventies some eighty boats were in the parade. Rumor had it that some owners spent upwards of fifty thousand dollars on their decorations. Even in boat parades, everything is relative.

The parade itself is one of the biggest social events in Newport. Parties rage at almost every house along the bay, and restaurants, clubs, and even the American Legion clubhouse flood with people eager to get a glimpse of the lights. Generations of people who have grown up in or near Newport mark this event as the traditional beginning of their Christmas holidays. Move over Pasadena. You may have the Rose Parade but Newport has its Boat Parade.

"It's a big boat," I observed. "We're going to need a lot of lights. Probably even an electrician."

"Nonsense," Elliot replied. "My father was an electrician. He taught me everything he knew. Let's go get some lights. You drive. I've heard so much about this Chrysler, I might as well ride in it once."

We drove the Chrysler down to the ferry at the Fun Zone and crossed to Balboa Island. From there we made our way across the island and onto Pacific Coast Highway to Dover. In a few short minutes we arrived in Westcliff. The ferry does have its advantages.

The old man knew the owner of the hardware store and I knew his son. They both helped us to load the car with every light they had. We ordered dozens of boxes more, which they assured us would arrive the following day.

"Deliver them to my house, please," Elliot said as he paid. The owner was falling all over himself to be accommodating.

We took the same route home through the business district of Balboa Island. In the middle of the block, the old man turned to me.

"You know I own this?"

"What? Balboa Island?"

He laughed.

"Not the whole island. Just these commercial blocks. I built them in the forties with oil money."

Then the old man told me how he got started. When he was nineteen he bought an oil lease in Long Beach and drilled a well. He had worked two jobs for a year to get the seed money.

"It helps to hit it big on your first well," he said. "And that well is still producing. Elliot number one. I sometimes drive over to Long Beach just to see her. To remind me of how it all started."

He talked more about his adventures as we crossed on the ferry. How he had once bought a chain of muffler shops and tripled his money in less than a year. Then he suddenly stopped and looked at me.

"Do you really think this jalopy can make it to Costa Rica?"

"I don't know. But whatever happens, it will be part of the journey."

Elliot laughed.

"That's good. That's really good."

I had to smile. The old man's words and expression reminded me so much of Perry. I couldn't believe that his other children never figured out that Perry was his daughter. I guess people believe only what they want to believe, even if the truth is staring them right in the face.

For the next four days I worked at Elliot's side stringing the lights as he barked orders.

"Don't you think we need another strand there?" "No, make it higher, Scotty." "That's good."

I climbed the masts and I climbed ladders. I ran to the hardware store and electrical supply store. It was turning into an enormous project. Elliot was acting like Michelangelo designing Vatican Square.

"It has to be just right, Scotty. This is important."

On two of the days I was only able to work until six because I had to go to work at the diner. I didn't want Pineapple coming down on me again.

Elliot smiled when I told him.

"How does it feel to be working two jobs?"

"It feels fine."

"I want you to take next week off from the diner."

"Why?"

"I need someone to help crew her."

"But I don't know anything about boats."

"You'll learn. It's not rocket science. All you need is intuition and anticipation, and trust me, those will serve you much better in life than rocket science."

On Friday I worked until eleven running extension cords and lights over the 100-foot boat. The extension cords had to be hidden and taped down with brown gaffers tape to match the wood deck. It was a big boat and the old man kept ordering more lights which meant more extension chords.

"No, the colored lights aren't right," Elliot commanded. "Replace them with white ones."

On Saturday, we finally had some help. Perry and Rodolfo were enlisted to string the lights on the railing. It was after dark when we were finished.

"Okay, let's light her up," Elliot said. "Scotty, you do the honors."

I flipped the switch Elliot had shown me how to install and the entire boat lit up like a Christmas tree. It was beautiful. A thousand points of lights twinkling like the stars in heaven, like the promise of

Christmas itself. To paraphrase Cary Grant and Katherine Hepburn in the movie *The Philadelphia Story*, the 100-foot schooner was simply "yar."

We walked back to the house and stood on the terrace admiring our work, Perry, Rodolfo, Elliot and I. And a smile the size of the Grand Canyon spread across the old man's face.

"Yes," he said. "It will do. Good job, Scotty."

86

Being a member of the Periwinkle crew was a turning point of sorts. I wasn't sure why the old man had asked me to join his crew. Maybe he knew something I didn't. After all, he did have a lifetime of experience.

Elliot hired a man named Dennis Gaily to skipper the boat. He was older, too, though not as old as Elliot, and had the appearance and demeanor of the original "salty dog", with a thick beard, an unruly mane of gray hair and a barrel chest that would make a pirate dream of rum. Gaily looked like he came straight from central casting. All he needed to complete the image of Long John Silver was Belfry on his shoulder and a peg leg.

But Dennis Gaily was the real deal. He had sailed the world. Hawaii, the Galapagos, the Caribbean, the Mediterranean, the South Seas, the Indian Ocean. He had sailed everywhere, crossing the equator to Tahiti, New Zealand and Australia several times. From pirates to skinny dippers, Dennis Gaily had seen it all.

"So, kid," he barked. "Are you willing to learn?"

"Yes, sir."

"First lesson. It's not the destination but the journey that separates sailors from mere mortals. We can teach you about knots and navigation. But that's just craft. That's not sailing. True sailing is in your heart and each man must find it for himself. When you find it, then you'll be a sailor."

He took a good long look at me.

"Second lesson. A good boat is like a good woman. Treat her with respect and she'll take you places you never dreamed possible."

There was also another deckhand. She was an older woman named Alice, who definitely knew her way around a boat. I never heard Dennis Gaily bark an order to her because Alice had already completed the task. Her power of anticipation was uncanny. What's more, she was taking time to teach me while completing her tasks.

My first night of work I followed Alice around the boat as she patiently taught me the basics of what I needed to know. We ran the Periwinkle slowly over the course we were to follow in the boat parade, carefully checking various depths. Starting at Bay Island, we headed down the Balboa Peninsula past the Pavilion, past Pirate's Cove and Channel Reef, past Harbor Island, Linda Isle and Bay Shores, past the Balboa Islands, both little and big, up the channel past the Newport-Balboa Club and bay front restaurants like the Stuffed Shirt, Ancient Mariner, and Rusty Pelican. Then back down the channel on the nord (north) side of Lido Island, and then back up the soud (south) side, and finally back down the peninsula to Bay Island. When we returned to our starting point, Dennis Gaily shouted at us from the helm.

"Sailing is the voyage into the unknown, only to find yourself back where you started."

"Aye, Captain!" Alice shouted and then she pointed at me.

"Aye, Captain!" I shouted.

We all laughed. It struck me that I was among people who were doing what they did because they loved it. It was their bliss and sailing had become the map by which they navigated their lives. I looked at Alice.

"Thank you for teaching me."

She smiled.

"You still have a lot to learn, kid. But don't let that deter you. We all do. You never stop learning. But you're not a sailor yet. You'll never be a sailor until you've been to sea under full sail."

87

Richard C. Elliot invited about forty guests the first night of the boat parade. There was a string quartet, a caterer serving everything from lobster to steak, and a bartender dressed in a tuxedo mixing any drink desired.

For me, the event was a job, but for Perry it was like a coming out party, and I noticed she stayed close to her father all night. A few times she sought me out. But I was on the bow making sure we didn't run over any drunks in rowboats. After a quick kiss and an affirmation of her love she returned to her father's side. Still, we ended the evening walking hand-in-hand to my car.

The next night was the same setup, only different faces. I saw Joey Bishop and the actor Lorne Green. There were other famous faces: Dean Martin and Sammy Davis, Jr. Seeing Dean Martin reminded me of the night Bobby and I watched *Rio Bravo* and how much Dean Martin's character made Bobby think of my dad.

This crowd differed from the first night. Where the first crowd had been doctors and lawyers, and politicians, these people were all from Hollywood and it seemed that the person who had invited the two groups could not have been the same person. Yet it was Elliot's boat and I knew the crowd had been hand-picked. It was, in a sense, a confirmation of the size of the life he had lived.

Perry was dressed in an expensive gown and she had on large diamond earrings that I'd never seen before, and never in my wildest dreams could have afforded. She looked every part the millionaire's favorite daughter. It was something I wasn't quite used to.

I wondered to myself what I was doing. A few short years ago I had been a kid standing on these beaches and docks watching the magnificent boats pass by. I remembered holding my mother's hand and her whispering to me what a thrill it would be to sail on one of these yachts. But it seemed so out of reach, so far away from who we were, that it was like wishing to fly to the moon. Now here I was, as if flying to the moon was possible, in love with a girl whose father owned one of these yachts. But why? I was only here because Perry had chosen to love me. I didn't really belong. I was just a beach rat who lived in a trailer park while Perry, with her beauty and poise, appeared to have lived this way all her life.

But like the night before, she sought me out. She was escorted home by her father's hired help, back to the trailer park from which we had come. I wondered if that was why Perry had chosen to live in the trailer park. To remind her of who she was, just an orphan from Louisiana.

The third night the crowd was different still. The men were dressed in three-piece suits and there was tension in the air. As if people were constantly sizing each other up and making judgments about who mattered. Various men approached Elliot, slowly, almost as if stalking a feral cat. But when they stood before him, their demeanor showed the kind of respect you would offer a cardinal or a pope. I expected one of them to drop to their knees and kiss Elliot's ring.

I didn't know who they were, but I finally understood when two men in their early thirties walked to the bow and I overheard their conversation. They were both dressed in dark, Brooks Brothers three-piece suits.

"Do you think the stock will hold up?" one man asked the other.

"Listen, he's already stepped down. The stock sold off, and then they reported earnings. Every person who shorted the stock got their heads handed to them. Shorting Elliot Enterprises is a death wish. When he dies, the stock will probably double."

"Yeah, especially with that daughter of his. You take one look at her and you know she's smart."

"Exactly, and you know she's getting everything. He's already made that clear."

"Too bad I'm married."

"Me, too."

They both laughed. Then they noticed me but pretended not to.

"Let's get a drink," one said.

"Good idea, we can drink to beautiful, rich women," said the other as they walked away.

As I watched the two suits disappear into the group, I thought, what a couple of dicks. Then I looked into the crowd and saw Perry and her father moving through the large group, taking time to talk to each person. It was like watching Fitzgerald's Gatsby working the room, as if there was some deeper purpose guiding their intentions. I realized these people were money and powerbrokers and Perry's father was teaching her the game. I also saw something else. Perry, as always, looked beautiful and I could see how proud her father was of her. This was the world she was to inherit, maybe not by choice, but because these were the cards she was being dealt, and I knew her circumstances came with enormous responsibilities.

While riding home in the Chrysler, I told Perry about the two guys along the bow who were commenting on her father's stock.

"I hated those people tonight," she said. "They were all sizing me up, wondering if they could trick me out of our money."

"Our money?"

Perry looked at me and smiled her perfect, imperfect smile.

"You're in this too, buddy. Don't think you're getting out of it."

I smiled. People who thought they could trick Perry out of anything were simply misinformed. Perry was too smart. She could also be tough, as tough as a tiger in a barroom brawl. Just like her dad.

88

The fourth night arrived and I assumed it was going to be more of the same, another group, another game. Then I spotted Lee Marvin in the crowd, and Elliot spent most of the evening talking to him without Perry.

At one point the actor left the party and walked to the bow. He stood a few feet from me looking at the people along the shore who were waving and yelling their appreciation of the boat.

"Excuse me, Mr. Marvin. But I just want to thank you for helping Bobby's mom with the funeral."

He looked down at me for a long moment. At first he seemed confused, then a smile spread across his face. His smile was like the sun as it appears from behind a cloud.

"I know you," he said.

"Yeah, Bobby Rowels and I swam to your boat last summer for a drink."

"Yeah, that's it. You're Scotty."

"Yeah."

He laughed. Then he grew serious.

"Your friend was a helluva football player. I was there the night he died."

We both grew quiet remembering the night as if a moment of silence was required. Then Elliot appeared.

"I see you've met Scotty," Elliot said.

Lee Marvin smiled.

"Scotty and I are old friends."

Elliot looked surprised. "Scotty, you're full of surprises."

"Yeah," Marvin answered. "He and Bobby Rowels reminded me of what friendship means. Do you remember what I told you?"

"Yes, sir. You said that a true friend will always tell you the truth."

"That's right. So you know that I know what you've lost."

Our conversation was interrupted by an attractive woman with sandy blonde hair and a beautiful complexion.

"Lee," she called. "We have a little disagreement about the Araner. Whether or not it was schooner, too. We need your help to settle it."

"All right," the actor said. "I'll be right there."

"Wasn't that Jack Ford's boat?" Elliot asked.

"Yeah, but it was a ketch, not a schooner. He used it in *Donovan's Reef.*"

Lee Marvin extended his hand to me and I shook it.

"Good luck, Scotty, and I'm truly sorry for your loss."

"Thank you," I said.

Elliot and Lee Marvin turned to walk away. After a few steps the actor stopped and turned back to me. He had that smile on his face.

"Hey, Scotty."

"Yes, sir?"

"If you ever need to borrow a towel, I have one you can use."

I smiled. "Thanks, Mr. Marvin."

"Don't mention it, kid."

The two men walked away, and I returned to my job of watching out for drunks. We were passing the north side of Lido Island. At every other house, partiers celebrated the start of the holiday season and the docks were filled with kids who yelled and whistled their admiration of our boat and decorations. I thought of Bobby. He would have loved seeing Lee Marvin again. Life was moving on, as it always does, as certain as the turning of the earth.

When we docked, the guests said their goodbyes to Elliot. Perry had returned to her father's side. I saw them say goodbye to Lee Marvin and the woman he was with. The woman gave both Elliot and Perry a goodbye hug. I returned my attention to securing the boat.

A little later, Perry sought me out. I was in the bathroom wiping down the sink and toilet with a rag and some Clorox.

"My dad wants to talk to you. I'll be up at the house waiting."

Perry looked beautiful. She had on a Chanel dress that I couldn't have afforded on six months salary from the diner.

"I love you," she looked into my eyes.

"Even when I'm cleaning toilets?"

She smiled. "Especially when you're cleaning toilets."

She kissed me on the cheek and was gone.

I searched the boat for the old man. The caterer and musicians had left. Alice and Dennis Gaily were gone, too. I was always the last to leave because I had to mop down the deck.

When I found the boat deserted, I looked on the dock and saw the old man standing at the very end peering into the sky. It was a clear winter's night and the moon hung like a half-eaten cookie over the cliffs of China Cove.

I climbed down the two-step boat stair and made my way to the end of the dock. He was still staring at the moon when I arrived to his side. Elliot must have sensed my presence, for without turning to me, he said, "Scotty, it sure is a beautiful world."

I looked up at the moon.

"Yes, sir. It is."

"Do you know if that moon is waxing or waning?"

"It looks to be waning."

He turned to me with a smile.

"So it is...as it should...like life itself. Well, I've said my goodbyes. The public life of Richard Elliot is a finished book."

I realized what these past few nights had been about, the old man's final farewells to some of the people he had shared his life with. At least, the ones who mattered most.

"Tomorrow is the last night of the boat parade. I'd like it to be just for us."

"Okay."

"And I'd like you to do something for me."

"What's that?"

"I'd like you to invite your dad and Bobby's mom to join us."

"All right."

The old man extended his hand for me to shake. I took it and noticed his grip was weak.

"Good," the tycoon said, "are you coming up to the house now?"

"I still have the deck to mop."

"Okay. Thank you, Scotty."

He turned to make his way back to the mansion.

89

Ellen and my dad joined Perry, the old man and me for the final boat parade voyage of the Periwinkle. Also on the ship were Rodolfo, his plump wife, their six kids and nineteen grandchildren. But the person whom I had most wanted to see was my little sister, Julie.

I had called The Dick's house and spoken to my mother about Julie coming on the final boat parade voyage.

"Oh," my mother said. "Are Dick and I invited, too?"

I paused.

"Mom, Mr. Elliot already invited Dad. I think it might make him uncomfortable if you and Dick were there."

"Oh." She was disappointed.

Still, she agreed to let Julie come. It was, after all, the <u>Elliots</u>.

My little sister looked beautiful. She wore a red Christmas dress with white stockings. We threw our arms around each other and hugged.

"Scotty, I've missed you so much," she said, squeezing me tightly.

I introduced her to Perry and her father, who stood greeting the guests on the dock. Perry hugged Julie too.

"Scotty's talked so much about you, Julie. I feel like I already know you."

"No working tonight," Elliot told me as I boarded the boat. Then he turned to Rodolfo.

"And that means you too, Rodolfo."

"Thank you, sir," the quiet little man replied.

It was quite a group. The musicians and caterers worked to make our evening special. Elliot had also arranged a Santa Claus for the kids. He walked around the ship making animals out of balloons, causing quarters to disappear, and presents to appear like magic.

One thing that worried me was the open bar. I didn't know if my dad was still drinking but he surprised me. All he drank was coffee.

We sat in captain's chairs on the deck talking while the kids ran amok yelling to people on shore and on the other boats. Elliot seemed so happy and I realized how much I had grown to like the man.

"Ellen," Elliot said. "I've heard many fine things about your son. I wish I could have gotten to know him."

"Thank you," she smiled sadly.

After dinner, Perry, Julie, and I walked to the bow to watch the lights and people on shore. Both Perry and I held Julie's hands.

"Scotty, will you ever come home?" Julie asked. "Dick thought you were going to be back in a week, and that was two years ago."

"Sorry, sis," I replied. "My home is with dad for now. After that, I don't know where I'll be. But no matter where I go, if you need something from me, I'll be there."

"I wish you were going to still be in high school next year."

"Me, too. But we can talk anytime. I'll fill you in on the best teachers."

It was a great evening and I was so proud of my dad. He seemed to have conquered something in himself, and Old Man Elliot seemed to genuinely like him. Julie also spent some time with our dad. It was almost like we were a family again.

There was another surprise for me. Just before we docked, the old man called me over and handed me an envelope.

"That's your pay," he said. "You better count it."

I opened it to find a stack of one hundred dollar bills. I counted it. It was three thousand dollars. I walked back over to him.

"It's too much," I protested.

"Nonsense. You made everything possible. Enjoy it. Go buy Christmas presents for the people you love."

I was a little stunned. The job had been so much fun that I probably would have paid Elliot to do it. Instead, I had been paid. That's the great thing about getting paid to do a job you love, it always feels a little like larceny.

90

It was a week into Christmas vacation and I still had not made a decision about Hawaii. I was leaning toward not going, and it was not only because of Costa Rica. Elliot had been good to me, and he wanted Perry to go with him to Hawaii. But I felt it should be a father-daughter trip. My presence could be disruptive to their experience. I spoke to Perry about it.

"Trust me," she said. "My dad wants you on the trip. He doesn't want me to be miserable the whole time worrying if you've been taken hostage by some senoritas."

I laughed.

"Like that's going to happen."

Then something occurred that settled the matter once and for all. On Christmas day Perry and I had planned on going to the Oakwood Apartments to have breakfast with my dad and Ellen. I decided to take the Chrysler. When I started her up, the car made a grinding noise and started smoking.

I got out and lifted the hood. The car was on fire.

"Get out of the car," I screamed to Perry who scrambled from the front seat to the safety of the driveway. I ran for the hose and turned the water on. Rushing back, I tripped. By the time I got up, the Chrysler was toast. The fire had spread, completely engulfing the entire car. Flames were reaching ten feet in the air. Perry and I just stood there watching in disbelief.

Neighbors, dressed in pajamas and slippers, came out of their trailers to watch the Chrysler burn. In the distance I could hear the sound of fire trucks. My eyes filled with tears and then I felt Perry take my hand.

"It's going to be all right," she whispered in my ear.

The firemen arrived and quickly doused the fire but the car was a smoldering heap. Even the tires had burned, and my wallet had been inside with two hundred dollars in it. I didn't care about the wallet or the money. What I cared about was the Chrysler. This pile of junk, this disaster of a car that had carried Bobby and me on a hundred surf safaris, was now finished, too. It was like that whole part of my life had been reduced to ashes, a life that I thought would go on forever; Bobby and me against the world.

Change is a funny thing. It creeps up on you slowly and all of a sudden there it is. You are always a little surprised when you wake up to the fact that everything has changed. It was with that realization that I made my decision. The Chrysler catching on fire was a sign of what the universe wanted from me.

"I'm so sorry," Perry said.

"Yeah, me too. The Chrysler's finished."

I took Perry by the hand and led her back to the trailer. We had decorated a small tree and had placed our presents for each other under it. I walked over and picked up Perry's gift and brought it to her.

"I thought you wanted to wait to open presents?" She said.

"I want you to open this now. The rest can wait."

Perry sat on the couch and carefully opened the long narrow package. It was a necklace. Not just any necklace; it was a hand-carved image of a goddess on old piano keys and green agate.

"It's Pele," I said. "The Hawaiian volcano goddess."

"It's beautiful. Where did you find it?"

"An antique store."

She immediately put the necklace on and it glowed against her white skin, more beautiful than any set of pearls.

"Does this mean you're coming to Hawaii or does this mean you're not coming?" She eyed me suspiciously.

I smiled.

"I hadn't made a decision when I bought it, although I was leaning toward Costa Rica. But I think what happened to the Chrysler is a sign that I'm supposed to go with you. It's like Pele herself commanded it. You have to admit, the Chrysler burned like a volcano."

Perry lit up like our Christmas tree, rushed over, and threw her arms around me.

"Scotty, this is the best Christmas ever."

91

We drove to the Oakwood apartments in Perry's new white convertible Karmann Ghia, a Christmas present from her dad, and spent Christmas morning with my dad and Ellen. Ellen made a simple breakfast of eggs and bacon and when we finished, my father made an announcement.

"Ellen and I are getting married."

I was surprised for a moment but then it made sense.

"That's great, Dad."

I looked at Ellen. I knew the pain of the losses she had endured would never completely heal. It was the same for my father. But together they might be able to face their losses, and what they couldn't rise above, they could learn to live with.

Then I made my announcement.

"After graduation I'm sailing to Hawaii with Perry and her dad."

"When did you decide?" My father asked. He looked pleased.

"This morning."

I told them about the Chrysler burning and how it seemed like a sign that I was supposed to go.

"Thank God," Ellen said relieved. "The thought of you driving to Costa Rica in that old car..."

"Yeah," Perry added. "We could have burned up inside."

"I guess she's done for," I said.

Suddenly, Ellen's eyes filled with tears

"I was always afraid one of you boys would end up dead because of that car."

I took hold of Ellen's hand and held it. She smiled sadly. I knew how much she missed Bobby.

We shared Christmas dinner with Perry's dad and some relatives. None of Perry's siblings were invited. They had been excommunicated. But an aunt and some cousins joined us. They were all very nice, especially to Perry whom they were meeting for the first time.

After dinner I sought out Perry's father and told him of my decision.

"That's fine news." he said. There was a twinkle in his eye. "Scotty my boy, we're going to have us an adventure."

"Yeah, but I intend to pull my weight. I don't want to be a guest."

The old man looked at me and smiled.

"On a voyage to Hawaii, everyone pulls their weight, even me."

On the morning of December thirty-first, I got a call from Jim Steiner. The boathouse was going to open to celebrate the arrival of a new year.

"My parents are going to chaperone," he said.

"Does that mean you have to keep your clothes on?" I laughed.

"Yeah, I guess it does."

Perry and I went and it was big fun. I saw the old crowd: Liza the Hurricane and her posse, Jim Steiner and Rickie Chandler. Even Tommy Watts put in an appearance. His parents had gotten him off of going to jail by agreeing to send him to a military boarding school. He was home for Christmas break and it was the first time I'd ever seen him dead sober at the boathouse.

"I've given up drinking," he said.

"That's good, Tommy."

"And, ah, Scotty."

"Yeah."

"Sorry for all the rug burns. I was stupid."

"No worries, Tommy. We all were. It was high school."

"Yeah, and Old English 800 didn't help either."

The live band King's Road played all our favorites and Perry and I danced to the sounds of the Grateful Dead, Doobie Brothers and the

Eagles. Toward the end of the evening, Bucko Shaw showed up. I had not seen him since the funeral. He stood next to the band. When they finished their song he took the mic.

"This song is dedicated to Bobby Rowels," he announced.

The crowd cheered and the band started playing. We immediately knew the song, The Beach Boys' "Surfin' USA" with Shaw singing the vocals. To say the place rocked out would be an understatement, and Shaw was great. He had a way of turning something fun into an experience you never forget.

Perry and I kissed at midnight and we stayed until two. So did practically everyone else. That's when she tugged on my sleeve and said, "We should go, babe."

As I walked up the tropical walkway, it dawned on me that I would be graduating in three weeks. This party was a farewell of sorts to the people who had shared my high school years. Like the burning of the Chrysler, there were endings all around me. I felt like the fool stepping off a cliff into the unknown.

92

I took on the attitude of finishing strong in school, two weeks of review and a week of finals. I felt confident.

The only struggle was in my English class. We were assigned to write a term paper on Henry David Thoreau. I had read *Walden* two years ago but now it left me cold. I turned to my favorite book, *The Art of Wondering*. In its pages I found an article on Thoreau, titled, "I Breathe After My Own Fashion."

It floored me. The article stated that in 1842, Thoreau's brother, John, the person Thoreau was closest to, died suddenly. It was a terrible and painful death, lockjaw brought on by a tetanus infection. John died in Thoreau's arms and the trauma of his brother's death caused Thoreau to experience a series of psychosomatic illnesses. I began to wonder. Is this why Thoreau went to Walden to conduct his experiment? His "personal business" as he called it. Was it to negotiate with his grief?

Walden came alive for me and I devoured it in two days. Like Thoreau, I had lost a brother, and the courage Thoreau had and the nature of his experiment could serve as a guide for me in reconciling my own grief and loss. I understood what Thoreau had felt - pain, loss, and regret - all the feelings that arise when you realize you have no control over death. Thoreau went to the woods to "live deliberately," but I believe it was also a way to say goodbye to his brother on his own terms. An act of rebellion against fate, society, and the world, and even death itself. When you've known a deep loss you see clearly the meaning of Thoreau's words, "Most people's visions do not penetrate the surface of things."

I got it. But there was one big problem. When I tried to write my paper, my words didn't resonate with how I felt. My "quiet desperation" just sounded like whining. My paper, flat and uninspired, failed to capture my feeling about Thoreau. Somewhere along the way, probably on the night I almost drowned, I had lost the connection between my feelings and my words. I knew I would get a decent grade. But for someone who values his words, as I do, it felt like failure, and it depressed me.

The last day of my high school career arrived without fanfare. This was supposed to be one of the biggest days of my life. But without Bobby there to share it with, the day felt anticlimactic and empty.

I said goodbye to some of my teachers and friends, Steiner and Chandler, and, of course, Liza. Instead of going to the library at lunch, I snuck in and climbed the rickety old stairs up to the old bell tower. The tower afforded an incredible view of the campus and I sat watching all the kids interacting with each other. The different groups, surfers, athletes, stoners, all off in their little cliques worrying about a million trivial things like pimples on their faces and who's hooking up with whom or whose parents weren't going to be home this weekend so they could party. It all seemed kind of meaningless.

I wasn't sure what I had actually learned here, pain, joy, anger, jealousy and, above all, insecurity, mixed in with some history, math and English, maybe a little science. I wasn't the same kid who had sat with Bobby that first day of school freshman year. I knew that. But how I had grown or what I had learned was a mystery to me. My most important teacher had been Bobby. He had taught me a million things; especially the meaning of friendship.

I looked around the bell tower and saw the names of those who came before me carved into the wooden wall. There were a lot of them. Some I knew: Shaw, Richardson, Christy, Mulroy, Patrick, Pantusso.

But there were many more I had never heard of, and it struck me that someday Bobby and I would be forgotten too.

That's when it happened. What possessed me I will never know. I stood and began ringing the bell. Its sound echoed across the quad and people looked up. Then I shouted at the top of my lungs,

"Bobby fuckin' Rowels."

The quad went silent. Then a mighty roar erupted from the quad as people cheered. Someone began to shout, "Bobby, Bobby, Bobby," and soon everyone was chanting "Bobby." I stood there looking down with a huge smile on my face.

High school had been a journey, a necessary step on the path of life. I wasn't graduating knowing what I wanted from life. Still, I now had a pretty good idea of what I didn't want. I only wished I had Bobby here to help show me the way.

It was the highlight of my day because I knew climbing the bell tower could result in expulsion if I was caught. It was an act inspired by some of what Bobby taught me. I had earned the right to rebel and the ability to act spontaneously made my last day memorable.

I was late to my final English class and the teacher, Mr. Bratton, was reading from Dylan Thomas. It was his final gift to us as the semester came to a close.

Do not go gentle into that good night.
Old age should burn and rage at close
of day;
Rage, rage against the dying of the light.

Suddenly, a student walked in and demanded I go to the principal's office. Of course, every smart-ass in class started yelling "Oooh. You're in trouble now."

As I stood to leave the room, Mr. Bratton looked at me and smiled.

"Good luck, Scotty."

I smiled back. He had been one of my favorite teachers.

I walked down the long empty hall toward the principal's office. My first thought was that someone knew I had climbed into the bell tower but I also doubted they would kick me out. What would be the point?

Mr. Doyle sat behind his desk with his heavy horn-rimmed glasses. He smiled when I walked in.

"Scotty...take a seat."

I sat in front of his large wooden desk. On the walls were several diplomas announcing to the world Mr. Doyle's journey to that seat behind the desk. There was also a Newport Harbor football team picture from 1956 reminding me of Mr. Doyle's long connection to the school.

"I understand you're leaving us today."

"Yep, I've served my time."

"We can't entice you with a series of electives?"

"Nope."

"How about valedictorian?"

"Nope."

"What about college?"

"Actually, I'm sailing to Hawaii."

"I thought you wanted to go to Stanford?"

I paused. It had been my dream once but now it seemed to be someone else's dream. Suddenly, I felt tears in my eyes.

"I did...but since Bobby died...you know..."

"I wish you'd reconsider. You had the highest SAT score in the school this year. Nearly perfect. It proves you have a gift."

"Well, it's just a test. Maybe I'll go to college next year."

"You need to be careful, Scotty. One year leads to two, and the next thing you know you're five years out and realize that you're never going to college."

"I'll think about it."

"Well, if you change your mind, I might be able to help you with some scholarship money."

"Thanks, Mr. Doyle."

"You're welcome, Scotty, and good luck."

I stood.

"Ah, one last thing, Scotty. Did you notice my name on the bell tower?"

"No, sir."

"Gosh darn it. I knew I should have made the letters bigger."

"Don't worry, Mr. Doyle. Mine are big enough for both of us. Bobby's too."

"That's good," he smiled.

As I walked out of the office, the bell rang and the halls filled with kids excited to be going home. Instead of sharing their joy I suddenly felt depressed. I knew I would never be back. But just for kicks, I rode the school bus home, knowing that this, too, was an ending. It would probably be the last time I'd ever ride a school bus.

93

March first was selected as the departure date for our voyage to Hawaii. School was finished, and though I continued to work at the diner, I didn't do much else. I didn't surf or write even though Perry encouraged me to do both.

What we did do was hang out in Perry's trailer and read. I read every sailing book I could get my hands on; *Two Years Before The Mast, The Dove, Mutiny on the Bounty, Moby Dick*. It was all about our trip to Hawaii. Perry, on the other hand, was reading books I suggested by Ayn Rand, *Atlas Shrugged* and *The Fountainhead*. She came away totally worked up and angry at the way society sets out to destroy or tear down those who are in one form or another different or talented. Alexis de Tocqueville, the french author who wrote *Democracy in America,* probably the best critique of American democracy ever written, called it the "leveling effect of the majority," and you can see it at work all around you, especially in high school.

We snuggled close as we sat reading on her couch, knowing that we were joined by something deeper than the words we were reading. At sunset, we always broke from our reading to walk to the beach and watch the day surrender to the evening. We felt close at those moments with the sky ablaze in red and the sun slowly slipping behind Catalina. It was as if the changes from day to night represented a growth of some sort which reflected itself in the deeper feelings we were sharing. These were good days, but Bobby still weighed heavily on my heart and mind.

One day, when Perry was out doing something for her father, I hopped on my bike and rode to Balboa. I wanted to relive the adventure Bobby and I had shared on Labor Day.

It was a sunny but cold winter's day, and a strong wind blew from the north. The deserted boardwalk and beach were a striking departure from the crowds that filled Newport's streets and beaches last Labor Day.

I rode past Blackie's and the Dory Fisherman, and past my old elementary school, stopping at the spot where Bobby had rescued the girl from the wet t-shirt brawl. The beach had been smoothed by the wind. The footprints, Bobby's footprints, were gone.

When I reached Balboa, I remembered how I used to think of this old business district as being sacred ground, the soldiers from World War II spending their final days of happiness here just as Bobby had. Balboa never felt more sacred.

At the Fun Zone, I stopped in the Bay Arcade. Two ten-year-old boys were playing our baseball game. I watched them for a long time as they competed, yelling superlatives in the joy of friendship and competition just as Bobby and I had. How Bobby always teased me for never taking a risk. But I wished I hadn't swung for the fences that last time so Bobby could have won. It was the last time he ever played Batter Up. I left the Bay Arcade knowing I would never play the game again either; that part of my youth had died with Bobby. I missed him, but still I couldn't cry.

On the ride home, I found myself listening to the clickity-clack of my bicycle chain on Bay Avenue. Suddenly, I remembered Bobby's words, "I can't really see myself in the future." Then I remembered him being happy that I had Perry in my life. "Now you will have someone to take care of your sorry ass when I'm not around," were his words to me. My thoughts were suddenly connecting the dots.

I slammed on my brakes, stopping in the middle of the street. The doctor had told Ellen that Bobby's aneurysm was genetic. "He could have died at any time," were the doctor's words and a question arose for me. Were Bobby's statements prophetic? Did he have a feeling or posses some subconscious knowledge that he would die young? And did this somehow inform his life and inspire him to take risks? How many seventeen-year-olds would blow off practice to ride eighteen-foot waves? Or take the crazy risk of dumping a dead body on a coach's doorstep? What about playing a football game while knocking on heaven's door?

My mind was racing until the blare of a car horn, loud and intrusive, startled me from my thoughts. I turned back to see a huge two-tone brown and white Pontiac station wagon with steer horns on the hood bearing down on me. The car had a large bubble over the driver's roof and the man inside wore a cowboy hat. He was motioning for me to move out of the way.

I waved and pushed my bike to the side. As the car passed, I read the words John Wayne painted on the side. I didn't get a good look at the man inside so I wasn't sure if it really was the hero of some of Bobby's favorite Western movies.

I watched the car fade away down the street and asked myself if it was a coincidence. But I don't believe in coincidences. Everything unfolds as it should, and I took John Wayne's car appearing to me as a sign. Some part of Bobby knew that his life would be short, and he wanted me to know that. I felt it was Bobby's way of helping me heal.

94

My training aboard the Perriwinkle began. I needed to learn a lot in a short time to become a full-fledged member of the crew.

"If you're going to crew then so am I," Perry said. "I'm not going to sit around all day and watch you work."

I smiled. She was with me in anything, win, lose or draw.

We met with Alice three times a week aboard the Periwinkle. She started with the basics, the various forms of knots, the difference between a rope and a line, how to effectively reef and trim your sails for the various angles your boat takes into the wind: in irons, close hauled, beam reach, broad reach and running.

"A lot of sailing," Alice said, "is learning how to trim your sail correctly for the direction of the wind. Until you learn that you'd best follow orders."

In a nice way, Alice was reminding us that we would be novices during the journey, and that we needed to respect the experience of those around us. Perry and I had no problem with that.

In mid-February, Dennis Gaily decided to take a run on the open ocean. It was a beautiful day, sunny and mild, and we met at the dock at eight. There were four additional people there besides Dennis Gaily and Alice: two women in their thirties, Sharon and Ann, and two men in their forties, Jeff and Mark. They were the other members of our crew and had previously worked with both Dennis and Alice.

Then a diminutive old man with a scruffy face strolled onto the dock. He looked ancient and could easily have been mistaken for a rummy like the character Eddie in the Howard Hawks' movie *To Have and Have Not.* He spoke with an Irish brogue, and I expected him to ask us if we had ever been bitten by a dead bee.

I had to smile while Dennis explained that this was Finius, our cook.

"Top of the morning to you me colleens and laddies. They say an army travels on its stomach," Finius announced. "The same is true for sailors at sea. But don't expect anything fancy. It will be good food that sustains you. If you want fancy, hire on with a cruise ship."

I stole a look at Perry's dad who was joining us for this practice run. He had a big smile on his face, like it was the start of his dream. There was a lesson in his smile. He knew he was dying, and intended to prepare for this challenge by spending the remaining days of his life living his dream.

But in a certain sense we are all dying. Death can come at any moment, as it did for Bobby, sudden and unexpected. So it only makes sense to prepare for death by living your dreams right now, this very moment. Live life and know that the honest joy in life is not so much in realizing your dreams but in the journey you take toward them.

We made our way out of the bay toward open ocean. To the north of us was the row of rocks that gave birth to the Wedge. To the south, another row of rocks separated the harbor entrance from Big Corona Beach. It's these rows of rocks, this feat of engineering, that established Newport as one of the premier yacht harbors in the world.

The wind blew steady at about twelve knots out of the north. Before we were even out of the harbor Dennis Gaily set us to work raising the sails. We worked hard and began to mesh as a crew. The other members were courteous and firm and a great spirit of cooperation quickly developed.

Little did I realize what a privilege it was to be a crew member on a boat like this. The Periwinkle was more than an outstanding boat. It was a millionaire's yacht in tiptop condition. A boat so fine that our skipper called out with glee, "She is fast. I will give her that!"

"Aye, captain!" we all yelled back.

When we returned to the dock and secured the boat, Dennis Gaily gathered us together.

"We'll end this fine day at the Snug Harbor. The beers are on me."

I approached the captain.

"Sir, I'm only eighteen."

"Nonsense. You're a crew member. We'll enter as a crew and the Snug Harbor will never know what hit them."

The Snug Harbor is a dive bar in Newport's Cannery Row, a sailor's bar run by two brothers who would just as soon grunt superlatives at you as serve you a drink. The Snug was crowded with salty dogs of every shape and size, but our captain had arranged in advance to have a table waiting. The crew of the Periwinkle, minus the old man, walked in as a group. As predicted, no one gave me a second look.

Everyone knew Gaily. It was like he was famous or something, and people started calling for a song from him. The next thing we knew, our captain climbed onto the bar and screamed:

"Suey sake, suey sake, hoy, hoy, hoy."

Like a group of parrots, the crowd threw his words back at him.

"Suey sake, suey sake, hoy, hoy, hoy!"

"Ohhhhhhhhh..." Gaily sang out and it was the longest "oh" I had ever heard. Then he broke into a song.

"What do you do with a drunken sailor
 What do you do with a drunken sailor
 What do you do with a drunken sailor
 Early in the morning..."

The whole bar sang the words with him in moments of magic as the crowd came together as one.

"Shave his chest with a rusty razor
 Shave his chest with a rusty razor
 Shave his chest with a rusty razor
 Early in the morning..."

When he was finished the crowd applauded wildly and raised their glasses to him. There was no doubt about it, Dennis Gaily was the best kind of sailor, and his love of the sea permeated everything he did.

95

March first arrived cold and misty. A thick cloud cover had blown in from the sea on a biting north wind. We'd spent the previous day loading provisions, gear, and sea bags so there wasn't anything for the crew to do except wait for Old Man Elliot to arrive. We stood as a group on the dock because Dennis Gaily wanted Elliot to be the first to board.

We didn't have to wait long. Elliot exited the house and limped toward us in brown deck shoes, khaki pants, and a button-down blue oxford shirt with a heavy navy blue jacket. He used a cane now because his gait was short and unsteady.

When he got to the ramp leading down to the dock, Perry met him. He turned and looked back toward his mansion for a long moment. I saw him wave. His man, Rodolfo, was standing on the upstairs balcony and waved back.

With Perry's help, Elliot walked down the ramp to the dock. He stopped to greet us.

"Good morning," he smiled.

"Good morning, sir," we chorused.

"I just want to thank you all for coming on this adventure with me. I've always wanted to sail to Hawaii."

Then he turned to Gaily.

"Are we ready?"

"Yes, sir."

"All right, then. Permission to board, Captain?"

"Permission granted, sir."

With Perry's help, the old man turned and boarded his boat.

"Scotty, cast off the lines," Gaily ordered.

I turned and began to untie the lines while the rest of the crew boarded. When the lines were pulled in, the engines started and I jumped onto the boat. We pulled away from the dock and were officially on our way.

I looked to the bow of the boat: Richard C. Elliot was standing at the tip. Again, he waved to Rodolfo. It was as if they were waving goodbye for the last time.

As we motored through the bay toward the open ocean, I, too, felt as though I was saying goodbye. My dad had told me he would be selling the trailer while I was gone and moving in with Ellen. This meant officially I was no longer a resident of Newport Beach. In fact, I wasn't resident anywhere. I wouldn't have a home when I came back.

For some reason, I waved to the city, too. I sensed that it would be a long time before I returned. It felt bittersweet, this farewell, for Newport was the place of my youth, the place that first nurtured me. I would always be grateful to her. But my journey required me to leave, to search the world for my dreams that were lost, and to find out who I was beyond the borders of this shining little city on the bay. I felt I had learned from her everything she had to teach. The umbilical cord was being cut.

96

The voyage to Hawaii was filled with blazing salmon sunrises and stunning vermilion sunsets. An ocean sky is like nothing you'll ever see on land; the sky simply dwarfs everything and is magnified by the deep blue colors of the sea. Surrounded by miles of vast, empty ocean, the sky is what you look to for perspective, and you can't help but realize how insignificant we all are in the face of the universe.

But it was the ocean that kept coming back to me, reigniting my immense pain. Bobby and I had never sailed together, but one thing we shared that deepened our friendship was the ocean. Being surrounded by it on all sides only served to remind me that I still had to find a way to make peace with Bobby's death, and Henry David Thoreau's words came to their full meaning for me:

"Men go back to the mountains as they go back to sailing ships at sea, because in the mountains or on the sea they must face up."

For the first few days, I felt an uneasy foreboding, a restlessness that caused me to withdraw. Perry had presented me with a new journal the night before the trip and I tried to write a couple of times. Nothing came, no words, and this worried me. Every hard thing in my life had always been successfully negotiated in my heart and mind through my words. But when it came to Bobby I just felt so empty that my lack of words left me feeling worse.

After three days at sea I thought that I might not make it through the trip, I was so low. I managed to make it through the days. Pineapple had taught me the lesson of physical labor as a way to still your mind, so I asked Dennis Gaily and Alice for every job I could get. From dawn to dusk I scrubbed every inch of the boat and washed the dishes after every meal. When an order was given I was the first to jump to the ready.

But it was the nights that took me down. We each had to stand a four-hour watch, and in the darkness, under incandescent stars, the demons of loss, fear and regret punished my soul. Searching for healing, all I found was anger. Bobby's death was just so unfair, so unjust, it was as if the ugliness of the world had swallowed my friend like the leviathan that had swallowed Jonah. Only for Bobby there would be no salvation, no redemption, no escape from the depths of oblivion.

I paced the length of the ship during my shifts, muttering to myself. It was a madness of sorts. I was not only mad at his coach, I was mad at the doctor who diagnosed Bobby with the flu, and mad at the school and society for encouraging him to play a football game with an aneurysm the size of a grapefruit. God did not escape my anger either.

But mostly the anger was directed inward. It was my fault.

"I should have stopped him...I should have stopped him...I should have stopped him..."

Thoreau was right. I had to face up. I hated myself for not protecting my friend.

I began looking at the ocean in a strange way, with crazy, nonsensical ideas, imagining that Bobby's spirit could be found in its healing waters. It felt almost like the night I tried to swim to heaven on the shimmering light of the moon. If I just jumped from the ship into the ocean, then Bobby and I would be together again, surfing waves, perfect waves that can only be imagined in your dreams. I knew these thoughts were crazy but they kept coming like the relentless incoming tide, threatening to drown me in their watery grave.

At meals, people asked me if I was okay.

"Maybe you should give up your night watch?" Dennis Gaily suggested.

"No," I shook my head. "It would just be worse."

I knew somewhere in my heart that I was negotiating with my grief. As much as it hurt, there was no other way. It was all part of the process of saying goodbye.

Perry started checking on me during the day and switched her watch to mine. She stood by my side and held my hand as I paced the ship.

"Goddamn it," I muttered. "Goddamn it, why?"

Perry put her arms around me and cried.

"Why don't you write about it, Scotty," she whispered.

"Because I can't. What are words compared to the death of your best friend?"

With every step on that ship at night, the memories of my life with Bobby burst forth, tearing my heart to shreds. Sometimes the memories were fragments of images or words, and other times whole scenes played through my head. Over and over again. Especially the moments outside the locker room on that fateful night. I felt like I had delivered Bobby to his death.

"I killed him."

Perry held me and cried.

"It wasn't your fault, Scotty."

If anyone suffered more than I did, it was Perry. During the day, she would stand with her father at the bow of the ship as he contemplated the last days of his life, and at night she would hold me tightly trying to protect me from myself. Even through my pain I realized that no one had ever loved me as much as Perry did. Not even Bobby.

After days and nights of watching me struggle, the little Irish cook, Finius, approached me.

"Scotty, me lad, it's bad luck for a ship to have someone on board who's possessed by a dark wind."

"I know, I just can't help it."

"It makes a crew uneasy and any bad luck will be blamed on you."

Many sailors, even some experienced sailors with scientific back-grounds, are superstitious. It probably has to do with the overwhelming power of the sea and mother nature and the fact that there are times when you realize you have no control. Bad luck happens, situations suddenly become dangerous, and sailors often look for reasons to explain the bad luck. It's a scary thing to be out of control.

Finius smiled. "Here, let me put this around your neck."

It was a string with a large silver medal tied to it.

"It's Saint Elmo. He's the patron saint of sailors. He'll ward off the demons, and by protecting you, he'll protect the ship."

"Thanks, Finius."

So far our trip had seen only calm waters and light winds. But that night a thunderstorm rose up. Powerful claps of thunder echoed through the heavens while great bolts of lightning shredded the sky. The sounds were deafening and the immense blinding white and blue streaks would have been amazing if they hadn't been so dangerous. Lightning is always looking to strike the tallest point and on the ocean that is the mast of a ship.

The entire crew filed onto the deck as a mighty wind picked up. We scrambled for the sails, pulling them in as quickly as we could. A fifty mph gust whipped up a deck chair and sent it flying like a missile across the bow of the ship. The ocean turned angry and spilled onto the deck.

The storm intensified. A giant swell crested and broke on top of the ship sending tons of seawater across the deck. Several people were knocked from their feet and clung to safety by whatever they could grab. Cloud to ocean lightning continued to strike all around us and the sound boomed like a Howitzer through my soul.

"By God," Dennis Gaily shouted. "It's a demon storm. Stand to the ready, boys and girls."

The storm boiled with the fury of hell, and I worried that if something happened, like losing a crew member overboard or the masts being cut down by a lightning strike, suspicion would fall on me: that I had brought this demon storm down upon us.

"Damn that Finius and his stories," I thought.

The boat pitched and groaned in the violent sea and I thought for sure that the Periwinkle would split apart at any moment.

Petrified with fear, the crew of the Periwinkle cried out for deliverance. Someone began shouting the Lord's Prayer. When I looked into their faces, they looked away. I was scared too. Not so much for myself but for the crew members around me. I was overwhelmed with guilt from the thought that by damning God, I had damned the ship. Holding tight to a line on the mast, I whispered my own prayer to the heavens.

"Please, God. I'm sorry. I was wrong. Keep us safe."

My prayer was answered in a strange way. It was Bobby's voice that came to me.

"Just relax, dickhead. It's almost over."

Then it happened. First, we noticed it in the ocean, a glow of sorts, a blue luminescence that seemed to spark on the tips of the waves as they crested around us. Then the entire ocean seemed ablaze with what looked like a gas fire, blue and white.

"I thought I'd seen it all," Gaily shouted. "But I've never seen anything like this."

Someone shouted, "The ship's on fire."

We looked toward the masts and sure enough, their tops seemed to be burning brightly with a blue-and-white flame.

"The ship's not on fire," Finius yelled. "It's Saint Elmo's fire. We are protected. Scotty is protecting us."

"It's not me. It's Bobby," I yelled back.

As suddenly as it had begun, the wind ceased and the waters calmed. The storm was dissipating and moving on.

The relief in everyone's face was priceless. They were now smiling at me and patting me on the back.

Perry had gone to her father in his cabin when the storm began. She had stayed with him, and when it was over she brought him on deck. He stood staring at the flames on the masts and Perry rushed into my arms.

"Thank God you're safe," I said.

"Hold me. Don't ever let me go," she said as she squeezed me with all her strength.

We were all too keyed up to go back to bed, so we sat on the deck watching the burning lights of Saint Elmo's fire, the fire that has been written about for a thousand years. It's mentioned in the *Rime of the Ancient Mariner* and in the words of Shakespeare, a natural phenomenon of electrical charges that has always taken on a deeper meaning to those who have witnessed it.

"The smartest thing I ever did," Finius repeated all night, "was give Scotty that medal."

For my part, I vowed to never damn God again.

97

After twenty-four days at sea we sighted land, the island of Kauai. This was the place in my heart and mind where I had always sought refuge. But I still felt so empty that we could have been entering the Port of Long Beach. The night watches had worn me out, numbing my reaction.

We sailed into Nawiliwili Harbor at around ten in the morning. A light rain was falling but the warm air made it feel refreshing. I wondered if it was an Ulalena rain, a rain the Hawaiians believe cleanses the spirit.

The old man searched me out and asked me to walk to the bow with him. Together we stood looking at the shore and green mountains beyond as the boat crept through the harbor. He turned and looked at me.

"How are you feeling?"

"All right, I guess. I hope I wasn't a burden."

"Nonsense. But it's been a tough trip. For both of us."

The trip had been anything but tough in terms of sailing. Except for the electrical storm, the wind had been fair and the ocean mostly calm. But I knew what he meant. Spiritually and emotionally, it had been torture.

"Yeah," I agreed.

"Thank you for coming with us."

"You're welcome, sir."

"I've been doing a lot of thinking and I've decided the past is a funny thing, Scotty. You can spin it and wrestle with it, but the truth is always there eating at you. Let me give you some advice. The only truth I see after all these years, the only thing that matters, is having the love and respect of the people you love and respect." He put his hand on my shoulder.

"Thank you, sir. I'll remember that."

98

The crew spent the morning unloading their gear and arranging transportation to various hotels. We were staying on Kauai for a week before we headed for other islands. The old man, Perry and I were staying on the north shore at a place called the Hanalei Hotel. A limousine picked us up and drove us up the Kilio Highway. We passed a cemetery, miles of beautiful beaches, and a lush rainforest. When we arrived at the hotel, we were greeted by two men playing ukuleles. There were also three pretty Hawaiian hula dancers. At the end of their dance they presented us with leis and kissed us on the cheeks. The old man intended for everything to be first class.

My room was next to Perry's and I told her I was going to take a nap.

"Are you all right?"

"I don't know."

"Maybe we should talk to someone."

"You mean, like a psychiatrist?"

"Yeah. Maybe. Or someone who's dealt with grief."

When I entered the room, I collapsed on the bed. The room overlooked Hanalei Bay and further beyond toward the mountains of Bali Hai. Through the open sliding glass door, I could hear the surf crashing against the cliffs somewhere below. I didn't feel like seeing any of it.

I was exhausted. Emotionally spent. I knew I couldn't go on like this. The trip had nearly ended in disaster, and could still be headed there. Perry was probably right. I was nuts.

I needed to get past Bobby's death. It was time, and I searched my heart. The priest at Bobby's funeral told us that the best way to get past grief was to be really good to yourself.

"Indulge yourself for a year," the priest had said. "If you want ice cream, eat ice cream. Take a trip. Just be good to yourself."

Even though I had indulged myself by traveling two thousand miles to a tropical paradise, my grief held me in its claws. Indulging myself wasn't the answer.

"How do I say goodbye, Bobby?" I whispered.

The trip to Costa Rica would have done the trick, a catharsis brought on by risk and adventure. That's what the memory of Bobby demanded of me, a tribute to his lessons of courage and fortitude. Nothing short of that would do. I knew this in my heart and soul. There had to be some kind of meaning to it all. Bobby's life, and his death, the way he died with such courage, had to mean something.

Then I knew. To honor his life and death required that I measure myself in a similar way, that I lay it all on the line.

"Please, Bobby, help me find a way to say goodbye."

Then I closed my eyes and drifted off to sleep.

Perry woke me in the early evening and we went to dinner with her father at the Hanalei Dolphin. With its open windows and lush setting, it has the feeling of old Hawaiian luxury. I savored fresh Mahi Mahi and artichokes so tender and sweet I could have eaten a dozen of them. I was indulging myself again.

"Sure beats what Finius cooked us," Elliot said with a smile.

We went back to the hotel early. We were tired from our journey and the old man had plans for us in the morning.

"Tomorrow we see the island," he said. "Get some rest."

Perry and I slept in each other's arms. But I awoke in the middle of the night and paced the floor thinking of Bobby. She tried to get me to come back to bed, but I couldn't sleep, and the morning light found me exhausted.

99

After breakfast, a stocky older Hawaiian man with dark, tanned skin and a thick mane of straight black hair met us in the lobby, our guide to the island.

"I'm Thomas," he said. "Today I will share my home with you."

Thomas owned a yellow 1950 Ford Woody, often called a "shoebox". Surfers in the sixties loved this style of car because it was big enough to carry their long boards. They were also cheap to buy because they had gone out of style and nobody wanted them. Surfers are always looking for a deal. They know that saving money means less time working and more time surfing. I wondered if Thomas surfed.

We drove an hour or so to the other side of the island to a place called Waimea Canyon.

"Mark Twain called Waimea the Grand Canyon of the Pacific," Thomas announced.

We stood at the edge of an overlook and the canyon, with its various shades of red, yellow and pink, spread out beneath us revealing a stunning view. Legend had it that this canyon was the Menehune's last stronghold where they hid from the encroachment of an expanding modern world.

"Do you think the Menehune are still down there?" I asked.

"You know about the Menehune?" Thomas's eyes sparkled.

"A little," I replied.

"What are Menehune?" Perry asked.

"They're the cousins of Ireland's leprechauns," Thomas said. "They were blown across the ocean by a powerful storm and they chose Kauai because it is as green as Ireland."

"Are they lucky?" the old man asked.

"Oh, yes. We believe that good fortune is associated with their kindness. If your visit is a good one, first thank the gods, then thank the Menehune. And God help you if you get on the wrong side of the wee folk. They're full of mischief."

As our group walked back toward the car, I lagged behind remembering the last time I had been happy as a child, here on this island paradise with my family still together, and where I whispered to the Menehune my hopes and dreams.

Quietly, I asked for the Menehune's help with Bobby. There was no response, only the sound of a warm trade wind rustling the wild vegetation, and I rejoined the group.

Thomas's plan was to start at Waimea Canyon and work our way back to the North Shore. We stopped at various places and points of interest along the way. It was a pleasant, leisurely journey with the Woody's excellent stereo playing the music of Cecilia and Kopono. We had drifted into island time. The old man sat in front with Thomas, while Perry and I sat in back holding hands. Maybe it was the music or the tropical beauty of the island, or maybe it was Thomas and the Menehune, I'm not sure, but I felt the cloud start to lift. For the first time in months I felt hopeful. Maybe, I thought, the old Hawaiian saying was true..."from destruction comes serenity and beauty," just like with a volcano.

"Will we be visiting the Fern Grotto?" I asked Thomas.

"Not today. The Wilua River is closed on Sunday. But I recommend you see it while you're here. A lot of people like to get married there."

"Don't get any bright ideas back there," Elliot said.

Perry and I looked at each other and smiled.

Thomas planned many other places to see like the Menehune fish pond, several heiaus, and the various locations where movies had been shot like *South Pacific* and *Blue Hawaii*.

"I met Elvis when he was here," Thomas said.

"Yeah," Elliot said. "He's a heck of a nice guy."

"He sure is," Thomas nodded. "He came to a luau at my uncle's house and sang for all of us."

But I especially liked the Hawiian legends. Each stop was filled with stories and the history behind them. The legend of Nounou, the legend of Kamokila and the legend of the spouting horn were just a few.

Thomas was a sweet man whose gentle spirit guided us back to the the North Shore, and we were enveloped in his love for his home and island. He was also a terrific storyteller, a talent I have always admired. This talent never fails to lift my spirits. My first teacher, my grand-mother Norma Jean, had been a great storyteller, too.

"If you look to your left," Thomas said, "you will see the mountain we call the sleeping giant. Try to find the nose. That's the demigod Puni who fell asleep there after helping to build the Kukui Heiau."

Our group wound its way past beautiful beaches and exquisite bays. Everywhere I looked was paradise, with water so brillant that postcards could never do it justice. At the Kilauea lighthouse we were greeted by a thousand seabirds who nested on cliffs while Hawaiian geese followed our every step along the path that wound itself around the lighthouse. Even a spectacular albatross put in an appearance. I thought of *The Rime of the Ancient Mariner* reminding me that Bobby's death was like an albatross around my neck.

We stopped for fresh coconuts alongside the road and watched a young Hawaiian girl use a large machete to deftly cut off the top of the coconut in mere seconds. We sipped the milk out of a straw while ob-serving sea turtles frolicking in an emerald bay which had been created by a protective reef.

Toward sunset we reached our final destination on the tour, a pretty little beach with chickens running everywhere.

"The end of the road," Thomas said.

I thought he had chosen this beach to watch the sunset. But Thomas had other plans.

"Follow me," he directed.

We trailed Thomas into the jungle. Both Perry and I took turns helping her father. The path was narrow, overgrown and not well marked and we found ourselves climbing higher and higher up a gentle slope until we came to a plateau. It felt as if we had come out of a dark tunnel into the light. The view of the coastline was stunning. To our left were miles of towering cliffs known as the Napali Coast, and to our right were more mountains framed by swaying palm trees. In front of us, the Pacific Ocean stretched as far as the eye could see. About a half-mile off shore a double rainbow smiled with their sparkling colors. Under the rainbows, a pod of whales circled and breached in the ocean.

"This heiau was built for the goddess Laka," Thomas announced. "She was the goddess who inspired and protected the spirit of the hula."

"It's a spot worthy of a goddess," the old man said with an enormous grin.

It was an ancient place with stacked stones all around us forming something of a low walled enclosure. A large boulder had been set against the sheer volcanic cliff that reached into the sky. On top of the boulder people had placed tea leaves and flower leis as if the boulder were a kind of altar. I knew instinctively that this place was sacred, as sacred as any church.

"The ancients came here to celebrate the hula," Thomas said, "the soul of Hawaii expressed in movement."

I pictured people dancing on the plateau at night to the sounds of the crashing waves, pounding drums, and the light of burning torches, their shadows reflected against the volcanic cliffs.

"The hula was a religious dance in the beginning," Thomas continued, "and only performed in ceremonies at special places and times."

"This is a special place," I said.

"Yes, it is. One of the most sacred on the island. Come on, let's watch the sunset."

We stood at the edge of the plateau watching the sun slowly fall into the sea. Below us, giant swells marched toward the island until they pounded the shoreline. I thought of Bobby and how much he would have loved this place. I whispered a prayer.

"Please, let me find a way to make my peace."

"The swell is building," Thomas said. "Tomorrow it will be twenty to thirty feet."

I thought of Bobby and his ride at the point.

"Where will people be surfing?" I asked.

"Just below your hotel in Hanalei Bay."

The sun drifted toward the cloudless horizon, providing a crystal clear sunset.

"Watch for the green flash," Thomas suggested.

"You know," the old man lamented. "I've spent a lifetime looking for the flash and I've decided it just isn't true."

"No, it's real," Thomas replied. "I've seen it several times. Watch. We may get lucky. The conditions are perfect."

Again, I whispered a prayer. "Please, God, let me find a way."

The sun started to slip away, only a small sliver of it remaining. We stood quietly, almost reverently, watching the end to a beautiful day. At the moment the sun fell below the ocean, a brilliant green flash lit up the horizon. We all gasped, the beauty reminding us that we live in a world filled with magic. The trick is to be open to it.

"The gods have smiled upon us." Thomas said. He had a big grin on his face and so did the old man.

"If I hadn't seen it," Elliot said, "I wouldn't have believed it. Now I've seen it all. St. Elmo's fire and now a green flash."

But I knew it was something more. It was a confirmation from the universe. I knew how I was going to say goodbye to Bobby. Kauai had once more offered me a gift. I had found a path out of the labyrinth.

100

I woke before dawn. It had been my first good night's sleep in a month. I reached out and held Perry's hand. Her fingers opened, allowing mine to slip between hers. She made a little noise and fell back to sleep.

Through the open sliding-glass door the sounds of waves crashing against the reef drifted in. It sounded like distant thunder or the faraway rumblings of cannons: powerful, foreboding, and dangerous.

For a moment I wondered about my plan. The thought of facing twenty-foot waves scared the shit out of me, there was no doubt about it. But it was the facing of my fear that would ultimately give meaning to my tribute. That was the rule Bobby had lived his life by: no fear. Or, more precisely, feel the fear but do it anyway. I remembered his excitement on the morning of Newport's epic waves.

"I hope I don't drown," he had said and then he ran toward his destiny.

I now knew my destiny as well. I gently let go of Perry's hand and slid out of bed and into my swimming trunks, t-shirt and slaps. I leaned over and kissed her on the cheek and peered at her through the dark, wondering to myself how I had come to deserve a girl like this. For a second, this scared me, too. If something happened, Perry would be left to pick up the pieces once more.

I decided to write a note and went into the bathroom, dug through my backpack, and found a pen and some paper.

"Perry," I wrote thinking of Thoreau and his adventure at Walden Pond being connected to his brother's death, "I have some personal business to attend to. Will be back as soon as I can. Love, Scotty."

I set the note on the dresser and left the room quietly.

The hotel felt like a tomb. I supposed people on vacation were sleeping in. The cavernous lobby, usually filled with tourists during the day and night, was empty. In fact, I was the only person in the lobby as I walked through it to the massive koa wood front doors with images of Pele, the volcano goddess, etched into its panels. It reminded me again that "Out of destruction comes beauty and serenity."

Outside, a lone valet stood by the curb. He was a little older than me, Hawaiian, and obviously sleepy.

"Good morning," his greeting was warm and friendly.

"Good morning," I replied.

"Can I get your car?"

"I don't have one. But would you know if there is a place to rent a surfboard?"

"You know there's a swell in. The waves are huge."

"I've heard."

"Are you going to surf by the pier?"

"I don't know."

"Are you from California?"

"Yeah."

"Every winter we get surfers from California who want to surf our big waves and every year one or two of them drown."

I knew if I told this guy my true intentions he wouldn't help me.

"Yeah, I'll surf by the pier. I just want to get in the water."

"Then the best place to rent a board is right next to the pier. They have every shape and size you could want."

"Thanks, and where is the best place to watch the big waves?"

"Just follow the path. It'll take you to the cliff overlooking the bay. From there you can see the swells lining up and peeling off the reef. But don't even think about riding them. I hear the swell is a monster."

"I won't."

"There's some stairs there. They'll take you down to the beach. From there, follow the beach around to the left and that will take you down to the pier. You'll have to cross a river but it shouldn't be too deep."

"Thanks."

"Aloha."

I walked down the sidewalk past the hotel's pool and found the path leading to the edge of the cliff. The path, lined with tropical plants and flowers, led across a large expanse of grass and plumeria trees. The early morning air felt moist and alive with the sweet smells of Hawaii.

After the long walk, I arrived at an observation point. There was a bench, so I sat staring into the darkness trying to see the lineup. It reminded me of the morning Bobby and I had arrived at the point and stood with the other surfers waiting for the waves to reveal themselves.

Slowly, the sky to the east turned a soft pink and dawn spread itself across the island. It was a few minutes before the first light crept into the bay. When it did, I gulped. The waves were enormous, just as Thomas had predicted. I didn't know how big they were, but clearly bigger than the waves Bobby had ridden at the Point. They were the biggest waves I had ever seen.

My mind was filled with uncertainty. Was I really going to do this as my tribute to Bobby? Driving the Chrysler to Costa Rica would have been easier. At least I would have, for the most part, been on terra firma. Maybe the valet at the hotel was right, this was a death wish. I had not surfed since Bobby died. I hadn't even been in the water since I nearly drowned on that cold November night four months ago.

I sat there for an hour contemplating the break. The wind was blowing offshore and the bay was smooth. The first surfers started to arrive. I watched them for the longest time as they rode these leviathans. The waves were rideable but one mistake, one miscalculation, could spell disaster. The amount of water and the power behind the wave could crush you onto the reef like a rag doll. Again, I grew afraid.

But my decision had been made. I was determined. I stood and headed down the stairs that led to the beach.

101

I waited outside the shack for Hanalei Surfboard Rentals to open. A couple with two young daughters waited as well. The father intended to teach his girls to surf, which meant I would probably have my choice of boards. They only wanted long boards for the shore break.

I knew enough about big waves to pick a 9'8 gun, a rhino chaser. Three strokes and you're up to speed, ready to crash the ledge. They're for bagging the elephant that's about to run you over. The board I chose was red with a yellow lightning bolt on it because it reminded me of Jerry Lopez and *Five Summer Stories*.

"I hope you know what you're doing," the kid renting the board said.

"I hope so, too," I replied.

I had never ridden a gun before so I spent some time by the pier practicing in the shore break. I quickly realized that a gun is not for tricks like roundhouses or bouncing off the lip. It's for the serious business of staying alive, charging forward in a straight line.

After my sixth two-footer, I decided I was as ready as I was going to be. So I started the long paddle, a mile or so to the outer reef of Hanalei Bay. It was a beautiful day, the sun was up and the warm air wrapped itself around me like my grandmother's quilt. The water, slightly cooler, was refreshing. In the words of a Bruce Brown movie, "it was so pleasant it made me want to throw up." But that nausea could also have been from fear.

During the paddle something happened. My fear suddenly subsided. Call it acceptance, or maybe it was resignation, but the knowledge

I was going to ride a big wave, or at least try to, became simply a fait accompli. Sure, I knew it could end in disaster, with me torn to shreds on a jagged reef that's as hard as concrete. But I was determined to honor Bobby's life. That was my purpose. That was my strength. Once I had made this endeavor a fact, then what would happen, would happen. It was now my fate. I was no longer afraid, because I chose not to be afraid.

My plan was to paddle out into the deep water of the bay and then over into the lineup. This would ensure that I wouldn't get caught inside where a monster wave breaks in front of you causing you to ditch your board and dive to the bottom in an effort to get out of the way of white water the size of Hoover Dam. Ditching could be as dangerous as wiping out, especially if you were sure to be pounded by additional waves. With your board halfway to east bejesus all you can do is dive and bob like a rubber ducky in a Jacuzzi, and hope you don't go down the drain. I did not want to get caught inside.

When I got to the deep part of the bay and changed course to paddle into the lineup, I saw that the waves were much bigger than I had imagined. They were huge swells sparked by fierce Aleutian storms thousands of miles away. It reminded me of Bobby's wave at the Point. The fate of my life coming face to face with a wave generated by a storm I had never seen. The sum of my eighteen years had led me to this confrontation. Bobby's life and death had led me to this moment, this moment of truth.

It was about five-hundred yards to the lineup, the place where the waves first break. Hanalei Bay is a point break that peels off for a long right. It's a world class wave, and surfers come from all over the world to challenge it.

But size always thins out the crowd, and today was no exception. The crowd was sparse, with only about seven surfers in the wolf pack. Seven brave, or possibly crazy, souls who decided they were up to the challenge of twenty-foot waves. But as I approached the group, I got the stare, the legendary Hawaiian stink-eye. Then there were words.

"What the fuck, Haole?" one man called out.

"Yeah, get out of here before you get hurt," another echoed.

But our one-sided conversation was interrupted by a giant set on the horizon. Like Pavlov's dogs, it triggered a conditioned response and they all scrambled out to sea for the safety of deeper water, paddling hard to make it over the swells before they crested. I scrambled as well. I trusted their experience, and I just barely made it up and over the mountain of water with my heart in my throat.

There were five waves in the set. Two of the surfers caught waves. The hoots and cheers of the others celebrated their courage and determination.

Then a lull arrived and I took it as an opportunity to move closer to the crowd. I knew they were in the best position to catch one of these monsters.

Again there were words, from a man twice my age and size.

"Get the fuck out of here before we take your board and make you swim for shore."

"No, I need to catch a wave."

"You know, every time it gets big some Barney from the mainland shows up thinking they have something to prove. They usually end up dead."

"I don't have anything to prove."

"Then why are you out here?"

"It's a tribute."

"A tribute to what?"

"To my friend."

"Who's your friend?"

"Bobby Rowels."

"The football player that died?" another man chimed in.

"Yeah."

If there's anything that Hawaiians love as much as surfing, it's football.

Another set arrived, but this one was not as big as the last so we didn't have to paddle. One by one the surfers caught waves, and I saw that it was not a competition. Rather, these riders were helping each other, taking turns so that each surfer would be the sole rider on his wave.

When the next lull came the wolf pack began quietly talking among themselves. Then one of them paddled over to me.

"Bobby Rowels was your friend?"

"He was my best friend."

"He was a rocket, bra."

"How do you know about him?"

"He's on the cover of Surfer magazine this month."

I had no idea. I had been out to sea for nearly a month, and the last thing I would have known was that Surfer magazine had done a story about Bobby. I wasn't surprised.

"I haven't seen it. I just sailed here from California."

"It was a good story. Your friend was da kine." Then the man looked at me for a long moment.

"How long you been surfing?"

"About ten years."

"Ever surfed big waves?"

"No."

"One wave, and then you get the fuck out of here. We're not babysitters."

"One wave," I said.

"Follow me, and do exactly what I tell you."

He never told me his name but someone called him Eddie, and he seemed to be the leader of the wolf pack. At least they let him decide my fate.

"The next couple of sets, just watch."

I sat next to him and he spoke about the waves.

"The reef starts at about twenty or thirty yards toward the shore, and the swells are coming in from really deep water. When they hit the reef they jump up fast. That's the moment you come to your feet. It's the critical moment. Big waves have a steep ledge at the top and that's the place most people eat it. Watch the other surfers and I'll call out so you can get the rhythm."

We watched one of the surfers paddling for a wave and the Hawaiian man named Eddie called out, "Now."

The surfer rose to his feet and disappeared down the wave. This was repeated several times, and I started to feel the rhythm.

"You have to paddle hard because big waves are moving fast, so you have to move fast. Whatever you do, don't hesitate. If you hesitate you're lost, and it's a long way to the bottom."

We watched a couple more surfers, and Eddie called out, "Now!"

"Besides the drop, the most dangerous part of this wave is the first section. Put your head down and drive hard through it. If the goddess smiles, you might just have a chance."

We watched some more surfers with Eddie saying "Now," and I felt I had the timing.

"I'm ready."

"You must have really loved your friend."

"I did."

"All right. Next set, fifth wave."

I knew he was doing this in case I crashed and burned. It would be the last wave of the set and he was buying me time just in case.

"Thanks."

"Hey, bra."

"Yeah?"

"If you make it, no crowing. That way it'll live in your heart."

"All right."

When my wave came, Eddie yelled, "Start paddling. Hard!"

I turned my board and started paddling as the wolf pack watched. I felt the rush of power and my board and tail begin to lift.

"Now!" Eddie yelled.

As I rose to my feet, I suddenly heard Bobby's voice in my head, "Yeah, Scotty, swinging for the fences."

Down, down, down the face of the wave I dropped, over the ledge, bull-egged, bully style. The speed was incredible. It felt like forever before I reached the bottom where I could see the reef rising up to meet me.

When I reached the bottom, I was almost surprised that I was still on my feet. I turned and shot myself up the face of the wave until I found the pocket. Then I trimmed my board and drove hard for the shoulder.

Just as Eddie had predicted, the section in front of me was already breaking. Twenty-five feet of water was about to come down on my head. I knew the next seconds were critical, and I wondered if I should bail.

Bobby's voice spoke to me.

"Trust it, bro. Trust the universe."

I crouched as the section came down, but the lip didn't hit me. Instead, I found myself inside the wave, completely covered. There was nothing for me to do but to ride. The universe, God, the wave and fate were all in charge now. My destiny had arrived. Just as it had for Bobby.

The sound of tons of water crashing into the sea exploded in my ears. Everywhere around me was the violent eruption of nature; disaster and destruction just inches away as if I was inside the eye of a hurricane. But all I could see was beauty in shades of blue, green, and white, a moment of such intensity and focus that I felt frozen in time.

I heard Bobby's voice again. There was glee in it.

"Yeah, Scotty. This is the place. You found me."

Suddenly, I emerged from the belly of the wave and found myself on the shoulder. I had come face to face with a volcano and found beauty and serenity. I was safe. I had made it.

The break at Hanalei allows for a long ride, and I rode the wave as far as I could until its power was dissipated in the deep water of the bay. I came to a stop and sat down on my board. I looked back toward the break. All the surfers waved to me. I waved back, and then started the long paddle back to shore.

102

On the paddle back, my heart raced from the adrenaline coursing through my veins. I thought of Bobby and how much he had meant to me and of Perry and how much I loved her. I also felt I had done what I needed to do. I had tested my courage in a way I knew honored Bobby.

I made it to the shore in a daze as a powerful feeling of elation swept through me. I walked up the beach with gratitude filling my heart. It had been an amazing experience.

"Thank you, Bobby," I whispered for I had felt his spirit during the ride helping me to conquer my fear.

The kid at the surfboard rental place looked me over closely when I arrived to return my board.

"How was it?" the kid asked me with a broad grin.

"Big," was all I offered as I remembered Eddie's advice, "don't crow." I wanted the experience to live in my heart.

"Yeah, I was wondering if you'd come back in one piece," the kid added and I just smiled.

Walking along the beach, I stopped a few times to watch the sets roll in. It was still pumping and the surfers were still riding. It amazed me how small they looked on these giant waves as the riders disappeared below sea level when they reached the bottom of the giant waves. I must have looked tiny, too.

I made my way up the stairs. Arriving to the top, I sat on the bench staring at the riders on the giant waves, trying to find some kind of meaning in everything that had just happened. I knew that in a hundred years people would still be here riding these waves. This spot would beckon surfers to test themselves for as long as man exists.

It's always a mystery to me, how life continues. Why had I been spared while Bobby was dead? This life-death cycle was constantly turning like the wheel of fortune. There could never really be an answer except maybe that it was part of God's plan. But what exactly is this plan? The question is simple and utterly complex. In the words of Churchill, "It is a riddle, wrapped in a mystery, inside an enigma."

And why do our lives require so much pain when all we are doing is seeking joy? It's the paradox of life but I think it has to do with what we are supposed to learn. Pain teaches us more than joy. But it is the memory of our joy that leads us from our pain, so that we come out the other side stronger and wiser.

What else had I learned? Well, I guess the first step is not only to accept the mysteries but to embrace them. To embrace the unknown, the uncertainty, and the doubt, fear, and despair that comes with being human. To love this magnificent adventure we call life knowing that it is not our destinations, but our journeys themselves, in all their messy and flawed glory, that ultimately give meaning to our lives. But part of me wondered if this was enough to live my life by.

What I did believe is that the most important part of our journeys, the only thing we can control, are our choices, and our most important choices are not about schools, careers, or money. It's not about hobbies or where we choose to live or what car we drive. Our most important choices are about the people we choose to love. Whom we choose to love so deeply and fearlessly that we are prepared to accept the pain if we lose them. Just as the old man had said, "the love and respect of the people you love and respect."

That is what Bobby taught me, both with his life and his death, that the courage to love is a choice, our most important choice. And in that moment I found meaning.

"I love you, Bobby. I'll never forget you."

"I know, dickhead," came the reply. "And if you ever need to find me, you know where to look."

"Thanks, bro. Thanks for being my friend."

Then I began to cry, for the first time since Bobby died I cried, really hard, for I knew Bobby and I were saying goodbye. Our journey, the physical part at least, had come to an end. My hands found my face as I wept. I wept for my loss, for the friend of my youth who had been beautiful, strong and brave and who taught me to swing-for-the-fences. My friend who taught me that life, to be fully lived, demands that you do something fearless.

I'm not sure how long I cried. It was a while. Then gradually I stopped as I saw another mammoth swell approaching the shoreline. Bobby was gone but the waves would keep rolling, the world would keep turning and somewhere in this mystery was Bobby's spirit, on the big trail, riding waves and sending me his love and courage.

"So long, Bobby. Until we meet again," I whispered.

"We will, bro," came Bobby's voice in my head and I was certain that the words were true.

A smile came to my face as I felt my grief being pushed aside by my gratitude for the time Bobby and I had shared. Like the storm that had ravaged the Periwinkle and then moved on, the storm that had raged in my spirit was moving on, too. Through my acceptance and the meaning I had chosen, I had made my peace. I was now ready to rejoin the living.

"There you are!"

I looked up and saw it was Perry. I gazed at her for a long moment, thinking how beautiful she looked. She was wearing a red Stanford Cardinal baseball cap and her blonde hair spilled out like a waterfall from beneath it.

"I like your hat," I said.

"I thought you would. I actually bought it for you. I was planning on giving it to you this morning. Where'd you go, anyway?"

"I went surfing."

Perry looked out at the waves and frowned.

"What? Are you crazy?"

"A little," I admitted.

Perry sat down next to me and snuggled close. I put my arm around her and kissed her on the top of her head.

"It's so beautiful here," she said.

"Yeah. Did you bring that new journal?"

"It's up in the room."

"Good. I want to write about this morning. I never want to forget it."

"It's about time. Let's go find it. I want to watch you write."

She stood and looked down at me.

"Hey, Perry."

"Yeah."

"Just so you know. Whatever happens, you'll always be my muse."

Perry smiled her perfect, imperfect smile and pulled me to my feet.

"Come on, hot-shot surfer-writer. I'll give you something to write about."

Perry took me by the hand and led me from that magical place, that point overlooking Hanalei Bay, where I said my farewell to my friend, Bobby Rowels.

Author's Notes

Bobby Rowles was a real person. We met in junior college on a cold bus ride home over a bottle of Peppermint Schnapps after playing in a football game at Mt. Sac on a rainy night. Bobby had snuck the bottle on the bus, and I liked him immediately. We became great friends and decided to go into business together building homes after I finished college. That dream ended with Bobby's illness. I held him in my arms three days before he died and told him I'd never forget him.

However, this is a novel, a fictional story. The events, as far as I know, never took place. Rather, I took the spirit of Bobby, his optimism and his fearlessness, and built a character based on my memories of his spirit, a mythic character of sorts.

There have been a lot of great football players and surfers to come out of Newport Harbor but no one has ever put it together with the consistency of the Bobby Rowels I created. Bobby was not the athlete I created nor did he do the things I wrote. Moreover, all the characters I surrounded him with are also fictitious. Scotty, Bobby's mom Ellen, Scotty's dad Ed, Coach White, The Dick and Scotty's mom, Liza and the posse, Jim Steiner, Tommy Watts, Rickie Chandler never existed in real life. Rather, they are archetypes based on stories and movies and hundreds of people I have known in my life. This is especially true of the antagonist, Coach Dale White. It has been my personal experience that the coaches and teachers at Newport were men of high moral character. Sure, they wanted to win, but never at the expense of their players. The antagonist was needed to propel the story, to make my heroes grovel. As in life, the stronger the challenges, the stronger the character.

However, something else occurred to me during the writing of this story. A teammate died (Richardson) and then another (Mulroy). About this time, I had a conversation with an old teammate from high school and we pondered the question of whether the teams from the seventies had a curse. A lot of guys had died, some tragically.

Suddenly, everywhere I turned in my story I found ghosts. From Dover Shores to the Balboa Peninsula, the spirits of these ghosts rose up and shouted to be heard, some asked to be mentioned and others asked for cameos. My tribute to them is the acknowledgment that they had been an important part of my youth and of my Newport. Like Bobby, I will never forget them.

This brings me to the use of Lee Marvin. In my first draft, a draft my mother, Norma Jean, loved, John Wayne played the hero/mentor part. On the surface this made sense since Wayne is synonymous with Westerns and Newport. But John Wayne wasn't available.

Although I like to think the Duke would have liked my book, this led to an epiphany of sorts. I had never met John Wayne but I had met Lee Marvin through Barbara Ford (daughter of Director John Ford). In my twenties, I had the privilege of being close friends with the director's daughter. She was in her sixties and I was just out of college and we worked side by side under very trying circumstances. Barbara was a tough broad, in the best sense of the term, and earned the nickname from me of PITA (pain in the ass). She loved this nickname which grew out of her love of Greek falafels that I had introduced her to and her strict demands that I fulfill my duties exactly as requested. She knew that in Hollywood details were important.

It was one of the closest friendships I have ever known and Barbara taught me about movies, her father and life. I became enamored with John Ford movies and read everything I could about the man. I must have asked Barbara a thousand questions about her father. She began inviting me to meet people and I remember driving with my girlfriend to a small cabin in the Santa Barbara foothills to meet the widows of Harry Carey and, I think, Tom Mix. I sat there listening to these women talk about the early days of Westerns, never realizing their stories would be part of my words some thirty years later.

But as so often happens, tragedy struck. Barbara, a film editor by trade, was hired as the editor on the film *Mask*. She worked hard but I began to notice she was tiring easily. One night she was so tired she collapsed on the editing room couch. I remember covering her with my jacket and Barbara whispering, "thank you, Steve." The next day she was so tired she could hardly move. She went to the doctor and was diagnosed with inoperable lung cancer. She was admitted into the hospital.

This is where Lee Marvin comes in. Although Barbara was working as a union editor, she didn't have enough days for insurance coverage. In fact, she had no insurance. Barbara was dying and the hospital wanted to kick her out. She became frantic and it was a crisis for all the people who loved her. What would happen to Barbara?

Then out of the blue, Lee Marvin appears. Who told him or how he found out, I will never know. He paid the hospital bill with cash and spent a whole day with Barbara talking about a lifetime in the movies.

I visited Barbara after Marvin left and she seemed to be at peace, almost happy. I think there were two reasons for this. First was Peter Bogdanovich. He had broken Hollywood's silent ageism rule by giving Barbara the job of editor on the film *Mask*. Barbara had so loved working on this movie. Every day during shooting she said to me with utter excitement, "It's a great movie." She felt productive in a way that connected with her entire life, a life spent in and around the movies. But Peter had not done it out of generosity alone. I asked him once why he had hired Barbara and he said, "If I get one good idea from her then she has earned her salary." Peter had faith in her, in her sensibilities, and I think Barbara knew this. For Barbara, this experience ranked high on her list of life's achievements, working on a big studio movie for a legendary director where her opinion mattered.

Then there was Lee Marvin who rode to Barbara's rescue like a white knight in her time of need, and I think it was more than just the money. His actions, like her hiring on *Mask*, told her in her final days that she mattered. This is why, as a writer, Lee Marvin meant more to me than Wayne in a deeply personal way. Marvin was a real hero to me, and to any writer worth his salt, a real hero is worth a thousand images on the silver screen even if it is John Wayne, one of the greatest actors and icons of all time. Marvin is not the icon John Wayne is but everything happens as it should and Lee Marvin has and always will be one of my great heroes. He was also a military hero and damn fine actor.

Over that year we sat side by side, Barbara had shared with me almost everything about her life. From an ex-husband who tried to burn down her house to her father hiding a bottle of whiskey under her dress when she was a young girl so he could sneak it past the guard gate at Fox. Her stories always revealed a wisdom that took a lifetime to earn. But the wisest thing she ever told me was actually words from her father. I had delivered something to her apartment in Sherman Oaks and she brought me in to see her father's six Oscars. Of course, I was duly impressed and Barbara noticed.

"You know, Steve, my dad put it all in perspective."

"How's that?"

"When he won the Oscar for *How Green was My Valley* it was sitting on the kitchen table the next morning at breakfast and I said, 'Daddy, you won the Oscar!' My dad looked at me for a long moment. Then he said, 'Barbara, that and ten cents will buy me a cup of coffee. The only thing that matters in life is having the love and respect of the people you love and respect.'"

I visited her in the hospital a couple of days before she died. She seemed in good spirits even though she knew she was dying. When I got up to leave, she said to me, "Here smile, here smile." She always said this when she knew I was sad or angry, and I was pissed that my friend was dying. I looked at her and smiled. She smiled back and said, "You know, I've had a pretty good run." I was happy she felt that way but I didn't really think about it for a long time. During the writing of this book I realize she felt she had earned the love and respect of the

P.S. Foley

people she loved and respected. Working on *Mask* and Lee Marvin's visit gave her that gift, the feeling that she had mattered to the people she loved, and like Bobby, I will never forget her.

Finally, there is Newport itself. It's interesting to me that I chose to write this book after I moved away from Newport. My wife and I moved to Northern California so our daughters could attend a Waldorf high school. I still visit Newport often, my family has a home there, but it's with different eyes that I see it now. When I was young I took Newport for granted like all kids thinking that everyone lives the way you do, in a sparkling city by the sea. Now I see it as a gift to be treasured and respected. Its people, its places, and its beauty are inspiring. *West Newport Blues* is a love letter to the town of my youth, warts and all, and on almost every page there is a tribute to my Newport of the seventies. I am eternally grateful for what she had to teach me, and I guess you could say this book chose me.

During the writing something else occurred. I realized *West Newport Blues* is part of a series of stories - my trailer-park stories. My first book, *Riding Godzilla*, explored the power of innocence and perseverance while *West Newport Blues* explores the power of friendship. My third book, *Angel in the Sand*, will explore the power of love in its many forms. I hope you've enjoyed the second installment of my trailer-park stories and I am grateful to you as a reader for sharing my world for a short time.

All the best,

P.S. Foley

Acknowledgements

I wrote the first draft of West Newport Blues in six months. It was thirty thousand words too long and it took over five years to edit it down. Subsequently, I had help from some very good editors. First was Jonathan Marmelzat who gave me some fine suggestions especially in my treatment of ALS. Next, Ana Manwaring took a shot and really cut out the words. Then I brought in the big guns of my dear friend Iris Chester who worked her magic. Finally, there was Esther Baruch, a fine editor, who really made my words sing and helped me clean up most of the inconsistencies. During the years, there were also readers including my daughter Storm who made some outstanding suggestions, Mike Wilsey and Ken Thurman who gave me a fresh perspective on Newport. Rick and Heather Concoff who's encouragement and insight I trust and value, and my wife, Kathy, my muse, who held my hand with notes, encouragement, and support every draft along the way. Finally, there was my mother, Norma Jean, who read the first draft before she died and inspired me to finish what I had started. As always, the people who have touched my life are in my words, always and forever.

More Praise for
West Newport Blues

"This is a familiar story about finding your gifts, your community, and your own way. It's profound because we share it, and it repeats endlessly in the lives of ordinary heroes and heroines everywhere. I didn't want to put it down."

Dr. Catherine Svehla, Mythologist and
Radio host of *Myth in the Mojave*

"A great read! *West Newport Blues* is a great story of the power of friendship and coming of age, and conjured up great memories for me of important friends and moments of my teenage years. It is simply a gift to readers."

Rodney Gillmore, Stanford graduate, lawyer, and
sports analyst ESPN

"*West Newport Blues* is real page-turner. It combines a sweet semi biographical coming of age story with an intriguing romantic fantasy. It's about two boys who have unique family challenges. They come together over common values of love, loyalty and trust. An unexpected turn of events separates this tale from those that may be similar and challenges the reader to open their hearts to the fate of the young men."

Rio Olesky, Author and Astrologer

"Seventeen-year-old surfer and writer Scotty Curtis narrates a moving story of living in a trailer park with a dejected father, going on escapades with blood brother Bobby Rowels, the school's star linebacker, and falling in love with the mysterious girl-next-door. How to outsmart troublemakers, sustain blows to one's spirit from misguided parental figures, and be a friend of true grit--P.S. Foley's *West Newport Blues* is entertaining, humorous, and poignant. Bravo!

Teresa LeYung-Ryan, 22-day writing coach, author, playwright

"I simply loved it!"

Pete Noble, Football Coach, Surfer, and Writer

"Fictionalizing a life is no easy feat. Sentimentality and nostalgia can be the writer's nemesis. Yet P.S. Foley has succeeded beautifully. His book *West Newport Blues* takes readers back to the bloom of adulthood on the California coast in a way that rings true historically and, more important, emotionally. This is a beautifully rendered coming-of-age story that avoids sugarcoating adolescence or demonizing adulthood. All his characters are multidimensional, engaging readers from page one and coaxing them to travel back to their own transition at this challenging time of life to excavate both the gold and the lead. Plus, it's a darn good story! I highly recommend this book."

Joan Parisi Wilcox, author and editor

"I totally enjoyed this book. I could not predict how the pieces would fit together."

Javier Esparza, Homicide Detective

"A unique perspective of "Happy Days" in another time and another place."

Roger Carlson, sportswriter

"P.S. Foley's characters continually surprised me starting with Scotty's love for his father, even when drunk and passed out. But it's Scotty's insights into people and his real empathy for them that won me. Scotty's loyalty to friends Bobby and Perry is profound and it's Bobby's fate and Perry's surprise that ensure Scotty's maturation. Foley's skill at putting all these surprises together against the backdrop of beautiful Newport Beach, California adds up to a fine read.

Ana Manwaring, writer, editor, and teacher

"Good characters. Well written. I enjoyed this book. The football scenes were very good."

Dan Ford, author of *Pappy: The Life of John Ford*

"A must read. I could not put it down. Two thumbs up!"

Buzzy Martin. Musician, Author - *Don't Shoot, I'm the Guitar Man*

"P.S. Foley has created an emotional coming-of-age tale that draws the reader into mid-70's Newport Beach. From a trailer park to Bayshores, from high school football to big-wave surfing, from a morgue to a yacht, from a young beautiful mystery woman to a rugged movie star, Foley's vivid characters draw you in from the first page to its cathartic ending."

Joe Mulroy – Musician, Lyricist and Composer, Born to Ride Waves

"An epic tale."

Brian Theriot – Athlete, Executive, owner of Castle Stone Cottages

"I got my copy of "*West Newport Blues*" on a Friday, and I finished it on Saturday. What a wonderful, uplifting and thoughtful tale. P.S. Foley brought Newport of the 70's back to life for all to enjoy!"

Jerry Hayden, Financial Advisor, congressional candidate.

"*West Newport Blues* generated warm and wonderful memories of the "Long Gray Line" as Roger Carlson* so aptly called the teams of Newport Harbor....

What visions you recreated in your book......and what marvelous events were recalled...THANK YOU VERY MUCH for putting into print for posterity what most of us can only think of in bits and pieces !!!!"

Marilyn Gust

"P.S. Foley's *West Newport Blues* is a coming of age novel, a modern Bildungsroman. His protagonist is a seventeen year old high school student living in Newport Beach, southern California. The temptations and challenges of adolescence along with the conformity and material-ism of the dominant upper class social scene, attempt to overwhelm the young man's life. His way out centers on writing, surfing and authentic friendship. It is a tale of dysfunctional families, loss, fidelity and love. Wisdom enters his life through exploration of the art of wondering by way of such figures as Thoreau, Steinbeck, Jung and Campbell. The other main focus is on the transformative power of surfing, a sort of Zen and the Art of Surfing.

Bob Flagg – Waldorf Educator, Thoreau Society Member.

"A wonderful book. I loved it."

Nadine Retmier

"P.S. Foley's writing is poetic, potent, and engaging - could not put this story down - *West Newport Blues* straight up needs to be a movie!"

Patrick Muldoon – Actor and Producer

"P.S. Foley's *West Newport Blues* takes me back to when I was a kid. I couldn't stop reading it. Great book."

Mousa Husary, Football coach

"Newport Blues is a touching story about love, loyalty, and coming of age. It resonated deeply with me primarily because of my connection to the brotherhood and love that unfolds between the three central characters. P.S. Foley paints a picture with words and he is able to masterfully weave in valuable lessons, old movies, and life growing up in Newport Beach! Newport Blues has heart and soul and the story grips you with its real characters and its unpredictable twist and turns. I highly recommend this book!"

Shane Foley, Athlete, Writer, and Banking Executive

"In his new novel, P. S. Foley has managed to accurately capture the feel of a time and a place that no longer exists and could never exist again. For a brief, magical time, from 1950 to 1980, Newport had managed to fight off the incursion of a freeway and thereby became a pocket of leisure and wealth: a small town whose residents were movie stars, sailors, surfers and enjoyers of the good life of all stripes and income levels.

Foley mentions my brother, David "Bucko" Shaw, several times in the book, again accurately portraying him as he was: "Mr. Newport", a true legend as an athlete and the ultimate fun-lover. Once he was waiting for me to get off work, and he struck up a conversation with the stranger sitting next to him. The guy asked Dave what he did. He thought for a second, then said: "You know how golf pros teach people how to play golf? Well, I teach them how to have fun."

When Bucko died in 2001, tributes poured in for weeks, including a huge group of surfers finally scattering his ashes off of 36th Street. I have never known anyone so universally loved. He touched and improved anyone he ever met.

"Our" Newport is long gone, but if you would like a long, loving look at how it really was, dive into *West Newport Blues*."

Bob Shaw

13436533R00216

Made in the USA
San Bernardino, CA
21 July 2014